THE CRISIS

A THRILLER

THE CRISIS

A THRILLER

T. O. PAINE

DARK
SWALLOW
BOOKS

Published by Dark Swallow Books
www.darkswallowbooks.com

Library of Congress Control Number: 2024927273

Paperback ISBN-13: 979-8-9866958-5-3
Hardcover ISBN-13: 979-8-9866958-6-0
eBook ISBN-13: 979-8-9866958-7-7

CHAPTER ONE

MATTIE

It's mornings like these I wish I could destroy the world and start over.

I finish checking the cash drawer to make sure the night clerk cashed out correctly and glance out the convenience store window. A whale of a mini-van rushes into the lot, stopping abruptly next to a gas pump. Its midnight blue body decorated with that drooping chrome molding ceases to shake when the driver shuts off the engine. A muscled-up bald man with a thin black beard, motorcycle cop sunglasses, and dozens of bird claw tattoos on his massive shoulders gets out, slips his credit card into the pump, and gazes back at the mini-van. He squints, trying to see into the passenger side. The shadow of a woman sits behind the windshield, motionless. The man's wife-beater tank top struggles to contain his broad chest, and I think to myself, *This is not . . .*

No.

It can't be.

No, this is not . . . oh, what's that kid's name? The new kid coming in today.

I can't remember his name, but no matter, this man can't be him.

First of all, this man is not a kid. Phil said my new coworker was young. A teenager and, as Phil put it, "super-excited" to start his career at the White Sands Pay-n-Save. I'll never understand why Phil named it "White Sands." We're smack dab in the middle of Florida, miles from any sands.

I miss living near the ocean. I miss my job—an actual marine biology position—at the nature museum.

I hate counting cash and refilling slushy machines. The bitter smell of coffee mixed with greasy roller hot dogs.

I miss my weekends.

Monday mornings are the worst.

I pull the kid's resume from beneath the counter. His name is Calvin, and he is eighteen, and he has almost no experience. His most notable skill—20/10 vision. I didn't know that was possible, but for working here, it hardly seems useful. *This is going to be fun—not.* The thought of spending the morning showing him how to refill the slushy and coffee machines makes me want to have a cigarette.

The muscle man at the gas pump has a cigarette tucked behind his ear. He's definitely older than eighteen. Thirty?

I want that cigarette.

I'd take any cigarette right now.

Columns of cigarette boxes taunt me from the walls above and behind the counter where I stand. Where I've been forced to work while I figure my life out.

No. No more cigarettes.

I've made it two days. I can make it another one. I don't need to let the minor stress of training some snot-nosed kid ruin my streak. My father always said, *If it is to be, it's up to me.* I'm the only one who can stop me from having a cigarette, but hey—where is that kid?

The passenger door of the blue Honda mini-van opens, and Mr. Muscles yells at the woman. She slams the door shut before I can see her face.

Knock, knock, knock.

Someone's at the back door.

Knock, knock.

"Coming."

I open the door and—this must be Calvin, the new kid. His curly brown hair shines in the hot Florida sun. He's much rounder than I pictured, not very tall, but definitely young, and he has that *super-excited-to-start-a-new-job* look on his face.

He points at my old Toyota Corolla wagon. "Is that your car over there?"

I nod.

"I love cars," he says. "Even wagons. They stopped making wagons, mostly, but I love them. Everyone wants an SUV, but I like wagons." He gazes at my car fondly. "I like sports cars and muscle cars, too."

"That's great."

"I'm Calvin." He holds out his hand.

"I'm Mattie. Come inside." He follows me through to the front. We stop behind the counter. "Welcome to the Pay-n-Save."

He gazes out the front window. "I don't like mini-vans. They're too big and clunky."

We look out at Mr. Muscles' vehicle. He's standing at the pump beside it, waiting. Our machines are slow.

"Especially like that one," Calvin says, shaking his head. "Ones with that bent silver trim running down the side. Makes them look like bloated hearses. Like there's a body inside filled with gas. Like they're about to explode."

I've turned to blink at my new coworker, struck by this weird and weirdly specific image, when something moves in one of the security mirrors above us. A man lurks by the antifreeze stacked in the far corner. He must have come in when I was out back. Though the bell didn't ring when the door closed behind him.

"Oh, there's a cricket." Calvin slaps the counter. "How'd that get in here?"

The cricket jumps, and Calvin catches it in the air. He squeezes his fist and throws the beast into a nearby waste bin.

No more cricket.

"That was . . . violent," I observe.

"Sorry." I can see in his post-pubescent eyes that he really *is* sorry. "I shouldn't have done that. Crickets are animals too, just like us. But it was him or me. They can get you killed the same as any other animal."

"Get you killed? How's that? They're so small, and they don't bite."

"Size doesn't matter. Crickets, mice, armadillos, cats, dogs, alligators, hippos—elephants. Even dinosaurs, if you believe in those."

"Armadillos? Really? They don't bite. Their mouths aren't big enough."

"I don't know about that, but I do know they can kill you. You have to watch out for them on the road. Sometimes, they run in packs."

"That's ridiculous."

"No, it's true." He puffs his chest out a little. "One minute, you're driving down the highway, free and clear, and then a hundred armadillos charge into your path and run you off the road. You crash and die. It happened to my dad." The shock on my face registers on his. He grins. "Well, not the dying part. My dad is still alive. But an army of armadillos did run him off the road once."

If Calvin is not the oddest person I've met, he has to be close. His cotton button-down shirt with subtle blue lines and pearl-inlay buttons stretches tight around his belly, and his black slacks barely cover the tops of his Converse running shoes. He clearly made an attempt to dress up for his first day at work. I return him to the back room, hand him the largest Pay-n-Save shirt I can find and tell him to put it on in the bathroom.

When he rejoins me up front, I feel bad for him. The shirt makes him look like an apple. Not a small apple. A rotund New York apple.

"Okay," I say. "We should get started. My name is Matilda, but I go by Mattie. I hate Matilda, so don't call me that. Today, we're going to start with refilling the machines."

"Hands up!" The man from the beer cooler appears on the other side of the counter. He has raised a handgun and is aiming it at my face. My heart jumps, but I smell fear rolling off of him. He's tied a red bandanna over the lower half of his face, and his arms are dirty. Greasy. He's desperate and mentally off-kilter. His squirrelly eyes make it look like someone else is running the show in his head.

I look around for help. The store is empty. Mr. Muscles out front is still glaring impatiently at the gas pump as it labors to fill his ugly mini-van.

No one else is around.

The man waves his weapon. "I said, 'Hands up!'"

Calvin and I raise our hands.

He points the gun at Calvin's face. "Open the register. Give me the money."

"I—I can't."

"He's new," I explain.

"Ah!" The man's face contorts, like I've just punched him in the gut. "Will *someone* open it?"

"Maybe you can ask that guy." I gesture toward the minivan. Mr. Muscles has opened the passenger door and is helping a young Latina woman out. "It looks like they're coming inside." As they approach, I realize she's not a woman. She's just a girl.

The gunman shakes his head. Squints. Rushes behind the counter and grabs Calvin by the shirt collar. "Get rid of them, Red," he says to me, "or I'm shooting your little buddy here." He pulls Calvin—jiggling muffin-top belly and all—into the back room and shuts the door.

My first instinct is to run. Get the hell out of here and not look back. Then I glance up at the sole security camera trained on the counter area. The monitor for it is in the back room with the gunman. He can see everything, if he's looking.

I think he looked crazy enough to shoot Calvin.

Poor Calvin. He hasn't even finished his first hour of work yet, and he's got a gun to his head.

The couple walk inside. Mr. Muscles holds the girl's elbow as they let the door close behind them—the monotonous *bing-bong* rings out as it shuts. With those sharp tattoos and tight tank top, he doesn't look like a helpful kind of man. He releases the girl's arm and gives her a stern look before heading toward the beer cooler.

She can help me.

I rip a piece of receipt paper off the register printer and grab a pen.

The girl—dark skin, dull brown eyes, long hair with tight coils running down her back to a pair of tight white shorts—drifts toward me. Her hair is curled like mine, except mine is a dark red, and I can't make it flow like hers. It sticks straight out in some places no matter what I do.

"Where are the bathrooms?" she asks.

"Over there." I gesture at the clearly displayed restroom sign hanging above the hallway. Her eyes are glassy. She has a number tattooed on the back of her left calf. It's more like a brand than a tattoo. Unlike her boyfriend, this appears to be her only art.

The two of them don't make for a good-looking couple. Maybe it's a case of opposites attract. I shouldn't judge.

"Hey," he shouts across the store to her. "Don't be long in there."

She glides toward the bathrooms.

I nod in her direction as she goes, as if she just said something. I write on the receipt as if she'd asked me to make a note of something. I am performing for the security camera.

Help me. Someone is holding my coworker hostage in the back room.

She returns from the bathroom and takes a lighter with a picture of Bob Marley off the display. She gazes at the lighter for a long, peaceful moment, then places it on the counter.

I want a cigarette.

Her boyfriend—armed with beer, chips, jerky, and other stuff—heads our way. She seems a little out of it. I should probably give *him* the note, but I don't trust him. Everything about him feels wrong.

I slide the note across the counter to her and she takes it, reads it before he reaches us. Her eyes open wide. They brighten a little. She gazes at the door to the back room, turns her head toward her boyfriend, then stuffs the note in her pocket. Just before he gets here, she takes my pen.

"Did you get everything you need, Lucía?" He drops his bounty on the counter.

She points at the lighter.

He smiles and shoves the lighter to the side. "Now Lucía, you know you don't need that."

I focus on her face. Is she covering bruises with that makeup?

He pulls his wallet out.

"Wait." She rushes down the miscellaneous traveler's aisle and rounds the corner, out of sight.

"Hurry, babe," says Mr. Muscles. "We've got to go."

I say nothing.

He says nothing.

Time moves slowly.

When she returns, she puts a box of feminine pads on the counter.

He rolls his eyes, and I'm drawn to the cigarette behind his ear.

I want that cigarette now more than ever.

My hands shake as I ring up their items. I hope they don't notice my nerves. They don't seem to. The look in Lucía's eyes reminds me of the time my cousin butchered a rabbit in front of us without any warning. I don't think I've ever gotten all the way over that.

"Have a great day," I say, shoving the bags toward the man.

"Thanks." He grabs them and turns toward the door.

Lucía stands still, staring at me as if trying to make me read her mind.

"C'mon, babe."

This man is so disgusting. I want her to tell him not to call her "babe," but she says nothing.

"Let's go," he shouts. "We gotta hit the road."

As she turns to follow him, she flips the receipt paper out of her back pocket.

It lands on the floor.

I act like I don't see it.

The door goes *bing-bong*.

I grab the broom and sweep the entire area in front of the counter as if a bag of dried beans had been spilled. I'm performing for the camera again. I want to win an Oscar and celebrate with a cigarette. Smooth, robust. Fully-flavored.

The broom catches the receipt, and I sweep it into the corner before I stoop for it.

No. You help me. Blue Honda mini-van going to Salt Springs. Someone named Stanley.

The Bob Marley lighter is missing, and Calvin is trapped in the back with a gun to his head.

Monday mornings are the worst.

CHAPTER TWO

LUCÍA

The white lines painted on Lucía's side of Highway 19 run together in the distance because there is only one line.

She blinks her eyes.

The two lines blur before becoming one.

They pass an adopt-a-highway sign. It's ironic. Highways don't know what it's like to be adopted. To be given from one person to another like some kind of toy. Highway 19 is just a road with one lane heading north and one lane heading south.

She can see the road clearly now. Salt Springs is north of Orlando, the direction Wyatt is driving. He's blasting the air conditioning and the mini-van hums like a microwave.

His beef jerky smells horrible. He has the bag open between his legs. She should have gotten some food at the convenience store, but it was so hard to think in there. What *happened* to her at the hotel this morning?

Things are clearing up now. Slowly.

A chunk of jerky falls out of Wyatt's mouth onto his crotch. He grabs it, the van swerves to the right when he looks away from the road, and he shoves the meat back inside his face.

She can't believe she fell for him. It was the drugs. It had to be the drugs.

No.

The truth is, it wasn't only the drugs.

He glances over and sees her looking at him before she can shut her eyes.

"What the hell was that all about back there?" he asks.

"What?"

"At the store. Maxi-pads? That's it?"

"It's all I needed."

"You need to eat. Here." He raises his bag of jerky. "Have some."

"I don't feel good."

"Take it."

"You know I don't eat meat."

"Oh, I've seen you eat meat." He tucks the bag back between his thighs. "You look like hell. Eat something. You need to look good for when we arrive."

"Why? Why are we going to Salt Springs?"

He puts both hands on the wheel. Gazes up the road.

"Are you going to answer me?" she asks.

"Shut up. I'm thinking."

This is the first time Lucía can remember him thinking. Thinking is not Wyatt's strong suit. It's also not what attracted her to him in the first place. His access to cocaine and other drugs. That's what did it.

No.

That's not true, either. It's only what she'd like to believe. What a mistake.

The truth? She fell in love with the idea of him in a single night. It was almost as if she'd planned it. She'd sought out the baddest boy of the bunch and turned him into a quest. From the moment she saw him at that party, she knew she'd wake up in his bed in the morning.

But that was supposed to be it.

And then it wasn't.

He was the opposite of every high school and college dude she'd ever dated. His tattoos. His motorcycle. His GED. The idea that life could be lived outside her wealthy suburban mold took hold of her. Living one day at a time, without any long-term plans. That kind of freedom consumed her. With only a month before high school graduation, she'd wanted to know what it would be like to go a different direction.

Now she knows.

The pavement whips beneath the mini-van's wheels. The motion makes Lucía sick. The jerky smell makes her sick. The fact she's ended up here with him—sick.

She just wanted to try a different direction in life, just for one night, and she's gotten what she wanted. The direction? North to Salt Springs.

But why Salt Springs?

His muscled jaws work over another wad of meat. The sickly sweet smell blends with the warm air coming from the heater vents. She can't believe she turned her life over to him. She'd only wanted a taste. A last hoo-rah before graduation. The ceremony must be sometime next week. She wonders if she'll be there. If the school will let her graduate. She hasn't seen her family or friends in three weeks.

Will they be at the ceremony even if she's not?

Has her dad sent anyone looking for her yet?

She's been gone three weeks.

The first week was a pleasant blur. She could have left then, but—it had only been one week. She remembers thinking how she had the rest of her life to live like a responsible adult, and Wyatt was totally into having her stay on with him.

So she stayed.

The two weeks since then have been a different kind of blur. Ragged, jittery.

Her memories of it come in flashes.

Some days, staying with Wyatt forever in his ancient, three-story Victorian seemed like the only way to live. Other days, sleeping in the basement to recover from the previous night's partying seemed like purgatory. More and more, she found the door to the basement locked when she tried to leave. Wyatt said he had to lock it for her protection.

Go back to sleep, Lucía. Get some rest, Lucía. You're not well, Lucía. I'm doing a deal out here, and we can't be interrupted.

"Before we talk about Salt Springs," Wyatt says, wiping his mouth, "what was up with that lighter? You know you can borrow mine anytime you want to smoke."

"It had a picture of Bob Marley on it."

"Whatever."

"Can we go back? I don't feel good. I need to sleep more."

"We're not going back." He glances at the dashboard. "We're already late."

"For what? What's in Salt Springs?"

"It's not what. It's who. Do you remember what we talked about the other night? The money?"

"I told you I'd never do that."

"I need the money."

"You need the money? What about me?" The air blowing from the vent is getting warmer. The A/C is breaking down. "Never mind. I told you. If you need money, let me talk to my father. He—"

"Shut up." His knuckles whiten on the wheel. "I like you." He eases the van around a sweeping corner. "It's been strange with you. I like everything about you." He glances at her leg. "I even like your tattoo."

"You do?"

"Yeah. What does it mean again? I forgot. Is it someone's birthday?"

"No. There are too many numbers for that. Did I—I don't remember telling you about it."

"We have time now. Shoot."

"If I tell you, can we turn around?" His glare says *no*. "I've had it for as long as I can remember. My father said it was there when he adopted me from Cuba. It's always been a part of me."

"You don't remember getting it?"

"I was a baby when he adopted me."

"What?" He studies my face. "Are you serious? You got a tattoo when you were a baby? That's hardcore."

"I guess."

"You see. That's what I like about you. You're a badass, and you don't even know it. So what does the number mean?"

"I don't know. My father once told me it might be the most important number in the world, but I think he said that to just make me feel better after I crashed on my bicycle."

"If it doesn't mean anything, why have you kept it?"

"It's always been there. It's part of me. I think I would feel naked without it."

"Naked." He grins. "You're so cool. I really do like you."

"Then let's turn around and go back."

The cords in his neck tense. "We can't." He swallows. "I don't *want* to do this, but"—he glances over at her, his eyes reddening—"you're so cool, but . . . no. You're a whore. I have to get the money."

Lucía slides her hand into her pocket. She grasps the lighter. "My father is rich. I'm sure he'd help us get started."

"You don't get it. There is no getting started. After today, there is no us."

He's breaking up with her.

This is great.

No, it's horrible.

It's a relief and terrifying all at once. He's breaking up with her, but he's driving her somewhere. Not just somewhere, but to whoever's waiting for her in Salt Springs. She's got to escape. It's been hard enough trying to run away from Wyatt. If he leaves her with someone else, it might be impossible.

She glances in the rearview mirror. The police should be coming any time now. She dropped that note on the floor of the convenience store. All that loser-girl behind the counter had to do was call the police. Wait. Something about her coworker, held in the back room. She'd wanted *Lucía* to call the police.

The convenience store is a fever dream. That clerk isn't going to do anything.

And, if the police aren't coming, Lucía's lost. Unless . . . her father. He will save her. He has to. He loves her—in his own Daddy Warbucks way. Saving her *is* his way. It will make him look good, and he won't have to do anything.

Yes.

He'll pay someone to save me.

She checks the rearview mirror again. There's still no police.

It's been three weeks. He must have sent someone by

now.

She checks the mirror again.

Still no police.

No other cars.

"What are you doing?" Wyatt asks. "Why do you keep jerking toward the window? Are you tweaking on me?"

"No. I'm pissed."

He laughs.

She wants to light him on fire. She wants to get out and light the whole damn van on fire.

"Just calm down. It won't be long, and we'll be there."

"But you're breaking up with me."

"We were never together."

That comes as a shock. What was it all about, then? *Nothing?*

"Where are we going after Salt Springs?"

"God, you're stupid. I already told you. After we get there, there is no 'we.' I'm leaving, and you're staying." He sniffs.

"Forever?"

He stares at the road.

He's close to six feet tall.

He can bench a Mercedes.

If there'd been a knife at the convenience store, she would have taken it. Scissors. She should have looked for scissors. This lighter won't help unless he's abnormally flammable.

Gas is flammable.

"I need to go to the bathroom again."

"You just went."

"Please?" She puts her hand on his thigh. "Can you pull over at the next stop?"

CHAPTER THREE

MATTIE

"Drop it, or I'll shoot him. I swear, I'll shoot him."

I look up from the note in my hand to see the gunman in the doorway to the back room, pressing his muzzle against the side of Calvin's head. The red bandanna still covers the lower half of his face, and he still holds Calvin by the collar, same as when he forced the poor kid into the back.

Calvin's cheeks tremble as if we're in a California earthquake, but we're not. We're in Florida.

"Drop what?" I ask.

"No," says the gunman. "Don't drop it. Bring it here. I saw what happened. I saw that girl drop it for you."

I take a step toward him.

"No. Wait." He scrunches his eyes shut. "Don't come here. Stay where you are. I'll shoot him. I swear I'll shoot him." He opens his eyes, squinting like there's something stuck in them.

"Calm down," I say. "You don't have to do this."

"What's that note say? Did you tell her about me? What about that guy? Did you tell him?"

"I—"

He points the gun in my direction. "You did. You told them. I can see it in your face."

I dive behind the Hostess snack rack, and the gun goes off. The sound is deafening inside the small store.

"Mattie!" Calvin screams.

"Be brave!" I shout back, my ears ringing. I don't know where the bullet went, but it didn't hit me. I peer out at the two of them between the Zingers and Ding Dongs.

"C'mon." The gunman jerks on Calvin's collar, pulling the round boy off balance and shoving his face down close to the cash register.

"Don't be afraid of him, Calvin. He's as scared as you are."

"Open the register." He presses the gun against the back of Calvin's neck.

"I can't." Calvin is shaking. Poor kid.

"He can't," I confirm. "It's his first day. Only I know how to open it."

"Shut up."

"Let him go."

"Do it. Now." He presses the gun muzzle harder against Calvin's neck.

I slide the Hostess rack across the floor toward the counter, staying low behind the assorted boxes of break-time goodness. The white metal frame scrapes the floor like fingernails on a chalkboard.

The gunman looks at the rack coming faster and faster his way, points his gun at it in confusion, looks at Calvin, and back at the oncoming rack.

"Run!" I shout.

The rack crashes against the counter. Twinkies and Ho

Hos fly off the shelves at him. When he raises his hands to shield himself, Calvin makes a break for it.

I dive into the coffee machine aisle.

The gunman fires at me and misses again.

As I scramble across the floor, Calvin runs past the broom I'd left near the front door. "Calvin! Grab the broom and—"

Before I can finish telling him what to do, he's out the door and bumbling across the pavement.

The door swings closed. *Bing bong.*

Curse him. Coward.

I crouch below the medium roast coffee machine and consider the chances this guy will miss a third time if I try to run. We start the till each day with less than two hundred dollars, yet this guy is willing to kill for it. He's willing to go to jail for the rest of his life for less than two hundred dollars. It's so incredibly desperate, I can't stand it. I've got to stop him, or he'll do this again at another place, somewhere down the highway. That's how these morons are. Desperate *and* stupid.

I'm not running.

I hear him mashing the register's buttons. He swears. He pounds on the counter.

Slowly, I rise and slide the carafe of hot coffee off the machine's hot plate. It should be hotter, but like everything around here, the coffee machines hardly work. Sometimes, I really hate Phil.

"Open," the gunman says to the register. "Why won't you *open?*"

I sidle up against the fresh donut display and peer around the corner just as he shoves the register off the counter. It lands with a *crash*, and the cash drawer pops open. He's frozen for a minute, stunned that something actually worked out for him, then kneels down and begins shoving bills into his pockets.

It's go time.

He screams and falls onto his back when I fill his face full of hot coffee.

I wish it was hotter.

He pulls his gun out, points it up at me, and begins scooting on his back toward the front door like a stingray stuck on shore.

I stand over him, pretending to be unafraid. I'm too close to suddenly move away without getting shot, and he's a coward. I see it in his eyes. "You're not getting away with this. Stop moving."

"No. You stop. I'll shoot you. I swear—"

"You haven't been able to hit me yet. You're a horrible shot."

He slowly rises to his feet, keeping his aim and taking a swipe at his face to shed some of the coffee. His cheek is bright red.

I raise the coffee carafe in the air. It's almost empty, but it's made of glass.

"Put it down," he says. "I'll shoot you."

I sling the carafe at him, and he turns his head to watch as it flies by, missing by three feet. I pick up the cash drawer and fling it at him. Again, he watches as it flies by at a distance, this time on his other side. It's like I have a disability. I've never been good at sports. Basketball was the worst. No, make that softball. No, make it anything requiring me to throw ... anything. I was banned from Frisbee golf at the University of West Florida. One of my crowning achievements, but not the worst. The worst was the latest catastrophe, when I was banned from the South Florida Aquarium. I loved that job.

He leans his back against the front door. "Looks like you're a horrible shot, too." The door opens.

I throw a box of Twinkies at him. I don't know why I did that. It misses him by a mile, and in my desperate stupidity, I grab a pack of cigarettes, take aim and . . . *Hmm. Cigarettes.* I haven't wanted one this entire time. Maybe adrenaline is a good substitute for nicotine. I could use that.

He laughs at me and runs out the door, sloppily pointing his gun behind him as he scurries across the lot.

I catch my breath.

He disappears into the bushes on the other side of the gas pumps.

I can't let him get away with this. It's not right. I drop the cigarettes and reach inside my pocket for my cell phone, but it's not there. Instead, I pull out the note.

No. You help me. Blue Honda mini-van going to Salt Springs. Someone named Stanley.

In the excitement, I'd almost forgotten about that poor girl. She must be miles away by now. Her and her wife-beater boyfriend. She'd looked so out of it, like he'd hit her in the head a bunch of times. But she didn't have any bruises that I could see. She only had that strange tattoo on the back of her calf. Those numbers. I'd tried to memorize them—208634 . . . that's all I got. There were more, but I can't remember them.

At least I can remember her name.

Lucía.

It was not a pretty tattoo. It was like a label. A brand.

Oh, my God.

I know about this.

Human trafficking.

It's the same thing that happened to my cousin.

This girl is a product, not a person. That man isn't her boyfriend. He's her pimp. He's going to sell her to someone. Someone in Salt Springs.

There's no time.

My pockets are empty.

I must have dropped my phone somewhere. It's not by the coffee machines. It's not in the back room. Under the smashed cash register?

Nope.

Whatever. I grab my wallet and keys.

After I catch up to the midnight blue mini-van, I'll memorize the license plate, pull over somewhere, and call the police. I'm certain they won't do anything unless I can identify the vehicle for them.

I can hear it now: *911, what's your emergency?*

I'd call them now, but I know from experience the men in blue won't do anything without tons of solid information. The gunman stayed well hidden behind his bandanna, and I'm caring less and less that he robbed us. That girl, Lucía, is more important. Unfortunately, this note is insufficient for the police to pull over that mini-van. I'd have to describe the nastiness of her boyfriend and how oddly she behaved to get them to do anything, and I still doubt it would be enough.

They have never believed me before.

What happened at the aquarium was not my fault.

What happened to my cousin was not my fault.

I've got to get on the road and stop that mini-van.

There's no time to hesitate. I'll call the police right after I find them.

I know that man is planning to hurt that girl if he hasn't already. He might be planning to sell her. He might sell her the way my cousin was sold years ago. Those human traffickers ruined my cousin's life.

I can't let that happen to Lucía.

That tattoo on her leg told me everything I need to know.

CHAPTER FOUR

DMITRI - 2007

Old-school tattoo designs cover the walls. Black ink on white paper. Dmitri Belkin sits on a bench in the tattoo parlor, the only light coming from a red lamp in the corner. He chose this place because of the old designs. They remind him of his heyday. Back when he was the best. Back when the Cubans talked about the one Russian whose tattoo art surpassed all. They did not care he was Russian. He was *el mejor tatuador.*

Now, Dmitri can't hold a needle steady if his life depended on it, and it does.

He'd been worried about holding the baby steady in his lap while waiting, but she's been no problem. She's a good one. His new friends, the crickets in his head, agree.

"Why did we have to meet so late?" Havana's current top tattoo artist sits on a round swivel chair with wheels and looks Dmitri up and down. He glances at the baby, parts his lips as if he's about to say something, but doesn't say a word. He appears anxious, like he doesn't want to be here. He is young, but to Dmitri, everyone is young. This artist's 2000s is Dmitri's 1970s. It's his heyday now. "Why couldn't you have come in during the day?"

Dmitri shifts his weight. The bench is uncomfortable. It needs more padding, but that's because he no longer has any of his own. He's emaciated, all skin and bone, but soon, that won't matter anymore. "No one can know I was here."

"Why not?"

"Do you know who I am?"

"I know you're paying double for this, right? That's the only reason I opened the shop this late." He leans over and switches on a desk lamp. The wheels on his chair squeak as he inches toward Dmitri, and Dmitri winces.

"So," Dmitri says, "you have no idea who I am. Is that true?"

"Hey, I don't know you, and I don't care who you think you are. I just want to get this over with and go home."

It's good the artist doesn't know who Dmitri is, but it also hurts. Everything hurts. His skin. His bones. His pride. He's lost his will to live. He's lost almost everything. Dmitri is no longer *el mejor tatuador*. His reputation is gone. His fame is gone.

His family. They're all gone.

"I was never here," Dmitri says.

The artist stares at him.

"I was never here," Dmitri repeats. "Say it."

"Huh?"

"Say I was never here. Make me believe you."

"Okay." The artist clears his throat. "You were never here."

"Good."

"But you are still paying double, right? Even though you were never here?"

Dmitri nods.

"Okay. Where do you want it, and what do you want? I have a lot to do tomorrow, and I need my sleep, so please, let me get started."

"It's a simple tattoo. It's just a number, but I will not pay if it is not done well. Make sure to outline each digit deeply so as the skin ages, they will still be readable.

"Here." The artist tears a piece of paper from a pad and grabs a pen. "Write the number down so I can see what I'm working with."

"No." Dmitri pushes the paper away.

"What? Why?"

"I will tell you the number, and you will forget it after I leave. No one can know the number. I was never here."

The headlights of a passing vehicle invade the parlor, causing Dmitri to squint. His eyes hurt. Everything hurts. He shifts his weight on the bench again. He doubts the car outside belongs to *them*. The lights disappeared too quickly.

"Are you all right?" asks the artist.

"I'm okay. For now."

"Why can't you write the number down? What's going on here?"

Dmitri grins. Usually, he avoids opening his mouth. Four of his front teeth are missing, and the rest are broken in half or cracked. "If I were to leave the number with you, it would eventually destroy you the way it has me. Is that what you want?"

The artist's eyes widen, he shakes his head and scoots his chair back. Keeping his eyes on Dmitri as much as possible, he picks up a vial of black ink and places it on a metal tray table. He picks up the needle. "Where do you want the tattoo?"

"Right here." Dmitri lifts the baby off his lap, turns her

face down, and points at the back of her left calf. "I think this is the best place."

The baby begins to cry.

"Are you insane?" The artist puts the needle down. "I can't tattoo a baby."

"She's almost a year old. She won't be a baby much longer."

"I don't care. I—I'll get arrested."

"No, you won't." Dmitri raises his voice over the baby's cries. "I was never here. Remember?"

"I don't care where you ever were, old man. I'm not tattooing a baby."

"Yes, you are!" Dmitri shouts. He grasps his head with both hands. The crickets in his cranium are scurrying over his brain, their feet poking into it like toothpicks poking into Jello. He must have the tattoo put on the girl.

"Are you okay?" the artist asks.

Dmitri glances back at the window. For years now—no, decades—*they* have chased him. This government. That government. His captors. Cuba. Russia. They want the number. He's unsure who has chased him on any one day, but it's okay now. He has a plan. His new friends, the crickets in his head—they help him. The chase nearly destroyed him, and that's okay, too. He wants to die. But first, he must have the number put on the girl. Then, he must send her to the United States. The crickets told him so. He can't write the number down on paper. The powers after him monitor everything and everyone. He can't send it in a letter or tell anyone the number or tell anyone what the number means.

If the wrong people obtain it, or someone destroys it, the world will end. The number is the world, and the world is the number.

The crickets assure Dmitri he's doing the right thing. He's removing the burden of carrying this number—this launch code—inside his head all these years. Once put into safe hands, he'll finally be free. He's saving the world. Soon, the nightmare will be over.

Dmitri lowers his hands. "I'm okay." He grins at the artist. "I didn't mean to scare you. I got excited because it's very important that you give her this tattoo. I can pay you triple."

"I don't know." He rubs his chin. "This seems like more trouble than it's worth."

"Quadruple."

"You don't look like you have the money, old man. I mean, those rags barely cover your chest, and your shoes—do you call those shoes?"

Dmitri grins again, purposely displaying his lack of dental care. "Don't worry about the money." He pats his front pants pocket. "I can pay quadruple."

The baby's crying has turned into wailing.

The artist stands up and heads for the door.

"Where are you going?"

"Don't worry. I'm just locking up. I don't want anyone to come in and catch me doing this."

Paranoid orange picker.

When the artist returns, he sits and wipes his brow. "Let's get this over with." He picks up the needle. "Lay her down over here and hold her still."

The crickets screech with joy.

Dmitri does as he asks.

The baby shrieks incessantly.

The artist sweats more.

Each time the artist wipes the blood off the baby's leg, he

also wipes his forehead. Before long, his face is covered in her blood.

He tattoos the numbers: 20863451—

"Wait." Dmitri grasps the artist's wrist and pulls it away from the baby. "Stop."

"Why? I'm almost done."

"I chose the wrong place."

The artist glances around the parlor. "What?"

"For the tattoo. The number will be out in the open anytime she wears a skirt or short pants. I should have had you put it somewhere else."

"Well, I can't move it now."

Dmitri thinks.

"Hey," the artist says. "I can't take much more of this. Her crying is killing me."

"Put the last two numbers on her inner thigh. Here." Dmitri flips the baby over and pulls her diaper down. "Put them right there by her crotch."

The artist blanches, then shakes it off. "Fine."

The needle breaks fresh skin.

The screaming reaches new levels.

Dmitri smiles.

Soon, it won't matter if *they* find him. Once she is delivered to the US, it will all be over. The code will be safe with the one person in the world he can trust. Someday, the code can be used to safely deactivate the missile. Any tampering without the code could cause a nuclear war. Dmitri made it that way. He made up the code, added the code to the circuitry, and made the code mandatory before memorizing it. Like his father, he was once a brilliant man. One of Russia's shining stars. This was long ago. Cuba in the '60s. Admittedly, the burden of keeping the code to himself all these years has driven him insane, but he doesn't care about that so much.

He just wants the crickets to go away.

He titters, then stifles a full-on laugh.

The crickets promised him this would work.

He can forget the code now.

He's finally to be free.

Free to die.

Even if *they* capture him now, they'll get nothing.

All he needs to do is forget the code.

Tomorrow, the artist will no longer have the code in his head either.

Tomorrow, the artist will no longer have a head.

Not one that works, anyway.

The crickets helped Dmitri arrange this.

It must be this way.

Dmitri smiles his toothless smile.

Maybe the crickets will leave him alone now.

The baby wriggles on his lap, sobbing, while the artist applies a bandage.

She's a good one.

This is going to work.

CHAPTER FIVE

JACK

Jack Clark presses gently on the gas pedal as he circles the Pay-n-Save convenience store, searching for the blue Honda mini-van. He's been at this for days now. The gas pumps in front have no customers. He's not surprised. No one ought to be here this early on a Monday morning in the middle of nowhere, Florida. The only car around is an old, faded Toyota wagon parked behind the store. Even the color black can fade.

Eventually, his Camaro's paint job will fade, too, but not today.

Today, his Camaro wants to roar. His Camaro wants Jack to find the mini-van and run it down before time runs out.

But Jack is not like his Camaro.

Jack wants to go home and sleep in his own bed.

He cruises slowly around the side of the building, heading toward the highway. A redheaded clerk with a Pay-n-Save shirt passes by the front window. At least, working for himself, he doesn't have to wear a uniform. He doesn't have to work at a place like this. He's grown to hate convenience stores.

They're all the same.

Well, not quite.

Some are red and white. Some are green and white. Brown and . . . white. He never noticed that before. Gas stations are like hospitals. They're all white on the outside but all the same on the inside. Convenience stores all sell the same junk food—not that it's bad. He's just tired of eating chips and jerky. Hot dogs and chicken fingers. Donuts and coffee. He's tired of staying in hotels with wasted desk clerks barely able to give out room keys. He's tired of many things. People. Paranoid women convinced their husbands are cheating on them. Cheating husbands convinced their wives are having them followed. Kleptomaniac employees. Embezzlers. Gamblers. Abusive step-parents. Stalkers. Predators.

Parents insisting their runaway teens were kidnapped.

Becoming a private investigator isn't all it was cracked up to be.

When he was a process server, he could sleep in his own bed most nights. That is, when he could sleep. Delivering summons to evil people didn't feel good, but it paid the bills. Capturing dirt on innocent people feels worse. Fortunately, no one in this world is innocent, so PI work is better. He's tired of it, but at least he can sleep now.

He made the right decision.

His Camaro purrs onto Highway 19.

It wants to roar.

Cypress and oak trees hang out along the sides of the two-lane highway, casting intermittent shadows. The morning sunlight on the road flashes on and off faster and faster as he accelerates. With his sunglasses on, Jack can't see what's hiding in the shadows. With his sunglasses off, the bright flashes of light make his eyes water.

He can't win.

He puts his sunglasses on the dashboard, and his cell phone buzzes. It's his client, Colter.

"Tell me the good news, Jack. Have you found her?"

"Yes."

"You have? That's great. When are you—"the connection falters and sounds robotic"—wetring rit were?"

"Sorry, I didn't catch that." Aside from the bad connection, Colter has an odd accent. It's been hard to understand him from the beginning, right when they first met. He must be from a part of Canada Jack's never been to. Maybe the French part, though Colter doesn't sound like Pepé Le Pew.

"When are you bringing her back?" Colter asks, raising his voice as if that were the problem.

"The good news is, I found her, but she's not with me. She's in a mini-van heading north on Highway 19. The bad news is . . . I lost the mini-van."

"You—this is not good. I want my daughter back now." His voice shakes. "If you lost track of the van, how do you know where she is?"

"She's in a van. I just don't know exactly where the van is, but I'm sure they're going north. They traveled north all day yesterday until they stopped for dinner at an Applebee's."

"They? Who's she with? How many of them are there?"

"Just one. She's with a muscle-bound, tattoo-covered biker type. He's bald and has a beard. Do you know him?"

"No. Absolutely not."

"Does he sound like someone she would hang out with? Date?"

"No. Absolutely not. She's not dating him. He kidnapped her. She's been gone for a month without calling or texting

. . . for the love of God, you've got to bring her back to me. What happened yesterday? How'd you lose them?"

"After Applebee's, I followed them to a hotel and sat in the parking lot all night. When—"

"When you saw her, why didn't you save her?"

"Save her? From what? She went inside the restaurant and the hotel room willingly. There was nothing to save her from."

"She's in danger, Jack. I expected better. Nathan said you'd be the best for this job. You came highly recommended, and now you're just sitting around watching her. That is, until you completely dropped the ball and lost her."

The trees surrender to the sun, pulling their shadows away from the road and exposing a grassy field stretching east and west.

Jack puts his sunglasses on. "I'm a private investigator. You hired me to find her, not kidnap her. The guy she's with looks like an evil miscreant, but he hasn't done anything to her I could see."

If Jack has learned anything since his time in jail, it's patience. That's what got him there. A lack of patience and an abundance of assumptions. He damaged the wrong guy and won't make that mistake again.

"I want her back, Jack. Lucía is only eighteen. She's never even hinted at running away before, and she's never dated anyone like the man you described. He's going to hurt her. I'm certain of this. Maybe he brainwashed her or something, I don't know."

"He's not going to hurt her." Jack presses on the accelerator. His Camaro begins to roar. "I won't let that happen. I just have to be sure she's in real danger."

"You're not listening to me." Colter sighs. "Maybe I

should go with someone else. Is it money? Am I not paying you enough?"

"No, it's . . . look. I messed up. When that guy came out of the hotel room this morning, he glanced my way. I wasn't sure he saw me, but then he and Lucía got in the mini-van and took off down the street. They turned onto random side roads until I lost them. It was my bad."

"That's not good, Jack. She—" Something catches in his throat. "She's—if he hurts her, her blood will be on your hands. Mark my words. It will be on your hands."

Jack looks at his hands. Blood trickles between his knuckles. It's his stepfather's blood. The memory comes back to him like it was yesterday. His mother's face, bruised and swollen. His stepfather's face, bloodied and broken. That man should never have hit her. Jack saw it coming, but he was too late. He knew it was coming, but that was before he realized his stepfather was evil.

Before he realized all men are evil.

The muscle-bound miscreant traveling with Lucía is evil.

Colter is not wrong. If that man hurts Lucía . . . the blood.

Jack eases off the gas.

Patience.

Don't let it happen again.

The trees return to the side of the road, obliterating the sunlight and casting deep shadows on Jack's path. He takes his sunglasses off and searches the shadows ahead.

"Are you sure it's not money?" Colter says. "I can double what I'm paying you. I just want her back."

"You can double it if you want, but you don't have to. I made a mistake, that's all. Whether you pay me or not, I'll make sure Lucía is safe."

"I'm not certain. There's something wrong here. Is it the

man? Are you afraid of him?"

"No."

"Nathan said you took down a guy twice your size for beating his sister up." Jack wonders when—or *if*—that guy ever got out of the hospital. "That's why I hired you. It wasn't for your investigative skills. It was because I thought you'd be the kind of man to get things done."

"I didn't know it was his sister." Jack's neck tenses to the point of pain. "And he didn't do it. I got the wrong guy."

"Whatever, Jack. You've seen this man with Lucía at least twice now. So, unless you're lying to me, you know he's the right guy. I think you're afraid of him. I might need to get someone else."

"You don't have to do that. Double what you're paying me. I don't care. Either way, I'm going to catch up with them and make sure nothing happens."

"I don't know, Jack. I still think you're afraid, or you would have done something last night."

"Okay. You're right. You got me. I'm afraid." A mini-van—*the* mini-van—zooms through the shadows in the distance. "I'm afraid, but I'm not afraid of him."

"Then what is it? What scares you?"

Jack hits the gas.

His Camaro roars down the highway.

"I'm scared of myself. I'm scared of what I'll do if he hurts her."

CHAPTER SIX

MATTIE

I turn the key, and my old Corolla comes to life. As old as she is, I've never worried about her starting up. She's also never broken down, either. I call her Dory—after my aunt on my mom's side, not after *Finding Nemo*. That woman lived to be one hundred and one, and she smoked until her dying day. I'm glad I took the cigarettes out of my car, or I'd light up right now. My emergency pack is gone. I'm not a smoker anymore. I will quit and stay quit this time. I guess that means I'll make it to one hundred and two.

The gas pumps out front don't have any customers. No one has come in since Calvin and that lame thief took off. A strange Camaro almost stopped in, but it left the moment I turned the CLOSED sign on. I made sure to lock the front door. Phil is going to be pissed, but I have no choice.

I have to find that blue mini-van and memorize the license plate number.

The radio plays Rage Against the Machine. Somehow, that's perfect.

I wait to pull onto Highway 19. It's not really merging.

I'm waiting for a beater farm truck to go by because I was too slow to get ahead of it.

And now I'm stuck behind it.

Ugh. Could this farmer go any slower? Whenever I try to pass, a car is in the oncoming lane. It's like these cars time it this way on purpose.

That's it.

I'm going.

I pull around the truck.

A semi is racing toward me, barreling through the shadows. He's far enough away. I can make it.

"Watch out!" shouts a voice from the back.

Calvin's curly-haired head fills the rearview mirror.

So that's where he went.

My convenience store trainee got the lesson of a lifetime this morning.

"What are you doing in my car?" I ask.

"Holy deathtrap, Mattie. There's a semi coming."

"Who are you, Robin?"

"Oh, you know that show?"

"Everyone knows that show."

"I only watched it because of the Batmobile. Did you know the Batmobile was a Lincoln Futura?"

The semi isn't slowing down, but it is still a fair distance away. "No. I did not know that." I press the accelerator all the way to the floor.

"Stop!" Calvin yells. "You're going to get us killed."

"Relax. We have time. What are you doing in my car?"

"Hold on." He grabs the back of the passenger seat. "I'm coming up there." Carefully, he wedges his hips between the front seats and plops down on the passenger side. I'm unsure how he made it, but he fits just fine. He puts his hands on the dashboard and looks down the road. His cheeks shake with fear, but there's nothing to worry about. "He's not stopping, Mattie. Please, back off."

I keep the gas pedal pressed to the floor. *C'mon, Dory, don't fail me now.* I can read the logo on the semi's nose now. It says, "Peterbilt."

"Please, Mattie!"

Dory cruises just ahead of the farm truck, and I pull back into the lane with inches to spare. No problem. I glance over at Calvin and wait until the blood returns to his face before saying anything. "Are you okay?"

"You didn't have to do that," he says.

"If I didn't, who would? No one else was going to do it."

He cocks his head at me.

I grin.

"Where are we going?" he asks.

"I'm trying to catch up to that mini-van from this morning."

"The one that looked like a hearse?"

"I guess."

"I don't like mini-vans. They're big and clunky."

I pass him the note. "The girl in that mini-van is in trouble. I'm trying to help her. Now tell me, why were you in my car?"

"I like wagons." He glances at the back seat. "I like your car. It's old, but nice."

"You're right. She is nice, and her name is Dory." He's so young. "What's your deal with cars, anyway? Are you—" I decide not to ask if he's autistic or something because I don't want to offend him. Then, I change my mind. "Are you autistic or something?"

"No." He glances at the ceiling. "Not that I know of. I

just like cars. I like them a lot." He lowers his head, and we make eye contact. "I like them a lot, a lot."

"I noticed, but does that mean you go around breaking into them?"

"No. It was open." This is true. As much as I love Dory, I never lock the doors. No one is going to steal her. She is too old and hard on the eyes. "I was afraid if I tried to run, that guy would chase me down and shoot me. I needed to hide somewhere, and this was the best place to go. You know he was going to shoot me, right?"

"No, I knew he wouldn't. He was a coward."

Calvin wipes his forehead.

It *is* a little warm in here.

I turn the A/C on, and a hint of rancid cigarette scent blows through the vent. I can't wait for Dory's lungs to clear like mine.

"Can you slow down?"

"No."

"Can we go back?"

"No." I point at the girl's note.

Calvin reads it again and nods.

"I'll take you back after we catch up with the mini-van and I get the license plate number."

"You know, that might not help. With practice, license plates can be switched in under three minutes."

"How do you know that?"

"I just know."

"First you break into my car, then you tell me how to switch license plates. Are you sure you're not a thief?"

"I'm sure. I just like cars."

"How about this one?" We're coming up behind a late-model Camaro. It might be the one I saw earlier. Now, it's in my way and going a lot faster than the beater farm truck was. Oh, well. Dory can do it. I mash the pedal down and swerve into the oncoming lane.

"Oh, no." Calvin grips the dash. "Not again. We're already going fast. We don't have to pass them."

"Yes, we do."

"Why?"

"Because if we don't, who will?"

"You keep saying that, and it just doesn't make any sense. If it's a joke, it's not funny."

It's hard to see anything down the highway because of the shadows from the trees, and a bend is coming, but I think it's clear. At least until a car rounds the bend. It's a mini-van, but it's not *the* mini-van. It's coming our way. This one is dark gray and nearly disappears each time it enters the shade.

"There's a car coming." The blood has drained from Calvin's face again. "It's a Chrysler Pacifica with a 3.6-liter V-6, and it weighs over four thousand pounds. It will crush us."

"How do you know all that? You can't even see the grill from here. How do you know it's a Chrysler?"

"I can see it. I have 20/10 vision."

Whatever. I'm not stopping. I pull up alongside the Camaro. The driver glances at me. I'm surprised by the way he looks. He has narrow, darkly decisive eyes and thick, shoulder-length hair, also dark. He's not a typical Floridian hick, and he's not happy with me. He gazes straight ahead and hits the gas. His Camaro thunders forward.

Dory lets out a moan. I push her, and she surges forward, her nose edging past the Camaro's front end.

The mini-van coming toward us blares its horn.

I push Dory harder, but she's not clearing the Camaro. The guy isn't backing off. I can't pull in front of him without running him off the road.

Calvin scrunches his eyes shut. Grips the dashboard. "We're going to die."

The mini-van positions itself in the middle of the road, horn blaring, coming straight at us. *Psycho.* A moment later, the min-van appears to be slowing down, but it's hard to tell, and it won't be enough in any case. I steer us onto the left shoulder, straddling it, making some room for the mini-van in the middle, but if the Camaro doesn't do the same, the mini-van won't fit between us.

Rocks fly up behind us, pinging off Dory's fenders.

I glance out the passenger side window at the Camaro. He isn't giving in. He's keeping his course straight down the right side of the highway, occupying the entire lane.

The mini-van veers toward Dory. We're almost nose-to-nose when it veers back to center, heading for the Camaro.

I swing back onto the highway and glance in the rearview mirror.

Smoke engulfs the Camaro's tires, and it swerves off the road, spinning to rest facing the other way as the mini-van resumes its voyage down the road as if nothing had happened.

The man in the Camaro should have backed off sooner. I hope he's okay.

Calvin's not okay.

He's still breathing, and he appears to be alive, but he looks like he could vomit or have a heart attack at any moment.

I press on the brakes and slow down just in time to take the bend in the highway without sliding off the road.

"You didn't have to do that," Calvin says, gasping.

"Yes, I did. If I didn't—"

"I know. I know. No one else would. But why would

anyone?"

After the bend, I search the horizon for the blue Honda mini-van, but there's nothing. "We've got to catch up with that girl. There's no time to waste."

"You don't have to rush everything. If we had crashed, you'd never be able to catch up with her."

"But we didn't, did we?"

"No." He lowers his chin. "But if something unexpected had happened, we would have run off the road, like that guy back there. What if an armadillo had run out in front of us?"

"But, it didn't, did it? In situations like this, every moment counts, and an armadillo wouldn't have stopped anything."

"What about a hundred armadillos?"

I shoot him a look.

"Never mind," he says.

"Did you see the tattoo on that girl's leg this morning?"

"No."

"It was a number. Like a stock number."

"So, maybe it was her birthday."

"No. The numbers were blocky. The style didn't fit her. Someone as pretty as she was wouldn't get something like that on purpose."

"So?"

"So, I think the man she was with is a human trafficker. It's the same thing that happened to a cousin of mine. I never knew her very well, but I do know she was sold into slavery by a man like that, and she was never the same. The experience destroyed her. I'm telling you, that man is taking that girl to Salt Springs for some reason, and from the note, she clearly did not want to go there. He might be selling her or—"

"I don't want to go to Salt Springs, either." He clears his

throat. It sounds phlegmy. "I want to go back. I don't feel good."

I accelerate, edging past twenty-five miles per hour over the speed limit. "We can't stop now. I'm sorry. Any hesitation could get her killed. You're going to have to trust me on this."

I think about the days leading up to the manatee's death. How I kept telling myself I'd get to it tomorrow. How I had hesitated, and then it happened. Those tiny, soulful green-gray eyes closed forever. I miss working at the aquarium so much. They put me through hell when I tried to keep my job, but that wasn't the worst part. Watching the manatee die, knowing I was too late to do anything about it. I hadn't acted fast enough.

That was the worst part.

CHAPTER SEVEN

LUCÍA

Wyatt throws the last piece of jerky into his mouth and swallows without chewing. Lucía is suddenly hungry, but not as hungry as she is nervous. Scared. Terrified, at times. Her heartbeat spikes every few minutes when she thinks of what will happen when they arrive in Salt Springs. Anything could happen after Wyatt leaves her there with someone else.

Longleaf pines form a thin veil over the clearings that sleep on the sides of the highway.

"We're not stopping again until we arrive," Wyatt says.

"But I have to go to the bathroom now." Lucía caresses the Bob Marley lighter in her pocket.

"You'll just have to hold it."

Caressing the lighter soothes her. Her heartbeat slows for a moment. Thoughts of the few Bob Marley songs she knows soothe her. He is one of those old sixties singers, crooning about peace and hope like that famous band, the Beatles.

Peace and hope.

Her lighter. Fire.

Wyatt isn't going to stop again. She won't have another

chance to drench him in gas and threaten him with the lighter.

She glances at the floor. Stale potato chip crumbs. A plastic grocery bag. Two empty cans of Monster. The only flammable items are some receipts from Applebee's. Lighting them on fire wouldn't do anything except make Wyatt stop the mini-van. He'd just take her lighter away and continue down the road.

He checks the rearview mirror.

She checks the passenger-side rearview mirror.

Wyatt sniffs, pinches his nose, and looks at his fingers to see if anything came off.

"I hate you," she says.

He looks in the mirror again.

Her heartbeat speeds up. "I don't understand why you're going to leave me. You still haven't told me why or with who. Why are you doing this to me?"

"Don't make it harder for me than it already is. I like you, but you knew this was coming."

"No, I didn't. I still don't know why we're going to Salt Springs. Why not Lakeland? Or St. Petersburg?"

"My boss has a place he uses in Salt Springs." He checks the rearview mirror again.

"Your boss?" She glances at her mirror. "You don't have a boss. You're unemployed."

"Why do you keep looking in the mirror?" he asks.

"Why do you?"

"Is there something I don't know? Did you do something back there at the Pay-n-Save?"

Lucía tries not to think about it, but thoughts of dropping the note on the floor for the clerk race into her head, and she begins to smile.

Hope.

Peace and hope.

"You did," he says. "You did something back there, didn't you?"

She shakes her head and covers her mouth.

"Tell me the truth. Tell me now." He slams his hand on the steering wheel and glares at her. "Tell me now, or I'll make you pay."

"I didn't do anything," she shouts. "You're paranoid. I keep looking in my mirror because you keep looking in yours. What's your problem?"

"Ah." He takes a deep breath. "Another hour, and it won't matter." He checks his mirror again. "I lost him."

"Who?"

"There was this muscle car following us yesterday. I thought I lost it this morning when we left the hotel, but I think it was behind us a little while ago."

Hope.

Maybe her father did send someone to find her.

Lucía looks in her mirror.

No one is back there, but maybe someone *is* coming for her after all.

"What kind of muscle car?"

He squints at her. "Do you know someone with a Camaro?"

"I have a friend in school with one, but they don't know where I am."

"Who? What kind?"

"No one. Never mind. I almost never talk to them."

"What kind?"

"An old one. Maybe from the sixties. He and his dad restored it so he'd have something to drive."

"Oh. The one behind us is a lot newer than that." He

relaxes his shoulders. Glances at her. "You haven't seen it back there, have you?"

"No." But if God exists, she will. Soon.

Hope.

She caresses the lighter once more and stops. No need to draw Wyatt's attention to her pocket.

She checks the mirror, this time looking for a newer Camaro.

Nothing.

"You're right," he says. "I'm being paranoid. I don't have anything to worry about. We'll be there soon, and if someone is following us, Stanley will take care of them."

"Who is he, exactly? Is he, like, your boss?"

"Yep."

The sunlight dances on Wyatt's shoulders. His tattoos are so lit, catching the rays through the windshield. He's fire. His thick arms and chest—so badass on the outside. She had no idea how rotten someone could be on the inside. Granted, she's not great, either. Not anymore. Hate wells inside her, but—he's not even close to being the person she thought he was. He's a . . . a—a kidnapper.

The basement. All the hours she spent in the basement. The walls closing in and opening up, expanding and contracting with her daily sleep cycles. The parties where he never—never ever—never left her side. Always holding her by the elbow. How could she not have seen what he was doing until now?

He is right.

They were never ever a couple. He only let her think that because—

She takes a hard look at his face.

This is not the bad boy she fell for. He's much worse. It's

like aliens came and replaced him yesterday morning. He's a kidnapper. A human thief. A predator.

And she's his prey.

His phone buzzes.

"Hey, I thought you might be calling." He smirks at Lucía as if she ought to know who's on the phone. "No, we're about an hour out. We'll be on time."

She can't hear what the caller says exactly, but it sounds like a man. "Who is it?" she asks.

"Shh." He covers the receiver for a second. "It's my boss."

She nods.

"No," Wyatt says into the phone, "no problems. That was her. She's fine—really fine, if you know what I mean. He won't be disappointed." He pauses. Listens. "Okay, yeah. There is one other thing. I—someone might be following us, but that's not a problem, right? I mean, if they show up, you can just have one of your guys tell them to go away, right?"

Shouting to the point of screaming comes from the phone. Wyatt holds it away from his ear.

Lucía's heartbeat spikes, and she gasps. She does not want to be left with this man. Wyatt's boss. Stanley. What a disgusting name.

"But," Wyatt raises his voice, "we're so close."

More shouting.

"Okay. Okay. I'll leave it somewhere and—" He waits for a new round of screaming to stop. "I know. You're right, we *will* be late now. He'll understand."

Lucía glances in her mirror, hoping to see that Camaro. Any Camaro.

Nothing.

Wyatt holds his phone to his face, taps the screen with his

thumb, and puts it back in his pocket. "Looks like you're going to get your wish."

"What? We're going back? It's over?"

"No." He laughs. "We're going to pull over somewhere. You'll get to pee or whatever, but you'll probably have to do it in the bushes."

"Why?"

"Because I doubt there'll be a bathroom."

"No? Why are we pulling over then?"

"We're upgrading." He turns toward her and lowers his chin. "My boss's client doesn't want us showing up in a mini-van."

"Is that so?"

He nods and begins scanning the sides of the highway. "We need to dump this heap and find something else."

She reaches into her pocket.

Grasps the lighter.

When they get out of the mini-van, she'll have her chance.

Bob Marley.

Hope.

CHAPTER EIGHT

Yans Rivero keeps his back straight against a fiery red-leather chair, his hands folded anxiously on a small, round tabletop, and his gaze on the striptease stage. The main stage. The only stage. All the other dances take place on shoddy tables scattered throughout the club. It's a wonder they don't fall more often. The place always looks more dangerous with the lights on. The stench of cheap perfume and stale alcohol lingers in the air from last night, and one of Yans's boots sticks to the floor. He shifts his foot, and the sole makes a plastic-wrap tearing sound.

Water droplets cling to overhead pipes, and sweat runs in a rivulet over the salmon scar on Yans's cheek. The basement club is hot in the morning before they open, and it is also quiet. So quiet, Yans can hear Darien breathing in the corner.

Yans calls out, "Next."

Darien startles. His green military uniform fits tight against his body, and he does not say a word. He keeps his mouth closed. A wise move.

No one comes out onto the main stage.

Yans sighs.

Two or three more times.

That's all.

Yans should only need to come back here two or three more times. By the end of the month, filling the tables with dancers won't matter, and he will no longer need to subject himself to appraising these whores. He'll no longer feel compelled to risk his position as Colonel in the Cuban military for the sake of this extra money. The money he needs for his family. He tells himself to have patience for one more month.

He tells himself, within a month, money won't matter.

The stage is still empty.

Darien stands in the corner with his back straight and arms at his side.

"What's the problem?" Yans glowers at him. "Where's the next one?"

"I'm not sure." Darien marches toward the main stage. "Let me check." He disappears around the corner.

One whore. Yans only needs to choose one dancing puta today, and he's out of here.

Darien returns to the corner. Stands at attention, his young eyes fixed on the stage. "She's on her way."

A thick Latina woman wearing a pink thong and torn black half-shirt—the underside of a lime green bra exposed—takes the stage. Her neck carries a roll of fat, bobbing as she struts.

Yans lowers his chin. Covers his eyes. Shakes his head.

"This is Estrella Verde," Darien says.

Yans looks up. "This is a nightmare."

Estrella begins to sway her hips. Her thighs are like oil barrels, and as she spins, one butt cheek appears to be larger than the other. She does not have a tattoo on either leg.

Yans can't do it. He wants to choose her and leave, but putting a manatee on a dance table is the same as leaving an empty table empty. No money. "I don't have time for this." He scowls at Darien. "We have other pressing matters to attend to today."

Darien nods.

"What do you mean?" asks the stripper.

"I mean," Yans says as he stands, "unless you've been to the US, get your zorra ass off the stage. Have you ever been to the US?"

"No."

"Then off with you."

"No." Estrella puts one hand on her hip and waves the other as she speaks, shaking her finger. "I came all this way. I need the money."

"You need surgery." Yans runs his eyes up and down her body. "I recommend you replace everything below your neck. But no, that wouldn't fix your face. Get off the stage."

"My face? What about yours? Is that a scar, or worms having sex?"

"*La puta.*" He reaches for his government-issue, a Browning Hi-Power seventeen shot. His favorite pistol. "You should not speak to me this way."

"Please." Darien extends his hands and goes to the girl. "Do as he says."

"No."

Yans pulls the pistol out of his waistband.

Darien takes Estrella by the arms and rushes her off the stage.

"No more of this!" Yans shouts as he returns his weapon to his waistband. "The next one had better be good so we can leave."

Darien leans forward as he rushes back to the corner beneath the sweating pipes. "But *señor*, we need to choose three today. Two more quit last night."

"You must think I'm a fool. You're telling me this now?"

"I thought you knew."

"How would I have known? I don't come to this place during business hours."

"I know, *señor*, but you, you always know so much. You have such knowledge at all times, I assumed—"

"We don't have time for this, Darien. We must check on your friends in the US. They're getting closer, aren't they?"

"It's hard to tell."

Darien's lower lip trembles faintly. He is not lying, but he is afraid. Fear rots a soldier's will. Darien may not be the man Yans had hoped.

Water drips from a pipe in the ceiling, splashing down next to Darien's military boots, just missing his head.

Darien does not move.

Yans sits. Clasps his hands on the table. Squeezes his fingers together until his knuckles hurt. "Next!"

No one comes out.

Yans shoots Darien a look.

"Sorry, *señor*. Please, let me see what is happening."

"Yes, you do that. How many more do we have to review?"

"Several from the street, and some arrived by boat yesterday." He heads behind the stage. "Close to ten."

This nightmare may never end.

"Anyone from the US?"

Darien appears on the stage. He pushes a woman forward. She stumbles and falls to her knees.

"Get up." Darien grabs her by the arms. "Dance."

The woman's skin looks like cracked earth under a relentless sun, bright but dark.

"Turn around!" Yans shouts at the whore.

She does as commanded.

She has no tattoo on her leg.

CHAPTER NINE

JACK

After spinning out and sliding down a grassy embankment, Jack's mighty Camaro backfired, and the engine died. He sat facing the wrong way, catching his breath and picturing that evil—black-as-night evil—Toyota wagon that ran him off the road. That frizzy-haired, redheaded woman who wouldn't back down. She had come out of nowhere right when he'd spotted the blue mini-van in the distance.

Now, it was gone.

Again.

He hits the START button, and a red light flashes, and the engine does not start, and he searches the instrument panel for a reason, and—cars won't start unless the transmission is in Park.

He's lost his patience.

He's in a frenzy, and that's when mistakes happen.

Jack closes his eyes, takes a deep breath, and puts the transmission into Park.

This time, the engine roars to life.

He shifts into drive, and his phone rings. Colter, again.

He slides the gearshift back to Park and answers the phone.

"I don't have time to talk right now," he says.

"I'm sorry to bother you again, Jack, but I wanted to apologize."

"For what?"

"For accusing you of being afraid. Given your history and my discussion with Nathan, I realized how wrong I was."

A wind rushes into the gully, bending the wild grasses at their base, beating the side of the car's hood. "Is that all?"

"Yes. I know you're doing your best. Have you caught up with them yet?"

"Hold on." Jack puts the transmission into Drive and hits the gas. Dirt flies up behind him, and he spins the wheel as the Camaro tears up the embankment. The rear wheels spin on the grass until they screech on the pavement, and he's off, thundering down the road.

The blue mini-van, the black wagon—both gone. Neither are on the horizon.

"Sorry about that," Jack says. "What did you ask?"

"Have you caught up with them yet?" Colter's voice has tightened.

"I had, but then this—wait a minute. Am I the only one you hired to find your daughter?"

"Yes."

"You don't have a backup? You didn't decide to replace me and not tell me?"

"Yes, I don't—I mean, no. I—there's no one else, Jack. I haven't hired anyone else. Why?"

"An odd woman ran me off the road." Odd, but familiar. Calmer now, Jack remembers seeing that woman somewhere before, but he can't place the memory. "I don't know why she was going so fast and wouldn't let me pass."

"You ran off the road?" Colter raises his voice. "What the hell? You've got to find my daughter. You don't have time to be playing Dukes of Hazzard out there with strangers."

"I know. It wasn't my fault. It'll be okay. After you and I talked, I spotted the mini-van, so I know I'm heading in the right direction." Jack pictures the redhead behind the wheel of her wagon, flying down the road ahead of him. His anger flares. "That woman has probably passed the mini-van by now, so I'm going to do the same. I'm going to catch up with her and give her a piece of my—"

"What? You don't have time for that. Forget about her. Bring back Lucía, or I'll fire you."

"But, that woman, she—I thought you called to apologize."

"I did, and thank God I did. You're losing your mind."

No, Jack is losing his cool. Colter is sort of right. Jack needs to refocus and let what happened with that woman go. Revenge won't finish this job.

He shakes his head and squints.

This is it. This is his last PI gig. After this, he's quitting for good.

A slow-moving tractor-trailer blocks the road.

Jack hits the brakes, slowing down just in time. The manila file folder on Lucía slides off the passenger seat and spills open on the floor. The printout with her photo and information leans against the wheel well. Copper, mahogany skin shrouded by curly, thick black hair, a bright smile, and deep, cocoa-colored eyes that make the sky over the beach in the background a brilliant blue. She looks like a springbreaker about to hit the beach.

"Did you hear what I said?" Colter asks.

"You're right. I'll forget about the woman in the wagon."

No, he won't.

Again, Jack gets that niggling feeling he's seen her before, and if that's the case, she might have something to do with Lucía. Could she have been following him while he was following them?

"Jack?"

"Don't worry. I'll focus on catching the mini-van."

"And then?"

Jack glances at the printout on the floor. "And then, what?"

Colter clears his throat. "I want my daughter back. Now. I know you said I didn't hire you to kidnap her from her kidnapper, but that's the job. It's what I want, so stop screwing up and get to it."

"Yeah, about that. I need to ensure everything is right before I can go that far."

When Jack first met Colter, he was impressed by the Canadian's presence. A tall man whose broad shoulders had cast a shadow over the table between them and whose piercing blue eyes had controlled the conversation. But, at the time, Colter was friendly in that Canadian way. He was one red jacket away from being Dudley Do-Right. Still, it was easier negotiating with him over the phone.

Jack glances at the photo of Lucía on the floor again. Curious.

"Your daughter doesn't look anything like you," he says. "How do I know I'm not being set up to kidnap someone else's daughter?"

"I thought I'd mentioned this already. She's adopted."

"Is that so?"

"Yes. Almost at birth. I love her the same as if she were blood-related, so I never think to bring it up." His voice nearly squeaks. He makes a choking sound. "I love her so much."

"I'll find her."

"And then?"

Jack scans the road ahead. Still no one. No min-van. No wagon.

No one.

"And then, I'll bring her back to you. Do you have any idea why they're going so far north? Any guesses?"

"I don't know. I can only let my imagination run wild."

"What's your imagination telling you?"

"I read these horrible articles on human trafficking. The man she's with might be a pimp. These men form relationships with girls and effectively trick them into slavery. That might be why you saw her *willingly* go with him into the hotel yesterday." He pauses. Sniffs. "Trust me. Lucía needs your help. After a time, the article said these 'groomers' often become violent to get what they want." Another pause. "Oh, Jesus . . . what if it is sex trafficking?"

"Is that why she has a number tattooed on her leg? Does it—"

"No, no. She's always had that tattoo, from the day we met her. It was some Cuban rescue thing." His voice sounds raw. "Think, Jack. Putting numbers on people would only call attention to what traffickers are doing. They wouldn't do that. It's a myth. The article said so. Please, you've got to find her."

Jack's been absently laboring behind the tractor-trailer. He mashes the gas pedal to the floor and whips around it with reckless abandon.

His Camaro feels good. It starts low before singing its way into a high-pitched whine, releasing a primal scream like a pterodactyl on fire.

The Florida sun beats down on the highway.

It's noon.

The highway stretches out straight into the distance, clear and narrow.

No wagon. No mini-van.

Lucía's picture stares up at him from the printout on the floor. Her innocent dimples beg him to find her.

To rescue her.

CHAPTER TEN

MATTIE

Whenever I left the front door to our apartment open, my mother would say, "Close the door, or we'll catch our death."

In the end, she was wrong. I continued to leave it open occasionally, and we didn't catch our death. Hank, however, the beloved forty-two-year-old manatee mascot of the South Florida Queen Museum and Aquarium, well—he did catch his death.

And it was my fault.

In a way, he died because I left the door open.

The pavement rushes beneath Dory's hood in a shiny blur. Water droplets from a sudden downpour scatter across the windshield as the rain subsides and stops. The pavement looks slick. It becomes mesmerizing if I stare too long at the road immediately ahead of the car. I need to focus my eyes down the highway. Find the hearse-like Honda mini-van. The midnight blue mini-van. The same blue as the thick carpet in the museum aquarium where I used to work. Where my degree in marine biology made the displays better by making the lives of the animals better. Animal lives matter. Then, they banished me to the Pay-n-Save because of Hank.

Because I didn't arrange for the panel to be fixed.

I didn't close the door.

Next time, I'll think ahead. Take action immediately.

Like now.

I need to focus.

I scan the road as far ahead as I can.

Where are you, Lucía?

The black clouds from the East darken the highway. It's hard to see far.

"Mattie!" Calvin shakes my shoulder, making me jump, which in turn makes us swerve.

"*What?*"

He's pointing out the passenger-side window. "Over there. It's a salvage yard. Look at all those cars."

A rusted chain-linked fence surrounds rows upon rows of abandoned cars, some stacked on each other like dead bodies in a mass grave. A chain hangs from the front gate, and a lock hangs from the chain, but the gate hangs wide open. Fresh tracks run in the mud, leading into the lot, disappearing around a corner. As we race past, a row of newer cars backed against the fence appears.

"Wait," he says. "We've got to go back." He twists in his seat and points out the back window. "The van. See?"

I glance in the rearview mirror, but by now we've gone too far. I hit the brakes and made an abrupt U-turn.

Calvin hangs onto the dashboard for dear life.

Sure enough, behind the fence, three cars down, a midnight blue mini-van rests in the mud next to a gunmetal-colored panel van. It's missing its license plates, but like Calvin said, those can be removed in seconds with practice.

"Do you think that's really it?" I ask.

"I know it is. I know cars."

We pull into the lot, and I park near the gunmetal panel van. Its broken headlights stare at me. The muted matte finish and dented sides reflect little light. This van looks like it was left here to die. It probably got stuck.

Stuck like a manatee in a cave.

Like Hank, when he pushed past the broken panel and swam into what we called "The Cave." I watched him on my computer. I don't remember why I was checking the underwater security camera feeds that day. Maybe I had a premonition something bad was about to happen. If so, I was right. His gray, gunmetal skin pressed hard against the sides of the cave.

He stopped moving.

I reached out for help, but no one responded. The tank was too far away for me to run to it.

Hank stopped moving.

He was stuck.

I could only watch helplessly on my computer screen as he drowned.

Hank couldn't have entered the cave if I hadn't put off scheduling the panel repairs. He wouldn't have died. They wouldn't have fired me.

I'll never put anything off again.

Calvin jumps out of the car and runs toward the mini-van.

The gray panel van sits next to it, staring at me with its broken headlights. Its sad manatee eyes.

I'll never put anything off again.

"Mattie," he shouts, waving to me. "Are you coming?"

Mud clings and flies off my shoes as I race after Calvin to the mini-van. Renewed. Reinvigorated. I'm unstoppable. The spot on the far side of the mini-van is empty, and tire tracks lead to the front gate.

Calvin has pulled the van's sliding door open and is rummaging through the back of the mini-van. It's trashed inside. They used the area right behind the front seats as a trash bin. Beer cans. Jerky wrappers. Empty bags of chips— all brands, but mostly Doritos. A few Fritos. Calvin holds up an unopened box of feminine pads and gazes at it curiously.

"You don't need those." I snatch it from him. "This is definitely the right car, though. These pads were the only thing the girl got from the store this morning." And a lighter. Maybe. A Bob Marley lighter. She'd really wanted it, and it was missing after she left. "Find anything else interesting?"

"They like Applebee's a lot." He holds up a fistful of receipts. "Oh, look." He reaches down and picks up an Applebee's gift card. "I wonder if there's money on it?"

I take the receipts from him. Based on the dates, Mr. Muscles has gone to an Applebee's once, sometimes twice, every day for several weeks. That much neighborhood steak can't be good for his stomach.

I open the front passenger-side door, and yes, more trash rests on the floor.

I search.

I hope to find another note written by Lucía. A plea for help. An explanation of what is going on. A reason they're going to Salt Springs. Something to confirm my suspicion she's being trafficked.

It's just past noon.

The rain has returned and drums on the roof.

"I'm done," Calvin says. He stands behind me, probably staring at my butt. If so, I take it as a compliment. Boys are boys. "Do you mind if I look around at the other cars? There are so many. It's like a museum."

I force my hand in between the seat and the center console. My fingers don't quite reach the floor, but something is down there. "You want to look at cars in the rain?"

"Why not?"

"We really don't have time." It's something small, smooth, and—oops. I almost had it pinched between my middle and forefinger, but it fell when I withdrew my hand.

"What do you mean?" he asks. "We lost them. Where do we have to go?"

"How about I treat you to lunch at the nearest Applebee's?" I slide the front seat back as far as it will go and reach underneath.

"What if they're not there?"

"Then we'll go to the next Applebee's. And the next."

He frowns.

I grasp the smooth item from beneath the seat and pull my hand out.

When I open my fingers, the song "Get Up, Stand Up" plays in my head.

Bob Marley.

Lucía needs to stand up for her rights.

She needs to hang on until I find her.

"Please?" he asks. "Can't we put lunch off just a little while so I can look?"

"No. We're leaving now."

I'll never put anything off again.

CHAPTER ELEVEN

LUCÍA

A disorienting feeling lifts Lucía above her seat. Heavy metal music plays on the car radio. She floats mid-air, knowing it's not real, before coming down. Wyatt must have drugged her this morning. He must have put something in the Monster he gave her. She drank half, took a shower, left it by the bed, and then drank the other half.

He had plenty of time to poison it.

"I'm hungry," he says.

Their new ride buzzes down the highway, the sound competing with thrashing guitars on the radio. At least this car is clean. Smelly, stale, but clean. It's a cheap Ford four-door. Something her father would never waste money on. The engine buzz irritates her. The guitars irritate her. But they're no longer complicating her headache. She's no longer loopy. Not like this morning at the convenience store. That was a fever dream. Slowly, throughout the day, she's become more lucid. She's almost fine now, but she's unsure why. Maybe Wyatt didn't slip her enough of whatever he's been using on her this morning.

Maybe it's adrenaline.

Maybe . . . she looks over at him.

Reality sets in.

He's not her boyfriend.

He's her kidnapper.

She's got to escape him.

She fumes.

Next chance she gets, she'll take her lighter and light him on fire. There's got to be a way, and she's got to make her move soon. They're hurtling toward Salt Springs now, late to meet Wyatt's boss and his "client." She shudders. She checks the passenger-side rearview mirror. If that Camaro is coming for them, it's looking for a blue mini-van, not a silver Ford Focus. It will never find her now.

"Aren't you hungry?" he asks.

The dark clouds overhead split open. A tiny patch of blue sky. The rain stopped only moments ago, but the chill has stayed. Wyatt hasn't turned the heat up, and Lucía doesn't want to touch it. She doesn't want to draw attention to herself. He lashed out when they stole the car, stunning her and unknowingly thwarting her attempt to escape at the abandoned car lot.

She glares at him out of the corner of her eye. He guides the car around a bend in the highway as if they're on their way to church.

He has her.

She's his.

The disorienting feeling returns for a moment. She floats and falls, and her stomach clenches.

The thought of it.

Him.

What he's done.

What he's become in the space of only one day.

He must have been drugging her for weeks, slowly increasing the dosage. Telling her she had come down with a cold to stem her complaints. Keeping her in that cold basement until she "felt better." Everything is coming together now. Clearer than ever. Especially now that he's admitted they were never a couple. Now that he's going to leave her in Salt Springs.

She closes her eyes and swallows.

He's going to burn for this.

Bob Marley is going to make him burn.

"We need to find an Applebee's," he says.

"Again?"

"Yeah. Why would we eat anywhere else?"

They pass a sign for Salt Springs. It's not far now.

Lucía thinks better than to say anything, but she can't help it. She should encourage him to stop for lunch, but Wyatt— the true Wyatt . . . he's a living contradiction. She can't stand it. "I thought we were in a hurry to meet with your boss. Aren't you worried about being late? Didn't he yell at you for being late? Now you want to go out of our way to eat?"

"Yeah. It's Stanley's fault. He made us dump the mini-van." Oh, how she hates his face when he talks. "I told him we'd be late, and he didn't care. We're going to be late no matter what now, and I'm hungry."

Another sign flies by. It lists restaurants. Applebee's is not on the list. "If you're so hungry, we should go to the next place to eat. I'm sick of Applebee's."

"You might be right. Not about Applebee's, but—I am hungry."

There are no cars in the rearview mirror. There are no cars in the distance.

Lucía catches Wyatt looking at her. She closes her eyes halfway and tilts her head to the side like she's woozy. He turns his gaze back to the road. It worked.

"Aren't you happy about stopping to eat?" he asks. "It'll be our last date. You should get something good to celebrate. Like a steak. I'll spring for it."

"Celebrate . . . what?" She lets her head bob to the side and gazes at the door lock on her side.

He grins. "Your new life."

Lucía groans, pretending to have trouble forming words.

"I'm gonna celebrate my payday." He glances at her. "When we get to Salt Springs, you behave, okay?"

"Your payday?"

"Yeah. I don't know why you're so important, but it's a lot. Stanley has been more on me about you than any other girl. It can't be that you're prettier than the others, because you're not. I don't get it."

Only two days ago, he told her she had a rocking body, like a new Harley Davidson. Now, she's a used scooter. "What does being pretty have to do with—"

"God, you're stupid." He shakes his head. "You're good-looking enough, though. I'm gonna miss the sex." He clears his throat and throws the last piece of jerky into his mouth. He doesn't need lunch. "It's not like I'm not jealous of Stanley's client or anything, it's"—he puts his hand on her thigh—"it's . . . okay. I'll admit it. I'm a little jealous."

"Sex?" She intentionally slurs the word. Shoves his hand away.

"Yeah." He laughs. "You're gonna have a lot of sex with your new beau. Just behave, okay?"

Her spine tingles. She shudders. She stares at the door lock. The tab sticks out. That must mean it's unlocked. She could open it right now and jump, but they're going too fast. Sometime yesterday, he started to keep the doors locked in the mini-van. When she'd drearily asked him why, he'd said nothing. Now, in this car, her door—it's not locked.

She sits up straight.

There are no cars on the horizon.

No cars behind them.

No Camaro coming for her.

She wants her dad.

She wants to sleep in her own bed tonight, wake up tomorrow, and have this all be a dream.

Panic sets in.

Adrenaline.

Run.

No. Think peace.

Think about Bob Marley, swaying to the calypso beat.

Think about using the Bob Marley lighter to burn Wyatt. Burn him, burn him, burn him—but she has nothing to light on fire. She missed her chance at the convenience store. At the abandoned car lot. Absurdly, she wishes Wyatt had long hair so she could jump into the back and light it on fire.

Rhythmic drums play on the radio. They sound like her heartbeat, but much slower. Frustratingly slower.

Wait.

If her door is unlocked, they're all unlocked. If she jumps into the back, maybe he'll stop the car and—

"He's gonna love you," Wyatt cackles. She recognizes the song now. It's Nine Inch Nails. "He's gonna love you like an animal." Wyatt sings along, butchering the lyrics.

She watches him closely as she unbuckles her seat belt. He doesn't hear the *click* over the music. In an instant, she lets the belt recoil, turns around, and thrusts her body between the front seats.

"Hey!" He reaches for her. Grabs the back of her shorts.

He can pull them off for all she cares.

She's getting out of here.

She fights her way into the back seat.

He loses his grip on her shorts.

She flops down face-first onto the faded cloth upholstery and inadvertently sucks in a slew of her frizzy black hair. She chokes on it and coughs.

He hits the brakes.

She tumbles off the seat onto the floor and faces the passenger-side door. She reaches up for the handle but misses when the car swerves and skids to a stop.

"Goddamn you, you bitch." He opens his door.

She can't reach the handle from here, but the door lock tab is up. The door's not locked. She extends her hand and stretches her fingers out but still can't reach.

"I can't believe you did that," he says from outside. Dirt crunches beneath his feet.

She inches her body forward, grasps the handle, and the tab sinks into the door with a *click*. She jerks on the handle, but the door doesn't open.

He locked it.

She rolls onto her back and looks up at him through the driver's side back window.

He holds the Focus's key fob in the air. "You're not going anywhere."

She kicks at the door and screams.

He presses a button on the fob—*click*—and opens the door.

She rolls over and reaches for the handle again, but he grabs her by the ankles and pulls her out of the car. Pain rushes into her head as her face bounces off the door jamb and hits the ground. She rolls over to face him and kicks wildly. He fights his way between her legs and grips her shirt just below the neck.

"Let me go!"

He pulls her face to his. His breath still reeks of jerky.

She reaches into her pocket for the lighter.

He makes a fist.

The lighter isn't there. Bob Marley isn't there.

Stars burst against a darkening sky. She's floating—disoriented once again.

Then, the stars disappear, and everything goes black.

CHAPTER TWELVE

YANS

A massive waterdrop falls from a rusty pipe and explodes on top of Darien's head. Darien does not move. The soldier boy doesn't even blink. The water runs down his face.

This pleases Yans.

Good soldier boy. Good.

The dank strip club basement closes in on Yans. The morning has left him. He's given too much time to hosting these stripper tryouts from hell. Pitted skin. Sloppy buttocks. Politically offensive tattoos. Twisted faces and broken-tooth smiles. He's chosen two dancers he'd never have sex with, even in the most desperate of moments, and needs to choose one more.

Just one more, and he's out of here. So help him God, if the next dancer isn't tolerable, someone might have to die.

"Next!"

No one comes onto the stage.

"How many more are back there," Yans asks.

"Only one," Darien says. "So sorry, *señor.* I thought she was awake." He heads toward the main stage.

"What are you saying, Darien? They're sleeping back there?"

A moment later, a girl glides onto the stage. Her eyes are at half-mast, and she sways to the right.

Darien returns to his post beneath the water pipes. "This is Aurora Snow."

The girl's skin glows, silky and smooth. Unlike the others, she's not dirty. She appears to be Latina, Cuban, but her hair is dyed blond and straight, and her body—it's not atrocious. It's not like the others.

She begins to dance, swaying like a drunken willow in the wind.

Yans stands. Glances at Darien.

Darien winces.

The boy has fear, but it's minor, and it's in honor of Yans's presence. With time, Yans might be able to remove it. Jerk it out of him like a rotten tooth and make him a true soldier.

Yans gazes back at the girl. "Have you ever been to the US?"

She stops dancing and points to her chest. Blinks slowly.

"Yes," Yans says. "I'm talking to you." He shakes his head. "I wasn't asking him. I know him."

Darien nods in agreement.

The girl shakes her head. Concern crosses her face. She squints and leans forward. "Are those bugs on your face?" Her Spanish sounds strange. Broken.

"Why does everyone think my scar is some sort of insect?" He covers his cheek. "Darien?"

"I don't know, *señor.*"

Aurora leans to the right and shifts back, attempting to stand straight as if thwarting some unseeable force pulling her down.

"What's wrong with her?" Yans asks.

"She does not speak Spanish well."

"Why?"

"She arrived from the US yesterday. I don't know much about her, but I don't think Spanish is her first language."

"What?" Yans raises both hands. "Why didn't you say something? You know we're on the lookout for girls from the US."

"You told me to speak when spoken to yesterday, so I—"

"Use your *cabeza*, fool." Yans turns his attention back to the girl. "Turn. Turn around."

She does.

A black tattoo runs down her leg—not just any tattoo, but a tattoo of a number: 3039334651.

"It's her," Yans mutters.

"We brought her in by plane from Miami last night. She said the flight made her sick, and she took some pills. I should have, but I did not ask my men what pills she took. She may have taken more this morning, by the way she's been behaving. My friend says—"

"Be quiet," Yans says. "Look. She has the tattoo."

"Many of the girls have tattoos."

Yans approaches the stage.

"My friend says she came willingly," Darien continues.

"Be quiet." Yans runs his fingers over the girl's calf. Numbers etched in black ink. They're perfect.

"She's beautiful and compliant." Darien holds his chin up. "Our incubator in Florida has given us better girls ever since you replaced Raúl."

"Be quiet. Didn't I tell you to speak when spoken to? Did

I speak to you just now?"

"No, *señor*, but—"

Yans opens his eyes wide at Darien.

Darien closes his mouth and directs his attention to Aurora.

She finally realizes Yans has been stroking her leg and turns to face him. She blinks once, and her eyes close. She wavers and forces her eyes open. Glassy, but aware, but not quite there.

"Give her more of whatever she's been taking," Yans commands. "We're going on a trip."

"May I speak, *señor*?"

"Of course. I spoke to you, so you can—never mind. What do you want to say?"

"If we leave with her now, we'll have an empty table for the day's first shift. We need another dancer."

Yans wants to pull his gun out and shoot Darien. Darien doesn't understand what's happening. It's not the poor boy's fault. Yans never told him the reason he ordered him to have his friends search the US for a Cuban girl with a tattoo. But, now that she's here and she has the tattoo, the boy ought to put *something* together in his head. Fearful and slightly stupid, but not a hopeless cause. Yet.

Aurora lowers herself onto the floor and sits with her legs crossed and her chin against her chest. Her long blond hair drapes over her shoulders. Her eyes close.

"I don't care about the club anymore," Yans says. "She's the one. Nothing here matters now. Load her into the SUV."

Darien doesn't move. He doesn't talk. He gives Yans a side-eye, checking to see if Yans is looking at him—and he is. The pipes over Darien's head rattle as if someone in an apartment high above flushed a toilet. It's that fear again. It's holding Darien back. Darien is holding himself back. He's hiding something. His fear stains Yans's opinion of him.

Water drops fall from the pipes, splashing down on Darien's head.

"Load her into the SUV, I said." Yans puts one hand on the grip of his pistol. "What's wrong with you?"

"The SUV is gone." Darien's voice shakes. "I arranged for a man to service it while we reviewed the girls this morning."

"What? Why didn't you tell me that before?"

"Because you said for me to speak only when spoken—"

"Be quiet. Stop being so literal. Call the serviceman and get the SUV back here."

Darien pulls out his cell phone and heads for the stairs to find a signal.

The girl appears to have passed out.

Her legs feel as silky as her face looks.

Yans whispers in her ear. "He said your name is Aurora Snow, but we know that's only a stage name, don't we?"

Eyes closed, she does not respond.

He pushes her chin up and down, making her nod in agreement.

"We know your real name is Lucía, don't we?"

CHAPTER THIRTEEN

DMITRI - 1990

Dmitri Belkin sits slumped in a shadow with his back to a tenement on the darkest street corner ever to curse Havana. The hot Cuban wind sweeps across the ocean, picks up sand from the island's shore and casts it into the city. The faint scent of salt and sea mixes with the humid stench of decay and sewage. The sun rises. The sun threatens to reveal Dmitri's location. Rotten, broken lives sleep in the stacked bungalows above. Their strained breathing creeps through the cracks. He can picture the stained walls. Though many house six, the malignant rooms are barely large enough to hold two people. Jail cells—that's what they are to Dmitri. He'll never go inside one of these buildings again, though it would keep him out of sight.

He'll never go inside any building again.

The streets are his home now. He has made his decision. *They're* coming. *They're* coming for him. *They* want to put him back in his jail cell.

That's not going to happen.

Footsteps.

Dmitri does not move. He keeps his eyes closed. His head down.

The footsteps grow louder, but it's okay. He can smell the man approaching. The man's not a member of the Red Star Society.

"Dmitri, my old friend. Is that you?"

Dmitri raises his head, and his neck pops.

The man stops at the curb and leans forward, his hands on his hips and twinkle in his eyes.

"It *is* you," the man says.

Dmitri recognizes him. He still has those white snowflakes on his face. Not freckles, not scars—maybe both. Maybe neither. The snowflakes have multiplied and grown larger with age, and, like Dmitri, wrinkles have set in. Over twenty years have passed since they lived in that tenement together.

Since they lived in those bungalows.

Those cells.

Those jail cells.

It wasn't a tenement then.

The cries of children fighting fall upon his ears from a window above. He wishes they would stop. He glances down the alley and across the street, but he can't see all the way from this angle.

They're coming for him.

He can smell it.

They want to put him back in his hole. His cell.

The crickets in his head told him this, so it must be true.

A twinge pecks at the tear duct in Dmitri's left eye. Then, a pain pecks at his right. He rubs them away and blinks.

He gazes up at the man. "Carlos. It's you."

"Yes, that's right. Here"—Carlos extends his hand—"let

me help you up."

Dmitri doesn't move. The sun beats its way between the buildings. Hot air hits his wet eyes.

Carlos leans in closer.

Dmitri shakes his head, and his neck pops again. "No." He shoves his hands down his pants. "No."

"It's okay." Carlos backs off. "How have you been, *compañero*? I heard you disappeared for a while."

Like a ghost, Dmitri thinks. He hopes he disappeared like a ghost.

"How long have you been out here?"

"Since he left."

"Your son?"

"Yes."

"Have you heard from him? How's he doing?"

"He hasn't talked to me."

"My son's there too. He's finishing his studies in North Carolina. You remember Miguel?"

Dmitri remembers everything and everyone all at once. He remembers the number the most clearly. The code. He gazes up at the sky. The morning heat rays wiggle in tight waves above the tenements. The prisons. He never told anyone the number. Not Carlos, and certainly not Miguel.

The number is his burden to bear, and his alone.

They're coming for the number.

They're coming for him.

"Remember when the two of them played together? When they were only *niños*?"

Dmitri lowers his head. "I remember everything. Thank you for saving the last piece for me."

Carlos cocks his head. "The last piece? Are you okay?"

"Yes." Dmitri shoots a look down the street. "It was a

piece of pie. That day at work."

"Ah. Yes." Carlos smiles. "If it helps, Miguel told me he talked to your son two or three years ago. He said everything was going great for him."

Dmitri nods. "He won't talk to me."

"Are you still giving tattoos?"

That's right. Dmitri used to paint the most intoxicating murals on skin. He was *el mejores tatuadores del mundo*. Ana hated his tattoo work, but that's because he was the best. She was jealous. It doesn't matter now. She's dead. She had his children and died. "No. I lost my customers when Ana left."

"I was sad to hear about her passing. Where are you living now?"

He's asking a lot of questions.

Dmitri looks up and down the street. Shakes his head and raises his hands. His ragged sleeves hang at his elbows, and his beard itches. His belly is round but no bigger than a saucer. He scratches his face. His home is here, and it's nowhere. Like a ghost's.

"I see." Carlos's eyes wander away. "And your daughters? I heard—"

"Whores!"

Dmitri stands.

Carlos jumps back.

"The whores left after their mother died. They're down there, selling themselves. Dirty, dirty whores."

"I don't think that's true."

Dmitri narrows his eyes at Carlos.

Is this Carlos?

The Carlos?

Or is it *them*?

Has the Red Star Society gotten to Carlos? Did they send

him here?

The ground shakes beneath Dmitri's feet like an earthquake, but it's often this way just after standing. What's unusual is how his chest is collapsing. He hunches his shoulders forward, closes his eyes, and wraps his arms around his body. Carlos's hand touches his shoulder. It's scorching hot, like the wind.

"The last I knew," Carlos says, "your daughters had jobs in Matanzas. Maybe you should go there."

"Maybe you should tell them I'll never get caught. Not here. Not in Matanzas. Not anywhere. Go and tell your friends."

"Who? My friends?" Carlos pulls away. "I'm talking about your daughters."

Look at him.

He doesn't know.

The snowflake-freckled, scar-faced bastard doesn't know. Dmitri never told him the number, and—it's Carlos, his old friend. His friend from the metal refinery. From the prison. His savior. He hugs Carlos. The scent of Carlos's cologne is sweeter than anything Dmitri has ever smelled.

The air clears.

Life is wonderful.

"Okay, okay," Carlos says. "Hold on, there." He places his hands on Dmitri's shoulders and gently pushes him back. "It's going to be okay. Let's get you somewhere where we can clean you up."

"We can't go anywhere." Dmitri looks across the street into an alleyway. The sun is pushing a shadow toward him. It's killing the shadow. "They're coming for us. They have re-formed, and they're coming."

"No one's coming for you. Who are you talking about?"

"The Black Crickets."

The twinkle in Carlos's eyes vanishes.

"The Black Crickets," Dmitri repeats. He glances at the alley again. "They re-formed. They're—"

Carlos shakes his head. "They're dead."

"They're after us."

"No one is after you. The Black Crickets disbanded long ago."

It's true, but it doesn't matter. They disbanded, but the Red Star Society replaced them. It is the Red Star Society that wants Dmitri now. But, maybe Carlos doesn't know this. Or maybe, Carlos is pretending not to know.

Dmitri jumps up and down. His feet slam against the dirt again and again.

"Calm down," Carlos says. "Let's find your daughters. They can take care of you. Don't worry about the Red Star Society. I think they're fictional."

Carlos knows.

He knows about the Red Star Society. They have sent him here. He's trying to trick Dmitri into going to Matanzas. Play into their hands. Go back to his jail cell.

Dmitri turns to run.

Carlos reaches for him. Takes hold of his arm.

"I'm not going back," Dmitri tells him.

"I'm certain your daughters are worried about you. They'll help you."

"I never want to see them again. They're like their mother, thank Jesus. They're dead to me. It's safer this way."

"What about your son? Why don't you go to him?"

"I can't go to the US. They'll"—he checks the alley again—"they'll send me to Mother Russia." He smells someone coming.

"Russia is gone."

"Russia will kill me on sight. They're too smart. Too advanced. I'd have nowhere to hide."

"Like you're hiding here?"

"Yes."

"I found you. Why won't they?"

A woman from one of the tenement cells above yells. "Quiet down there. I have *niños* sleeping."

"Go away, you filthy *puta*!" Dmitri yells.

A Ford Falcon with Lada headlights coasts out of the alley and rounds the corner, heading for the tenement.

Dmitri runs.

CHAPTER FOURTEEN

Calvin and I are at a crossroads. Literally. Highway 19 runs north to Salt Springs, but according to my maps app, there are no Applebee's in that direction. Lucía and Mr. Muscles have some strange fascination with Applebee's. We can't be too far behind them. The tracks in the mud at the abandoned car lot seemed fresh, but I'm not exactly a professional trail tracker. I don't even know if that's a thing. Either way, we're at a crossroads.

Literally.

Highway 40 runs east and west from here, crossing Highway 19, which runs straight north. Several Applebee's restaurants wait for us only forty minutes in either direction. Ocala or Daytona Beach.

"Daytona," Calvin says. "We can go to the car racetrack."

"We don't have time."

"After we find them, we can go to the car racetrack. NASCAR."

I'm not taking him to any racetrack. After we find them, we're going to the police.

"I'm hungry," he says. "Which one is closest?"

"There's several in each place, but the closest is Daytona, so I guess you're in luck."

He grins.

It's a 50-50 whether Lucía went to Daytona or Ocala. If going to Daytona makes Calvin happy for a while, that's less of him for me to contend with. Underneath all of his blabbering, he's a sweet kid. "Daytona it is." I hang a right.

Close to an hour later, we're standing at the hostess station inside an Applebee's. I casually stroll toward the tables while Calvin waits for the hostess. Lamps with yellow, opaque glass shades and intricate patterns hang over each booth, dimly lighting the tables. The curtains are drawn to block out the afternoon sun. I check the booths on both sides of the bar. Lucía's not there. Neither she nor Mr. Muscles are anywhere in sight.

"Just one?" the hostess asks.

"No," Calvin says. "I'm with her. We need a table for two."

"No, we don't." I approach the hostess's station. She's young. So young, she's still in love with makeup. Too much eyeliner, lip gloss, blush—everything.

"Is something wrong?" she asks.

"Have you seen a girl with a number tattooed on the back of her leg?"

"No." She wrinkles her nose. "No one like that. There was a tough-looking guy with a butterfly tattoo on his shoulder. I thought it was kind of ironic."

"Okay. Thanks anyway." I turn to go.

"We need a table for two," Calvin says.

"No, we're leaving. Let's go."

"But, I'm hungry."

"C'mon, Calvin." I walk out.

He follows.

I walk fast.

"Hey!" he shouts after me. "When can we eat?"

I unlock the car door and hop inside.

He leans into his stride as if trying to hurry, afraid I might leave him here, which I'd never do. His heavy body slows him down. It holds him back. He's too young to be this big, but who am I to judge? I never strutted down any fashion runways when I was in high school. Like him, back then, my heavy body held me back.

But right now, he's slow, and we need to go.

I hit the horn and start the car.

He gets inside, panting. Not a lot, but enough for me to know he either never exercises or he just came down with COVID.

They should have named the next place "Applebee's Déjà Vu." Not only were the layout, the booths, and the lamps the same, but the hostess was eerily similar, and we had the same experience. No Lucía. No Mr. Muscles. I asked about the tattoo, and the hostess hadn't seen Lucía. I rushed to the car, and Calvin complained about being hungry.

Now, we're three blocks from the ocean, driving through Daytona Beach on our way to the next, and last, Applebee's.

"Can we get a table this time? I'm still hungry."

"Sure," I say. "If Lucía is there. That's the plan. We can't stop until we find her. Then, I'll order whatever you want." Of course, I'm lying. I'll pay for one, and only one, entree.

"I'm so hungry, even that looks good." He points out the window at the road ahead. "Roadkill."

A bloated armadillo lies on its back with its legs in the air.

"Where are its friends?" I ask.

"What do you mean?"

"I thought you told me they run in packs of a hundred." I laugh.

He doesn't. But he does grin a little, like he knows his story about the armadillo horde running his dad off the road is a bit exaggerated.

The next Applebee's is not a complete repeat of the first two, but only because of the lampshades and the curtains. The shades are red, and the curtains are wide open. Light streams in, crossing the bar and glinting off the golden trim.

No Lucía.

"C'mon, Calvin, let's go."

"No. I need something to eat." He follows me outside. "Wait." This time, he runs. He gets to the car before I do. "Please, please, ple—" He struggles to breathe. "Please, can't we stay? I'll starve if I don't eat soon."

"I doubt that."

"What do you mean?"

"I think it might be good for you to starve for a while. Look at yourself."

My father's words. Not mine. I can't believe I just said that. All the times my father condemned my weight growing up, and now I'm him.

Suddenly, I want a cigarette.

Calvin wants to eat, and I want a cigarette.

He lowers his chin.

"I'm so sorry. I didn't mean that."

"I know I'm fat, but I still have to eat."

"Hop in. We'll go somewhere and get it to go." I open my door. "I'd get something here, but I'm not a fan of chains."

We leave Daytona Beach, heading west on Highway 40.

"What about the racetrack?"

"We were wrong. Mr. Muscles must have gone to Ocala for an Applebee's. We don't have time to get food and go to the racetrack."

"But, I like race cars."

"I know, but you're hungry, right? That's the first priority."

The number of houses dwindles as we leave town, and the number of trees alongside the highway increases.

Getting food is not the first priority.

Somewhere on the other side of this state, a girl's life is being destroyed. She asked me for help when she dropped that note at the store, and now, no matter how fast I drive— no matter how much I push Dory down the highway—I feel like I'm too late. That evil bald man is selling her to someone right now. I just know it. I can't get the tattoo out of my mind. She's a number, not a person to him. He's selling her like a piece of meat, yet I promised Calvin we'd stop because he's hungry. What a waste of time, but then again, maybe not. Maybe I'm already too late.

"There," he says. "That's the last place for miles. Pull over."

A rustic wooden restaurant crowds the side of the road. A patch of pavement near the front door has a few faded parking spots, outlined in classic parking lot yellow, but most of the lot is dirt. Only a few cars sit scattered about.

"Look at that one," he says, pointing at a wagon. "Park over there."

"You'll have to walk farther to the door." I immediately put my hand on his shoulder. "That wasn't a crack. I swear. I didn't mean it like that." As he suggested, I park next to a shiny black Volvo wagon. It looks brand new.

"You *did* mean it like that, and it's okay." He grins. "I know I'm fat. I know I need the exercise." He makes eye contact, still grinning. "I like that you're honest with me."

"It's the stress." I put my hand to my forehead. "I really wanted to help that girl. I'm sorry you ended up tangled in all this." The sign reads A.J.'S PUB & GRILL – CLOSED SUNDAYS. "You're having a hell of a first day at work, aren't you?"

"It's not what I expected," he admits.

"Let's go inside and get a table."

"But you said we don't have time to stay."

"We'll get to the Applebee's in Ocala when we get there. We'll ask if anyone saw Lucía, and if so, we'll continue on. Otherwise, I think we're probably already too late. Don't worry, it's not your fault."

We get out of the car, and he gazes at the Volvo for a while before we go inside.

Long fluorescent lights covered in hippie sixties tapestries hang from the ceiling. No lamps. The sign by the door tells us to seat ourselves, so we do. The orange Formica tabletop has a few broken spots, revealing plywood stained to match. It's seventies puke orange. The waitress appears next to our table. Her goth bob haircut hides her forehead. Her cotton top with small pockets hugs her chest, and her skirt ends above her knees. She's all in black. Her clothes, hair, mascara, lipstick— all stained black to match.

Calvin opens the menu.

"What can I getcha?"

"I want the—"

I put my hand on his wrist. "Wait." It's a long shot, but I haven't entirely given up. "Did a Latina girl with a tattoo on her leg come in here today?"

The Goth gobby waitress glances around. "Yeah. Probably." The light catches her nose ring. "A lot of people have tattoos on their legs." She turns and shows us her calf. An 1800s locomotive blowing steam with a grinning cattle guard for a face stares up at me. How nice. "I think leg tattoos are a requirement for spring-breakers. I sort of regret getting mine."

"No, I—did anyone have a tattoo of a *number* on their leg?"

She thinks for a moment.

Calvin pipes up. "I want the double cheeseburger with fries and a chocolate shake, and—" He glances up at me. "No. Make that fruit. No fries."

"Got it," the waitress says.

"The girl," I say to her. "Did you see a girl with a number on her leg?"

"Hey." Calvin puts the menu down. "Whose station wagon is that out there?" He points at the Volvo parked next to Dory. "It's amazing."

"The one on the right?" asks the waitress.

"Yeah," Calvin says. "The Volvo. The V90."

"What about the girl?" I say, my neck feeling hot. I don't want to shout at her, but— "Did you see a girl with a number on her leg?"

"That's my uncle's car." The waitress has no lines on her face. "He works here, too. It's nothing special."

"Yeah, it is. It's fast, I bet." Calvin seems so happy. Good for him.

I'm not happy.

I'm seething.

I wave my hands until I get Wednesday Addams's attention. "Did you hear what I said? About the girl with the number tattoo on her leg?"

"Oh, right." She circles her hand around her head. "There was a girl. With the crazy permed hair like yours?"

"Yeah, that sounds like her."

"And yeah, she had a tattoo of a number. I remember. They sat over there." She points at a booth near the front door.

"Was she with a muscle-bound bald guy?"

"Yeah."

I reach across the table. "That's it, Calvin. They ate here. They must be back on their way to Salt Springs now. We've got to go."

His face goes dark. He grips the menu with both hands. "I'm not leaving without food."

"Calvin—"

"I'm not leaving."

"And what would you like to order?" The waitress casts her listless eyes in my direction.

"I'm fine. How fast can we get his order to go?"

CHAPTER FIFTEEN

JACK

The world Jack had known has disappeared. One minute, he had them in his sights. The next, he was racing north on Highway 19 by himself.

Disappointed roars escape his tailpipes each time he hits the gas.

He was right behind the Honda mini-van all day yesterday, and it was only a matter of time, but no . . . he had to be patient. He had to make sure Lucía was really in trouble. He had let himself be seen. And now they're gone.

Patience is a virtue.

He reminds himself that patience is *his* virtue. It is the only thing that will keep him out of jail the next time the rage comes.

He laughs. He doesn't believe he'll ever be that angry again. He believes he will always be patient, but . . . yesterday. Yesterday, patience bit him in the ass.

No. That black Toyota Corolla wagon bit him in the ass.

The driver was so familiar, yet not. Something about her told him she knew about Lucía. It's a strong feeling. He promised Colter not to let the highway incident derail his investigation, but if he can find that woman, not only can he get even with her, he might get some information.

An hour turns into two.

No mini-van. No wagon.

At this point, he can't remember if he saw any other cars. The Camaro's air conditioning keeps him cool. The sun's rays shine across a brilliant blue sky. It looks hot outside as the trees race by. He turns east onto Highway 40. He's unsure why. Continuing north didn't feel right anymore. However, after a while, he realizes he still hasn't seen any other cars. It's like a nuclear bomb went off and eradicated everyone. It's like he's in a dystopian movie and—

His phone rings.

Why won't Colter leave him alone long enough to find Lucía?

"Hi, Jack." Colter sounds hurried. "I've got some important information. I need you to—where are you?"

"I'm headed east on . . . just a second."

"You don't know where you are?"

"Hold on, there's a sign up ahead. Let me make sure."

"Look, it doesn't matter. I need you to—"

"I'm on Highway 40."

"You're going the wrong way. I need you to go to the airport in Miami."

"What?" Jack eases off the gas a little. "No way. She's not there."

"You're right. She's not there. She flew out last night." He lowers his voice. "I don't want to get into it now, but you messed up again. You've been chasing the wrong girl since yesterday."

Jack takes a good look at the road ahead before leaning

over and snatching Lucía's file off the passenger-side floor. He looks at her picture on the printout. Colter is wrong. This is the girl Jack followed to the hotel last night. No doubt.

Colter goes on. "My housekeeper was coming back from visiting friends in Miami when she saw Lucía walk down a jetway and board a plane to Cuba."

Jack continues east, pressing down on the accelerator harder now. "That's not possible."

"Valeria panicked when she saw her and froze, not knowing what to do.

"Did she get a good look? Are you sure you can trust what your housekeeper saw?"

"Valeria has been with us for years. If anyone could recognize Lucía, it would be her."

"It's not possible. I saw your daughter this morning near Orlando."

"Jack, listen carefully. Valeria saw Lucía's tattoo just as she turned the corner and stepped onto the plane. I trust Valeria. I can't say the same about you."

Jack flips to the second page of the printout. There's a close-up of a Mickey Mouse tattoo on Lucía's back, and another of her leg tattoo: 20863451.

"She got onto a plane to Cuba last night," Colter says. "Stop wasting your time and my money, and go there. Now."

"But I saw her this morning."

"You saw someone that looked like her."

"Maybe your housekeeper saw someone that looked like her. We all make mistakes."

"The tattoo, Jack. How many girls in Florida have a number tattooed on their leg like Lucía's?"

"There could be thousands. I saw an article last week saying Florida has over twenty-two million people."

"Most of those are gray-haired retirees. You're not looking for a retiree. You're supposed to be looking for my daughter. What's wrong with you?"

"I am looking for her." Jack can't honestly say he saw the tattoo at the hotel this morning, but he shouldn't have to. He saw her face. Lucía's face. He saw *her*. Colter is dead wrong. "I think your housekeeper is mistaken."

"No. After all your screw-ups today, I think you're mistaken. You're a mistake. This is your last chance, Jack. Go to the airport, find out where she flew, and find her. Do you think you can get into Cuba?"

"She's not there."

"I need to know you're going to do this. If you don't, you'll get nothing. I won't pay you a single cent. When you arrive at the airport, send me a picture of the current flights to Cuba with your phone so I know you actually went there. I still want you to find her, Jack. We're running out of time. I'll buy plane tickets for you if I have to—just get my daughter back!"

Jack's neck tenses.

Patience.

Patience will make the rage go away.

He slows down and leans over the steering wheel. He gazes into the sky and takes a deep breath.

Colter is not going to give in. It's no use arguing.

Jack hangs up the phone.

He's not going to give in either. Whether Colter pays him or not, he'll find Lucía and make sure she's okay. He's invested now. He leans back and glances at her picture on the printout. Part of him hopes Colter is right about her not going willingly in the mini-van. Part of him hopes the future gives him a reason to unleash his rage on the driver who took her.

He passes a sign for Daytona.

It doesn't matter how he finds Lucía, only that he finds her.

She was not in Miami yesterday. No way.

A dirty-looking roadside cafe is coming up on the right. He could sure go for some real food, but—

There it is.

That woman's Toyota wagon sits innocently in the sun, soaking up the rays.

A.J.'S PUB & GRILL.

He swerves into the parking lot and screeches to a stop on a patch of pavement.

Good thing he slowed down, or he might have missed it.

Good thing he had some patience.

CHAPTER SIXTEEN

LUCÍA

The passenger-side window slaps Lucía in the temple when they hit a bump. She opens her eyes and sits up straight.

"Good," Wyatt says. "You're awake. We're here."

Wyatt guides their new ride between a cluster of mobile home trailers scattered across a dirt lot. Peeling paint. Broken windows. Dented aluminum sides. Muddy tracks in all directions. A lake lies in the distance. Maybe it's only a pond.

They hit another bump, and Lucía almost cries out. She touches her cheekbone. The place Wyatt hit her.

The sun beats down on the lot, highlighting the grime of the trailers. A particularly filthy one with two cars parked in front lies near the water. The cars don't belong here. One is a Lexus, and she's unsure about the other, but like her, they don't belong here.

Wyatt parks next to the Lexus.

They must be somewhere in Salt Springs. She's not sure how long she slept.

He looks at her and taps his fingers on the steering wheel. "Is there something you can do about that?"

"What?"

"Your cheek. It looks worse."

"It's your fault."

"You shouldn't have kicked me. Don't you have some makeup or something to hide it?"

She looks at herself in the mirror. "You can't hide swelling."

"Well, at least try to make your eyes the same size. Can't you open that one a little more?"

She shakes her head.

He unlatches his door.

"Please, don't do this," she says.

"I told you. I don't have a choice. You meant more to me than the others. I—I've grown to like you, but a deal is a deal. Man, I wish you hadn't made me hit you." He releases the child lock mechanism. "Let's go, and don't try to run again." He puts his hand on her shoulder. "I don't want to have to hit you again."

"We had a lot of good times, Wyatt. Please. I'll stay with you. I won't try to run away again. I promise. Please, let's leave now." She gazes out the windshield. Bright sunlight plays on leftover rain running down the trailer's door. Droplets hang from the steel doorknob before falling onto a wooden packing crate that serves as the front step. Each window has a different closed curtain. Yellow daffodils on a red background. Periwinkles on a white background. The British flag. The pond lies on the other side.

"Get out," he says.

She pulls on the latch, and her door pops open.

Wyatt gets out, glances at the trailer, and walks around the car. He pulls her door all the way open and grasps her elbow. "Here, let me help you."

"No." She jerks her arm away and gets out.

"Whatever you do," he says, "don't make a scene."

She follows him to the door. While he knocks, her future passes before her eyes.

Shackles on her wrists. Her ankles. Disgusting men ogling her and more. A lot more.

When the door opens, her fears are affirmed.

"You're late," the man says.

"Stanley, this is Lucía." Wyatt motions in her direction. "She's ready."

Stanley runs his eyes up and down her body. She does the same to him. He's wearing a tight-fitting, white button-down shirt, a short red tie, and black slacks. His belly hangs over his belt—that is, if he's wearing one. She can't quite see it if it's there. His skin is greasy, with blood-red blemishes and odd-shaped pores, some so deep they appear black. He's so evil looking, when he smiles, she imagines that even the alligators in the woods behind her cower and hide.

"What happened to her face?"

"She tried to—"

"Wait." Stanley glances around the trailer park and holds up his hand. His pinky ring has a square cut stone with sharp-looking edges. It's dark red like his nose. "You can explain inside."

She takes one last look at the trailer park as she crosses the threshold. Six or seven trailers lie haphazardly between here and the road they came in on. Her face aches. Her arms feel weak. Her tongue is dry.

Once she's inside, Wyatt pulls the door closed.

It's dark.

Her eyes adjust.

Her head swims.

A slender man in a black suit and slim tie stands on the other side of a dining table, holding a black briefcase. Four chairs sit tucked under each side of the table. Black folding chairs beneath a black table. The kitchen wraps around the far end of the trailer behind the slender man. All the curtains are pulled. No light can get in, and everything is so small. The sink. The fridge. A microwave. They're all miniatures.

"This is Mr. Suzuki," Stanley says.

"Hey." Wyatt reaches over the table, but the man does not shake his hand.

Stanley pulls a chair out. "Sit her down here."

Lucía makes eye contact with Wyatt and shakes her head.

He grabs her by the wrist, and she sits. He steps behind her. Puts his hands on her shoulders.

"Okay." Stanley turns toward Mr. Suzuki. "I sincerely apologize for her face. I was not expecting this. Wyatt, do you want to tell us what happened?"

"Honestly?"

"Yes."

"Okay. She tried to—"

"Wait." Stanley turns his back to Mr. Suzuki. Raises his eyebrows at Wyatt. "Start at the beginning. Where were you?"

"Oh, right." Wyatt licks his upper teeth. "We were at lunch. We went somewhere other than Applebee's, and she tripped coming out of the restaurant. I tried to catch her, but she hit her face on the railing when she went down." Mr. Suzuki blinks. "Isn't that right, Lucía?" Wyatt nudges her shoulders.

She nods.

Stanley presses his lips together. "Hm."

"I am not concerned about the damage to her," Mr. Suzuki says. "It's not her face I'm interested in."

"Yes." Stanley chuckles. "I understand. So we're good?"

Mr. Suzuki places the briefcase on the table and opens it.

As rich as her dad is, Lucía has never seen this much cash in one place before. So many portraits of Ben Franklin.

Stanley pulls a stack from the case.

Wyatt steps up to the table. Holds out his hand.

Stanley begins to give him the money, then pulls it back.

Lucía glances over her shoulder. The living room leads to a narrow hallway running to the end of the trailer. She could run down there, but then what? There's no door. No window. Only a few side doors along the way. But, if she's going to escape, she's got to do something soon.

"What gives?" Wyatt asks, his hand still extended.

"Hold on." Stanley peels about a quarter of the bills off the stack and holds it out.

"That's not enough."

"Neither is that." Stanley waves at Lucía. "She's damaged."

"He said he didn't care."

Lucía glances down the hall again.

"This isn't between you and him," Stanley says.

Mr. Suzuki removes two stacks of money from the case.

"What are *you* doing?" Stanley asks. "You said you weren't interested in her face."

"I cannot pay full price for someone who is not fully willing."

"She's willing," Stanley says. "What's your concern?"

"If she were willing"—he slips the two stacks of money into the breast pocket of his jacket—"she wouldn't be checking the hallway. She's about to run."

Stanley eyes her.

Her nerves light on fire.

Stanley reaches under the table and pulls out a tote bag.

"I've been with her for over a month," Wyatt says. "You want to be here, don't you, babe?"

Stanley opens the bag and takes out a roll of gray tape.

Stomach acid fills Lucía's throat. She chokes it down, stands, and turns toward the living room.

"Wyatt," Stanley snaps.

She manages only two steps before Wyatt brings her down. Her face smashes into the thick pile carpeting. Rotten fish. The carpet smells like cat food mixed with cat litter.

She hears the *skritch* of the tape as Stanley pulls a piece off.

She can't move. Wyatt weighs too much.

"Here," Stanley says. "Hold her hands behind her back."

Wyatt eases off her shoulders but keeps the pressure on her backside with his knee.

"Please," she pleads. "Don't do this."

Wyatt pulls her hands behind her back, and Stanley wraps the tape around them.

"I'll do anything you want."

He gets off and rolls her onto her back.

He stands over her and looks down.

Stanley steps next to him.

When Stanley lowers his head and gazes into her eyes, his double chin inflates like a croaking bullfrog's. Streams of sweat run in and out of his pores, pooling and overflowing. His cologne smells worse than the carpet.

"Anything you want," she repeats. "Anything, Wyatt. I'll do anything. Please, just help me. I'll do anything you want."

"No," Stanley says to her. He kicks her in the side and licks the sweat off his upper lip. "You'll do anything Mr. Suzuki wants."

CHAPTER SEVENTEEN

YANS

Yans's scar itches. He scratches it as the SUV rumbles over a bump in the road, causing him to rub too hard. His cheek burns.

"Watch the road, you orange-picker."

The driver slows down.

"No." Yans braces himself against the dashboard. "Don't slow down. Just watch the road. *Maneuver.*"

"Yes, *compañero.*" The driver speeds up.

"I'm not your *compañero.*"

"Sorry, *señor.*"

Yans gazes at the countryside. He always enjoys the trip from Havana to Guanajay. The royal palm trees along the roadway, tall and proud, reach for the sky with their slender trunks and their feathery green-topped crowns. It makes him feel at home. It reminds him of his childhood. Of his father.

His scar itches.

He scratches it.

"How is she back there?" Yans reaches up and tilts the rearview mirror so Darien and the stripper—Lucía—appear.

The boy's shoulders are still wet from the club's leaky water pipe.

"Still asleep," Darien says.

Lucía has her eyes closed. She passed out onstage while dancing for Yans and hasn't woken up yet. Drugs. Her self-sedation made putting her in the SUV easier—she couldn't fight Darien—but now, Yans wants her awake. The tattoo on her leg says she's Lucía, but she said her name was Aurora. Yans wants to make sure she is the right girl. Darien said she flew in from Miami late last night, and he wasn't happy that he had to stay up late to pick her up.

Yans glances at her leg. It must be her. After years of searching, fortune has once again blessed him, and she flew right into his hands.

"After she arrived, did you see her ticket?" Yans asks.

"What ticket?"

"Her flight ticket. Did you see the name on it?"

"No," Darien says. "She didn't show me her ticket. I believed her because of her accent and difficulty speaking Spanish. We had a tough time talking. I'm certain she's from the US."

"So, she is lying about her name."

"I don't think so. I saw her identity card. She wouldn't have been able to get past security with a fake. Not these days."

Darien is wrong. He must be wrong about her identity card. It's a fake, or . . . it's got to be her. This girl must be Lucia.

Yans faces forward and cracks his window. The warm air rushes into the Chinese SUV's cabin. The sweet scent of coconut mixes with the faint fragrance of the royal palms. Together, they smell like vanilla. Red hibiscus flowers dot the countryside. Cuba can be beautiful. The land, not the people. Not the weak security at the airport. Not the politicos running everything.

Nothing is like it used to be in Cuba.

"And what name was on her card?" Yans asks.

"Aurora Snow."

"That's obviously a stupid stripper stage name."

"Right. I'm sorry. It was Aurora Arenas."

"No. It can't be. Perhaps one of your friends saw her ticket before they put her on the plane. Can you contact one of them?"

"My friends didn't send her. She came on her own. They're still looking for Lucía."

Yans believes in good fortune. He's overcome everything to be this close by using his good fortune wisely. But, Lucía flying into his grasp without any help, suddenly feels *too* fortunate.

"Wake her."

Darien shakes the girl's shoulder with one hand. Gives up. "It's no use. She's out."

"What's wrong with you? Were you raised by women?" Yans lurches into the back seat, takes the girl by both shoulders and shakes her hard. Her head lolls back and forth, bouncing off the headrest. "Wake up."

She does not.

Yans returns to the passenger seat and eyes the driver. "What are you looking at?"

The driver keeps his eyes on the road.

"You didn't answer me, Darien."

"What?"

"Were you raised by women? Dirty Cuban women?"

"My mother, I—she's Cuban."

"And she's young, right?" Yans gazes out the window, searching for something beautiful besides the trees. "Don't answer. You're young, therefore she's young. Neither of you know how it used to be." His scar itches. "I was raised by a man." He spots a church in the distance. The building kneels before Guanajay on the edge of history. White, cracked bricks. A crooked cross on top. Broken windows. "My father taught me to take what I was given and make more of it. That's something we lost when Fidel died."

He rubs his cheek.

Fidel was the only leader who ever got it right. He was the single greatest factor in Cuba's development, according to Yans's father. Take your rations, your bruises—your scars—and make something out of yourself for the good of Cuba.

But then, everything changed.

Raúl lost the mantra because of Obama's sweet words. Everyone got it in their heads they could live like Americans. Like Yumas. Capitalist pigs. Then, Trump took the hope out of everyone's heads, and Cuba was left alone again. Díaz-Canel didn't stand a chance. Then, Biden kissed the warm winds with his warmer words. And so on, and so on. Back and forth, these *Gusanos de político* and their promises. With Fidel gone, Cuba has oscillated like the ticking of a bomb.

The church sits empty on the side of the road.

Yans will take no more.

He will end the politics.

Real power comes from action. Not words.

His father was a great man.

Yans learned how to make something of himself with what he was given by his father.

He scratches his scar.

His cheek burns.

He misses his father.

"Where are we?" Lucía asks.

Yans spins around. "What is your name?"

She rubs her eyes.

He grasps her by the shoulders and shakes her. "What is your name?"

Darien attempts to push Yans away. "Stop it," he says. "She doesn't understand you. She barely speaks Spanish."

Yans slaps him hard across the face.

"Where am I?" she asks, looking out the window.

"Tell me your name," Yans says in English.

"I'm Aurora." Her lower lip trembles. "Aurora Arenas."

"Stop lying." He reaches down and grasps her ankle. He jerks her leg up. "What's this?"

Darien sits with his hand pressed to his cheek.

"What's this?" Yans demands of the girl, yanking on her leg.

"It's my"—she kicks and pulls, but Yans won't let go— "it's my brother's dog tag."

"*¿El Perro?*"

"He was in the Marines." She frees her leg. "It's to remember him by."

The SUV hits a bump.

Yans is rocked back into the front of the cab. He shoves the driver in the shoulder. "Watch the road."

The SUV swerves.

"Let me out of here," Lucía cries. She beats on her window.

"Darien. Control her."

Darien gently touches her on the back. "Please, calm down."

Yans turns toward the back seat. Glares at Darien. The

pendejo doesn't know English, yet he stupidly keeps telling her to calm down.

She does not calm down.

The driver asks, "Should I pull over, *compañero?*"

"I'm not your *compañero.*" Yans punches him in the ear. "Keep going."

"But it's not her," Darien says.

"She's lying." Yans faces forward. Looks out over Guanajay. Straightens his uniform. Calms his voice. "Her name is Lucía Tremblay. It is her. It's Lucía."

"Please," she screams.

"Those aren't dog tag numbers on her leg," Yans says. "She's a lying *gringa.* They're all lying *gringos,* and they're all going to pay for what they did to our Cuba. It's only a matter of time now."

CHAPTER EIGHTEEN

Having sat across from Calvin at A.J.'s Pub & Grill for the last half hour, I know everything I never wanted to know about the Volvo V90 wagon parked out front. Calvin will not shut up. Time is speeding by, and it's taking forever for the cook to make a burger and a shake to go. I glare at the door to the kitchen, and I'm about to lose it. I'm about to go inside and make Calvin his lunch myself when the door swings open, and the Bride of Frankenstein saunters toward us with a brown paper bag.

"Here you are," she says, dropping the bag in front of Calvin.

I stand.

Calvin opens the bag, pulls out a Styrofoam box, opens it, and shoves the cheeseburger into his mouth.

"Hey," I say. "We got that to go. Let's go."

He chews.

"Calvin?"

"Here's your tab." The waitress places the bill on the table. "I can take it here or up front."

I pick it up. "There's a 'To Go' charge on here."

"Yes. That's for people who don't tip."

"I was going to tip."

Calvin takes another bite.

"Thank you," she says. "I appreciate that."

"But you already charged me for the tip."

"I know." Her face sours. "That's why I appreciate it."

Calvin sucks on a straw. I stare as his chocolate milkshake travels up the tube and into his mouth. It's been two days since my last cigarette, and this waitress—this Night-of-the-Living-Dead waitress—she's not making things easy.

"Pack up, Calvin. We've got to go."

The waitress holds out her hand.

I give her my credit card, and she walks to the register at the bar.

"What's wrong with you?" I ask Calvin.

"Nothing." He wipes ketchup off his chin. "You knew I was hungry." He puts the burger back in the box and the box back in the bag. "I'll finish eating in the car."

I don't wait for the waitress to return. She finishes swiping my card as we approach the bar. I sign for it—no additional tip—and we burst into the parking lot. The sun is hotter now. It's melted the clouds. We're about an hour from Salt Springs, maybe a little more. My faithful Dory can take us there faster than that, if I speed, and—who the hell is *that*?

A man stands between me and my car, snapping pictures of Dory with his phone.

"Excuse me." He turns toward us. "What are you doing?"

"I'm taking pictures of your license plate." He raises his phone and aims it toward us. "Now, I'm taking pictures of you."

"Stop it," I say.

"No."

"Who are you?"

"Who do you think you are?" he counters.

Calvin tips his head. "I'm Calvin."

The man has thick, shoulder-length hair, darkly disturbing eyes, and a goatee mustache combo that doesn't actually look bad. In fact, he in no way looks bad, other than his flaring nostrils. He nods once at Calvin and then focuses on me. "Who do you think you are, driving like that? You could have killed me back there." He points at the highway.

Not far from my car, a Camaro sits parked cock-eyed over one of the few paved spots. Black tire tracks run up to the rear tires, and the burnt rubber smell hangs in the air. It's the guy I passed on the highway. He's hot, but not only in a good way.

I feign ignorance. "What?"

"You ran me off the road." He takes another picture of us.

Calvin and I look at each other. No way will Calvin go along with my ruse, pretending we've never seen this man before.

"I don't have time for this," I say.

"What year is your Camaro?" Calvin asks. He pulls the chocolate shake out of his doggy bag.

I attempt to walk past the man to my car, but he grabs me by the elbow. "Why were you driving like that?"

"Why were you driving like my Grandma?" I pull my arm away.

Calvin sucks on his straw and drifts toward the man's car.

"If you weren't a woman . . ." The guy puts his phone in his pocket.

"If I weren't a woman, I'd still be stuck behind you on the highway."

"I think it's a 2019," Calvin says. "Am I right?"

"You're right, kid." The man looks up at the sky. "Let's slow down, here." He takes a deep breath. "Are you going to tell me why you were driving like that? It can't be how you always drive."

"Are you a cop or something?"

"No. Well—I'm a private investigator."

"Yeah, right. Me too." Calvin reaches into his to-go bag, hunting for something more. "Stop it, Calvin. Let's go."

"All right." He heads for Dory.

"I'm trying to find this girl." The man holds up a piece of paper. "Have you seen her?"

My heart drops.

The paper shows a picture of the girl with the leg tattoo. The name at the top is Lucía Tremblay. I need to double-check the image. I take it from his hand. Long, black, frizzy hair. Warm olive skin with hints of copper and bronze. Eyes that say the sun will come out tomorrow.

It's her.

The man sees it on my face.

He knows I've seen this girl.

Calvin stops walking toward Dory, turns around and returns to stand next to me.

The man gently pulls the paper from my fingers and folds it. "Let's go inside and talk."

"We don't have time for that," I say.

As he stows the paper in his chest pocket, he deliberately pulls his jacket back far enough for me to see a gun tucked in his waistband.

"Oh," he says, "I think we have time for that. Besides, that shake looks terrific. Is it chocolate?"

CHAPTER NINETEEN

JACK

Jack has it now. His memory isn't completely flawed. The woman seated across from him inside A.J.'s Pub & Grill stood inside the Pay-n-Save convenience store earlier this morning. Her tangled red hair had filled the window. He hadn't gone inside, but he should have. Now, she sits next to the amiable young guy who immediately introduced himself as Calvin in the parking lot.

She hasn't been as forthcoming with information.

"Can I get another cheeseburger?" Calvin asks.

"Really? You really think you need another one?" the redhead says. "Wait. No." She puts her hand on his wrist. "I'm sorry."

"It's okay. It's just that my first burger is cold now."

They're both still wearing their Pay-n-Save shirts. Suckers. Jack will never work for someone else again. Sure, he's working for Colter now, but not really. Colter is not the boss of him. He's only a client. Jack can fire Colter as easily as Colter can fire him. Jack will find Lucía on his own if he has to, but getting paid sure would be nice. It would help his retirement.

"We don't have time for this." Red pulls out a piece of paper and slides it across the table toward him.

No. You help me. Blue Honda mini-van going to Salt Springs. Someone named Stanley.

"She gave you this?" Jack asks.

"Yes."

"Did she tell you her name?"

"No, but the guy she was with called her Lucía." She points at the note. "Look. She needs our help *now*. We shouldn't be sitting in here."

"But I'm still hungry," Calvin says.

"Patience," Jack mutters.

He reads the note again. He balls his hand into a fist. He wants to hit the table, but he stops himself. He should have believed Colter. He should have done something when he tracked the couple to the hotel. *Stanley*. It had better not be *the* Stanley. He should have saved Lucía when he had the chance, but he just wasn't sure. She'd looked so willing.

"What's wrong?" Red asks.

"Nothing," Jack says. "Just that, after reading this note, you took it upon yourself to save her and ran me off the road in the process."

"That's right. You were going too slow."

"No, I wasn't. I was—" He leans back and lets his shoulders drop. "Why *were* you going so fast? You don't know exactly where to go in Salt Springs, do you?"

"I saw her get into a blue mini-van. We were trying to catch up to it." She raises her voice. "C'mon, we've got to go. They're trafficking her."

A waitress approaches the table. "You're back." She's dressed all in black and holds an order pad. "And you brought a friend."

Jack is so sick of convenience store food. He was really looking forward to eating here, but this waitress . . . she's not instilling much confidence. It's probably because of the face jewelry. He hopes the cook doesn't have a snotty nose ring.

"I'll have another cheeseburger," Calvin says. "No fruit this time."

"Hold on." Red holds her palm up to him. "We don't have time to wait. The last burger took half an hour."

"How long does it take to make a chocolate shake?" Jack asks the waitress.

"Look, the food here takes as long as it takes, but yeah, a shake is quicker."

"Fine," Red says. "Get one of those."

"I want another one, too," Calvin says.

The waitress writes on her pad. "Anything else?"

"No." Red slumps back in her chair. "Please go."

The waitress rolls her eyes and sashays away.

As soon as she's out of earshot, Red leans forward. "That girl is being *trafficked*. You know, *human trafficking*? That guy— he was like her owner. Like a pimp. Like he marked her 'on sale' and is taking her to Salt Springs for a Spring Sales Event. A Toyotathon Sales Event for humans, not cars."

"I like cars." Calvin glances out the window at the parking lot. "I like that Volvo."

"You might be right, Red." Jack looks over at the bar. They've begun to make his shake. If the Stanley on the note is Stanley Owens, then Red is one hundred percent right.

And Stanley is one hundred percent dead.

"Don't call me 'Red.' My name's Mattie, if you have to know."

"It's really Matilda," Calvin says. "But she doesn't want

you to call her that either." He removes a half-eaten burger from a brown paper bag and bites into it.

"I'm curious," Jack says to Mattie. "What makes you think she's being sold?" He hopes she's never heard of Stanley Owens. The man is too dangerous for these two, and if she has heard of him, there's a lot she's not saying. And, if Stanley is trafficking Lucía, Jack can't be weighed down by a couple of convenience store workers when he moves on him. He's got to go alone.

"I saw a number tattooed on her leg," Mattie says. "It was ugly. It wasn't like anything anyone would do to themselves."

"I've got news for you. Human traffickers don't number their victims. She's had it since she was little. Like, really little. A baby."

Mattie's jaw literally drops. "*What?* Why?"

"I don't know. My client didn't either. He said it was there the day he adopted her. She wasn't even a year old yet."

"That's crazy. Someone gave a baby a tattoo?"

"I know, but look, it doesn't matter. At least I know where she's going now. Thank you."

"You're welcome." She places her palms on the table as if she's about to stand up. "Grab your shakes. Let's go."

"Hold on. You're not coming with me."

Mattie stands. "Oh, yes, I am."

The waitress approaches with the milkshakes.

"Please, sit back down," Jack says. "There's no reason to rush now."

"Yes, there is."

The waitress puts the fountain glasses—tall, sweaty fountain glasses with double-sized straws—on the table. Calvin takes the last bite of his burger, grabs a shake, and begins sucking on the straw.

"Wherever they're going in Salt Springs," Jack says, "they're probably already there. We have time to talk about this." His shake is heaven. Chocolate heaven.

"Why aren't these in paper cups?" Mattie asks. "We need them to go."

"Do you always order everything to go?" the waitress huffs.

"It won't be necessary," Jack says. "Mattie, please sit back down."

The waitress saunters over to the next table.

Mattie sits.

"If you really want to help Lucía," he says, "you'll go to Miami for me."

"What the hell? Miami?" She raises her voice. "What's in Miami?"

"My uncle has a condo in Miami." Calvin takes another pull on his straw. "He moved there when he retired." His shake is already half gone.

"My client wants me to go to the airport in Miami and ask about Lucía. He thinks she flew out of there last night."

"But she didn't. She left that note." Mattie takes the note back and holds it up. "That's her on your report there. I'm sure of it. She's in Salt Springs."

"I know." Jack nods reassuringly. "But another girl with a tattoo on her leg went to Cuba last night. There could be a connection."

"I don't care about any connections. I need to tell the police where that girl went. I promised myself I wouldn't wait around and do nothing."

"Slow down," Jack says. "We don't know for absolute certainty she's being trafficked."

If it's Stanley Owens, Jack knows. He knows exactly

where to go in Salt Springs. And he knows exactly what a man like Stanley Owens will do with her. She will be sold and sex trafficked. This could be Jack's chance to rid the world of another evil man. A big one.

"That's right," Calvin says. "We don't know. That's why Mattie hasn't called the police yet. He could just be a bad boyfriend. We'll call the police after we find her. After we know what's really going on."

"No." Mattie shoots Calvin a look. "I haven't called the police because there isn't any time to drag them into this. They'll waste hours asking us questions and filing reports. Trust me. Lucía will drown before they even start looking for her."

Jack cocks his head. "Drown?"

"I mean, be sold."

Jack forces a smile. "I can find her. I have contacts in Salt Springs. But I need you to get my client off my back. Just go to the Miami airport and find out about the girl who left last night. Talk to the ticketing agents, the baggage handlers—anybody who might have seen her. You know, a girl with a number on her leg." He takes a quick drink of his shake. "Give me your phone number, and I'll text you. I'll keep you posted on what I find. I promise."

"They won't tell us anything at the airport." Her face is turning the color of her hair. "Customer privacy agreements or whatever. This is insane."

"Okay. Calm down." Jack pushes his milkshake to the side. Leans forward. "Let me put it another way. I'm getting paid a lot to find Lucía. I'll give you a substantial percentage if you go to the airport and send me proof you went there. My client asked for a picture of the current flights. I know Lucía didn't go to Cuba last night, but that doesn't mean she isn't next. Like I said, there could be a connection."

"I like money," Calvin says. "That's why I got a job." He glances at his Pay-n-Save shirt, then turns to Mattie. "Maybe we should go to Miami." Mattie sits back and folds her arms. "Jack can find Lucía. He's got a gun and everything. He's the professional."

"Well?" Jack asks.

"Let me think." Mattie gazes out the window.

"It sounds like a good deal to me." Calvin loudly finishes his shake. "I'm saving for a car."

"How much?" Mattie asks Jack.

"A lot. Several thousand."

"Okay. Let us talk in private." She stands. "C'mon, Calvin. I think we can figure this out."

"You're making the right decision, Mattie."

Jack hopes to never see her again.

He's not going to send her text messages.

He's not going to keep her posted.

It's for her own good.

He's going to Salt Springs, and if it works out, he's going to put the hurt on Stanley Owens. He can't think of a better ending to his PI career than to take down one of Florida's most infamous sex traffickers.

CHAPTER TWENTY

Six years is a long time not to see the sun. Dmitri has seen *a* sun, but not *the* sun. Not the golden sun he knew growing up in Russia. He hasn't seen that sun since 1962. Sometimes, they make him work outside in that deplorable Cuban heat beneath the oppressive Cuban sun. It's a blessing and a curse.

The Black Crickets.

Those misguided, doomsday nihilists. Dmitris prays for the day Castro discovers them, but that day may have long passed like a whisper in the wind.

He makes a circle in the dust on the floor with his finger. He adds lines to it. Rays. It's a sun. It's a simple sun, but it's oppressive. It's ugly, yet he loves to draw. He drags his finger across the floor, making a smile for the sun, and his fingertip catches on an edge.

He gazes up at his cell door.

No one is out there. Noises come from the corridor, but they're faint.

He can't believe he has exposed the groove again.

Quickly, he spreads dust over the floor to hide it. Then,

he erases the entire picture and moves back onto his cot. He lies down. Stares up at the concrete ceiling. It's dark up there.

Six years is a long time to go without a sun.

He closes his eyes.

He's going to die in this place.

Other prisoners have come and gone, but they'll never kill him. On days like this, he wishes he were dead. He's played this mind game before. It always comes down to three options.

He could tell them where it's hidden and how to activate it. Then they'd have no use for him. They'd kill him like the others who came with him to work on the base, and he'd be free.

Or he could kill himself. This option would protect the world from the Black Crickets, but it's so hard. It's one thing to wish you were dead, and it's another to take your own life. Especially when you're locked up.

So far, Dmitri has always chosen the third option. He pictures the Tserkov' Znameniya Presvyatoy in Dubrovitsy—the church of the Sign of the Blessed Virgin. He's holding his father's hand. He's eight years old, and the church's stone carvings—angels and saints—soothe his soul. This was the day he realized he had a soul. The dome reaches into the sky. It goes all the way to the sun. He and his father walk hand-in-hand, circling the church.

The Black Crickets can take his freedom, but they can't take his memories.

They can't take his soul.

He circles the church in his mind.

It brings tears to his eyes, but it gives him hope.

It gives him the strength to—

Bang, bang, bang.

"Wake up." A prisoner stands outside Dmitri's cell. "Wake up, old man." The prisoner shakes the wrought iron door against its frame, and—he's outside the cell. How can that be? This man is in the corridor, standing outside Dmitri's cell.

He's a free man.

Dmitri leaps off the bed.

The prisoner inserts a key into the lock and opens the door.

The cries of men with ragged voices spill into the corridor.

"This way." The man motions for Dmitri to follow him.

Dmitri is stunned. The man is young. Too young to be locked away in a place like this. But he's not locked away. Not anymore. He's right there. Free. His threadbare clothes match Dmitri's. His gaunt face and stick arms match Dmitri's. He's weak. Malnourished. Like Dmitri.

He's a prisoner, but he's free.

Dmitri takes a step forward. Odd, white freckles dot the man's face. They're like white stars. No. White snowflakes.

"I'm Carlos." The man steps inside and grasps Dmitri's hand. "It's okay. Come with me."

Together, they join a group of other prisoners near the stairs. They hustle. At the top, they scurry down a hall and outside. There, everyone disperses into the wilderness, running in different directions—everyone except for Dmitri. He follows Carlos. They enter a morass of weeds, bushes, and trees, causing them to lift their knees to avoid falling down. Dmitri quickly loses his breath. He's used to working at a slow pace, not running fast.

Carlos ascends a hill and lies down on the other side.

Dmitri joins him.

They do nothing but suck in air for a while.

Dmitri rolls onto his back and gazes into the sky.

The sun is out.

The sun from his childhood is out.

He's free.

"What happened?" Dmitri asks.

"Soldiers came." Carlos sits up. "They overtook the prison. The entire compound. They—it's over."

"The Cuban military?"

"No. Some other group. Rebels of some sort." He stands. "It doesn't matter. We're free."

Dmitri stands.

Carlos runs into the jungle.

"Wait." Dmitri runs after him. "Wait!" Vines twist around his legs, and he goes down. He gets up again, spots Carlos, and chases after him. He makes it a few meters before tripping and going down again. He lies in a dip beneath fluctuating shadows from a royal palm caught in the wind. This time, Carlos returns and helps him up.

"I can't keep coming back for you," Carlos says. "Go your own way."

"No, I have to know who attacked. Are you certain it wasn't the government?"

"Yes."

"What do they want?"

"I don't know. To take over. They killed most of the Black Cricket's men. Sergey said it was a bloodbath. They call themselves the Red Star Society. They're just another militant group."

"Why did they come here?" Dmitri grasps Carlos's shoulders and shakes them. "I've got to know."

"Let go of me." He pushes Dmitri back down.

The ground is soft. Soft compared to the concrete floor of his jail cell. He tries to stand but slips on the wet leaves. He reaches for help.

Carlos shakes his head, leans over, and grasps Dmitri's hand.

"Please," Dmitri says. "Let me come with you. We need to find out why these soldiers freed us."

"They weren't trying to free us. They were taking over." Sweat glistens on his brow, his cheeks, and his neck. His snowflake freckles shine in the sun. "Try and keep up." He takes off into the jungle again.

Dmitri does his best to stay with him.

Each time they emerge from the shadows, Dmitri checks the sky, and each time, the sun appears to have changed position. Time is moving fast. As he runs, he thinks about the rebels' motives for releasing all of the prison's inmates, and the more he thinks, the more the sun resembles the one he drew on his cell floor.

The freedom sun from his childhood.

He hopes he covered the groove well enough.

He knows what these rebels want.

They want him.

This new society. This Red Star Society. They're the same.

They want to know what Dmitri knows, just like the Black Crickets had.

They'll come after him. It's only a matter of time.

He's free, but he's not *free*.

He will never truly be *free*.

CHAPTER TWENTY-ONE

"You're not supposed to be in here," Calvin says.

"Would you rather we went into the women's restroom?" I ask.

"I don't know. Maybe. I've never been in one of those. Is it nicer?"

Soggy cigarette butts lie in the corner nearest the stall. I'm so glad I quit smoking, and the sight of those butts helps. The grout in the floor beneath the urinal is stained a deep yellow. There's a puddle. The place smells like someone mixed Fabreze with ammonia and a urinary tract infection.

"Yes," I say. "It's nicer in the women's restroom. Men are disgusting."

"No, A.J. just needs a better janitor. I cleaned the bathrooms at school once. There's a way to make it better in here."

"Yeah. It's called mopping. It's not rocket science."

He shrugs. "What if someone comes? You're not supposed to be in here."

"Don't worry about it. I'll hide in the stall."

"What did you want to tell me?"

"We're not going to Miami."

"What? Why not? That guy said he'll pay us a lot of money. Don't you want money?"

"I don't care how much he said. I don't trust him."

"You don't think he'll pay us?"

"No, I don't think *he'll* get paid. I don't think he's going to find Lucía. Something's not right with him. He ought to be in a hurry, but he's out there sipping on a chocolate milkshake instead."

"They make great shakes here."

I step toward him. He's not listening to me. He leans away, unsure what I'm intending. Damn. I've scared him. That's not what I wanted to do. I back off and nonchalantly place my hand on the edge of the sink, as if that's all I'd intended to do.

"We need to help Lucía," I say. "Going to Miami isn't going to help anyone. We've got to make sure this *Jack* goes to Salt Springs and, if he does, he'll lead us to her. He said he knows where to go. If he doesn't do it, we'll stop him and make him do it."

"It's too dangerous. Why are we doing this?"

"You don't understand. I had a cousin who was . . . she was sold into slavery. It was human trafficking. She escaped, but she was never the same. They're going to do that to Lucía. I'm sure of it. We must follow this guy to her and stop them."

"But he wants us to go to Miami, and he has a gun."

"Calm down. He doesn't have to know we didn't go to Miami. In fact, we can't let him know. If he does what he said, we can use him to lead us to Lucía, and then we'll find out whether she's really in trouble or not. We still don't have enough solid information for the police to convince them she's been kidnapped. When we find her, we'll call the police like we planned."

"I don't want to. If we're not going to Miami, I want to go home. He doesn't want our help, and he doesn't need our help. He has a gun, Mattie."

"I'm not afraid of him. He's a coward, and he's not right in the head. Think about it. He made us come back in here at gunpoint for a milkshake. He doesn't want our help, but he clearly needs all kinds of help. He needs therapy. He's wasted so much time already. Lucía might already be gone. It might be too late, but we don't know. We can't stop now, Calvin. We need to help her."

"I want to go home." He runs his hand through his curly locks and looks at the door. "I'm done."

"Do you want to go home, or do you want to drive that Volvo out front?"

"What?" His eyes light up. "What do you mean?"

"The sports wagon. Do you want to drive it?"

"Of course I want to drive it."

I've got him. He's coming to Salt Springs with me. "Jack can't know we're following him, so we need a different car. We might as well take that Volvo for a spin."

"I don't know." He bounces on his toes. Averts his eyes.

"You'll never have a chance to drive one of those again. No matter how much that guy pays us, I doubt you'll ever be able to afford a car like that."

"Yeah, but . . . how?"

"Don't worry about that. I'll handle it. First, we need to tell Jack we're going to Miami. We'll tell him you want another cheeseburger, and we'll be here for a while. He'll leave, and after he does, you wait in the parking lot. I'll grab the keys to the Volvo, and we'll catch up with him on the highway. I'll drive first because I know I can catch him."

"I still want the money."

"Fine. If you're so sure he's telling the truth, then he'll find Lucía. After we know her situation and call the police to come save her, we can race to Miami as promised and send him the picture of the flights he requested. We can still get the money, and you can drive the entire way. I promise." He shifts his weight. Bounces again. "Hurry and decide. We need to go."

"Okay," he says.

The door to the restroom opens, and a man with a gray beard and a red flannel shirt beneath a puffy vest enters, then stops short. He stares at me with this stupid look on his face.

"What are you looking at, Skippy?" I push past him, pulling on Calvin's wrist.

Our table is empty. Not only did the waitress come by and take Calvin's empty glass, but Jack is missing.

I look out the window, and his Camaro is missing.

The bastard.

"Wait outside," I say.

Calvin nods and heads for the door.

I rush over to the bar and peruse the venue. It's too early for a bartender, or at least that's what I assume since I haven't seen one yet today. So her uncle, the owner of the Volvo, must work in the kitchen. That Night-of-the-Living-Dead waitress takes an order on the far side of the restaurant. I thought I saw another waitress earlier, but she's not around now. She must be on a break somewhere. She's probably smoking a cigarette. A jealous pang hits me. I picture the butts in the restroom.

I'm good. I can do this without a smoke.

But, because Jack has already left, I don't have time to ask nicely for the keys to the Volvo.

I ease my way into the kitchen and just inside the door find a set of cubbies situated beneath a row of coat hooks. Our waitress's cubby is obvious. A black handbag with a pink skull painted on it. She said the Volvo belonged to her uncle, so I ignore her cubby. None of the others have anything that looks like a good place to hide their keys. But when I search the pockets of the largest, man-looking jacket, a lime green raincoat—bingo. A fob with the word Volvo on it.

"What are you doing?" The Bride of Frankenstein stands in the doorway, holding a pile of dishes on a tray. "You're not supposed to be back here."

I run toward her.

I barely bump her, but she drops the tray anyway.

The sound of the ceramic plates breaking against the floor unnerves me.

I burst into the restaurant and race toward the front door.

"Hey," she calls after me. "Like, come back here."

"Sorry."

Calvin's standing by the Volvo outside. He's making what we're doing look so obvious.

I click the unlock button on the fob.

The Volvo's brake lights flash.

"Get in!" I shout. I open the driver's side door.

The waitress yells from the open front doorway. "Stop, or I'll call the police."

"Mattie!" Calvin opens the passenger door. "What did you do?"

"I did what I had to." I hop inside. "No one else was going to do it. Get in."

CHAPTER TWENTY-TWO

Yans shoves the table as hard as he can. Canisters fly off the shelves when the table slides across the underground chamber and smashes into them. One canister pops open when it hits the concrete floor, sending a plume of ancient food powder into the air.

Yans drops to his knees and begins sweeping the floor with his hands. He finds a groove and follows it, clearing the way with his fingers.

Darien stands in the doorway at the bottom of the bomb shelter stairs, holding his government-issued gun against Lucía's head like a good soldier. Four cots run down the middle of the room, and metal shelves line the walls. Food containers. Battery packs. Flashlights. An extension cord. Gas cans. Yans started the electric generator when he entered the shelter for lighting. It rumbles. Cages protect the dust-covered light bulbs mounted in each corner of the room, and a refrigerator shakes in the corner. It's empty. Yans checked it the last time he came here, ten years ago.

"I've only ever heard about this place," Darien says.

"Why are we here?" Lucía asks.

"Shut up." Darien pushes his muzzle harder against her head and glances at Yans. "I told you only to speak when spoken to."

That's a good soldier. There's hope for him yet.

Yans retrieves a long iron rod from behind a shelf. He shoves the slender end into the groove on the floor and pries it up. A blanket of thick gray dust slides off a wooden plank as it rises to reveal a tunnel. Yans drops the rod and kicks the plank out of his way. He goes to a shelf and grabs an extension cord. He puts one end into the generator and carries the other to the tunnel.

Darien stands wide-eyed, still holding his gun to Lucía's head.

"Wait for me to yell from the other side, then follow," Yans says.

Darien nods.

"Mind the cord when you come."

Yans drops onto his hands and knees. He pulls his father's Zippo lighter out of his pocket and flicks it on. The round tunnel is dark and narrow, almost not big enough to crawl through. Roots poke through the dirty, damp walls. His shoulder scrapes against a rock as he rounds a corner, pulling the cord behind.

A hatch lies at the end of the tunnel.

Yans waves the lighter over the hatch until he finds the latch.

He swings it open and climbs through.

His chest swells with anticipation.

He searches the nearest wall for the box.

He finds it.

He opens it.

He plugs the extension cord into it, and the room comes alive.

Bright lights hanging from the ceiling illuminate everything.

"Darien," he shouts. "Come, now."

The nuclear missile, in all its glory, points toward the heavens on the other side of the room. A set of launch bay doors are set into the ceiling above the missile. Rust adorns the doors' edges. It's unlikely they open anymore, especially with the decades of sand and debris that's settled on the ground above. Yans rushes to the missile. Places his hand on the cool surface. He closes his eyes, breathes in the moment, and gazes downward. A bundle of wires with tattered cloth insulation runs across the floor to a control panel mounted on the wall.

Yans opens the panel.

Lucía tumbles out of the tunnel and thumps onto the concrete floor.

Darien follows her, gun in hand. He gathers her off the floor and presses the muzzle against her head.

Yans looks over the controls in the panel. A keypad. Five buttons. Two bulbous, unlit lights. One red. One green. Legend says the launch software only allows three chances to enter a code without launching the missile. This must be what the button labeled "Test" does. His index finger shakes as he holds it over each control in the box. His nerves rarely affect him this way, but he's not afraid. He's excited. The legend also says the original protectors of the missile used one of the codes already, leaving him with only two.

But, it's all legend. He might have an infinite number of chances to test the missile. He doesn't know.

"Read her tattoo to me."

"Is that what I think it is?" Lucía asks.

"Shut up." Darien pushes her forward and looks at her leg. "30 . . ."

Yans types in the two numbers and waits for more, but Darien says nothing. "What are the next numbers?"

"We can't do this." The blood has drained from Darien's face. *Bad soldier.*

"We're not," Yans says. "We're not launching the missile, you *idiota*. We're validating the launch code."

"Aren't you concerned the missile might launch? How do you know it will only tell you if the launch code is good?"

"If you must know, weasel, I've entered codes before, and the red light came on without launching the missile. I fully believe the green light will come on the same way with no launch."

"Wait." Lucía turns and faces Darien. "What are you guys doing?"

Yans tries, but he can't read the code on her leg from here. "Hurry."

"Turn back around." Darien waves his Browning pistol at her. "Show me your tattoo."

"It's not what you think it is," she says. "It's my brother's dog tag."

"Turn!" Yans shouts, and pulls his gun out.

Lucía shakes her head, spins around, and faces Yans. She moves her left leg backward, tipping it up on her toes so Darien can see it better.

"Read it." Yans has one hand on the keypad and aims his gun at Lucía with the other.

"3933," Darien says.

"Yes."

"4651."

"That's all?"

"That's it."

"It's not going to work." Lucía giggles. "You guys are idiots."

"You won't be laughing if it doesn't." Yans's trigger finger tenses. "If it doesn't work, we won't need you anymore." He hovers his index finger over the button marked TEST and stares at Darien. "Ready?"

A bead of sweat runs down the side of Darien's face. He touches his throat. Nods.

Yans presses the button.

A green light flashes twice.

A red light comes on and flashes twice.

The green light does not come on again.

Only the red one. It stops flashing and stays lit.

Yans closes his eyes in dismay. It's not possible. She's—she's not Lucía. It's the wrong code.

Her name is Aurora.

She was telling the truth.

"Well?" Darien asks.

"I told you," Aurora says. "It's not what you think."

Yans stands. Aims his weapon at her. "Get her out of here."

Darien grabs Aurora by the shoulder from behind, spins her around, and shoves her into the tunnel.

"Wait for me in the shelter," Yans says.

They disappear into the dark hole.

Yans stows his gun and lifts his chin. He marches across the room. *You do your best with what you're given.* Fortune gave him the wrong code and the wrong girl. He flicks his father's Zippo lighter on and unplugs the extension cord. Standing in the flame's light, his resolve strengthens.

He climbs into the tunnel.

On the other side, Darien did as told. *Good soldier.* He waited for Yans at the bottom of the stairs to the surface, holding his gun to Aurora's head.

It's still unbelievable, but the missile controls did not lie.

She's not Lucía.

She's Aurora.

She's wrong. She's all wrong.

Yans takes a blanket from a cot and spreads it on the floor.

"Let go of her."

Darien does as told. *Good soldier.*

Yans pulls out his gun and waves it at Aurora. "Move." He motions toward the blanket.

"No way, scar face." She talks tough.

He aims his gun at her, holding it with both hands.

Darien stands there like a statue. A statue with fear in his eyes. *Bad soldier.*

"Move, or Darien will move you for me."

Darien shakes his head.

Yans points his gun at Darien. "Move her."

Darien shakes his head.

Yans strides to Aurora, grasps her by the collar, and thrusts her toward the blanket.

She stumbles and catches herself by grasping a metal shelf.

Yans fires.

His bullet rips through her head and hits a canister on the other side.

A plume of ancient food powder bursts into the air, and she falls to the floor.

CHAPTER TWENTY-THREE

A warm stream runs over Lucía's upper lip and into her mouth. Her nose is bleeding. She sniffs. The trailer's cat-dander carpeting odor won't leave her nose. The blood doesn't stop running into her mouth, and she can't stop it. Stanley taped her hands behind her back with the roll of gray tape he took from his tote bag. The bag rests on the table before her. It rests next to Mr. Suzuki's cash-heavy briefcase. Part of her is embarrassed by the blood, but then she remembers what Mr. Suzuki said earlier.

I'm not interested in her face.

Mr. Suzuki sits across from her at the black dining table in his black suit and tie, smiling his black smile. Wyatt sits to her right, and Stanley sits to her left. She has never felt smaller. She's as small as the appliances and sink in the kitchen behind Mr. Suzuki. Smaller, maybe. It's all so cheap looking.

She licks her upper lip.

She twists her wrists, and, yes . . . she can reach the edge of the tape with her long fingernails. No one can see what she's doing. She begins to pick at the tape.

"You can go now, Wyatt," Stanley says. "You've done your part. I don't need you here to wrap things up with Mr. Suzuki."

"No. You haven't paid me."

"I paid you."

"Not what you promised. I want the rest of it."

"Mr. Suzuki?" Stanley gestures toward the slender man. "Are you willing to pay me the full amount for this?" He gestures toward Lucía. His maroon pinky catches her eye. It looks painful.

"No. I will not pay the full amount."

Wyatt lowers his chin and shakes his head.

"She has blood on her face," Mr. Suzuki says, "and you were forced to restrain her. This is not what you promised."

"You see, Wyatt?" Stanley licks his lips. "I'm not getting paid the full amount, so you're not getting paid the full amount. We'll discuss this later. Do you understand? It's because you didn't do your job."

Wyatt groans.

"You can leave now," Stanley says.

"I'm not going anywhere."

"Fine." Stanley wipes his greasy forehead. "But be quiet." He's the only one in here who's sweating. It's because he's fat. He's a fat, disgusting slob of a man. Lucía wants to vomit. He pulls a piece of letter-sized paper from his tote bag, then places the bag under the table. He runs his thick finger down the paper, skimming the text, and puts it down on the table. He reaches for Mr. Suzuki's briefcase and eyes him. "May I?"

Mr. Suzuki nods.

Stanley slides the briefcase into his lap, closes it, and places it under the table.

Lucía tears the tape with her fingernails, and it makes a

noise, but no one notices.

Wyatt looks destroyed. She wishes he were dead.

"First of all, let's go over the rules." Stanley picks up the piece of paper. "One. You must return her to me one week from now. Two. You never met with me"—he glances up at Wyatt—"or him. Three. If you are arrested, you're on your own. If you tell anyone about us, we will take appropriate action."

"I'm not a snitch," Mr. Suzuki says.

"Four. Be kind, rewind." He strokes his tie and grins like he thinks he's funny. "You will return her in the same condition as you took her so she can immediately move on to my next client."

"But she's already damaged."

"I understand that. Please, don't cause any more damage than my associate here has already done."

"I didn't do anything," Wyatt says. "I spent a month of my life grooming her, and everything only happened today. It's not my fault."

Another tear in Lucía's tape. She'll free her hands soon. The only way out is the way she already tried. Down the hall behind her and into one of the rooms. With some luck, she'll be able to fit through a window. But, to get there, she'll need a head start. A distraction.

"I told you to be quiet." Stanley glares at Wyatt. His double chin shakes when he speaks. He strokes the smooth, dark red stone in his pinky ring. "Can you do that?"

The front door flies off its hinges and crashes onto the floor. Light floods the room, and yelling ensues. Men's voices. Boots on steps.

Wyatt stands, already facing the doorway. He raises his hands.

Stanley attempts to spin around and stand at the same time but fails, falling back into his seat.

Two men surge into the trailer, wielding guns.

"No one move," says the first.

Lucía almost doesn't understand him because of his thick Spanish accent. She turns her head toward him and focuses on his lips.

Mr. Suzuki calmly raises his hands also and slowly stands.

"Mr. Owens," Mr. Suzuki says. "What is this?"

"I don't know." Stanley gets to his feet, hands also raised.

"*Siéntense.*" The two men step into the trailer and stand side by side. They wave their weapons. "Sit."

One holds a sleek black handgun pointed at Stanley, and the other carries a silver revolver. Both men are young, not much older than Lucía, with dark curly hair and olive skin. Fitted beige-brown shirts, baggy green-black camo shorts— their sharp jawlines tense and serious. The shorter one with the silver gun steps next to Lucía.

"Mr. Owens," Mr. Suzuki says. "I do not like this."

Wyatt's lips tremble like he wants to speak, but he says nothing.

"Who are you?" Stanley demands.

The one with the black pistol says something in Spanish.

The other one sticks his gun in his waist and grabs Lucía by her wrists. He pulls her up. The tape almost tears. Almost. Her shoulders bind, and she cries in pain as she stands.

Without letting go of her hands, he kneels by her leg and touches her tattoo. He says something in Spanish to his partner. She understands the word *numero*. He's very interested in the number on her leg, and she hopes he doesn't go looking for more. She hopes he doesn't know about the other two digits tattooed on her inner thigh.

"Sit," his partner says again, waving his pistol.

Everyone does so this time. Everyone except Lucía. Her new friend hasn't let go of her yet. She hopes he's a friend. She hopes these are the men from the Camaro Wyatt said he saw this morning. She hopes her father hired them to rescue her.

"Is this some kind of trick?" Mr. Suzuki asks Stanley. "Do you know these men?"

"I've never seen them before in my life," Stanley says. He shifts his weight and bumps the table, exposing Mr. Suzuki's briefcase. "What do you want?" He quickly pulls the table toward his belly to hide the money.

The man with the black gun points his finger at Lucía.

The other man lets go of her hands, pulls out a cell phone, and holds it up to his partner. It's clear the man with the black gun is the leader. He nods, and Lucía's new friend begins thumbing his phone.

"Wait a minute," Stanley says. He stands up.

The leader slaps him hard in the face. Sweat flies into the kitchen.

Stanley sits back down.

Mr. Suzuki stands up and takes a step back.

Wyatt sits there, shielding his face with his arm like he's watching a horror movie he wants and doesn't want to see.

Lucía's new friend puts his phone to his ear. She wishes she'd taken Spanish last semester. Sometimes, because of Valeria, her family's Spanish-speaking housekeeper, she can understand a lot, but now, the only words she recognizes are "Miami" and "Darien."

"Are you here to save me?" she asks.

The muzzle of the leader's pistol fits neatly between Stanley's eyes. "In a way. I suppose you could say that."

CHAPTER TWENTY-FOUR

MATTIE

The road sign confirms what the maps app on my phone already told me. Salt Springs is straight ahead, north on Highway 19. Neither piece of information is all that helpful, though. I've got to catch up with Jack, that bastard. I knew I couldn't trust him. He left us at the restaurant after making up some story about wanting us to go to the Miami airport for him.

I feel so stupid.

His Camaro must be on the highway somewhere. I've been pushing the stolen Volvo to over one hundred miles an hour for a while now. He's slow, so I should catch him soon.

"Could you slow down?" Calvin asks. "Just a little?"

"You were right about this car. It has a lot more power than mine." I speed up to a hundred and ten.

"Mattie, please. Why do you have to be in such a rush all the time? It's going to get us in trouble."

"No it's not. Here, hold this." I hand him my phone. "Watch the map and make sure we don't miss a turn. I can't watch the road and—"

Red lights flash in my sideview mirror.

Then, blue lights flash.

Then, I'm impressed with the brilliance of the police cruiser's headlights. Here we are in broad daylight, and those headlights outshine the sun. I push the Volvo to one hundred and twenty miles an hour.

The cruiser's siren comes on.

I press harder on the gas, and the cruiser reacts slowly and falls behind.

"Pull over," Calvin says. "What are you doing?"

"You know we don't have time to stop."

He drops my phone on the floor and grips the dashboard while I guide the wagon around a sweeping bend in the road. The cruiser disappears from my mirror for a second, then returns with a vengeance, its siren blaring.

I gun it.

I stop looking at the speedometer.

The cruiser keeps coming. It occurs to me they want more than to give me a speeding ticket. That nasty waitress probably honored her threat and called them. She probably reported her uncle's Volvo stolen and described me to the police.

I glance over at Calvin. I think of Lucía.

Getting caught isn't an option.

Once we help Lucía, I hope they'll understand why we ran.

"Watch out," Calvin yells.

I take my foot off the accelerator. "For what?"

"Animals. If one comes out, you'll hit it. You're going too fast."

I put my foot back on the accelerator. "I'll worry about that if and when it happens."

He looks so scared. Maybe the story about his father

getting hurt after running over an Armadillo army *is* true.

No.

It's ridiculous.

"Hold on," I say.

Up ahead, a narrow dirt road takes off to the left. I slow down until the cruiser is riding my bumper. The policeman announces something over his loudspeaker, but I can't understand him over the road noise. It sounded like *Pull over.*

Whatever.

I whip into the left lane and slam on the brakes.

He didn't expect that. The cruiser screeches past me on the right, and I pull off onto the dirt road to the left. Heavy greenery hides the edges. I turn on the headlights to fight the shadows from the thickening forest. The road winds this way and that, causing me to repeatedly hit the brakes.

I no longer see the police cruiser in the rearview mirror, but I can hear it back there.

Calvin doesn't anticipate the next turn and slams into the door when I take a hard right.

"Are you okay?" I ask.

"I'm never going to be okay."

"Yes, you will. Don't be so dramatic."

"Me? Dramatic? You're trying to kill us."

"I'd think this would be fun for you, with how much you like cars."

He holds on to the dashboard for dear life. "There's nothing fun about dying, Mattie."

A rickety wooden bridge appears around the next corner. This is perfect. "Then hold on tighter. We're leaving the road."

He grips the armrest with his right hand and keeps the other on the dashboard.

The cruiser hasn't caught up with us yet.

Calvin closes his eyes.

Right before the bridge, I swerve off the road, and we rumble down the embankment beside it and ease into a stream. The water can't be more than a half a dozen feet wide. Hardly worth the bridge. Maybe the creek was larger a long time ago. I turn the wheel and navigate the wagon under the bridge. Once we're completely out of sight, I turn the engine off.

The bridge has seen better days. Boards and posts hang from the underside—rotted and broken. I'm glad we didn't try to drive over it.

"You can open your eyes now," I say.

We sit in the darkness and wait, but not for long.

The cruiser's siren sounds above us.

Without a pause, the cruiser rumbles over the bridge.

A thick wooden beam falls onto the Volvo's hood and bounces into the stream with a splash, leaving a magnificent dent.

"Oh, no," Calvin says.

"What?"

"What if the car doesn't start?"

"It'll start. Just wait a minute."

"Why?"

I listen to the siren fade into the forest. It doesn't sound like the cruiser is turning around.

I turn the key.

The engine purrs to life.

"See? Everything is fine."

"What's wrong with you?"

"Now, we just need to reach Salt Springs and find Jack."

I reach over to his side and pick my phone up off the floor.

"Here. Which way does the map show we should go?"

He glances at the phone. Then, he looks out the windshield.

The stream flows from under the bridge into the sunlight and disappears in a cluster of cattails ahead.

"We should go up." He points at the ceiling and hands the phone back to me. "The phone didn't show it, but the only way is up."

CHAPTER TWENTY-FIVE

JACK

A few years ago, Jack served papers in Lake Kerr Village. He remembers it well because he knocked on the flimsy door of nearly every mobile home here. The park smelled like an aquatic rotting corpse, like a beached whale bloating in the sun, especially on the north side. He had wanted to leave immediately, but he'd also wanted to investigate.

Now he's back, cruising through the park years later. Coming here has made him realize this is probably where it all started. The bug to quit serving court documents and become a private investigator had bitten him on this very site.

Now, he wants to quit working as a PI and become—he doesn't know. Something else.

The trailers are how he remembered them. Crooked, leaning—paint peeling from metal siding beneath sagging roofs. Windows covered with a menagerie of curtains running the gambit from Confederate flags to black garbage bags to rainbows. This is the right place, based on the research he did the last time he came here. He served a man who hadn't returned his custodial daughter to his ex-wife by the agreed-upon date. To locate the right mobile home, Jack asked around the place, and several people told him to leave. They said if he happened to knock on the wrong door at the wrong time, he'd likely be shot on the spot.

Stanley Owens rules over Lake Kerr Village. Stanley Owens doesn't like strangers. Stanley Owens takes no prisoners.

Jack researched Owens.

Stanley Owens is an evil man. He hurts women.

And now, Jack is back.

Looking for a man named Stanley because of a note.

No. You help me. Blue Honda mini-van going to Salt Springs. Someone named Stanley.

He navigates his Camaro between the buildings slowly, taking each one in. He searches for the mini-van to no avail. He doesn't want to go from door to door knocking like last time, and as he rounds the last corner, he sees he won't need to. It seems like Stanley would be more cautious, but maybe he's become lax with power. A shiny new Mercedes SUV sits in front of a trailer on the park's north side, sticking out like a diamond in the rough. It's parked next to a Ford Focus and a sleek sedan. None of the other trailers have more than one car near them. Most don't have any, and none of them are anywhere near as nice as that Mercedes. It's got to be Stanley's.

Even if it's not his, this is as good a place to start as any.

Jack considers parking far away but doesn't. If Lucía is in trouble inside, he'll need to get her out of there fast. He won't have time to drag her across the park to his car. Instead, he decides to quietly park close to the trailer, run inside, and act fast.

He idles the Camaro, backs it in next to the SUV for a quick getaway, cuts the engine, and counts to thirty. None of the curtains move, and the trailer door does not open. He gets out, closes the door softly, and sneaks onto the front steps.

Men's voices argue inside. The conversation sounds intense—not your normal drunken trailer-trash talk.

They're arguing about a girl. They're fighting over her.

Jack takes out his gun and reaches for the doorknob, but the door to the trailer is not on its hinges. It's leaning forward in the frame, tilted at the top. A thin strip of carpeting runs along the bottom of the door. He places his free hand on the door, keeps his weapon raised, and pushes the door in. It falls into the trailer, and the first thing Jack sees is a tall Latino man standing next to a black dining table, pointing a gun at a silhouette's head.

Then, the tall Latino man swings his arm around and suddenly points his gun at Jack.

Jack returns the favor.

"Freeze," the Latino says with a thick Spanish accent. He sounds like he might be from Cuba.

Before Jack responds, his eyes adjust to the darkness. The silhouettes take human form, and he sees her.

He's found her. Lucía.

She sits on a chair at the table with her hands bound behind her back. Another Latino man stands at her side. He's shorter and wearing the same clothes as the other man. They look like army men on vacation—camouflage shorts and black military boots. White shirts. The bald bodybuilder from this morning is also at the table. He does not look happy. Next to him, an Asian man dressed in a black suit has his hands raised and—

Stanley Owens. The scourge of Florida.

He also has a seat at the table. Jack knew Stanley was big, but not this big. It's a wonder the cheap dining chair doesn't buckle under the load.

"Drop your weapon," Jack says, waving the business end at the tall Latino.

Stanley heaves himself off his chair. "Who the hell are you?"

"Lucía," Jack shouts. "Are you okay?"

He already knows the answer. She's not okay. Whatever is going on here is not okay. They've bruised her face. They've hurt her. They—

He tightens his grip on his gun and steps forward.

"*¡Para!*" shouts the Latino who pointed his gun at Jack.

Jack shakes his head no. "Get up, Lucía. You're coming with me."

A second, short Latino pulls out a silver revolver. The sunlight through the door glints off the revolver and momentarily blinds Jack. He carefully steps sideways into the shadowy living room so he can see everyone better.

Lucía stands.

Shorty grasps her arm.

His partner motions toward the door. Jack has no idea who these men are or why they are here. The Asian man sits calmly on the other side of the table next to the bodybuilder with his hands raised. Clearly, the bodybuilder brought Lucía to Stanley, but these Latinos . . . none of this makes any sense.

Shorty pulls Lucía toward the front door.

"Stop," Stanley says. He rumbles to the opening. The trailer shakes as if it's about to collapse. He turns around, spreads his arms, and blocks the way. He glares at Shorty. "You can't take her."

"That's right," Jack says. "Because I am." He aims his pistol at Shorty and holds his hand out to Lucía. "Come here."

"Wyatt," Stanley stammers. "Do something. Get my bag."

The bodybuilder—*Wyatt*, apparently—sort of disappears under the table. He's too big to fit and knocks the table over while trying to grab a tote bag on the floor.

The tall Latino steps forward.

Jack resists the strong urge to shoot. There are too many people here who could retaliate in an instant. Jack can't cover them all.

"*Baja el arma*," the tall Latino says.

"What?"

The Latino has dense amber eyes with an unnerving seriousness. He's young but experienced.

"Give me your gun," the Latino says.

Jack freezes. He can't do it. The rage comes. Lucía has blood on her upper lip. He's got to—

The Latino rips Jack's gun away from him in one swift move, lets it fall to the floor, and shoves Jack in the chest. Jack stumbles back into the living room and regains his balance quickly. He lowers his body and runs to the front doorway, burying his head in Stanley's gut. Together, they tumble out of the trailer and roll onto the ground. Stanley's body is immense, but Jack manages to roll him and climb on top. He straddles Stanley's waist and throws a punch, his hand sinking into the fat man's thick chest.

Stanley wraps his hands around Jack's neck.

Jack hits him again, but it's like pounding sand. He struggles to breathe.

Stanley squeezes.

The stars inside Jack's head come out. He grasps Stanley's

hands and tries to pull them off his throat. He makes progress with the left hand, but it slips away when a ring slides off Stanley's pinky finger. Jack makes a fist around the ring and punches Stanley in the face again and again.

Stanley is not fazed.

Jack is choking.

He tips his head back as far as he can, lifts his knee, and manages to put one foot flat on the ground. He presses upward.

Stanley holds tight.

Something hits Jack in the head from behind.

Stanley lets go of his grip on Jack's neck, and Jack falls to the side. His shoulder hits the ground with a *thud*.

Wyatt stands over him, holding the tote bag.

Jack, still struggling to pull air into his lungs, rolls to his stomach and begins to crawl. He sticks Stanley's pinky ring into his mouth and hides it in his cheek.

"Quick," Stanley says. "Get him. Give me the bag."

Wyatt jumps onto Jack's back and pulls on his arms.

Jack can't move. He can't breathe.

Wyatt tapes Jack's hands together.

He keeps fighting—kicking, twisting—but it's no use.

Wyatt puts his forearm on the back of Jack's neck and pins his head to the ground.

Lucía's feet come down the steps, followed by a pair of army boots.

"Wait," Stanley says. "I'll make you a deal."

"*¿Qué?*"

"You speak English, right?"

"A little."

"Leave the girl, and I'll give you this guy. He's in much better shape. He can join your cause. What do you say?"

CHAPTER TWENTY-SIX

The shovel's head clangs against a rock, making Yans stop pacing and turn toward Darien.

Darien tries again and plunges the blade deep into the earth.

Yans looks away.

The warm Cuban wind begins to blow again. The royal palms sway on the hills outside Guanajay. Yans looks on longingly, remembering the way the trees used to be, dense and deep. The way they were when he was a child. The way they were before Cuba turned on him.

He didn't ask for this.

Darien tilts the shovel, and the dirt falls into the hole. The wind ferries dust across the field. Darien's jacket blows open—a chaotic jumble of green, black, and beige patterns. His jacket grapples with the wind, flapping and slapping his neck and torso. He's a good soldier—now. But not before.

She had to die.

She was in Darien's charge. His responsibility. At the penultimate moment, he allowed fear to affect his judgment.

He was a bad soldier. He did not follow Yans' command, and Yans had to shoot her.

But, since then, Darien has done as he's been told. He knows he made a grave mistake. To teach him, Yans made him dig alone. Yans made him bury Aurora here, not far from the bomb shelter. Not far from the solution to all Cuba's problems. The missile.

Yans rubs his neck.

Since leaving the shelter, Darien has obeyed every command without complaint. He's been a good soldier.

Darien pauses to wipe sweat from his brow and notices Yans watching him. He quickly returns to stabbing the ground with the shovel, heaving dirt . . . erasing what happened.

"Why did you refuse to kill her?" Yans asks.

"I don't know. I thought we needed her."

"For what?"

"For the club. We still do not have enough dancers for tonight." He drops another load of dirt on Aurora's tomb.

Yans hadn't thought about the club since they left it this morning. Filling the dance tables tonight no longer mattered because he thought they'd found Lucía. Darien's small mind is fixated on small things, but at least he's thinking.

"So," Yans says, "we will have an empty dance table tonight. That is okay."

"We'll have two empty tables." He drops another load of dirt into the hole. He's almost finished.

"That is also okay."

"It's never been okay before." He stops shoveling. Sweat drips into his eyes. He removes his black cap and wipes his face with it.

"When did we begin flying candidates in from the US?" Yans asks. "I thought we always took them from the streets."

"We don't fly them in." He begins to shovel again. "A few months ago, we decided to put men in the airport to catch potential dancers getting off the planes. Girls come to Cuba looking for work and an inexpensive lifestyle but usually end up on the streets, broken. By the time we recruit them, they're damaged. So, we decided to get them while they're fresh."

"Aurora was one of those, yes?"

"Yes." He sticks the shovel in the ground. "I'm done."

"Come, sit with me."

Yans strides away up the hillside. He doesn't want to be near Aurora's grave. He sits, and Darien sits next to him. He gazes out over the countryside. The wind slows down, but the evening heat does not relent. A concern tugs at his mind. If the heat penetrates the shallow earth, Aurora's decay may begin to smell. Hikers or other commoners might notice and alert someone. Ah, but not to worry. He reminds himself this has never happened before. At least two girls and several traitors are buried on the other side of the hill. He's letting his foolish thoughts detract from the moment.

Sitting with his backside firmly planted on the ground, his gun protrudes from his waistline. He puts his hand on the hilt.

Darien sees this, and though he sits similarly against the hill, he straightens his back and squares his shoulders.

"Don't concern yourself," Yans says. He takes his hand off his gun. "I don't plan on shooting you." Darien relaxes. "But I am not all pleased with you. Why didn't you kill her when I commanded? Apparently, we have strippers for the club arriving all the time."

"I don't know."

"I need to know you will do as I say in the future. Why didn't you kill her?"

"She was innocent."

"No," Yans yells. "No one is innocent. Especially not whores. You didn't have the strength to do it. Admit it."

"I could have. I needed time."

"When I am commanding you, I control your time. Do you understand?"

"Yes."

"What will you do next time?"

"Whatever you say."

The wind picks up—one last gasp—and blows the cap off Darien's head. He doesn't take his eyes off Yans. He doesn't react. This is good. The sun shines through the trees and glints off one of the Revolutionary Armed Forces medallions pinned to Darien's jacket.

"You've done well for yourself," Yans says. "Serving the *Fuerzas Armadas Revolucionarios*."

"Thank you."

"But after earlier, I'm concerned about your place in the Red Star Society."

"I will do as you say next time. I promise." Darien turns his head toward the hills. The sun is continuing its descent. The wind gusts, and his cap tumbles away across the packed earth. Yans can tell he wants it back, but he doesn't move. "I will do as you say—especially now."

"I would think so. You didn't believe the legend before today, did you?"

"I don't know what I believed before I saw it."

"I am in command of the missile. No one else has access or knows where it is—no one other than you, now." He glances at the mound. "You see why she had to die."

"Yes. I understand." His cap rolls up against a fallen tree branch and stops. "May I ask a question?"

"Now is a good time. Otherwise, you should only speak

when spoken to."

"If you were the only one who knew about the missile before today, how did you find it? Where did it come from?"

"A former member of the Black Crickets, a man named Dmitri, told me before he died on the streets of Havana years ago. Do you know who the Black Crickets were?"

"Yes. I've heard of them. One of those anti-Castro groups that never got anywhere."

"That's correct. You see, before Dmitri died, he was the only one who knew the missile's location. Working for the Russian government as an engineer in the 1960s, he helped install the missile. Somehow, at the end of the crisis, Cuba neglected to return that missile. Legend says the Black Crickets stole it, and the Red Star Society found out about it later on." Yans lifts his chin. "No one else knew its exact location until I took over the Red Star Society and found Dmitri. We've been waiting for this opportunity for a long time."

"Opportunity?"

"It's time for the Red Star Society to relieve the government of its failed duties. It's time to save Cuba. Now is perfect. All sides are arguing like children. Without a real Castro in command, the government is fractured."

"I understand. It's time for a Rivero. For you."

"Don't flatter me." Yans gazes toward Guanajay. Toward Havana and the rest of Cuba. "But, you're correct. It is time for a Rivero." He makes eye contact with Darien. "Did you know we are related to Castro?"

"No."

"My great, great grandfather was a Castro. This is my destiny."

"I see."

"We're only missing the launch code. Once we have it, and once we validate that it will launch the missile, we'll have leverage. Everyone will be forced to negotiate with us or we'll threaten to use the code. You understand better now why we must have it? The importance of it. The importance of your friends searching for it in the US."

"What if the government finds out?"

"Do not concern yourself. They trust me. I am a general, and I've made many friends. Some know about the Red Star Society. When it's time to negotiate terms with the US, the other generals will leave Miguel and come to me."

Darien's cell phone rings. "*Hola.*"

Yans stands and sidesteps down the hill.

"You have?" Darien says into the phone, pressing it hard against his ear. "That's most excellent news."

Yans retrieves Darien's cap.

"Wait," Darian says. "Are you certain?"

Yans shakes the cap. He rubs the dirt off with his hand and holds it up in the breeze to check for more.

"Great. We'll be waiting for you." Darien returns his phone to his pocket.

Yans returns to him and hands him his cap.

Darien places the cap on his head, straightens the bill, and puffs out his chest. "They found her, *señor.*"

"They know where she is?"

"Yes. She's with them. They have her."

Yans keeps his emotions in check. "How do they know?"

"She matches the description perfectly."

"She's Lucía?"

"She answered to that name. Yes."

"And the tattoo?"

"Yes." He takes his cap off. Runs his fingers through his

hair. "Ooh. I forgot to ask for the code."

"No matter. We need her here, as planned. We must be absolutely certain the tattoo is correct before we try again. We can't make another mistake. Legend says we may only have one more chance to test the launch."

"But, forgive me for saying, the code is the code."

"After today, we must be certain. If it doesn't work, we'll need to find out why. If it doesn't work, we'll need to interrogate her. We need her alive to tell us everything she knows."

"Alive?"

Yans glances at Aurora's grave.

Darien does the same. "I understand."

"When will they bring her?"

"Tomorrow, maybe the next day. They're coming by boat for safety."

"Excellent."

Darien is a good soldier.

He's Yans's only true soldier. His most loyal soldier.

Yans goes to him.

"I need to know you'll be loyal to me. What will you do next time?"

"Whatever you say."

"I want you to be *mi mano derecha*. You will have a place in the Red Star Society. A high place."

"I am honored."

Yans places his hand on Darien's shoulder and points toward the hills. The setting sun paints the sky pink and orange and purple. The colors streak across the horizon like watercolors. The silhouettes of the royal palm trees stand tall. They stand still in the dying breeze. They stand at attention before Yans and Darien.

They stand looking over the future of Cuba.
"Tell me," Yans says. "What do you see?"
"The future."
Good soldier.

CHAPTER TWENTY-SEVEN

I have Jack's Camaro etched in my brain. It's one of the newer ones. I guessed it to be around one or two years old, but Calvin insists it's five, and he would know. We're cruising through the third neighborhood in Salt Springs, looking for Jack. When we came in on Highway 19, we nearly missed the town. It took less than a minute for us to go from one end to the other on the highway.

"There's one," I say.

"That's not it." Calvin leans forward. "Too dark. His car is a lighter shade of gray. Almost silver."

We approach the next house. From what I can tell, Salt Springs is so small that it doesn't have a downtown area. I saw a post office next to a pizza joint, and that was it. Since then, we've been looping through the neighborhoods, hoping to spot his car. The lots are large, and the homes are small, often surrounded by enormous trees. But if anyone can spot Jack's car, it's Calvin.

He has a gift.

Nevertheless, before long, we have searched everywhere.

Maybe Jack didn't come here after all. That would surprise me because he seemed so excited when I showed him Lucía's note. He said he had contacts in Salt Springs, but he could have been lying. Without finding him, we have no chance of finding Lucía.

I pull up to a dirt intersection and stop. We're on the edge of a large pond. It's almost large enough to be a lake, but the blankets of algae floating throughout make it look like a pond. We have nowhere to go from here.

"Why are we stopping?" Calvin asks.

"Hold on. I need to think."

I can't stop picturing Lucía leaving the Pay-n-Save. I should have done something sooner, but I didn't know. She and her supposed boyfriend were gone by the time I read her note, and Calvin was trapped in the back of the store with a thief. I should have run out, jumped in Dory, and taken off after the mini-van. I should have called the police. Calvin would have been okay. That thief was a coward.

By the time I decided what to do, it was too late. The thief brought Calvin out of the back with a gun to his head.

I shouldn't have hesitated.

It's Hank the Manatee all over again.

I head for the highway.

It's over. I can't believe it's over.

"Look." Calvin points at the pond. "Over there."

"Where?"

"Way over there."

It's not a huge pond, but I can barely see the other side. I slow down.

"We didn't search over there," he says. "It looks like a trailer park."

"It does?" I don't see what he sees over the water and

into the trees, but I trust him. If he sees mobile homes, there are mobile homes. And, sure enough, when we arrive on the other side, we find the Lake Kerr Village entrance. Paint hangs in strips on the weather-worn sign, making it hard to read. A rusted chain-link fence surrounds the mobile homes. If there was ever a gate to the entrance, it's long gone.

We wind our way into the park, cruising toward the pond.

"Up there," Calvin says, beaming. "That's Jack's car."

The late model Camaro sits next to a big black SUV with heavily tinted windows.

I whip in behind an RV with an orange stripe painted down one side. Like all the places here, the RV is rusted and probably hasn't moved since the 1970s.

We exit the Volvo and peer around the corner.

"Oh, no," Calvin says.

"What?"

"See that Mercedes? The SUV with the tinted windows?"

"Of course I see it."

"I want to go home."

"Hold on. What's wrong?"

"I've never seen a movie with a car like that that didn't belong to gangsters or the CIA. Either way, they always have guns, and they always kill the cannon fodder."

"The what?"

"The cannon fodder. Characters who show up out of nowhere and have nothing to do with the movie except to be killed. They always get killed." He glances back at the Volvo. "Don't you get it? That's us."

Yelling comes from the trailer across the way. Jack's car is over there, but I don't know for sure he's inside. If he is, it doesn't sound good. We have no time to waste.

"Something's going on in there," I say.

"Yeah. They're fighting. They're going to start shooting soon. Let's go."

"No. I need to hear what they're saying."

"I want to go home."

"Wait in the car. I'll be back in a minute."

The way I scamper across the road is ridiculous, keeping my upper body low to the ground like I'm running to a helicopter, but it's also appropriate. I *am* sneaking around, after all. I move as fast as possible and dart around to the other side of the trailer. It backs to the pond Calvin and I saw earlier, and none of the neighbors can see me here.

The yelling inside stops, but muffled voices continue.

I reach up and slide open a small, frosted glass window.

"No, you take him," says one voice.

"We don't want him. We're taking the girl."

"You can't have her," the first guy replies.

"If you touch one hair on her head—" It's Jack. That's his voice. I'm sure of it. "If you touch her—"

"Shut up." There's a *smack* and a grunt.

"If you touch her, I swear to God, I'll rip your arm off and strangle you with it."

You go, Jack. You tell them. He must be talking about Lucía.

A different, booming, older voice says, "I'd like to see you try. Don't you know who I am?"

"I know who you are, you lech. You're Stanley—"

Smack. Grunt.

Jack's grunting sounds like he's hurt.

"What should we do with him?" another, younger voice asks.

"Mr. Suzuki? What do you recommend?"

"The solution is simple. We kill him. Then, we'll negotiate who will take the girl."

CHAPTER TWENTY-EIGHT

LUCÍA

Misery loves company. Lucía's housekeeper has always said that, and it's true. Lucía feels better sitting next to someone with their hands taped behind their back like hers, but she also feels bad that he was caught. Like these Cuban guys, he came inside the trailer and demanded she leave with him. Then, they beat him up. Unlike these Cuban guys, he seemed to be trying to help her. He defended her, and he got mad when he saw what they'd done to her face.

He got really mad.

And then there's the Camaro. Wyatt had said they were being followed by a Camaro, and now there's a Camaro parked outside. It must be this guy's car.

She leans over to get closer to him.

"What's your name?" she whispers.

"Jack."

"I'm Lucía."

"I know."

Everyone else is standing around the dining table in front of them, arguing. They've been arguing about what to do with her and Jack for a while now. The Cuban guys insist on taking her with them, but Stanley isn't letting that happen. He's tried to give them Jack instead. Then, he tried to bribe them, and that almost worked. The creep in the black suit and tie keeps leering at Lucía like he thinks Stanley will win the argument. He stares at her like she's in a circus freak show.

That's what this is.

A circus.

That's all it takes for delirium to take over. Everyone's appearance changes before her eyes. Stanley is an elephant, Wyatt an ape, and the Cuban guys trapeze artists.

Mr. Suzuki stays the same.

She closes her eyes and shakes her head.

When she opens them again, Wyatt is no longer an ape. He's staring at her. He hasn't said anything in a while. He doesn't belong here with these other creeps. He's not up to their level.

She waits until he looks away before leaning toward Jack again.

"Did my father send you to find me?" she whispers.

"Yes."

She knew it. She knew her father would try to rescue her.

"Quiet!" Stanley shouts at them. "Wyatt, aren't you watching them?"

"Uh, yeah. Sorry." Wyatt puts his angry face on. "Shut up."

Lucía recommits to sawing through the tape around her wrists with her fingernail. In only another minute, she's nearly broken through. She can feel it. She twists her wrists and the tape snaps. She glances around for a reaction, but no one heard it. Not even Jack. She keeps her hands behind her back where no one can see.

She can leave now, but she's got to time it right.

She's got to run, but . . .

If she tries to go past Stanley to the front door, they'll catch her outside just like they did Jack. The kitchen on the other side of the table is a dead end. The best she can hope for is a room in the hallway behind her with a window. Bathrooms always have windows. Maybe not in mobile homes—she's not sure—but she plans on finding out.

It's the only option.

The men are coming to a decision.

Time is running out.

She reconsiders the kitchen, but the window is too small. Everything in the kitchen is too small. She wonders if everything in the bathroom will be the same. Too small.

"He's not worth anything dead," Mr. Suzuki says.

"What do you care?" Stanley asks. "As long as you get her, we have a deal."

"No one is taking her," says the tall Cuban guy. "She's ours."

He has his gun aimed at Stanley.

Stanley has his gun aimed at him.

Wyatt stands there like an idiot, his bald head glowing red.

Another wave of delirium hits her, and she thinks, *Boys will be boys. Boys and their toys. Boys always make noise.* The guns are lollipops, and Stanley is a bullfrog. She shakes it off. She's unsure if these bouts with reality are the after-effects of the drugs Wyatt had her on or if they're coming from the concussion he gave her. She licks her upper lip. The blood from her nosebleed has dried. She wriggles in place. Glances at the hallway over her shoulder.

"That's negotiable," Stanley says. "But to be sure, there is no way you'll take him instead of her. Correct?"

The tall Cuban guy nods.

"Fine, then. We'll dispose of him. Wyatt—you can do cleanup, right?"

"No." He shakes his head violently. "No way. I'm a groomer, not a cleaner. You were right, Stanley. I should have left when you told me to."

"Go to hell," Jack says.

"Wyatt, can you at least shut him up?"

Wyatt makes a fist and slams it into the palm of his hand.

"I was thinking of the tape," Stanley says. "Put it over his mouth. But whatever."

Wyatt stands up, rears back, and hits Jack in the temple with his meaty fist.

Jack's head lolls. "Hey . . . "

Wyatt hits him again, and he slumps into the chair with his eyes closed. Like a good boy expecting a treat, Wyatt turns toward Stanley, practically wagging his tail. "Can I leave now?"

"No," Stanley says. "You're too late."

But it's not too late for Lucía.

Wyatt lowers his head and trudges toward his seat, turning his back on Lucía.

Now is her chance.

She scrambles to her feet and runs toward the hallway.

At first, she can't bring her hands in front of her body. The tape is broken but sticky. She runs awkwardly and almost trips over the coffee table. The tape's glue finally lets go of her wrists, and she enters the hall with her hands free.

"Stop her!" Stanley shouts.

"*¡Para!*"

They're all still behind her, maybe jockeying for who gets lead position.

Four doors. Two on the right, two on the left, and none at the end.

"No one shoot," Mr. Suzuki says.

The first door on the left—locked.

The second door on the left—locked.

The tall Cuban guy is marching down the hall with his gun drawn and Wyatt on his heels.

She tries the handle of the second door.

The knob turns. It's the bathroom, and she's inside.

She slams the door behind her and locks it.

The bathtub-shower combo are normal in size, but the window is not.

It's small. Really small. But open, at least.

The fishy odor of the trailer park mixes with the smell of soap residue.

A faint, delirious spell comes and goes.

She steps into the bathtub and wavers.

Bang, bang, bang.

They're going to beat the door down.

She gets it together.

"I'll just be a minute. I had to go real bad."

She steps up on the tub's edge and looks out the window. All she sees is water. A pond spreads out far and wide. She knows how to swim, but she's never swam that far.

"Lucía. Down here."

Her heart flutters.

The woman from the convenience store is outside, kneeling beneath the window. She got the note and came. She must have followed them here somehow.

"Quick," the woman says. "Climb down."

Lucía sticks her head and one arm through the opening, but her shoulders are too broad for her other arm to fit.

A gunshot rings out, and the porcelain beneath her feet shatters.

Her ears ring.

Voices from the hallway sound like they've traveled a long way to get here.

"You fool. *¡Idiota!*"

The door flies open and slams against the sink.

"Get her."

The woman outside grabs Lucía's hand and pulls.

She hadn't thought it possible, but her other shoulder pops through the window.

The woman takes her by both hands and leans back, pulling hard.

Lucía's shirt rips down the side, and so does her skin. Her ribs feel exposed. She's almost through, but now her hips catch. The ground looks far away. Inside the trailer, hands seize her ankles, and she kicks. She screams.

The woman pulls on her arms.

The hands pull on her legs.

She kicks.

The hands let go.

Then, the hands grab her again.

She kicks again, making contact with what she hopes is someone's face.

Wyatt's face, with any luck.

She twists, and her hips pop through.

The woman lets go and falls backward.

The earth rushes up and slams Lucía in the face. Her neck cracks. Her knees bounce off the ground.

Slick grass slimes her cheek.

She rolls onto her back, and the sky disappears when the blackout comes.

CHAPTER TWENTY-NINE

DMITRI - 1969

The machine grinds away, day after day, spitting copper chunks and other metal pieces onto the conveyor belt. Dmitri sweeps the deep reddish-brown chunks to the side, where they drop into a hole. A bucket fills beneath. The belt moves. Dmitri sweeps copper chunks. More chunks fall into the bucket.

The belt moves.

Dmitri sweeps.

Somewhere up the line, another car arrives. It could be a '55 Chevy with a blown crankcase. It could be a rusted Packard Super Eight from the 1940s. It could be a Model T. The unlucky cars go to the car crusher. The other unwanted, broken-down cars go into the garage whole and come out in parts. The belt delivers the parts to the shredder. Dmitri's shredder.

Dmitri scans the belt for copper chunks.

The belt moves.

Dmitri sweeps.

His knowledge is wasted here, like so many cars. He's

seen the cars they send into the garage. With effort, many of them could have been repaired. But they're worth more torn to pieces. Most people don't realize how many things they depend on come from the copper chunks of a discarded car. They don't know the wiring for their rock-n-roll radios comes from Dmitri's sweat as he stands day after in the hot Cuban sun, scanning the belt.

Sweeping the chunks.

Filling the bucket.

Looking over his shoulder.

Wondering if the Red Star Society has found him.

Dmitri smiles up at the sun.

He will gladly stand here, burning in the heat, for the rest of his life if it means never returning to that jail cell. The sun above shines with freedom. His pale, Russian skin has grown dark over the past year since he escaped.

With each passing day, he looks more like a Turk.

A tap on his shoulder.

"Dmitri," he hears over the machinery's thunder. "Dmitri, it's me."

He knows better than to turn his back on the shredder when it's feeding. Dmitri pulls the lever down, the shredder halts, the belt stops, and then he turns around.

"Remember me?"

"I do." Swept with emotion, Dmitri hugs the man. "How could I forget? Carlos. What are you doing here?"

"I started work yesterday. I can't believe it's you."

The young Cuban's face has filled in nicely. No sunken, starving cheeks beneath his scattered snowflake freckles. No knobbed knees or nicked elbows. He looks human now, just like Dmitri. He looks like Dmitri's savior, because he is. This man rescued Dmitri from the Black Crickets, and he'll never forget that.

Carlos.

"I had a hard time finding you," Carlos says. "They told me a man named Feridun ran the shredder, but here you are. Is that you?"

"It is," Dmitri whispers. "And it isn't." He leans in close. "It is me. My name is Feridun."

"Huh?"

The tubby boss comes out of an office across the lot.

"Feridun. My name is Feridun."

"Oh." Carlos glances around. He doesn't seem to see *Señor* Chapa, or maybe he does. "I understand. Tell me, 'Feridun,' where are you from?"

"Turkey." Dmitri smiles and gently slaps Carlos on the shoulder. "I've been here for years."

Carlos smiles cheekily. "And do you ever plan on going home?"

The Sign of the Blessed Virgin church appears in Dmitri's mind. His father, his mother, his brother—the church . . . they're all home in Moscow, but—no. Cuba is home now. He can never return to Mother Russia. He's never been to Turkey. The Russians have most likely lost interest in finding the missile, or they may never have known about it, but Dmitri's paranoia knows no bounds. He could never take the risk of returning for fear of what they might do to him for deliberately modifying a nuclear warhead for Cuba. They might kill him.

However, the Red Star Society would do worse. They'd lock him back in that dank, underground tomb. His old jail cell. His living nightmare.

No.

Based on what he knows, he's not Dmitri. He's never

been Dmitri.

He's Feridun.

He's an uneducated immigrant from Turkey who loves his freedom.

"Feridun." His boss, *Señor* Chapa, has succeeded in waddling over. "Why have you shut the shredder down?"

"Sorry, *señor*. I did it to talk to . . . what was your name again?"

"Carlos."

"Right." Dmitri's face is glowing, glistening with sweat. "Carlos just started yesterday."

"I know." *Señor* Chapa does not glow. He turns to Carlos. "And you're assigned to Alberto in the garage."

Carlos nods and leans into a run. After a few strides, he glances back and winks at Dmitri. Having a friend—a true friend—working here fills Dmitri's chunk bucket with joy.

The sun above is shining on him today.

He reaches for the lever.

"Wait," says *Señor* Chapa. "Don't start it. I have a question for you."

"Yes."

"Were you ever in the military?"

"No." In the distance, the car crusher squeals, taking another automotive victim. "Why?"

"Two men in army fatigues were asking about you this morning."

"Why would they ask about me? I don't know them."

"That's what I thought. They asked to see your file, but there was nothing about any service to the revolution." The fat man checks the front of the lot, glancing toward the garage. "Are you in some kind of trouble?"

"No. It must be a mistake."

"Okay." Chapa waves his hand dismissively. "Carry on."

Dmitri pulls on the lever.

The belt moves.

He scans the belt for copper chunks.

They've found him. They're asking about him.

The shredder shreds.

Dmitri spots a healthy-sized chunk of copper.

Either the Cuban government or the Red Star Society has found him. Either way . . .

The belt moves.

The chunk falls off the end.

Dmitri calmly walks away from his station. Having only just reunited with Carlos, his heart aches at what he must do now. In another few moments, he'll have put the recycling plant at his back, never to return.

CHAPTER THIRTY

MATTIE

"Wake up."

I don't want to slap Lucía, but I don't think I'm strong enough to carry her to the car. The poor thing blacked out when she hit the ground. Above us, two men's faces fill the trailer's bathroom window, one atop the other. Blood runs down the aluminum siding beneath them. Lucía's blood. It's a miracle she was able to fit through the opening.

The men yell at me, knock their heads together, fighting for a better view.

I take Lucía by her wrists and drag her across the slick green grass. She's heavier than she looks.

"Wake up," I say. "We've got to *go*."

The men's heads vanish from view.

Lucía opens her eyes.

A gun barrel appears in the window, and a shot is fired, but it goes wide. Then the barrel is swinging back and forth outside the window. The men are fighting with each other. If they keep it up, we might have a chance.

I help Lucía stand up. "Can you run?"

She nods.

We take off around the corner of the trailer.

Lucía doesn't keep up with me, though, and when I turn around, she's leaning on Jack's Camaro.

"Don't stop!" I shout.

"Can't we take this one?"

"No. That's Jack's car." I read her face. She knows who Jack is, and what she knows isn't good. He's trapped inside the trailer. "I parked down there. C'mon."

The front door to the trailer bursts open.

"Duck!" I pull her onto the ground behind the Camaro. We lie down all the way, and I peer beneath the undercarriage.

"Do you see them?" an older man's voice asks.

"No."

Someone with a thick Spanish accent joins the conversation. "Get out of my way."

Coming down the other side of the car, black boots pound the earth. They move at top speed around the trailer, heading toward the pond. The boots' owners think Lucía and I are still back there.

"Get up," I hiss at Lucía. "Run!"

We find our feet, I take her hand, and we sprint down the road in the other direction.

"There," shouts the older voice. "Get them!"

Crap.

We pass several haphazardly parked RVs and mobile homes, weaving between them until I spot the Volvo. It sits in all its glory, ready to take us away with its powerful engine. This wagon is no Dory, but it's strong. Reliable.

However . . . it was too much for me to ask Calvin to be reliable.

He's not in the car.

I scan the homes, the trees, the bushes—he's nowhere to be seen.

He ran away.

Lucía gets in the passenger side.

Calvin said he wanted to go home. He got scared and ran. The coward.

"Calvin," I call.

Nothing.

"Hands up." The voice comes from behind.

I raise my hands and slowly turn around.

Walking now, two heavily breathing Latino men approach the back of the Volvo with their guns drawn. They're young, strong, and determined. A whale of a man and Lucía's muscle-headed boyfriend follow at a distance behind them.

I shouldn't have stopped to check for Calvin in the car. I should have jumped inside and driven away. I parked the Volvo in the direction of the exit for a reason. The key fob is in my pocket. All I had to do was get in and drive, but I didn't.

"Get out." The taller man waves his gun at Lucía. He must be the main man because the soldier boy purposely lags a few steps behind.

"No," I say. "You can't have her."

The fat man and Lucía's boyfriend stop running several paces behind the Latinos. The whale puts his hands on his knees and sucks in some air. Mr. Muscles fares better, but he's not used to running either, his face red and chest heaving.

"Get out," the main gunman repeats.

I want to tell Lucía to stay in the car. I want to tell her these men are cowards and will not shoot her, but they're not cowards. They're serious, and if they take her, they won't need me. They might kill me. The thought of having a last cigarette prances into my mind, and for a brief moment, I desperately want a smoke at any cost.

"Ah!" Something hits the main man in the head, and he puts his hand over his ear. The rock that struck him bounces off his foot. "Ow."

I look where the rock came from, and there he is—Calvin. He's hiding behind a bush with orange flowers. The gunman looks in the same direction, but I don't think he sees Calvin. I take this opportunity to pick up a rock of my own.

"Hey," I yell. "Over here."

I throw my rock at the other gunman, but it misses by—oh, God. It's so embarrassing. The rock lands way to the right of the men, and I mean *way* right. They laugh and say something in Spanish about baseball. But, while they're looking at me, another rock flies through the air. This one strikes the second gunman in the neck, and he drops his gun.

Thanks, Calvin.

The fat man hunches over and starts hustling back to the trailer. "Let's go, Wyatt. I don't want to get hit."

Coward.

I jump into the driver's seat and start the car. "Lock your door."

The back window explodes.

No one was shooting at any of the men, but now, one of them is shooting at *us*.

I gun it and wave out the window at Calvin, motioning for him to go into the woods. If he runs in the right direction, he can cut across and meet us on the other side.

Another gunshot rings out.

Mud flies from the front tires, battering the side panels.

In the rearview, I see the two gunmen turn around and run back to the trailer.

I hope Jack got out while everyone was gone.

I hope we get out of here before it's too late.

The road bends this way and that, and sure enough, Calvin pops out of the woods on the other side. I stop the car, and he climbs into the back seat.

"Is everyone okay?" he asks.

"We're fine." I glance at Lucía. "You're fine, right?"

"I'll be okay."

The side of her face is swollen and she has a bloody upper lip, but she's smiling. Her shorts are also red with blood from the deep scrape down her left side. That bathroom window was way too small, but it was worth it. We're going to make it out of here.

The road slants to the right and makes a hard turn toward the exit. The tires lose their grip around the corner and we begin to slide on the mud, forcing me to ease off the gas. I make the turn and slam the accelerator to the floor.

The exit comes fast. The road leads to an opening in a rusted chain-link fence. There is no gate to stop us.

But there is a black SUV with tinted windows.

The beast sits sideways in the opening, blocking our way.

"That's a Mercedes like the other one," Calvin says. "I think it's brand new."

"I see that," I say.

I slow down.

The doors to the SUV open, and four men step out.

I stop the car about thirty yards from them.

They aim their guns at us. They have huge guns.

I glance in the rearview mirror.

The other Mercedes SUV suddenly appears around the corner and barrels toward us.

CHAPTER THIRTY-ONE

YANS - CUBA NOW

The Red Star Society sits in shadowed rows, their faces obscured by the blindingly bright lights beating down on the stage. The bright lights beat down on Yans. Ernesto told him before his address that nearly one thousand members were in attendance. This is the most ever. They sit in the abandoned 1950s cinema, revering Yans and his leadership. As the lights from the stage burn, he lets the sweat drip down his cheeks. His back is drenched. The silhouettes—a sea of black figures on the brink of destiny—sway with the beat of his words.

". . . and after twelve long years—a significant portion of our lives—the next and final stage is at hand. The New Cuba is at hand!"

A smattering of applause drifts up from the crowd. Yans had hoped for more.

"The world will no longer treat us with disrespect. They will invest in us rather than toy with our economy. This tit-for-tat policy will end. They will consult us rather than issue demands. We have the strongest medical care system in the world, and they will beg us to share our wisdom. We'll cure their cancer. They will stand in awe of our spirit. Our way of life. The New Cuba.

"Our friends to the north will—"

"We've heard all this before," an older man's voice bellows from the seats. "What has changed? How many more promises are you going to make and break?"

Yans squints into the darkness in vain. There's nothing more disgusting to him than untamed dissent, except, perhaps, an outright revolt. A second jeer from the same, ragged old voice claims Yans's speech is nothing more than repetitive rhetoric. This man is a dissenter. Yans wishes he could see him. This man must be dealt with.

"Ahem." Yans begins again. "Our friends to the north will cower because of our power." He decides to take a risk. This promise he will keep. "With progress made just earlier today, we will begin negotiations within a week's time. The United States will do as we say, or they will suffer."

Darien's friends in Florida—his little troop—said they have her. They have Lucía. They have the missile launch code.

He said his friends will deliver her within one or two days.

He had better be right.

Yans glances offstage.

Darien stands in the wings next to Ernesto, his hands at his sides, his back straight, and his chin up.

Respect.

Yans did well to make Darien his right-hand man.

"We will move into the *Palacia de la Revolución*. We will a forge a new path for our New Cuba. We will take our place in history. All of you, and more, will become gods on earth when Cuba takes over the world economy."

This time, the applause swells. Keeps swelling until it shakes the stage. The dissenter has been forgotten—by everyone but Yans.

Yans bows his head and makes his exit.

He walks past Darien and Ernesto and hammers down the stage steps toward the old movie reel storage room. "Follow me."

Once inside, he closes the door behind the two men and turns toward Ernesto. None of the lines in the old man's puffy, russet-colored forehead are parallel. His cheeks are pocked and deepened with age, and his ever-present smugness shows on his pursed lips. He's a buffoon. The dust-laden boxes and crates stacked around the windowless room are in keeping with his decrepit looks and abilities. He's only ever been good at repeating information gathered from others, and he's never been very good at that.

"Who was it?" Yans asks.

"Who?" Ernesto cocks his head like a dog.

"Who accused me of breaking promises? We have a dissenter."

"I do not know," Ernesto says.

"Darien? Did you see who said those words?"

"Permission to speak freely, *señor*?"

"You have been spoken to."

"The Red Star Society has many dissenters. Mostly older, like the man yelling tonight."

"Is that so?" Yans turns, lowers his chin, clasps his hands behind his back, and begins pacing the floor. "Ernesto. Do you agree?"

"Yes, *señor*. I've been told some of the older men have met multiple times. They've been waiting a long time, they say, and their patience has been exhausted. Twelve years is a long time."

"Who are they?"

"I do not know."

"Who told you they met?"

"No one." His voice has a slight tremor. "I found a note. It was their meeting minutes."

Yans stops pacing. "What did it say?" He advances on Ernesto. "What did it say?"

"Not much. Only things like, 'Introduction by Estefano,' and 'Proposals by Katya.'"

"What good are you?" Yans slaps him.

Ernesto takes a step back.

Yans raises his hand again. "You're part of this older group. How do I know you weren't at the meeting?"

"If I were, would I be here?"

Yans ponders this. How far has this gone? This coup? How much planning have these *idiotas* done? "Tell me everything you know."

"I have," Ernesto says.

"It's not enough." Yans pulls his gun out. "Tell me everything. Now."

Ernesto raises his hands. The tremor in his voice becomes a full-on earthquake. "Please. Don't. I beg you."

"Talk."

"Some of them know—all of them know. They know about the payments."

"What payments?" Yans waves his Browning in Ernesto's face, clipping the man's nose.

"I don't know how, but they've seen the amount of the Red Star Society's donations you send to the US every month. They believe it could be used for other purposes. They're not happy."

"Obviously." Yans slaps him in the face again. It stings Yans's palm, and the sting feels good. "You can tell them I stopped payment. We are close enough now. The payments are no longer necessary. What else?"

"What?"

Yans slaps him again. "What else? That can't be their only concern."

"Some say we shouldn't negotiate. As soon as possible, we should launch our attack. Without hesitation. Make it a surprise."

Darien draws himself up at this. "Do you know what that would mean?"

Yans turns toward him. "You weren't spoken to."

"Sorry."

Yans returns his attention to Ernesto. He aims his gun at the buffoon's belly. "Do you know what that would mean?"

"I think so, yes. But the others. They may not."

"It would mean millions dead. I will not allow New Cuba to become an anti-Christ nation. We will not control the world with fear. We will do it with admiration. Loyalty. We must negotiate."

"You may not have a choice. We've already chosen a prospective new leader."

"We've?"

"I meant, 'They've.'"

Yans lowers his gun and steps away from the waste of space formerly known as Ernesto. He stares at the floor. Only a few more days. He can stop this madness once Lucía arrives and the code passes the launch test. Once the code has been validated, Yans will have the confidence and proof to begin making his demands of the world inside and outside Cuba. But right now, this is madness. As worthless as Ernesto has always been, part of Yans will miss him. It's a shame Ernesto has gone mad like the others.

"In a few days," Yans says, "we will have nothing to worry about."

"But—"

"But nothing, Ernesto." Yans puts his hand on the man's shoulder and feels it sag.

"But, I—"

"You, on the other hand, do have something to worry about."

"No."

Yans turns and heads for the door. "Darien?"

"Yes."

"Take Ernesto here to see Aurora Snow over in Guanajay. I'd like him to meet her face-to-face by morning. Will that be a problem?"

"No, *señor.*" Darien draws his weapon. Aims it at Ernesto. "The shovel is still in the SUV."

CHAPTER THIRTY-TWO

MATTIE

I feel like I'm in another country. Not the US. One where modern-day desperados roam the countryside, stealing drugs and money from innocent travelers. Four men in matching white T-shirts, camouflage shorts, and black army boots form a line in front of the Mercedes SUV. They raise their weapons. The two men flanking the line have larger guns. I've never seen an AK-47 before, but I've heard about them in the news. Rippling muscles and fierce expressions—the men step toward the front of our car in unison, shouting at us in Spanish like some kind of hellish chorus line.

"What are you going to do?" Lucía asks me—her voice weak and troubled.

I accidentally respond by revving the engine.

The chorus line stops moving.

It's come to this.

I've saved Lucía, but we're trapped.

Behind us, the matching Mercedes from the trailer also sits sideways in the road, blocking our way back into Lake Kerr Village.

This place is going to receive a seriously bad review from me on Yelp when this is all over.

I can't believe how close we are.

This can't be happening.

Lucía's right here with me, sitting in the passenger seat.

Calvin tries to hide in the back seat, but it doesn't work. He's too big.

I can't let them take Lucía.

We've come too far.

I consider ducking under the dashboard and driving straight ahead, blind and fast, running these guys over, bullets flying through the windshield, but we'd never make it. Their gigantic SUV sits sideways in the road, blocking the opening in the chain-link fence. If I tried to take it on, the fence would wrap around the Volvo, and its rusting jagged wires would probably pop the tires.

In the rearview mirror, I watch the gunman from the trailer and his buddy get out of the matching Mercedes SUV barricading the road behind us. The stalled chorus line ahead joins us in watching these two advance on us, guns in hand. Each takes a side of our car, and the one on my side—the gunman from the trailer—taps on the glass.

"Stay in the car," I say to Lucía and Calvin. "Don't leave."

I start to open my door and raise my hands when I'm met with resistance. "Excuse me. Can you move?"

The gunman scowls and creases his forehead.

"Excuse me?"

He finally steps back far enough for me to get out. Then, he shakes his gun at me as if I hadn't noticed it. What a jerk. I stand up and get in his face.

"Take me," I say. "Leave her alone. You want somebody? A girl? Take me."

He shakes his head. "No. We want her."

"What's wrong with me?"

"Nothing, baby," calls one of the men from the chorus line. He's the only one wearing a cap. "You want to go on a date with me?"

They all laugh.

"What is it?" I ask the gunman before me. "Am I too tall? Too short? Too fat?"

The gunman glances at my legs.

I lean in closer to him. I might be able to knock the gun out of his hands, but I'm actually starting to wonder—what *is* wrong with me? Why wouldn't they want me instead? Am I really not good enough?

"You don't have the tattoo," he says. He cocks his head and shoots a look over the top of the car to his buddy.

His buddy opens Lucía's door.

"Get out."

"No!" I shout. "Leave her alone. I can get a tattoo. You can number me." I place my hands on the gunman's shoulders and push him. "Take me."

He catches himself quickly, putting one foot back. He keeps his gun aimed at my face. A sick grin crosses his lips, and he shakes his head.

His buddy pulls Lucía out of the car.

"No!" I shout again.

Calvin sits in the back seat, watching everything play out like he's at the movies. The fear on his face makes me glad he hasn't gotten involved.

Two chorus line guys take Lucía by the arms and march her to their SUV.

"You're not taking her," I shout. "You can't. I—I will follow you. I'm going to—"

The gunman places his finger over my lips. "Shh. If you follow us, we'll kill you both."

"Why?" I watch as they load Lucía into the back of the SUV. The last thing I see is her tattoo. "Really, take me. I'll get a tattoo. Anything you want."

"You don't have what we want. We need the number."

"Why don't you just write it down and leave us alone? How stupid are you?"

The sting of his palm is harsh on my face. The pain is worse than I thought it would be when he raised his hand. I cover my cheek and back off.

"My boss wants the girl alive in case her marking is flawed."

"Flawed? It's a number. How could it be flawed?"

He turns to go.

I shove him in the back. "Answer me!"

He whips around. "I don't know. Flawed. In some way, it won't work for him. Maybe the number is encoded. Maybe there's a . . . what do you call it? A riddle behind the number to make it work? Maybe it's only part of a bigger number, and the rest is somewhere else. He wants her alive in case the number doesn't work. He'll want to ask her questions if it is flawed."

"Why is he so paranoid? It's just a number. Please."

The gunman narrows his eyes and lowers his voice. "I was told the tattoo on the last girl my boss captured did not work. She's no longer with us. The only thing keeping your friend alive right now is the chance her tattoo is also flawed and she'll know how to make it work for him."

He turns toward the SUV blocking the exit and circles his hand in the air. "*Vamos.*"

"No," I cry out. "You can't have her."

The SUV's engine starts, and the hellish choir takes off out of the trailer park with Lucía in tow.

My slap-pal and his buddy return to their SUV, get in, and drive away.

Lucía's gone.

Again.

The deafening silence left behind attempts to crush my hope of ever seeing her again.

I return to the Volvo and take my seat behind the wheel.

"What are we going to do?" Calvin asks.

I gaze at him in the rearview. "We're not going to give up. We just need to give them a little time to get ahead, then we'll follow them."

"What about Jack? Shouldn't we go back for him?"

CHAPTER THIRTY-THREE

Something is poking the inside of Jack's cheek. He lets his jaw relax, and something falls out. It hits the floor. He opens his eyes. Everything comes rushing back to him when he sees the square-cut stone. Stanley's pinky ring. When they fought outside, Jack stripped the ring off Stanley's finger and kept it, thinking he might need the sharp edges to cut himself free if they tied him up. And, he'd been right. Unfortunately, the blow to his head from Wyatt came before he'd had a chance to free himself.

A fog settles inside his mind, and he shakes it off. He sits up straight and tries to pull his hands forward, but they're taped behind his back. He's seated at the dining table in Stanley's skeevy trailer next to—she's gone.

Lucía is gone.

Everyone is gone.

He struggles to pull his hands free from the tape. He needs a knife. Something sharper than the pinky ring. It would take forever to whittle his way out with that thing. The dining table is useless. It has rounded edges. The cabinets in the kitchen look like they're made of particle board. He could rub the tape on a door's edge, but that would still take too long.

He stands, leans uncontrollably to the left, and sits back down, his head throbbing. His shoulder flares. It might be dislocated. Wyatt brought him down hard on the ground outside.

He's running out of time.

They could return any minute.

He attempts to stand again, and this time, he finds his balance. He steps around the table, heading for the kitchen, and the solution to his problem presents itself. A cigarette lighter lies on the floor near Wyatt's seat. It has a picture of Bob Marley on it. He drops to his knees, rolls onto his side, gets hold of the lighter after some awkward contortions, and, once he's figured out how to manage it without setting himself on fire, he's burned through the tape within a minute.

He's free.

He checks his pockets. Everything is there. He's glad he left his cell phone in the car. He pulls his car keys out and goes to the window. It gives him the creeps to touch the Confederate Flag curtain, but he does it.

He moves the curtain to the side.

All the cars are gone except his.

His shoulder aches. He rolls the joint forward, stretching the muscles to determine if it still works, and it does, but it hurts like hell.

Where did everyone go?

He rushes to his car but doesn't get in. Every ounce of him wants to be on the road chasing after Lucía, but he doesn't know what happened to her. She could be anywhere with anyone. She could have left with Wyatt, or Stanley Owens, or that weird Asian man, or—those army guys. The

Latinos.

Rushing out into nowhere isn't going to work. He needs to take his time.

Back inside the trailer, he goes down the hall. The rooms are all locked except for the bathroom. The window is open, and the frame has blood stains. A lot of blood stains. No one could have fit through that opening, but someone obviously tried. Maybe it was Lucía. If so, she was probably caught. He hopes it was Stanley Owens and not the Latinos.

Wyatt, Stanley's muscle-monkey, put the hurt on Jack, but it was Stanley's doing.

Stanley, that disgusting, flabby, horrible, sick man. Evil. Evil like all men, but worse. Evil like a stepfather. Like all stepfathers.

He caused all of this.

Jack's rage wipes out the pain in his head and his shoulder.

He wants Stanley Owens.

He returns to the front room and retrieves Stanley's pinky ring from the floor. With any luck, the ring didn't give him a disease when he'd hidden it in his mouth. The thought makes him want to vomit. The dark red stone resembles the dried blood in the bathroom.

He's running out of time.

He searches the kitchen for addresses, names—anything that might tell him where to go and what to do next. It wouldn't hurt his feelings if he found some money. He checks under the living room couch, and the miracle of patience pays off. Had he rushed away earlier, he wouldn't have found his gun. It must have slid under the couch after the Latino took it from him.

It's time to go.

He's found all he's going to find.

The Camaro starts with no problem.

The engine thumps and thunders as he swerves through the trailer park, dodging the mobile homes like a slalom skier. Just after the last bend in the road, he hits the brakes and slides to a stop at the gate next to a black station wagon, not believing his eyes. It's not quite dark yet, but nightfall is on its way. He switches on his headlights. That redhead and her Pay-n-Save lackey step out of her station wagon, but—it's not the right wagon. He could have sworn she drove an old Toyota. Not a Volvo.

He exits his car before Mattie can come around and beat on his window. She's yelling obscenities and waving her hands in the air.

Calvin follows behind her, unconcerned.

"What the hell?" she asks. "Why'd you leave us back there?"

"Hold on." Jack raises his palms in defense, and his shoulder smarts. He winces. "You're supposed to be going to Miami. You promised."

"You left us for dead at that pub in Daytona! Don't act like you didn't do it on purpose."

"You said you were going to Miami like I asked."

"I wanted to go to Miami," Calvin says. "She said I could drive the Volvo there."

Jack takes comfort in the fact he's not going crazy. They do have a different car, and other than the shattered back window, this one is much nicer. He understands why Calvin wanted to drive it.

"We didn't promise anything." She leans close and narrows her eyes. "Are you okay? One of your pupils is way bigger than the other one. What did they do to you?"

"It's nothing. I bumped my head." He touches his temple and winces. "I've got to go." He reaches to open his car door. "Send me pictures from Miami. Remember our deal."

"Oh, hell no." He has his hand on the handle, but she's planted her body against the door so he can't open it. "You're just trying to get rid of us again. Lucía never went to the airport down there. You're a liar."

"No, I'm not. I told you what my client told me."

"Lies. He told you lies. We saw her. We rescued her."

"Yeah," Calvin says. "Mattie rescued her."

"Then where is she?"

"They took her," Mattie says.

"Who? Stanley?"

"The fat guy? The whale?"

"Yeah."

"No, it wasn't him. It was this band of army guys. I think he sold her to them. We didn't have time to talk." Angry tears well in her eyes. "It all happened so fast. One minute, we were on our way out. The next minute, we were surrounded by this militia."

"South Americans?"

"No, you insensitive jerk. Latin Americans. They had Cuban accents."

"Whatever. Where'd they go? It's getting dark soon, and—"

"Hey," Calvin says. "Do you think I could drive? I'd love to drive your Camaro. I've never been in one before."

This conversation is going nowhere.

The Latinos took Lucía. That's all he needs to know.

He reefs on the door and tries to power his way past Mattie into the driver's seat, but she whirls and hip-checks him and throws herself behind the wheel. He wishes he hadn't left the engine running. She grins up at him like a Karen who got her way.

"Move," he says. "You're not coming with me."

Sirens sound in the distance.

"Yes, we are." She hits the gas. The engine revs. "I'll drive. Let's go."

"I think the police are coming for us," Calvin says.

"Get in!" Mattie yells at them both. "Calvin's right."

Jack grabs Mattie's arm and pulls, but she doesn't budge. He'd have to hurt her to move her, and he's unwilling to do that. It's maddening as hell.

"Get in," she says. The sirens grow louder. "We don't have any time."

"Yes we do!" Jack yells.

His patience has worn thinner than thin. He wants to smack her like an evil stepfather, but he never would. Instead, he focuses on his hate for Stanley. "Why would the police be coming for you?"

"She stole the Volvo," Calvin says as he opens the Camaro's passenger door and hops inside.

"*We* stole the Volvo." Mattie leans forward and pulls the handle beneath her seat. Her backrest folds forward, clearing space for Jack to sit down behind her. "Last chance, Jack. Get in, or I'm leaving you here like you left us in Daytona."

Not far now, the trooper's sirens wail. Jack doesn't want to explain anything to the police. He can't. He hardly knows what's going on. His concussive brain fog is returning, and he still has no idea why those Latinos were at Stanley's trailer. They weren't the kind of people to trade in sex trafficking operations. They wanted Lucía for some other reason, and the way Stanley tried to negotiate with them . . . it was clear Stanley had no idea who they were, either.

Jack slips into the back seat, and Mattie drives through the gate. To his surprise, she takes it easy, chatting away to Calvin in nonsense words until the police pass by.

Then, she's off to the races.

"Please slow down," Calvin says.

"Where are you going?" Jack asks.

"I'm going after that militia. They're driving these big black SUVs."

"But you have no idea where they went." Jack slides over to sit behind Calvin. "Slow down until we know where we're going."

She turns onto the highway, heads south, and floors it. "We're going to lose them if I don't go fast."

"You're going to *really* lose them if we go the wrong way."

"Ah!" She slams her hands on the steering wheel. "I want a cigarette. Tell me you have a cigarette."

"I have a lighter," Jack says, "and we can stop for cigarettes. Let's stop somewhere and think this through."

"We're not stopping for anything. They took her, and I'm going to get her back. She was so scared, Jack. You should have seen her."

He did see her. He sat right next to her and, yeah . . . she was scared. She was hurt. Her face was damaged. Stanley Owens hurt her like an evil stepfather. The Latinos took her, and Jack wants to rescue her for himself and, of course, for her father, but—

He wants to hurt Stanley first.

The pain in his shoulder flares.

"Look," Jack says, "you're lucky. You're going in the right direction, but you're going after the wrong people. We won't find the men who took her this way, but I know where we can go. We can find her."

She slows down a little. "I'm listening."

"Like you said, Stanley probably sold her to those Latinos."

"We don't know for sure they're from Latin America, do we?" Calvin asks. "Just because their accent sounded Cuban doesn't mean—"

"Shut up, Calvin." Mattie shoots him a look. "Go ahead, Jack."

"If Stanley sold her to them, then he probably has an idea where they took her."

Jack meets her eyes in the rearview mirror. They're as red as her hair.

"Where's Stanley, Jack? Where is he?"

"He has a mansion up in First Coast. It shouldn't be too far. I'll have to call someone for the exact location. Can you hand me my phone?"

While Mattie reaches for his cell, Jack checks his waistband to ensure his gun is still there.

It is.

CHAPTER THIRTY-FOUR

Night has fallen.

The lights along the base of Stanley's palatial home shine upward, illuminating white walls between Greek columns stretching up to the second floor. The lights flicker, shimmering gold on the darkened windows. As I ease Jack's Camaro down the drive, the mansion looms over us, resting atop a hill, overlooking a black, wrought iron fence that separates Stanley's world from ours.

Jack is awake again in the back seat. For a while, he didn't want me to drive, but something overtook him, and he slept. He refused to tell us what happened to him in the trailer park, only saying he bumped his head. I doubt that happened. It was obvious someone had hit Lucía since meeting her at the convenience store this morning. Someone obviously hit Jack since then, also.

"Let me do the talking," he says.

I pull up to the gate and line the back window up with the intercom so he can reach it. He lowers his window, leans out, and presses the button.

Calvin sits patiently in the passenger seat, gazing at Stanley's mansion.

I hope this isn't a waste of time. Moreso, I hope being here doesn't get us killed. But we have no choice. Somewhere, rumbling across the Floridian countryside, those men have Lucía in their SUV. We just don't know where or exactly why. Jack said he agreed with my theory that Lucía's kidnappers plan to traffic her, but he seems unsure. He *is* a liar, I remind myself. I still think he made up the story about seeing Lucía at the Miami airport only to rid himself of Calvin and me.

He'd better not be lying about Stanley.

"Hello?" Jack says into the intercom. "You there?"

"It's late." The attendant's voice sounds like a sleepy sloth mumbling. "What do you want?"

"We need to speak with Mr. Owens immediately. It's very important."

"He's not expecting anyone."

Calvin leans closer to my window and says, "Expect the unexpected."

"What was that?" the attendant asks.

"Shh," I say. I gently give Calvin a shove to get his belly off me.

"Nothing," Jack says. "Tell Stanley it's Jack from earlier today. We have unfinished business."

"Mr. Owens has finished his business for the day. I cannot speak with him now. You'll have to come back tomorrow."

We don't have time for this. This guy is giving us the runaround. I don't believe a word he says. Coward.

"Why not?" Jack asks.

"The master has taken to his nightly bath."

"Oh, my God," I say. "The master? When are we? 1935?"

"Excuse me?" The attendant sounds like he's sick and falling asleep. He coughs into the intercom. "Come back tomorrow if you wish to speak with Mr. Owens."

"No," I say. "You tell that whale to get his blubber butt out here now and—"

"Mattie," Jack says. "Stop it."

He's right. I hold my tongue. It's just that we're running out of time.

Jack leans even closer to the intercom. "Tell Stanley if we have to come back, then we'll bring the police with us."

Silence, followed by a door slamming. We wait. I think the attendant went to find Stanley.

Wow. Jack is good at this.

The intercom crackles. "I spoke with Mr. Owens."

"And?" Jack asks.

"And he said to come back tomorrow with the police. They'll be interested to know why you spent yesterday and today stalking a girl and her boyfriend across northern Florida. They'll want to know why you sat outside the couple's hotel last night. We have pictures."

Two black dogs—Dobermans—appear on the other side of the gate. They must have been hiding in the darkness this entire time. They move with purpose, their muscular bodies rippling beneath their shiny black coats. Their ears are up, and their intense gaze is unblinking as they slink back and forth, searching for a hole in the fence.

"What's he talking about, Jack?" I ask.

"I'm a private investigator. I staked out a hotel last night." His face reddens. "It's my job."

"Okay, okay," I say. "Calm down."

"Have a good night." The intercom clicks.

"Can we go get something to eat?" Calvin asks. "I'm

hungry."

Jack sits back. He wipes his face, and his chest swells as he draws in a long, deep breath. "Let's go. I'm tired."

I've had it with these two.

The Dobermans and I stare at each other.

I'm not afraid of them.

They start barking their heads off when I open the door and step out.

"Mattie!" Jack yells. "What are you doing?"

"This is our only lead. We can't wait until morning. I refuse to waste another minute listening to your guys' bull."

The dogs follow along the other side of the fence as I make my way toward the backyard.

"Oh, Mr. Owens," I call out to the mansion above me. "Mr. Stanley Owens . . ."

I pick up my pace, heading around the corner, pausing to check whether Jack and Calvin are coming. They are not, so far.

Stanley's neighbor is not as well-off as he is. Their house is smaller and doesn't have a fence. They probably don't need a fence to hide behind like Stanley.

I hear a commotion behind me. Calvin and Jack are exiting the car. Jack stops and grabs something from the glove compartment. It's a flashlight, and he shines it on me. "Mattie, wait. Let's take our time."

"No time, Jack."

"What?" Jack asks.

Apparently objecting to us having a conversation, the dogs begin to bark, weaving back and forth, occasionally running into each other.

"We don't have any time," I call back at him. "They could be taking their turns with Lucía right now." I can't believe I said that, but it's true. It's my fear. If we don't act now, something bad will happen to her. Something really bad.

I sprint to the backyard. The dogs keep up with me on the other side of the fencing, barking and gnashing their teeth. Sloping concrete steps sweep down from the mansion and surround a heart-shaped pool. Something about the pool creeps me out. It's picturing that sweaty whale of a man floating in it, sipping daiquiris, or bloody Marys or blood . . . plain old blood.

Ew.

I pick up a rock.

"Don't!" Jack yells, waving his hands as he rounds the corner with Calvin lumbering after him.

I throw the rock at one of the windows as hard as possible. It falls short, splashing down in the pool. As usual, I'm way off target. I should never have quit softball. Actually, I should never have started. I've never been able to throw anything on target.

I pick up another rock.

"What are you doing?" Calvin almost can't speak. He's out of breath.

Jack reaches me and attempts to grab my arm, but I step to the side and throw the rock.

It bounces off the fence and almost hits Calvin in the head.

The dogs are practically having strokes on the other side. Their mouths sling froth with greater accuracy than I can throw.

"We need to get Stanley's attention," I say. "Calvin, do you think you can hit the house?"

"No doubt." He picks up a rock.

"We should wait and come back later," Jack says. "I don't

want any trouble. I don't want to deal with the police."

Calvin throws the rock. It's a direct hit. The glass in the door beyond the pool cracks.

"Well," I say, "I think it's too late." A shape has appeared behind the door. "I think we got trouble." I turn toward Jack. "Why are you so afraid of the police? What haven't you told us, Mr. PI?"

"Look." Calvin points at the mansion.

Stanley, wearing a white, monogrammed robe, trudges down the steps. Just as he nears us, Jack lurches forward and shines his flashlight in the whale's face. Stanley recoils from the glare, then glares into it and barks at his dogs. "Heel!"

The dogs reluctantly move away from the fence, not taking their eyes off us.

"Sit," Stanley commands.

He advances on us again and when he stops a few paces away, the dogs sit down on either side of him.

"What do you think you're doing?" he asks us.

"Come closer," Jack says, motioning with his flashlight.

"No. I'm good here."

Out of nowhere, Jack drops his flashlight and grasps the bars with both hands, violently shaking them.

I startle.

The Dobermans erupt into a mad, horrifying fit of barking.

Calvin puts his hand on his chest like he's having a heart attack.

"Get over here, Stanley." Jack continues to ravage the fence, making it *clang* loudly, over and over. "So help me God. If you don't come here . . . "

Then, like a wave coming to rest upon the shore, Jack stops shaking the fence and tilts his head back. He closes his eyes.

"Well," Stanley says. "Suppose you tell me why I shouldn't call the police right now, you psychopath."

Jack bends over and calmly picks up his flashlight. He lifts his shirt and shines the light on the gun tucked into his waistband. "This is why."

The whale's cheeks bounce up and down when he laughs. He opens his robe, and I cover my eyes.

"It's okay, Mattie." Calvin puts his hand on my shoulder. "He's not naked. He's got boxers on. They have pictures of a cartoon cat. I think it's Garfield."

"No," Stanley says. "It's Heathcliff."

Calvin cocks his head. "Who?"

"It's Heathcliff." Stanley points at the dog on his right. "This is Garfield."

"What's the other dog's name?"

"Felix."

"Shut *up!*" I scream.

"Go ahead, Stanley." Jack puts his hand on the butt of his gun. "Make your move."

"Are you sure?" A leather shoulder holster spans Stanley's chest. He has a gun over his heart. "You want to see who's faster?"

"Yeah."

Sometimes, I really hate men.

CHAPTER THIRTY-FIVE

They could have at least given her a cushion to sit on. The floor of this vehicle is unbearable. Lucía's had some time to calm down. She spent the first part of her trip in a panic. Now, physical pain swarms throughout her body. Her face. Her neck. Her left side. The skin over her ribs burns, And there's more. Internally, her ribs ache. She's never had a broken rib, and she's only ever heard of "separated" ribs. She might have both.

Everything hurts.

At this moment, her backside hurts the most.

She wants a cushion.

She's unsure if she's sitting on the floor of a van or in a truck with a canopy. It's probably a van, based on the muffled road noise. The last thing she saw when they took her was the leather back seat of a Mercedes SUV. Then, the blindfold went on. She misses that seat. Somewhere along the way, the Cubans dragged her out of the SUV and threw her in there. Listening to them talk, she has decided they're definitely from Cuba. Their Spanish is too much like Valeria's to think otherwise.

The van hits a bump.

Her butt smacks the floor.

"Can I have something to sit on?" she asks.

"*¡Cállate!*"

"Where are we going?" she cries.

"*¡Cállate!*"

Whoever is answering is getting louder. Angrier. She can't tell how many men are there. Five? Maybe six? She asks where they're taking her one more time, and she's told to shut up again. Then, someone slaps her in the face.

She'll shut up now.

The tears come.

Someone grasps her hair, pulls her head back, and shoves a rag into her mouth. She blows snot bubbles out her nose, trying to breathe. The air smells like dirty gardening gloves. She gags, but she can't cough. Someone tapes her mouth shut with the cloth inside. She focuses on sniffing slowly until she can catch her breath, and then she lets her head drop to her chest, panting.

A man's voice says, "Baseball . . . Marlins . . . game . . . return to Cuba."

It sounds like the one who told her to shut up. He wants to go to a baseball game.

If only Lucía had let their housekeeper teach her Spanish. Valeria tried to teach her, but growing up in Canada, it hadn't made sense to her to know anything other than English. None of her friends had to learn another language. So, no Spanish. Now, she regrets it. She can only understand a few words here and there.

". . . restaurant . . . movie . . ."

"No. Dance . . ."

"... baseball!"

"*No hay tiempo para eso.*"

?

"Yans ..."

"... women ... ooh ..."

"... Yans! Cuba ..."

"... girls ... dance club."

A lizard-like voice laughs at the mention of girls dancing. He wants to go to a club. At first, Lucía thought they were talking about a "dance club," but now she thinks "strip club." She's not entirely sure, but it sounds like another man wants a massage with a *"feliz"* ending. The angry one who slapped her in the face desperately wants to go to a baseball game. The Marlins. She's sure it's him because of the anger in his voice. He's begun to yell. A fourth man speaks calmly, like he's trying to keep the peace. He sounds friendly, like he might be nice to her at some point.

She can't believe they are arguing about what to do. Have they forgotten they've kidnapped her? She's sitting right here. She doesn't know how long they're going to keep her tied up and gagged. Baseball games can take a long time, and it must be too late at night for a game. It was already after five when they took her.

Oh, no. They're going to keep her like this all night tonight and all day tomorrow.

What about the next day after that?

The panic returns. Her nostrils aren't big enough for this. She can't breathe. She tries to speak. She tries to scream, but it's all muffled.

She kicks her legs and receives another stinging slap to the face.

At least they know she's still here.

"Yans . . . stay . . . USA."

"No . . . girl sell . . . work."

"Cuba trip . . . vacation."

"Marlins *manana*!"

"The Golden Hookup . . . sexy . . . Club XXX . . . gentlemen's . . ."

"Box."

The conversation shifts. They're discussing her now, and it doesn't sound good. As best she can tell, some of them want to stay in the USA and put her in a box. Others want to go to a Marlins baseball game, and the snaky one wants to take her to a strip club and sell her.

None of it makes any sense.

Why can't they just let her go?

CHAPTER THIRTY-SIX

JACK

No way could Jack miss from here. Stanley stands on the other side of the fence with his robe open and his hand on the butt of his gun. His Doberman puppy pals, Felix and Garfield, sit at his sides. Jack has never seen a bigger target. He has his hand on the butt of his gun, and he could easily shoot Stanley in the chest, in the head—in one of those tree-trunk legs . . .

"Stop it!" Mattie shouts. "Put your guns away."

Stanley glances at her, taking his attention off Jack.

Now would be a great time to shoot, but Jack holds back. If he kills Stanley now, they may never know where those Latinos took Lucía. It's better to kill him later.

"I'll stop if he stops," Jack says.

Stanley smiles a crocodile smile. "I'll stop if you leave my property." He takes his hand off his gun.

Jack reciprocates. "Not until we're done talking."

"I have nothing to say to you. Please, leave now." He reaches down and pats one of his Dobermans on the head. Garfield.

"Who are you working with now?" Jack asks. "Who were those men that took Lucía?"

"I have no idea."

"Yes, you do." Mattie steps up to the fence. Here we go. She's going to lose it. "Where did they take her?" Her voice rises.

"I honestly have no idea."

"What are you doing, Stanley?" Jack asks. "Just tell us. Are you building up your business? Trafficking to foreign gangs now? Who were they?"

"I told you. I have no idea. They showed up out of the blue and wanted her. I don't know why."

"He's lying, Jack." Mattie grips the fence with both hands. "Look at him."

"I know, I know. Calm down."

"Oh, let her go on, Jack." Stanley folds his robe over his gut and ties the belt in a bow. "It's fun to watch."

Jack resists the urge to pull his gun and shoot. He imagines the bullet burrowing into Stanley's forehead and how good it would feel to rid the world of another evil man.

"I know you sold her to those men." Mattie lets go of the bars. "You scum. You brand girls like cattle and sell them."

"Like cattle?" Stanley chuckles. "What are you talking about?"

"The number on her leg." Mattie waves her hand over Stanley's palatial estate. "All this. You paid for all this with the suffering of—"

"I don't brand girls and sell them." His laugh carries deep into the night. "But if I did, I certainly wouldn't put numbers on them." He fixes his eyes on Jack. "That would only attract unwanted attention."

"Then why does she have that tattoo on her leg?" Mattie

asks.

"How would I know? You should ask those men. They're the ones who were interested in it."

Mattie is right. He's lying. He knows who those men are, and he's covering something up. Jack can sense it. He can envision Stanley watching as a tattooist needles the number onto Lucía's leg. She's screaming. Screaming like his mother screamed when his stepfather hit her.

Jack walks away from the fence. "Mattie. Come with me." He turns after a few steps and points at Stanley. "Don't you move."

"Can I come?" Calvin asks.

"Yes."

Just beyond Stanley's earshot, Calvin and Mattie join Jack in a huddle.

"Listen," Jack says. "I want you two to leave."

"No," Mattie says. "He's lying."

"I know. I need you to leave so I can take the lying out of him." Jack pats his waistband.

"What are you going to do?"

"I don't want you to know. Don't worry about it."

"We could go get something to eat and come back," Calvin says. "I'm hungry."

"Right." Jack pats him on the shoulder. "That's right. Go get something to eat and come back."

"Absolutely not." Mattie narrows her eyes. "Stanley's not the only liar here. You're trying to get rid of us again."

"No I'm not. I promise."

"Hey," Stanley calls to them. "I think we're done here. Felix. Garfield. Come."

Jack breaks away from the huddle and strides up to the fence. "Stop. We're not leaving until you tell us where those men took Lucía."

"So." Stanley turns back toward the fence. "They did take her."

"Don't play stupid."

"Yeah," Mattie says. "Don't play stupid."

"Mattie." Jack has lost his patience with her. "Take Calvin and go. Now."

"Goodnight, everyone." Stanley turns to go. "I'll see you in the funny papers."

Calvin steps up to the fence. "They don't make funny papers anymore."

"Stanley," Jack yells. "Look at this."

The dogs continue trotting up the hill toward the mansion, but Stanley hesitates and looks over his shoulder.

Jack holds Stanley's pinky ring up and shines his flashlight on it. The deep red stone captures Stanley's attention.

"Is that . . . ?" Stanley asks. "Is that my—" He marches down the hill for a closer look. "It is. Give it here." He holds his hand out. "Throw it through the fence."

"Not so fast." Jack switches off his flashlight and puts it in his pocket. "Where's Lucía?"

"I have *told* you, I don't know. I never saw those men in my life before. That's the truth."

"Don't give it to him," Mattie says. "He's totally lying. Look at his face shake."

Jack closes his fist around the ring and puts it in his pocket. "Well, I guess we *should* be going."

"No, no." Stanley rushes the fence. "I'll tell you."

Jack instinctively grips the butt of his gun. For a moment, it had looked like Stanley was planning to charge the fence and knock it down like a rhino. Jack wishes he had, but he didn't. Jack wants to shoot him so bad . . .

"I'll tell you everything." Stanley sticks one hand between the bars, palm up. "Give me the ring first."

Jack takes the ring out of his pocket and holds it up. "This ring?"

"Yes, yes."

"Tell us where they took Lucía."

"Fine. They took her to Miami. There's a dance club run by man named Jenkiles down there. He's, uh … he's my business associate on this new business endeavor. You were right, Jack. I'm trying to grow my business with foreigners. We use Club XXX as a waystation for women."

"You mean innocent young girls," Mattie says.

"I want to go now." Calvin hunches forward and puts his hand on his stomach. "Can we go now?"

"Sure," Jack says. "You two go wait in the car."

Mattie glares at Jack and shakes her head no. She's not going anywhere.

"Give me the ring." Stanley extends his hand farther between the bars.

Calvin gently tugs on the back of Mattie's shirt.

"Go wait in the car," Jack says.

"Not without you." She's so damn stubborn.

Jack gives up.

He drops the ring and it bounces through the fence into Stanley's yard. Stanley looks down, and Jack grasps Stanley's wrist. He pulls as hard as he can, bracing himself with one foot up on the fence. The fat man's face presses against the bars. With his other hand, Jack pulls out his gun and shoves the muzzle against Stanley's forehead.

Stanley lets out a squeak.

"Calvin," Jack says. "Close your eyes."

"No!" Mattie tackles Jack from the side.

He loses his grip on Stanley's wrist, and the gun fires. The bullet flies wide, shattering part of a Greek column near the back door of the mansion.

The dogs bark and come running down the hill.

"Get off me." Jack pushes on Mattie's shoulders, but she doesn't budge.

Stanley bends down and picks up his ring.

"I'll be in the car," Calvin says. "I think Applebee's is still open." He runs. "I'm still hungry."

Mattie rolls off Jack.

Stanley lumbers up the hill and around his pool, heading for the back door.

Jack raises his gun, but the rage is gone.

Mattie stares at him like he's from another planet.

As much as he would like to watch Stanley die, he can't shoot the sicko in the back.

Not in front of Mattie and Calvin.

Not now.

Not yet.

CHAPTER THIRTY-SEVEN

Nothing but half a can of red beans, a few wilted peppers—too hot for Yans's palate—and three cans of tomato paste grace his refrigerator. It's moments like this he misses women like Augustine. It's been months since she found out about the Red Star Society. Since then, he hasn't trusted any new whores to live with him. They're good at grocery shopping and cleaning the apartment. The bedroom activities. But, disposing of her was more difficult than usual. She wouldn't shut up.

He doesn't have time for female nonsense these days.

This is why he has no food.

He needs to eat. It's late.

He closes the refrigerator door and returns to the dining table. The plans for the missile test launch are stacked in the upper right. The best-case negotiating plans with the US sit in the center, overlapping the worst-case scenarios off to the side. His ashtray and cigar rest on the table, but the Red Star Society's personnel files fell on the floor a while ago. Over a thousand profiles. The Red Star Society is at capacity.

He's at capacity.

He's been at this all day, and he's hungry, and he has no food, and he has no woman to cook him food.

It's after midnight.

He puts on the first jacket he sees—his militant camo by the door—then he thinks better of it. Inside his closet hangs a light, black jacket he rarely wears. It's so civilian, but that's who he'll be in a moment. Just another civilian looking for food in downtown Havana. It's a humbling and oddly freeing thought. For the next few moments, he won't be the answer to Cuba's problems. He won't be the chosen leader of the Red Star Society.

He'll just be him.

Yans Rivero. Son of DeMarco Rivero. Heir to the Castro aristocracy. Destined to—oh, never mind.

He rushes out onto the street, climbs up a steep hill, and searches for somewhere to buy food. Water from a midnight rain runs in the gutters. Colorful lights outside most businesses have been extinguished this late on a Tuesday, but some remain lit. A cloud drifts across the moon. It's a full moon tonight. Ornate archways glow above doors bearing closed signs hanging in the windows of restaurants and other businesses. His stomach threatens to hurt him if he doesn't eat soon. He's humble. He doesn't need a fancy restaurant. A food truck would do. Someone on a blanket selling burritos.

He heads for the tavern district, assuming street vendors will be there waiting to serve the drunks leaving the pubs. If a drunk stumbles into Yans's path, he'll be sorry. It's happened before. Yans has his hunting knife with him.

He always has his hunting knife with him.

At the next intersection, Yans turns right and steps onto a short street with only one bar and one alley, followed by a dark corner at the end. No food for sale anywhere. No one around, but—there is someone. There are always people, homeless drifters, but tonight . . . Yans's senses go on high alert. His stomach be damned. He passes the alley, and shadows—bum-shaped shadows—line its walls. Short, round, vagrant silhouettes, and one tall silhouette.

One tall shadow.

It's a man, and he doesn't fit in with the rest.

Yans does not turn his head. He continues to walk with purpose. He trudges up the hill toward the dark corner, thankful for his knife, regretful he did not bring his gun. He's a wanted man now. Ernesto tried to warn him. On the cusp of opening talks with the US, dissenters in the Red Star Society want someone else to lead them. He wasn't sure he believed it before, but he does now.

He rounds the corner and stops, pressing his back against a wall.

He listens.

Paranoia exists to protect him from the unseen, the unknowable—the unbelievable. But Yans is not paranoid. Someone is coming up the hill. Heavy-sounding boots hit the ground, growing louder with each passing moment.

Yans pulls his knife out. He slips beneath a hotel awning and sits in the dark, attempting to take on the shape of just another tramp.

A man wearing a tight camouflage jacket—a poor choice, a dead giveaway—strides heedlessly around the corner and passes by Yans. He does not look at Yans. He looks this way and that like a tourist searching for a bathroom, but he does not see Yans. The man is a member of the Red Star Society. This is not a happenstance.

A noise comes from inside Yans's body. A guttural noise.

His stomach sends him a hunger pang, reminding him why he left the safety of his apartment. He places his hand on his stomach and leans forward. His pursuer, moving away from him now, comes to an intersection and turns right. Food will have to wait. Yans removes his boots, quickly ties the laces together, and hangs the boots over his neck. He refuses to be heard trudging down the street like a moron.

He crosses behind the man to the other side of the street and hustles down an alley. He's going to cut him off.

He waits.

Boots beat against the street.

Rookie.

He tightens his grip on his knife.

His stomach protests, and he doesn't care.

The man passes in front of Yans, and just like that—he's got him. Yans shoves the man's face against a brick wall—his forearm on the back of the man's neck, the tip of his blade sticking into the man's side.

"Who sent you? Give me a name."

"No one."

"Liar." Yans applies pressure to the knife.

"Stop."

"Are you ready to die?"

"No. Are you?"

"Who sent you?" Yans presses harder on the back of the man's neck with his forearm.

The man coughs. "Let go. I can't breathe."

"Very well." Yans grasps the man's shoulder, spins him around, and shoves the blade into the man's midsection, piercing the jacket but not the skin. Yans pins the man's head to the wall by placing his hand over the man's throat. "I will control your breathing for you from now on."

The man's eyes bulge.

"Who are you?"

"I—I'm Juan."

He's familiar, but many young men have joined the Red Star Society lately. "Tell me, who sent you?"

"No one."

Yans pushes the blade deeper, and when Juan's brow furrows, Yans recognizes someone else in the boy's face. "I know who you are."

Juan has deep lines on his forehead for someone as young as he appears to be. He can't be more than twenty-four. His rounded jaw and squinty eyes tell Yans all he needs to know about who sent him. The Red Star Society certainly sent him, but he made them choose him specifically. Revenge is a strong motivator.

"What have they told you?" Yans asks. "How much do you know?"

Juan's eyes begin to water.

Yans eases off his neck.

"I know everything. You're as good as dead." His eyes sparkle beneath the fresh sheen of tears. They have far more life in them than Ernesto's did. Otherwise, the father-son resemblance is uncanny. "I know about the missile. I know about the launch code. I know about Darien's team in the US."

"How?"

"I know about the girl with the leg tattoo."

Yans squeezes his throat.

He chokes.

"How? Ernesto didn't even know about the girl. How do you know?"

"You'll pay for what you did to him. He was my father.

You used him like a puppet, tricking him into spying on us, but he didn't tell you everything. He knew what you were doing. You think everyone believes your lies. You think you can go on, year after year, making your empty promises. We're not doing it anymore. The world will be ours once you're out of the way."

It's true, then … the coup. And it's more robust than Yans thought. He refuses to believe the entire Red Star Society has gone against him, but this—this ugly faction … they want to blow up the world in the name of Cuba. Buffoons.

"And," Yans says, "how do they intend to, as you put it, 'get me out of the way'?"

"Take your hand off my neck, old man, and I'll show you."

Yans thrusts the blade deep into Juan's abdomen. The sparkle vanishes from the young man's eyes. His devious eyes. "Tell Ernesto I said hello." Yans pulls the knife out, twirls it once betwixt his fingers, and thrusts it into Juan's chest. He pictures Juan's heart pouring blood into his pristine young lungs, filling them like water balloons, and, sure enough—Juan's cheeks fill. He coughs, and blood spews all over Yans's face.

The blood is warm.

Yans licks his lips.

He wipes his knife clean on the boy's ridiculous camouflage jacket, stows it, puts his boots back on, and gazes into the alley.

He's hungry.

He needs to find somewhere to get some food.

A street vendor would do.

CHAPTER THIRTY-EIGHT

DMITRI - 1970

Dmitri doesn't see anyone suspicious on the street below. He closes the curtain but leaves the window open. It's too hot inside, though it makes little difference at this time of day. The buttery aroma of his half-eaten lunch hangs over the dining table—the only table in their one-room tenement. He sits at it and waits for his wife to come home.

Ana hates this place.

Dmitri hates this place.

The tapestry on the wall, the one of the ocean sunset, made their home seem bigger when they first moved in two years ago, but now, it couldn't be smaller. Dmitri drums his fingers on the table. He checks the time. He pulls out his art pad and opens it to his latest drawing. A tiger's head surrounded by roses. The animal stares at him like it knows where Dmitri used to live. Like it knows who Dmitri really is.

Like it knows what Dmitri knows.

The nuclear missile launch code.

He goes to the window and pushes the curtain aside.

Nothing suspicious.

No Ana.

No mysterious automobiles.

He waits.

And waits.

And finally, Ana appears. She crosses the street and heads for the tenement building.

Where has she been?

He rushes back to the table, closes his art pad, sits down, and drums his fingers. The gentle *tap, tap, tap* of his fingertips on the cracked wood surface does nothing to ease the tension in his neck. He tips his head to the right as far as it will go. Then, he tips it a little farther until it pops.

The door opens.

Ana places her handbag on the table and sits across from Dmitri.

He glances at the window. She's safe now. He can't imagine what he'd do if something happened to her. If *they* came for her.

"It smells good in here," she says. "How were the plantains?"

"There's more in the kitchen. You can have the rest of these if you want." He scoots his plate toward her. "They are a bit dry, but decent. How was it out there?"

"Hot."

"I meant—is it busy out?"

"No more than usual." She pokes the inside of her cheek with her tongue and sighs. "Why aren't you at work?"

"I quit my job."

"That's the fourth time—" She's on her feet, has assumed that all-too-familiar pose. One hand on her hip, the back of her other hand on her forehead. "You can't keep quitting. Especially now."

"I've made a decision. Please, sit back down." She yanks the chair away from the table and sits. "We must leave this place."

"We've been over this," she says.

"We've got to leave. I don't like it here. You don't like it here."

"That's true." She scans the tenement, letting her eyes settle on their couch. Their bed. The kitchen. "We need a bigger place, but we've been over this. We can't afford to leave if you keep quitting. Why don't you go back to the metal plant? You liked it there, and your friend is there."

Dmitri pictures Carlos for a moment and glances at the window. He has one good friend and a million enemies looking for him. "Feridun" is not so much popular as he is infamous. *They're* always looking for him. Four jobs ago, *they* came to the metal plant where he and Carlos worked together and asked questions. Then, *they* began to show up everywhere "Feridun" worked. This morning, a man in military fatigues stood by the bus stop outside the hotel for far too long. Dmitri had no choice. He had to quit his job cleaning sidewalks.

Ana doesn't understand, and he can't explain it to her.

She sits across from him—safe.

She must never know about the missile. The Black Crickets jailing him before surrendering to the Red Star Society. The Red Star Society looking for him for the same reason the Black Crickets had jailed him. His knowledge of the missile. The truth behind the nuclear crisis—Castro, Kennedy, and Khrushchev. No one can ever know his part in it. He shudders to think what would happen. The worst-case scenario—world annihilation. The best-case scenario? The Red Star Society kills anyone who knows so they can protect the secret location and the code.

"I can never go back to the plant."

"We can't afford to save up and move, then."

"We could if we left the city."

"No." She shakes her head. "Absolutely not. My family is here in Havana. They've always been here."

"I've always given you what you want, and I can give more. I want to give you more, and I can, but only if I work for myself."

She reaches across the table, picks up his art pad, and waves it at him. "With this? You waste so much time with this. No one wants it. No one can afford to pay for your silly little drawings. People are too concerned with getting enough to eat."

The curtain sways slightly. Dmitri shifts his gaze to the tapestry of the ocean. He remembers the day he stole it and brought it home. He hung it up, and she threw her arms around him. Those were better days. Days before *they* started following him from job to job. Days before *they* started closing in on him.

Days before the walls started closing in on him.

"They're not drawings. They're tattoos, and people will pay for them." He stands and puts his hands on the table. "We have to leave."

"Where?"

"Somewhere away. Away from people. To the countryside."

"Are you saying farmers want tattoos?"

She has a point. The two things aren't connected, and it sounds ridiculous when she puts them together. Farmers and tattoos. He won't have customers for his art in the country, but he'll have peace of mind. Safety. The shame of being forced from this hovel pushes Dmitri to the window. He gazes down at the street.

The real and only reason to leave is the fact.

The undeniable fact.

They are coming.

A red and white Volkswagen bus parks across the street. It could easily hold eight armed men.

Dmitri closes the curtain. Turns to her. "We must go."

"I don't think doctors in the country want tattoos, either." She averts her eyes. "I don't even think they have doctors out there."

"Why do you care about doctors?"

"Because I just came from one."

"And?"

"Dmitri . . . I'm pregnant. It's a boy."

CHAPTER THIRTY-NINE

JACK

Club XXX hides behind four short palm trees on a main road with a small parking lot on the side. It's not at all what Jack expected. When Stanley had said it was a waystation for moving trafficked women, Jack assumed it would be larger. The main floor isn't much bigger than a Subway sandwich shop. Stucco siding. No windows. An odd golfing green with fake grass near the front door.

Jack pulls up to the stop sign at the nearest intersection. He sits and thinks.

"What's the problem?" Mattie asks. "Let's go."

The streets are empty this early in the morning, yet half the club's parking lot is full. They must have a loyal contingent of morning regulars. Jack doesn't want to go inside. There's something about going into a nightclub in the light of day that feels wrong. After Applebee's last night, they came here, and he parked in the parking lot. The owner, Mr. Jenkiles, wasn't in. The bouncer said to come back in the morning, so here they are. Mattie, Calvin, and the last chance to find out where the Latinos took Lucía.

"Are you going to park or what?" Mattie asks.

The closest parking is across the street. A chain-link fence surrounds the lot next to it. Construction signs hang from the fence bordering the concrete foundation and red girders of a new building. The workers haven't shown up yet, and Jack doesn't want his car near the worksite when they do.

He pulls into the Club XXX parking lot and slides his Camaro into a spot as far from the front door as he can. His back is tight from sleeping on the floor in the hotel last night. Mattie and Calvin shared the king-sized bed because the clerk messed up and didn't give them the two queen beds they'd requested.

"I'll be right back," he says.

Calvin and Mattie nod.

Inside the club, it looks the same, sounds the same, and smells the same as last night, yet it's different. The people are different. There are fewer of them, of course, but they're also older. The sound system blares "Livin' La Vida Loca," but no one here lives the crazy life. They look bored. Scant chairs surround three dance tables bathed in the low light of a disco ball shifting from green to blue to red to purple to yellow to green to . . .

Most men sit on benches against the walls. They're older. Aged leather skin draped beneath watery, baggy eyes, earlobes twice the size of a young man's, and noses cratered like the moon. One man has a strange discoloration throughout his face. Something like what Michael Jackson had, when the pigmentation disappears, leaving behind a smattering of splotchy white freckles.

Not everyone was born in the last century, though. A group of younger men sit at the dance table, watching the only dancer in the place. Two of them wear matching yellow vests, and Jack realizes they're all probably late for their construction job across the street.

He walks to the manager's door and raps on it.

"Mr. Jenkiles? Are you in there?"

Nothing.

"Mr. Jenkiles?"

Jack turns around and scans the room for anyone who looks like a manager. The man with the white freckles stands and limps toward him. He looks like he's going to ask for money.

Jack tries the door, and the knob turns.

A man with a thinning black widow's peak and an equally angular chin is snorting cocaine off a desk. Posters of nearly naked women advertising Club XXX adorn the walls along with a calendar celebrating twelve months of Dalmatian dogs dressed as firemen.

The freckled man continues to approach, but Jack closes the door on him.

"What the hell are you doing in here?" says the man behind the desk. He wipes his nose and stands. He still has white powder on his upper lip.

"Jenkiles?"

"What's it to you? Get out." He waves his hand.

"Where is she? You have a girl here with a tattoo on her leg. Where—"

"What the hell are you talking about?" The man walks around the desk and grasps Jack's elbow.

Jack pulls his arm away. He pushes Jenkiles away. The touch of this evil man, this exploiter of women—it brings the rage. "Where is she?"

Jenkiles opens the door.

The freckled man sits on a chair just outside. His odor

instantly rolls through the doorway. He smells like old bread. Rotten yeast.

"Go, now," Jenkiles says to Jack.

"Not without the girl. I know a Latino brought her to you last night."

"Latino? I don't know any Latinos, and I don't know you."

"But you know Stanley Owens."

A light goes on behind Jenkiles's eyes. He does know Stanley. He shakes his head and looks at the floor. "So, that's what this is about."

"Where is she?"

"There are no Latinos here. Follow me."

Jenkiles leads Jack to a dressing room. Three women sit facing a wall mirror. They dab their faces with makeup, their eyes with mascara, their lips with lipstick. Dozens of G-string outfits hang on a rolling rack.

"Do you see any Latinos here?" Jenkiles asks.

He's right. None of these women look remotely Hispanic.

"The closest one," Jenkiles continues, "is out dancing right now, and I know she's from Wisconsin. Not Cuba."

"But Stanley Owens said you were expanding the operation. You're hiding them somewhere."

"Operation?"

"Sex trafficking."

All three women stop what they are doing and look at Jack.

Jenkiles takes Jack's elbow and pulls him toward the door.

Jack jerks his arm away. "Touch me again . . ." He lifts his shirt to show his gun.

Jenkiles strides out onto the main floor, heading for the front entrance. "Stanley Owens is a big fat liar. He's had it in for me for years." He opens the front door.

The sharp light of day invades the club.

Jack squints. He steps into the doorway with Jenkiles.

"I've tried to work with Stanley in the past, and he has screwed me over every time. Do you think I'd be sitting here in this shithole if I could make money selling women the way he does?"

Jack looks back inside the club. It is a very sad place.

Jenkiles licks the last of the cocaine off his upper lip.

The freckled man limps toward them.

"But Stanley said this was a waystation for transporting women."

"Stanley lied. Look again. Where would I put them? There's no space here. If you see him again, tell him I'm done trying. I don't want anything from him." He sniffs himself into a snort. "And I don't want him sending donkeys like you to my establishment." He pushes Jack outside and slams the door.

When Jack looks up, the hot sun slaps him in the face.

The humid air coats his lungs.

He curses Stanley.

He closes his eyes, relaxes his shoulders, and waits for his rage to die down.

Mattie and Calvin are parked out of sight around the corner.

They can wait.

They don't need to see him like this.

Not again. Not like last night.

Never again.

CHAPTER FORTY

MATTIE

"Where the hell is Jack?" It's rhetorical. I don't actually want Calvin to answer. We've been waiting in the Camaro outside Club XXX forever.

"He's been in there for five minutes," Calvin says.

"No, it's been longer than that."

"I don't think so." Calvin leans forward between the front seats. "Do you think he'll let me drive his car sometime?"

I turn around in the passenger seat to face him. "Do you think you could talk about something besides cars and food for once?"

"I could." He gazes at the driver's console. "But why would I want to?"

"How about the armadillos, again? I'd rather hear your story about the herd of armadillos blocking the road than some random car's engine specifications. At least armadillos have personality."

"That's not funny, and no they don't. They're murderers."

"How about Jack?" I ask. "You could talk about him.

He's got personality."

"He does. He's a great guy."

"Really? You think so? Did you happen to notice how he tried to kill someone last night? You were there, right?"

"Yeah, but I was hungry. I needed to eat."

"Weren't you scared?"

"No. Not of Jack. I'm afraid of Stanley and those Latino guys, but not Jack. Besides, food makes me feel better."

I don't mean to stare at his gut, but I can't help myself.

He looks down at it, too, and sighs. "I guess I feel bad a lot."

It's cold of me, but I can't concern myself with Calvin's eating issues right now. Jack is taking too long.

"Applebee's was great, wasn't it?" he asks. "I like the riblets. Doesn't eating make you feel better?"

"We should be careful." I face forward and look out the windshield. I wish we had parked across the street, where I could see the front of the club. It shouldn't be taking Jack this long. All he had to do was find the manager and ask where the Latinos took Lucía.

"Are we going to lunch after Jack comes back?" Calvin asks.

"It had better not take him that long. It's not even noon yet."

"He's only been gone about five minutes."

"I don't trust him. He's lied to us about so many things, and he's capable of murder. You *did* see him last night. That look in his eyes. He's got an anger problem."

"Everyone has an anger problem. Are we going to lunch after he comes back?"

"I'm going inside." I open my door.

"Wait." Calvin grasps my arm. "Why are you always in

such a hurry? Why do you always have to do something?"

The air here has a hint of salt. Brine. We're far from the ocean, so it can't be that. Maybe a seafood platter is rotting in that dumpster over there. Whatever it is, the smell reminds me of the aquarium. So does Calvin's question. It reminds me of my old job there. Of Hank the Manatee.

It's not right. I suddenly want to cry.

I pull my door closed and turn to him.

"Do you know what a manatee is?"

"Yes."

Maybe if I talk it through, the tears won't come. Calvin might be a perfect sounding board. Other people's emotions never affect his two-track mind. I wonder if he was born without empathy, or if he built a wall around it, growing up.

"When I was working as a marine biologist, one of my jobs was to take care of a manatee."

"Manatees are the big fat sea cows, right?"

"You could say that." My throat tightens. "They're big, yes, but they're also precious and cute."

"Do we use them for their blubber?"

"No. You're thinking of whales. Shut up and listen. I put off scheduling the underwater gate for repairs. I procrastinated for weeks, and one of the manatees got stuck and . . . and he died."

"That's it?"

"What do you mean, that's it?" I swallow. "He got trapped in the gate and drowned. It was all my fault. I lost my job and had to move away from the coast."

"Can't they breathe underwater?"

"No." I turn away from him. This isn't working. "They're not fish."

"When Jack comes back, and we go to lunch, I'm not

going to order fish, in honor of your sea cow."

"Manatee."

"Right. Manatee. I won't eat fish today, in honor of your manatee. Does that make you feel better?"

"The only thing that will make me feel better is if Jack comes back and knows where they took Lucía."

"Lucía's not a manatee, Mattie. She's a girl."

CHAPTER FORTY-ONE

LUCÍA

Time moves slower when you're trapped in a van, blindfolded, gagged, and your hands are zip-tied behind your back. Time moves so slowly. Lucía can't tell how long she's been stuck here, listening to the Cubans argue about their immediate future. She's terrified to fall asleep. The only thing she has left is her awareness.

And her aches and pains.

And her innocence, if you can call it that.

But time—it moves so slowly.

The van rumbles down the road so steadily.

Time moves so . . . and she's so sleepy.

She kicks a soccer ball. The ball flies into the air and lands by the goalkeeper. The goalkeeper easily blocks the shot and picks up the ball.

No.

She must wake up.

She jerks her head to one side. Then, to the other. She licks the inside of her gag rag. The coarse material irritates her tongue. The van hits a bump, and her backside smacks against the metal floor, firing a fresh shot of pain up her back. She winces. She listens, but the Cubans have stopped talking. Her head aches. She—she drifts away . . .

The soccer ball flies into the air and bounces off a wall. It must be wintertime. She's playing soccer on an indoor field in Canada. A re-purposed hockey rink with artificial turf. She must be eight years old again because Roanne, her nemesis, is here. Lucía seizes the ball and heads for the goal. Roanne cuts her off and steals the ball, but not before plowing into Lucía. Lucía trips and falls. Her head hits the side wall.

Her head hits it hard.

The pain is unbearable.

All is quiet.

She opens her eyes to the darkness that is her blindfold.

The Cubans have stopped talking, and her headache reaches new levels, as if the dream had been for real.

She shakes her head, but it only makes the throbbing worse.

When she was younger, she played soccer indoors, and one day, she collided with the side wall. The doctor had said she'd suffered a concussion then. Now, she realizes Wyatt must have given her a concussion when he punched her.

The pain just won't go away.

All is quiet.

The van hasn't moved since she awoke. How long was she asleep? Did they leave her here alone?

A chill courses through her.

The van was warm before, but now, without the engine running, there's no heat. She's not cold, but the air has a chill. It must be late at night or early morning. She assumes she's still in Florida. It must have cooled down outside.

All is *not* quiet.

Someone is breathing near her.

Warm air passes over her cheek.

She tries to speak with the gag in her mouth, but all that comes out is, "Mm. Mm."

No response.

She waits.

More breathing. More warm air.

Her skin bristles. Her head throbs.

Something touches her left breast.

She screams, but the shrill of her voice can't escape her gag.

Her cry is muffled.

She falls onto her side to get away from the touching. To get away from the hand. Someone's hand is touching her body. She kicks and squirms away. The zip tie digs into her wrists as she flails. As she kicks.

"Oh, stop," someone says in a strong Spanish accent. "It's not worth it."

She listens to the van door open and slam shut.

Then, all is quiet.

The breathing is gone. He must have taken his warm breath with him.

She waits.

And she waits.

Time moves slowly.

So slowly.

She worries the concussion Wyatt gave her caused permanent damage. Was she just assaulted, or was that a dream, too? She needs to see a doctor. Her memories of the past two days blur into a wave of confusion. She's so foggy, but that could also be from the drugs Wyatt slipped her. She needs medical attention. By now, under normal circumstances, her dad would have taken her to Dr. Jensen, and Dr. Jensen would have given her something to stop the pain.

Her dad . . . fresh tears stream down her cheeks.

Where is he? Why hasn't he sent someone to save her?

What happened to the Camaro? Where's Jack? Did they kill him in that trailer like they said they would?

Is he dead?

The van's door makes a *ka-klang*. The hinges squeal.

Someone says something in Spanish.

Another person responds.

Thank God, there are two of them. Maybe more.

"I have to go to the bathroom," she shouts, but her voice is muffled. She shouts again, and the Cubans stop talking. She shouts again and again, and finally, someone pulls her gag out. "I have to go to the bathroom." She drums her heels on the floor. "*El baño. El baño.*"

"No."

"*El baño, por favor.*" She wonders if they can understand her attempt at Spanish.

The voices speak quickly. They sound like they're arguing.

The van door squeals, and a faint light penetrates her blindfold.

One of them seizes her elbow. When he speaks, she realizes he was the one breathing on her earlier. "Don't be a stupid," he says. "We have somewhere you can go."

He pulls her out of the van.

She can barely stand.

"*¡Quita la venda!*" a different man says. "*Ahora.*"

"*¿Qué?*" The Breather says.

She can't understand what they're saying.

"*Es sospechoso.*"

The blindfold comes off, and the light of day attacks her eyes. One of the Cubans holds her blindfold with his fingertips, letting it swing back and forth inches from her face. He has a sickly grin. He's taunting her. His crooked teeth are taunting her. She turns away, but before she can take in the scenery, another Cuban pulls on her arm, and she stumbles toward him.

"*Allá*," he says. He points at a port-a-potty leaning against a chain-link fence. The fence has yellow-and-black slashed signs hanging from it. They've taken her to a construction site. The brown earth has holes surrounded by mounds—or are the mounds surrounded by holes?

Her brain aches.

The man pulls her to the port-a-potty.

Her mind is not her own.

He opens the door.

She steps inside and turns around.

As the door closes, she gazes across the street. A cute little building sits beside a cute little parking lot behind a cute little golfing green. The place looks fantastical in the bright morning light until she reads the sign.

CLUB XXX.

It's a strip club.

The door closes.

Lucía manages to pull her shorts down even though her hands are still zip-tied behind her back. It's not easy.

She sits.

She thinks.

The stench is intolerable. A blend of antiseptic, urine, and motor oil.

She worries.

Earlier last night, one of the men had insisted they go to

a baseball game. She'd worried they would leave her in the van for hours, but now, it's much worse. Another man had said they wanted to go to a strip club. They had talked about selling her, presumably for sex. Maybe this is why she's here. Maybe they'll sell her to someone in that club across the street.

She doesn't want to leave the port-a-potty.

Bang, bang, bang.

"*¡Date prisa!*" a man shouts.

She doesn't want to leave, but she can't stay here forever. If it wasn't for that stench . . .

She also doesn't want to be slapped again.

Lucía stands and opens the door.

Outside, one of the Cubans—The Breather—grabs her wrists and shoves her forward. The holes in the ground trip her up, but she keeps her feet. She gazes across the street. She scans the parking lot, looking for help, and—she sees it.

She sees help.

The Camaro sits there. Jack's Camaro.

Now it's the mounds in the ground that trip her up. She's forced to look away from the parking lot to keep her balance, but when she looks back, she sees that unmistakable red hair behind the windshield of the Camaro.

Mattie.

It's Mattie. She's across the street, sitting in the Camaro.

She's come to rescue her.

"Help!" Lucía shouts. "Help!"

A drab gray semi-truck with the Amazon smile on the side glides down the street. The damn thing stops at the intersection in front of the club. She can't see Mattie anymore, and Mattie can't see her. She yells, but the semi's droning engine drowns out her voice.

The Breather pushes her up against the back of the van

and slaps her in the face.

The other Cuban opens the door and grabs her by the ankles. Together, the two animals force her into the van. As the door closes, she glimpses the Amazon semi-truck pulling away. Someone steps out of the shadow in the front of the club and onto the cute little golfing green.

It's Jack.

He's still alive.

He's come to save her.

CHAPTER FORTY-TWO

JACK

Jack steps into the sunlight outside Club XXX. He's calm enough now to tell Mattie and Calvin the bad news. They're at a dead end. Stanley led them astray when he claimed the Latinos had taken Lucía to Club XXX.

That fat liar.

Jack steps onto the little golfing green in front of the club and stops to think. He needs to focus, but his concentration is broken. The club door opens behind him with a loud *creak*. Before he can turn around to see if Jenkiles has followed him outside, a black panel van across the street catches his eye. He doesn't remember seeing it at the construction site when he entered the club. The rear wheels spin, kicking up dirt as it powers off the lot and onto the road.

He turns around.

The man with the odd white freckles stands in the doorway. He looks like he wants a handout. Then, the man literally holds out his hand. "Excuse me, sir."

Jack doesn't have time for this. He heads for the parking lot.

The freckled man limps after him. "Please, sir. Wait a moment."

"Sorry," Jack says. "I don't have time for urban campers."

"For what?"

Jack stops at the edge of the parking lot and turns around. He doesn't want the guy to follow him to his car. "Urban campers. You know, homeless people. I'm sorry, buddy, but I have nothing for you right now."

The freckles dance on the man's face as he laughs. His face looks like a snowstorm. "I'm not homeless. I don't need your help. You need mine."

"I'm sorry, but—"

"You're looking for a girl with a tattoo on her leg, yes?"

"What the hell took you so long?" Mattie walked up behind Jack when he wasn't looking. "We've been out here waiting forever."

"Who's your friend?" the freckled man asks.

"Who are you?" she says.

A gust of wind catches Mattie's hair and thrusts it into Jack's face.

He brushes the frizzy red strands away from his mouth. "Where's Calvin?"

"He's waiting in the car."

The freckled man holds out his hand to Jack. "My name is Carlos Espinoza, and I think I know who you're looking for."

Jack reaches out to shake Carlos's hand, but before he can, Carlos pulls away. He covers his nose and sneezes. Snot oozes between his fingers. "Excuse, me." He sniffles.

"Bless you," Mattie says.

"Thank you." Carlos extends his hand to Jack again.

"No, thanks," Jack says. "I'm good."

"Are you sure? I believe I can help you find the girl with the tattoo *números* on her leg. We should become friends."

Mattie takes Carlos's hand. "I'm Mattie, and this is Jack. What do you know?"

Carlos's sleeve slides up, revealing three wristwatches—two silver, one golden.

Mattie releases her grip and wipes her hand off on her pants.

Jack does not want to spend any more time with this man than he must. Something's wrong with him.

"I know quite a lot," Carlos says.

"Look, we don't have much time." Jack studies Carlos. The man says he wants to help, but there must be something in it for him. "Tell us what you know so we can go."

"Oh, I know a lot." He has a twinkle in his eye as if he *thinks* he knows a lot. "I know too much to discuss here."

"How do we know you know the same girl we know?"

"I didn't say I know her."

The Camaro's door opens, and Calvin gets out. Great. That's all Jack needs. Another participant in this conversation. "If you know something, say it now."

"Please," Mattie says. "We don't have much time."

Carlos raises his hand and lets his sleeve slide down. His wristwatches twinkle in the sunlight. Here it comes. The sales pitch. He said he wasn't homeless, and maybe he's not, but he's acting like an urban camper. Jack senses a scam about to unfold.

"Time doesn't matter," Carlos says. "See?" He points at his arm. "What time is it?"

"It's 11:32 in the morning," Calvin says as he joins them. "I saw it in the car before I came over here. It's 11:32. What are you guys talking about?"

"Ah, but it's not 11:32." Carlos gazes at his wristwatches. "None of these say 11:32."

"That's because they're wrong," Jack says. "If you're not going to talk about the girl, then we should go."

"Her name is Lucía Tremblay, is it not?" Carlos asks. "Her father's name is Colter. Correct?"

"Yes," Mattie says. "That's right, isn't it, Jack? His name is Colter."

"It is." Jack grumbles. This won't end until he ends it. "Listen. Tell us everything you know, and do it now."

"I know I'm hungry." Carlos places his palm on his belly.

Jack hadn't noticed the man's ribs showing through his shirt before. Carlos's body screamed homelessness at first, but now Jack sees the details. The dirt under the fingernails. The matted hair above the left ear. The yellow around the eyes. For a PI, details can mean everything. Carlos is not as decrepit as he first appeared.

Jack is losing his touch, and that's okay.

He's done.

He's quitting this business right after they find Lucía.

He's made up his mind for sure this time. He'll never have peace of mind as long as he must deal with individuals like Carlos.

"I'm hungry, too," Calvin says.

"Of course you are." Mattie rolls her eyes.

Impatience heats Jack's neck. He doesn't know exactly what it is, but something about Carlos has set him off. It's more than the usual evil he sees in mankind. It's an arrogance. An attitude of privilege. A holier-than-thou spirit riding on top of the common evil. He wants to stay calm, but he unconsciously hovers his hand over his concealed weapon. "I don't care who is hungry. Where is Lucía?"

"I have an idea," Carlos says. "Let's discuss her over lunch. Who wants Outback for lunch?"

"I do," Calvin says. "I love the bloomin' onion."

"No." Jack's hand trembles. "It's not even noon yet."

"It's 11:32, and I'm hungry."

"It's not 11:32 anymore." Jack begins to lift his shirt.

"No." Mattie grabs Jack's wrist. She lowers her voice to a whisper. "Don't do it, Jack."

He looks her in the eyes and slowly releases his shirt, letting it fall over his gun.

"Who's buying?" Calvin asks.

A broad smile stretches across Carlos's face, warping his misshapen freckles.

Mattie stares into Jack's eyes.

"Colter Tremblay is buying." Jack adjusts his shirt to make sure his gun is hidden from view. "I'll expense it."

CHAPTER FORTY-THREE

Rich Cuban coffee—the finest in the world—fills the air with its aroma, blending with smoke from Yans's cigar. He lies back on a pool lounge chair and gazes at the sky. The May Day speeches by the leaders of what he calls "Old Cuba" did not stay with him today as they had in years past. No, today, he could not listen to the rhetoric. He could only think of how things would be when he became the leader.

He's so close.

He puffs on his cigar and extinguishes the stub in a copper ashtray stand.

His negotiations with the US could begin early next week, depending on when Darien's friends arrive with the launch code.

Lucía the Launch Code.

He adjusts the lounge chair so he's sitting upright. The sparkling blue pool and the floating bar beyond simultaneously put Yans's quaint apartment to shame and make him proud. He enjoys visiting his sister and her family, but he would never live this way. He lives the way of the working man, eating beans in his tiny abode downtown. That's what May Day is all about.

In recent years, he's had little time to spend with family, but he always comes to Suelo's Miramar mansion after the May Day celebrations.

He's a good uncle.

His nieces and nephews run around the pool, jumping in and out, splashing around without a care in the world. The way it should be. He's proud to give them his time. He's proud to have provided them a glimpse of Cuba's future by purchasing this estate. He's proud of what he will do for Cuba in the future.

Mansions for everyone.

It used to be a dream.

Now, it's becoming a reality.

Once Yans discusses his newfound power with the US—his newfound *nuclear* power—Washington will lift the economic blockade. The unrelenting war on Cuba's economy will end. Cuba will be removed from the list of countries sponsoring terrorism, and tourists will flood the shores with money.

Cuba is not a terrorist nation. Terrorists negotiate with guns and knives. World powers negotiate with nuclear arms.

It's always been that way.

Yans pulls another cigar from the box and lights it.

He has but one concern in life now, and it's not much. If those impatient buffoons of the Red Star Society get what they want, Cuba will forever remain on the terrorism list. They don't want to negotiate for economic freedom. They want to launch a nuclear attack. They want to destroy the US, and that retaliation would destroy Cuba.

Idiotas.

He puffs.

It's okay, though. Removing Ernesto and his son from existence . . . that sent a strong message. The opposition within the Red Star Society will be scared and scrambling for at least a week, and that's all the time Yans needs.

Lucía the Launch Code will be here by then.

"Enjoying yourself?" Suelo approaches. "Do you want something to drink?"

"Yes. That would be nice."

She snaps her fingers. A servant nods and heads toward the pool bar. Suelo's tangerine swimsuit doesn't cover her swelling thighs, and her ass cheeks hang out when she turns to yell at Giselle, her youngest *niña*. Time and relaxation have softened and ballooned Suelo's body. Like all women, she blames her weight on having had children—four girls, one boy—but, like all women, it's an excuse. She has no reason to become unattractive due to child-bearing. Women were created to look good for men *and* have children.

Those are their only two jobs in life.

The servant returns and lowers a tray filled with drinks. Yans chooses the flute filled to the brim with an aqua-blue fluid. He doesn't know what's in it exactly, but he smells Tequila, so he knows it will do the job.

This is the one time a year he allows himself to soften and relax.

Suelo puts her hands on her hips. "The closet doors in Tomás's room are broken. They're hanging off the rails, and one of them has a hole kicked in the bottom."

"Have a repairman come." Yans sips his drink. "Certainly, you can afford to pay for it out of the allowance."

"Money isn't the issue. It's Tomás. This is the third time he's ruined the doors."

"I didn't know that."

"You would if you were ever here."

Insolent bitch.

Yans stands up, drink in hand. His swim trunks sag, making him uncomfortable. He'd feel better in his canvas fatigues right now. She can't talk to him this way. He can't allow this.

"Do you see me?" He points at his eyes. "Am I here, or am I a figment of your imagination? I *am* here, right? You *can* see me?"

"Tomás is your only nephew, and he's at that age when he needs a man to teach him." She turns away. "I don't think his father is ever coming back."

Yans knows Raphael is never coming back.

Yans knows where his men buried Raphael.

"Send Tomás to me," he calls to Suelo's back. "I'll talk with him."

"Thank you." She waves to the boy. "Tomás. Come here. Your uncle wishes to speak with you."

"Do I have to?"

"*Mijo*, now."

The boy climbs out of the pool and leaves a wet trail on the concrete as he strolls past his sisters. Funny how their faces assume he's in trouble. If anything, they should be jealous. Someday, they'll understand. The day Yans hands the world over to his nephew.

"Sit," Yans says. "Tell me what you've been doing."

"I've been doing art. Drawing, mostly."

Oh, no. Tomás could become one of those. A waste-of-space picture peddler on the sidewalks of Havana. A starving artist. Perhaps Yans should visit more often after all, and he will. Once he's dethroned the "Old Cuba," he will have time.

"What do you draw?"

"The ocean, mostly. And birds."

"Do you go to the beach a lot?"

"No. I draw from memory in my room. *Mamá* won't let me go to the beach alone, so I usually don't go."

"Why won't she let you go alone?" The blue margarita has a kick to it. Yans feels okay. Better than okay.

"Because I need to take them." Tomás points at the pool. Yans's nieces bob up and down, screaming at each other with their high-pitched voices, playing some kind of girly game.

"I understand," Yans says. "I wouldn't want to go with them either."

Tomás rises up on his tip-toes. "Really?"

"They're annoying and stupid, am I right?"

"Yep." He bounces on his toes. "I hate them."

"That's good. What do you do when they go to the beach with them?"

"They always go shopping, too."

One of the girls—the troublemaker Giselle—runs by, shrieking as she goes. She acts like someone is chasing her, but she's an *idiota*. Her older sisters don't care about her.

"So, when they're not here, you stay in your room and draw?"

"Yes."

"She told me about your closet doors. Why do you kick them in?"

The happiness drains from the boy's face. "It makes the room bigger."

"Why don't you go to the *sala de estar*? It's much bigger in there."

"I can't." He glances at his feet. The big toe has a bandage on it. "Mama locks the door to my room whenever they leave."

"I see."

Yans puts his drink in the lounge's cup holder.

He stands up and smooths his swim trunks.

Suelo sways on the other side of the pool, laughing with a friend. She chose a red drink.

"Where are you going?" Tomás asks.

"To speak with your *madre*."

"When will you come back?"

Yans did not buy this mansion so Suelo could lock up the heir to the Rivero legacy in a small bedroom. Tomás is not only the heir to the Rivero legacy but also to Cuba. Maybe to the world. She wasn't wrong that Tomás needs a man to teach him. He needs Yans, and he needs to be safe.

Suelo has gone too far.

The giggling gaggle of girls crisscross in front of Yans, impeding the way to his insolent sister. The girls form a line, scampering along the pool's edge. He wants to kick them in one by one. Drown them like cats.

All of them.

They're nothing but worthless women in the making.

He grasps Suelo by the elbow and pulls her up the steps into the mansion.

Her feet slap against the marble floor.

"Let go of me."

She slaps his shoulder.

He barely feels it.

She's so weak.

They enter the foyer near the front entrance.

Two servants stand near the dining room hall, staring.

Yans makes fierce eye contact with the servants, and they scatter, but he doesn't trust others won't appear.

Sunlight shines in through the vaulted ceiling windows. A crystalline dome splits the light into rays. He can't believe he funds his sister's elegant lifestyle only for her to mistreat Tomás.

Tomás. The heir to the world.

"What are you doing?" Suelo asks. "Let go of me."

He opens the front door and tosses her down the steps.

She catches herself before falling and spins around. Face red and trembling.

"Never lock Tomás up again. Do you understand me? He is the man of the mansion now. You do what he says."

"What?"

Yans can't believe his eyes.

Beyond Suelo—beyond the circular drive, through the security fence, and across the street—an SUV screeches to a halt.

"*What* did you say?" she asks. "He's only twelve. I'm not doing what he says."

Two men wearing green camouflage exit the SUV.

"Are you listening to me?" She waves her arms in the air.

The men are carrying AK-47s.

Yans recognizes the SUV. He recognizes the men.

It's the Red Star Society opposition.

"Shut up, Suelo."

The men aim their guns at the gate and fire.

Suelo screams and hits the ground.

The gate blows open.

May Day is the one time a year Yans allows himself to soften and relax.

Just look what that's got him.

He raises his hands in the air.

A coup.

CHAPTER FORTY-FOUR

Jack, Mattie, Calvin, and Carlos weren't the only people at the Outback Steakhouse to begin lunch with a blooming onion. The place reeks of beef grease and spices. Carlos and Calvin pull petals off the appetizer as if they've entered a competition. Jack decides he can't stomach the deep-fried calamity, and Mattie focuses on Carlos. The old Cuban has a permanent grin plastered across his freckled face. He shoves the greasy, golden-brown onion strands into his mouth.

Somewhere out there, the Latinos have Lucía. A niggling in the back of Jack's head tells him they're doing something to her. They're hurting her. They're doing something evil. He doesn't know what or where, but Carlos might. This old Cuban knew her name and all about her tattoo, but he refused to talk unless Jack bought everyone lunch.

Sitting across from this manipulative, weather-worn, elderly Cuban man gives Jack the creeps. This had better not be some kind of con.

"What do you know about Lucía Tremblay?" Jack asks.

"I know a lot." Carlos pauses his chewing and raises his

eyebrows. "Where should I start?"

"Start with where those Latinos took her," Mattie says.

"I'll start at the beginning."

"Do we have time for that?" she asks. "How long will that take?"

Carlos pulls his sleeve back, exposing his wristwatches. Two silver, one golden. "Time doesn't matter. It's going to move on, whether you like it or not. I have time to start at the beginning."

"Whatever," Jack says. "Tell us about Lucía."

Calvin grabs the last of the onion.

Carlos frowns at him.

"Well?" Mattie asks. "Are you going to tell us?"

"Dmitri Belkin came to Cuba in the early 1960s," Carlos says.

"Who?" Jack can't believe this guy. "We want to know about Lucía."

"I'll get to her." He flags down a waiter. "When will our meals arrive?"

"The order is in, sir. It won't be much longer."

"Good," Calvin says. "I can't wait for my steak."

"Go on," Mattie says. "I have a feeling that you will tell us everything, whether we want to hear it or not, so you might as well start. Who's Dmitri?"

"The greatest tattoo artist to ever wield a needle in the streets of Havana." He leans back in his chair. "And, my very good friend." He averts his eyes. "They killed his entire family, you know."

"I'm sorry to hear that," Mattie says, "but we don't—"

"Let him finish," Jack says.

"Fine," Mattie grumbles.

"I met him the day we escaped from the Black Crickets'

prison." Carlos's sallow cheeks swell with pride. "He'd still be there if it weren't for me. I got him out, and he started a new life. The Black Crickets were a group of political rebels in the late 1950s and early 1960s. They imprisoned anyone they thought might let on they wanted to overthrow the government. Castro wouldn't have treated them very nicely if he'd know about them.

"Dmitri and I later worked together at an automobile recycling plant and became the best of *amigos*, but he couldn't stay. He became paranoid. Years earlier, a new group of rebels, the Red Star Society, had taken over the Black Crickets. Dmitri was convinced this new group were looking for him. They weren't, of course. Not at that point. But he still feared for himself and his wife. They moved to the country and had children. It was lovely for a while."

"I'm sorry," Jack says. "I don't see what this has to do with anything. What about Lucía?"

The waiter passes by the table.

"What about my steak?" Calvin asks.

"Soon, sir," the waiter says without skipping a step on his way to the kitchen. "It'll be out soon."

"When Dmitri came back to Havana, our children played together, but Ana, his wife, she . . . "

"She what?" Mattie asks.

"She passed away. It destroyed Dmitri. He took to the streets, supporting himself with his tattoo skills. His children grew up and left him. He lost touch with them, and later, they had their own children. And then . . . then, they killed them all." He closes his eyes. "His three children. All his grandchildren." He opens his eyes and gazes at Jack. His pupils are as black as black can be. "Dmitri never recovered. I tried to help him before that, but he wouldn't listen. He went insane. He swore the Red Star Society wanted to lock us up like the Black Crickets had. Of course, that wasn't true. Not at that point." Carlos slaps his palms on the table and bursts into a maniacal laugh.

"What is it?" Mattie raises her voice over the old Cuban's cackling.

"It's true what they say about dreams into reality." Carlos catches his breath. "Dear Dmitri spent the 1970s and 1980s convinced the Red Star Society searched for him because he was the only one who knew about the missile, but he was wrong. They didn't come after him until the next century. Had he not dreamed they were looking for him for so long, they might never have come after him. Dreams into reality can be bad."

"Missile?" Jack asks.

The waiter places Carlos's lunch on the table before him. Filet Mignon, mac-n-cheese, a baked potato, and sweet potato fries. All extra. Jack rarely passes expenses on to his clients. He likes to build goodwill and work at a fair rate, but after what this case has put him through, he's going to make Colter foot the bill on this one.

The waiter gives Mattie her chicken sandwich and Jack his ribs.

"Where's mine?" Calvin asks.

"I'll be right back with that."

"I don't like this place." Calvin grips his steak knife, ready to eat the second the waiter returns. "It's taking too long, and I don't like . . . I mean . . ." He gazes at Carlos. "Jack is right. Your story has nothing to do with Lucía, and you ate all the appetizers. You smell bad, and—"

"That's enough," Mattie says.

Carlos puts his nose near his armpit and sniffs. "I don't

smell that bad, and my story has everything to do with Lucía, fat boy." He quickly cuts into his steak and eyes Calvin as he puts a greasy chunk of meat in his mouth. He licks his lips.

"Hey," Mattie says. "Don't call him that."

"The missile." Jack raises his voice. "What about a missile?"

"Oh, this tastes good," Carlos says. He chews. He stares at Calvin, and he chews.

Calvin reaches across the table and grasps Mattie's wrist. "I want to go home after this. I'm done. Can we go back to the convenience store?"

"It depends," she says. She eyes Carlos. "Are you going to tell us about Lucía or not?"

"It was one of the missiles that came to Cuba during the crisis." He puts another piece of steak in his mouth. "You *gringos* called it the Cuban Missile Crisis, but it wasn't our fault." He chews. Meat juice gathers in the corners of his mouth. "Well, actually, it was a little bit our fault, but mostly Russia's." He slices the baked potato in half. "Dmitri came from Russia at that time and worked on installing the missiles. After the crisis, we gave the missiles back. All except for one. It's rumored to be buried in a hillside east of La Boca. It fell into the Black Cricket's hands, but they couldn't launch it without the launch code." He shovels half the potato into his mouth. Sour cream runs down his chin.

"You're disgusting," Calvin says.

The waiter delivers Calvin's steak to the table. He digs in.

"So what does that have to do with—" Mattie tips her head back. Gazes at the ceiling fan spinning above. "Oh . . ."

"What?" Jack asks. "Why didn't they have the code?"

Carlos talks without looking up from his plate, chewing quickly as if a new eating competition with Calvin has begun.

"Only Dmitri knew the launch code. Now, only Lucía has it."

"Not true." Mattie looks at Jack. "Those Latinos have her, so they have the launch code, too."

"Why do they need her?" Jack asks. "Why haven't they taken the code and gotten rid of her?"

"They won't do that. They told me whoever is running the show wants her in person in case the launch code doesn't work. They want to be able to interrogate her about the code."

"I don't think she knows anything about any of this. Her father would have told me. Or, he should have told me if he knew."

"What are we talking about?" Calvin asks. "A nuclear missile? Are we talking about launching a nuclear missile?"

"That's right, *chico.*" Carlos leans forward. He puts his elbows on the table—a steak knife in one hand and a fork in the other. He grins. "They're going to blow up the world, my little friend."

"Stop it," Mattie says.

"Where exactly is the missile? How far east of La Boca?" Jack asks.

"Don't know." Having had fun with Calvin, Carlos leans back in his chair and picks up a claw full of sweet potato fries. "But I wouldn't think it would be very far. I'm fairly certain they never moved it out of the country." He fills his mouth with the fries.

Jack stands up. "That's where they're taking her."

"You're right." Mattie stands.

Calvin begins to eat faster.

"How would they get her there, though?" Jack asks. "It's not like they can just waltz her past TSA without them realizing she'd been kidnapped, could they? She has that bruise on her face."

"I doubt they would try that," Carlos says.

"Then, how?"

"They'll probably smuggle her into Cuba the way refugees are smuggled out. By boat."

"Where?"

"We've got to stop them," Mattie says. "They can't have her."

"If they get the launch code, will they really destroy the world?" Calvin asks.

"There's a small port south of Miami before you reach the keys." Carlos lays his knife and fork on the table. "I wouldn't know for sure if the port is still in operation, but they used to make a daily transfer just past noon. That's where I would go to find her. If they don't do it anymore, you could ask around."

Jack checks the time. It's past noon now. The soonest they could arrive would be tomorrow.

Mattie grips Jack's elbow. "We've got to go now."

"It's too late today."

People in the restaurant are staring at them. Jack pries Mattie's hand off his arm and holds onto it while he sits back down.

She sits, and he lets go of her.

"Where is this port, exactly?" Jack asks.

"I'm getting a to-go box," Calvin says. "And, I want to go home. I'm not going to Miami. You can't make me go to Miami."

"Good," Carlos says. "You can stay here with me, chico." He's down to his veggies, having eaten the last bite of his filet. He dabs at a broccoli spear with his fork. "You don't have to go to Miami."

"Where in Miami is this port?" Jack demands.

"It's down under," Carlos says.

"What?"

"It's down under Miami"—he picks up the dessert and drink menu—"just like this Chocolate Thunder cake is from Down Under. You are buying us dessert, aren't you?"

CHAPTER FORTY-FIVE

Hurry up and wait. One of the worst phrases ever conjured by mankind. Not only do people use it to confuse me with its paradoxical discomfort, but an inherent truth lies behind it like an impassable wall. Time is the one thing I can never change. I can't speed it up or slow it down.

It drives me crazy.

Carlos said boats carrying illegal immigrants only used the port south of Miami after noon and before four o'clock. That was all Jack and Calvin needed to hear to form their "hurry up and wait" excuse. After watching Carlos devour a ridiculously large piece of chocolate cake, we hit the road for Miami but only made it a few hours in. I was glad to get away from that creep. Calvin came away from the lunch shook, also. It was like Carlos was hitting on him. Calvin had the creeps worse than me. I hope he's asleep in his hotel room now, dreaming of good food and fast cars.

Last night, we crashed in a single hotel room for only a few hours. Jack had to sleep on the floor. This afternoon, the sun beat in through the Camaro's windshield until Jack couldn't keep his eyes open. Weary and frustrated, he took us to another hotel and splurged on two rooms this time. Two very nice rooms. One for Calvin and one for us "adults" with two queen beds each. Jack will be sending his client the room bills and any other expenses we have. He's been coming through for us lately, and he's kept his cool. I can tolerate him as long as he doesn't get overly angry again.

I wish I knew his damage.

Our room overlooks the ocean and comes with a stocked mini-bar, an iron, a hair dryer, the usual microwave and refrigerator setup, and robes—luxurious fluffy robes. This is close to the nicest place I've ever stayed.

"I'm taking a shower," I say.

"Okay."

Jack lies on the bed, putting the large-screen TV through its paces with the remote. He seems dismayed by the programming options.

I slip into the bathroom and undress. The steam heats me up, and the water washes away two days of frenzy. My mind clears for a brief moment, and I don't think of what they might be doing to Lucía. Instead, I eat a slice of peace pie and breathe easily as I soap up my legs. The waiting part of "hurry up and wait" has its advantages. I imagine what a literal slice of peace pie would look like. For me, it's a piece of blueberry pie à la mode. Smooth and rich. The berries burst in my mouth, and the buttery crust melts on my tongue. The ice cream is ice cream. So good. The most amazing part is I don't crave a cigarette after eating my imaginary dessert. Instead, I just want more pie.

I should have eaten a real dessert at Outback with the others. It's not like I didn't have time.

Hurry up and wait.

I wash my hair and step out of the shower. The fluffy robe is a bear hug from heaven. Jack hasn't moved and still hasn't found anything on the TV to watch.

I sit on the desk chair and swivel to see the TV.

"A million programs, and not one of them worth a damn," he says.

"Wait, there's *Forensic Files.*"

"No."

"Why not? Isn't that right up your alley?"

"It is, but I've seen them all." He continues to flip through the channels. The screen scrolls. "I thought watching it a lot would be good research when I started out as a PI, but after a while, I realized they're all the same."

"You couldn't have seen them all. There're too many."

"If you seen one, you've seen them all."

"That's not true. They nail the bad guys with different stuff all the time."

"Mostly DNA." He shifts the pillow wedged between his back and the wall. He doesn't look comfortable. "It's always blood and hair and some lab analysts showing off their equipment. I hate it."

"I suppose you're right, but you can't say all the episodes are the same just because of that. The reasons for the crimes are always different." I brush my hair. They haven't made a brush yet that can comb through it on the first pass, and this brush is no exception. As nice as this place is, it's not perfect, but it's super close.

"Actually," he glances in my direction, "if you think about it, that's not true either. Underneath the details of each crime, the killers all do it for the same reason."

"What's that?"

"How many episodes have you seen?" he asks. "A lot?"

"Yeah. I went through my *Forensic Files* phase in college."

"How many can you remember where the killer wasn't a man?"

He has a point. "Not many."

"If any. How many can you remember where the victims weren't women?"

"There are more of those."

"Yeah, but not many. It's always men killing women."

He puts the remote down. Analysts on *SportsCenter* argue about an upcoming football draft. I scoot my chair over to the side of the bed to hear him better. Though he had a good nap this afternoon, he still has bags under his eyes. I'm refreshed, and I'd leave for Miami right now if I thought he would come with me, but—

Hurry up and wait.

He gazes down at his hands and mutters, "It's always men killing women."

I can't take any more of this conversation about *Forensic Files*. I need to know what his damage is. We have all the time in the world to talk, but I can't wait. "What happened to you last night?"

"What do you mean?"

"Why did you shoot at Stanley? You don't seem like one of those murderers on *Forensic Files*."

"If I was"—he grins—"I'd be a bad one. I'm glad I missed."

"Yeah, but why'd you do it? He had already told us where the Latinos took Lucía. Then, you still shot at him."

"He was lying."

"We didn't know that then. Why did you shoot at him?"

"I was angry."

"I know, but you could have gone to jail for life." I make

a pass at my hair with the brush, and it gets stuck.

"That's true. Like I said, I'm glad I missed."

"What about him made you so angry?" I tug on the brush, but it doesn't come loose. "I've never seen anyone lose their temper like that."

His voice goes grave. His eyes are black stones. "He hurts women."

This sends a chill through my body. An oddly comforting chill, but a chill nonetheless. My robe has no problem warming me back up, but I realize I may have gone too far. I can't pull the brush out of my thick red hair. Jack's shoulder-length hair hides his neck. His thin, dark beard hides his sharp jaw. His darkly deceptive eyes hide his past. I can't tell if he's angry at my questions or not. He's certainly not like he was last night.

Tonight, he's like an anti-villain. A troubled hero from a cheap crime novel.

"I'm not defending that sleaze bag," I say, "but a lot of men hurt women. You can't kill them all."

"Hm." He shuts the TV off. "Are you sure about that?"

I tug on the brush. "I don't think you're being as noble as you think you are. It's not your responsibility to rescue the women of the world. Just Lucía." There's more to his feelings around women than he's letting on. His deep-seated anger for Stanley apparently applies to all men. I decide to drop it before he becomes angry, but then I reconsider. I can't help it. I've got to know. "Besides, you're not a woman. What's it to you if the Stanleys of the world are hurting us?"

"My mom was a woman."

"Was?"

"She was murdered just after I turned sixteen. My stepfather beat her to death with his fists."

There it is.

His damage.

Ask, and ye shall receive.

He reaches over and pulls the brush out of my hair.

CHAPTER FORTY-SIX

LUCÍA

Lucía comes out of a deep sleep. Her scraped side hurts first, followed by the familiar throbbing beneath her eye where Wyatt hit her yesterday. The pain of her predicament comes rushing into her mind, and none of her ailments hurt as much as losing sight of Mattie. She saw Jack. They had come to rescue her, but they hadn't seen her. They hadn't known to stop the van.

Nothing hurts more than that.

She'd screamed like never before when the van left the construction site. She screamed until she fell asleep. Until she—did she pass out? Or, fall asleep?

She's not sure.

She inhales freely. The air soothes her lungs. While the rest of her body hurts, her mind is fresher than ever. Thoughts and memories emerge with clarity and speed. It's been more than a day now since she's seen Wyatt. He must have drugged her for weeks, slowly increasing the dosage so she wouldn't notice. Making her docile. Preparing her for sale. Grooming her.

That's over now.

He's gone.

She has bigger problems.

She tests the zip tie binding her wrists. It's still strong. She has no idea where the Cubans have taken her now, but the van is not moving. They're talking outside. The faint aroma of beer and brine floats in the sticky air. She can't see through her fresh blindfold, but she can breathe freely. They didn't gag her this time. Instead, they let her scream herself to sleep, not caring who might hear as they drove away from Jack and Mattie.

Away from hope.

Hope or despair. It's up to her.

Having come so close to being rescued, she'd lost her mind, but she was feeling much better now without Wyatt's drugs clouding her thoughts. During one of his pearl-of-wisdom sessions, her father once said, "Your mind can be your greatest friend or your worst enemy. It can give you hope or banish you to despair. No matter the situation, your mind can go either way. If you can control it, it's up to you where you go. Hope or despair."

Lucía misses him. She wants to go home. She wants to hug her father.

After seeing Jack across the street, and after the van's back doors slammed shut without him seeing her, she had chosen despair. She'd let it all out and passed out. But now, it's not too late to choose hope. Jack is still alive. He is with Mattie, and they must be looking for her.

They must be coming for her.

They must be.

A new pain comes. Her stomach. It's empty, and it's not happy. Spikes dance on the inner lining. They wail on her insides.

The Cubans' voices suddenly become louder. The grating sound of the van's side door ends with a shrill *clang*.

Oh, no.

What are they going to do to her now?

They sound excited. Their Spanish speech is fast. She can't understand most of what they say.

"Marlins . . . game . . . win tonight."

"Little Havana . . . best . . . good . . . play . . . park."

A new spike stabs Lucía's small intestine.

"Girl . . . time . . . tomorrow . . . boat."

Boat? Why are they talking about a boat?

"Marlins . . . Dodgers . . . "

They're going to a baseball game. The jerks plan to leave her here while they root for the Marlins. They talked about baseball before, and now it's happening. Because it's the Marlins, she must be in Miami. Wow. They drove all the way to Miami while she slept.

Lucía slams her heels against the van's floor, banging them as hard as she can.

"Hey, I need to eat," she says.

"Ah, *pobrecita niña.*" The jerk's mocking tone comes through loud and clear. "*Tienes hambre?*"

"I need something to eat. You're starving me!"

A different Cuban speaks up. He sounds like the one from the trailer who tried to take Lucía. The leader. "We'll bring you a hot dog after the game. Okay?"

"When? After the game? That will take hours."

A grating noise comes from the side door.

Her stomach strikes again. The pain wraps around her insides, and she can't think about anything else.

"Are you still there?"

She can choose to listen to her hunger pains in despair, or hope someone brings her a hot dog before the game ends. It's her choice. Hope or despair. Pain or promise. Patience or anxiety. It's all in her mind.

"Please, bring me something to eat."

The side door *clangs* shut.

All is quiet.

She's alone.

Stomach acid creeps up her throat.

She chooses hope, but hope can't stop vomit.

CHAPTER FORTY-SEVEN

MATTIE

The door to our room automatically locks when I pull it closed behind me. I hope the sound didn't wake Jack up. The complimentary two packets of hotel coffee weren't enough. I finished my second cup an hour ago, and I want more. It could become an addiction. We're headed for Miami today to rescue Lucía, and everything is looking up. We will find her at the port Carlos told us about, put her in Jack's Camaro, and take her to her father, Colter.

It's going to happen.

Today.

I stride down the hallway, heading for the lobby in search of caffeine. I feel like I'm flying and don't want to come down.

Just around the corner, Calvin stands with his back against the wall. I stop. Teenagers never wake up this early. He's talking to someone on his cell phone, his eyes darting this way and that. He keeps his phone pinned to one ear and holds his other ear closed with his right hand. Not only do teenagers never wake up this early, but I've never seen one talk on a cell phone. They only ever send text messages.

I slink back around the corner and listen.

"No, you don't understand. I don't have a nuclear missile. They do. They said it's in Cuba, um . . . west of somewhere called 'La Boca.'" Calvin pauses. "Uh, huh. Yes, by the shore. Or, no. Buried by a hill. I don't know." His voice is stressed. "Uh, huh. I understand. I know it sounds crazy, but you have to believe me. They took her, and now they have the launch code. I think it's a launch code." He presses his phone harder against his head. "No, the Cuban men. At least eight. Can you send someone for me?"

This is unbelievable. How could he do this?

"Okay," he says. "I'll be here."

At that, I charge around the corner.

He sees me coming.

Who the hell was he talking to?

The blood drains from his face. He's scared, and he should be. He taps on his phone and shoves it in his pocket. He's going to try to play this off. I can't believe it, but then I realize he doesn't know what I heard.

"Good morning." He forces a smile onto his face. "I was hungry, so I—"

"Is it?" I walk right up to him and put my face in his. "Is it a good morning?"

"What's the matter, Mattie?"

"Who were you talking to?"

"A friend?"

He's so unsure of himself. What a horrible liar.

"And what were you talking about?"

"Stuff."

A young couple with a baby stroller walks toward us. I hadn't noticed how close we were to the lobby. I can see the desk clerk from here, and he can see me. He raises his hand to the next person in line and looks my way. He could have heard Calvin's entire conversation. This is bad. The young couple could have heard everything he said, too. The woman pushing the stroller gives me a long, steady stare as she passes us.

My lack of patience escalates from a calm three to an excited eight. Two more levels, and Calvin will be begging for mercy. "Come with me." I bound out of the hotel into the drop-off area. An elderly man pops the trunk of his Mercedes coupe and tugs on a suitcase. Engraved planters the size of soldiers border the hotel. Each one contains a shrub groomed to perfection. Each spire stretches toward the sky. I walk to the farthest one and turn around.

Calvin comes out of the hotel and looks both ways.

"Over here," I shout.

He makes his way over to me. "What's the matter, Mattie?"

"You. I heard what you said on the phone."

"Oh." He shoves his hands in his pockets. Looks down.

"Who were you talking to?"

"I don't want to tell you."

"Why?"

"You're going to get mad at me."

"I'm already mad at you. What's wrong with you? The people in the lobby could have heard you."

"I don't think it matters. No one would believe me."

The elderly man slams his trunk lid. He's too far away to hear what we're saying, but he sees we're arguing. I can't believe Calvin did this.

"Who were you talking to on the phone? Don't lie." He freezes up. He won't look at me. "I promise. I'll calm down if you tell me."

"I called the police."

"You *what?*" I yell.

He jumps back. Puts his hands up.

A bellhop had come out of the hotel to help the elderly man, but stopped and turned in my direction when I yelled.

"Please," Calvin begs, "you said you wouldn't get mad."

"Okay, okay," I say. "I'm sorry." I back off. "But you shouldn't have called them."

"I can't take it. I just want to go home. Those guys are going to blow up the world."

Carlos, that ancient, freckle-faced Cuban—he really got inside Calvin's head. It's way worse than I thought. "You're talking about the missile."

"The nuclear missile."

"Don't worry about that. For one thing, that missile is so old now that it probably won't work. Second, even if it did, the only way to stop them is to rescue Lucía. Nothing has changed. We still need to save her. I need your help to save her."

"I can't do this anymore."

"What did the police say? Are they coming for you?"

"They didn't believe me, but"—he glances out at the street—"they said they'd send someone to talk to me in person."

In the interviews I went through when the police investigated Hank the Manatee's death, I had assumed I was speaking with detectives, but sometimes, they tricked me into spilling my guts to psychologists. They wasted weeks painting an evil picture of me, forcing us to close the museum until they finished.

"We've got to go now. We can't tell them anything until we find Lucía. We're so close." I take him by his shoulders. If he doesn't understand what I'm about to say, I'll shake it into him. "If they find us and 'talk' to us, we'll never see her again. Do you know what will happen then?"

"What?"

"The Latinos will take her to the missile and launch it." I'm totally making this up to scare him, but it's the only way we can save Lucía. "You'll be right. They will blow up the world."

His head looks like it's about to explode.

I let go of him.

"I'm so sorry," he says. "Can't I please go home? I'll never say anything to anybody."

"You promise?"

"I promise."

Poor kid. He only wanted to make some extra money at the Pay-n-Save this summer. Since then, he's been held at gunpoint, chased by the police, and witnessed an attempted murder. Now, he's terrified of nuclear war.

At least he ate well and rode in an awesome Volvo, so there's that.

"I'll order you an Uber." I pull out my phone and find a location a few blocks away. "I'll have them pick you up on the corner of Azalea and Mockingbird Drive." I point west.

"I won't make it." Sweat beads on his forehead. "I'm too slow."

"You have time. It won't arrive for a while. Just go now so you're not here when the police come. I'll make the Uber take you back to work, and Jack can pay me back later. Go, now."

I wish the bellhop and old man had gone inside. I hate that they're watching us.

"Bye, Mattie."

"Goodbye, Calvin. It was nice knowing you. I'll send you a text when we find Lucía."

"Should we hug or something? I don't know what to do."

"It's all right. Just go."

He runs away, looking over his shoulder a couple of times. With his eyesight, he'll see the police before they see him. I'm not worried about his loose lips anymore. He's getting what he wanted, but Jack and I aren't. We must leave.

Now.

My skin tingles all over.

I've come back down to earth from my coffee rush.

I need more.

I grab a paper cup in the lobby, put it under the Golden Blend carafe, and flip the spout tab up.

Nothing comes out.

They only have decaf.

Worthless decaf.

CHAPTER FORTY-EIGHT

JACK

Jack's mother died over twenty years ago, but she's here with him now.

He rolls over. Pulls the pillow tight under his head. Forces his way back into the dream. He wants to spend time with her, though she's not real. She stands in the doorway of his childhood apartment. A song by Sublime—"What I Got"—plays in the room behind her. She's holding Jack's leather jacket. "It's going to be cold out later, Jackie. Take this."

"I'll be all right."

She has a carpet burn on her jaw. She holds her head tilted to one side like her neck hurts.

Jack's stepfather steps up behind her. He puts his hand on her shoulder.

She winces.

"Don't you touch her!" Jack yells.

His stepfather lifts her hair and sniffs it.

Jack charges toward them.

"I knew you'd change your mind." She holds his jacket up. "It's going to be cold out later." The jacket flops open, exposing a gun in the inner breast pocket.

"Jack!" a voice shouts. It's a female voice, but not his mother's.

He reaches for the jacket. For the gun.

His stepfather pulls his mother inside, but it's not his mother anymore. It's Mattie. He pulls Mattie into the apartment, and the door slams shut.

Bang.

Jack jerks awake. Sits up in bed.

The door to the hotel rooms slams shut.

Bang.

Mattie stands in front of the door, breathing heavily. Jack is ready to kill whoever chased her here. His stepfather, or Stanley Owens, or the Latino who punched him in the face. His gun is on the nightstand. He thinks about reaching for it, but reality washes over him like a Spring shower, clearing the divide between his dream and reality.

This is not the Mattie from his dream.

His stepfather is not in the hallway. Neither is Stanley Owens or the Latino kidnapper.

"Calvin's gone," Mattie says. "We've gotta get out of here, now."

"What are you talking about?"

She walks into the bathroom. "Calvin won't be coming with us to Miami. I sent him home in an Uber."

"Why?"

"He didn't want to come with us. You heard him complaining yesterday. That creepy Cuban guy scared the hell out of him with all that nuclear missile talk."

Jack's temper flares. He didn't sleep well. His temples pulsate. He stands, walks to the bed's other side, and puts his clothes on.

"Where did he go?" Jack asks.

"Home, I said." She comes out of the bathroom carrying a plastic grocery bag filled with her woman stuff. "Let's go."

"Where's home for him?"

"It doesn't matter. He's gone, and we have to go." She opens the door and rushes into the hallway.

Jack takes a quick look around to see if he's forgetting anything before grabbing his gun and wall charger. He nearly snaps the cord when he yanks the charger's plug out of the wall.

"Mattie," he shouts down the hallway, "*stop*. Let's talk about what to do."

"We'll talk in the car."

She slows down near the front desk.

Jack catches up with her. He walks next to her, acting as if they are a couple. The bellhop at the entrance makes eye contact with him. Then, he stares at Mattie as if he recognizes her. Jack wonders what happened here while he fended off his stepfather in dreamland.

Mattie jerks on the Camaro's door handle. "Unlock it, Jack. Let's go."

"How do you know Calvin took the Uber? Did you see him get in?"

"No, but he promised. C'mon, open the door."

Jack scans the parking lot, gazes up and down the street between each building as far away as he can see, searching for movement.

"C'mon, Jack. Open it."

"We don't know he left. What if he's still here? I could talk him out of leaving."

"I doubt it." She jerks on the handle. "Please, Jack. Open it."

"Do you realize what will happen if we don't stop him? You stole a car, Mattie. What if he goes to the police? What if he tells them about the missile and Lucía?"

She glares at him.

He prays for tranquility to dissolve the impending rage inside him.

He tells himself he has nothing to worry about. Calvin's departure was a surprise, but Jack suspected something like this would happen. The kid was more of a hindrance than a help, anyway. But now that he's gone, a new threat emerges. Jack remembers an adage about keeping secrets. Something Benjamin Franklin said. It's strange. Ben invented electricity, not philosophy. Why was he making up quotes about lying? George Washington was the liar.

Jack laughs to himself.

All men are liars.

No man can keep a secret. Any man who says he can is lying.

The adage: *Three people can keep a secret if two of them are dead.*

"We need to stop Calvin," he says.

Mattie lets go of the door handle.

She focuses on something behind him.

He turns around.

A police cruiser is pulling into the hotel parking lot. It moves like a serpent. Bright white paint with blue lettering. Sheriff. The light bars are off. The officer sees Jack looking at him and turns the steering wheel their way.

Jack unlocks the Camaro doors.

The policeman pulls up and rolls his window down before he and Mattie can jump inside the car.

"Excuse me, have you seen a teenager out here by himself? He was supposed to meet me out front."

"No, sir. I haven't seen anyone."

The officer looks over at Mattie. "How about you?"

"Nope. Not me."

He gives them the, *You know I'm a cop, are you sure?* look.

"Anything else, officer?" Mattie asks. "We're in a hurry."

"Oh, yeah? What's the rush?"

"No rush," Jack says. "She's always in a rush." He glances at her. "Aren't you, honey?"

She smirks and gets inside the car.

Cute.

"Have a great day," the officer says. "And let me know if you see something." He rolls his window up and backs into a parking spot facing the front of the hotel.

Jack gets inside the Camaro. "What was that all about?"

"Nothing." She doesn't look at him. "Can we go now?"

Jack starts the car and drives out of the parking lot.

"Did you know Calvin already talked to the police?"

She shrugged. "It doesn't matter. He left before they came, and he won't tell anyone anything until we find Lucía. He promised."

"And you believed him?" Jack struggles to keep the anger out of his voice. Mattie thought she was doing the right thing. "I can't believe you not only let him go, but paid him to leave."

"He was leaving either way. I bought his silence."

"You bought nothing. Calvin won't keep his mouth shut. You've doomed us. You've doomed Lucía."

Three people can keep a secret if two of them are dead.

They've got to find Calvin before he ruins everything.

"Oh, don't be so dramatic," she says. "We can reach the port and stop them from taking Lucía to Cuba before Calvin tells anyone. He's scared, but he won't do anything. Trust me."

Jack wants to trust her.

He takes a deep breath.

He does trust her.

She listened to him talk about his mother last night. After their talk, she held his hand and told him about her work situation. Something about a manatee and being banned from an aquarium. He listened to her, and she listened to him. He's not sure, but she might like him.

It's a strange feeling to be wanted.

It's a strange feeling to trust someone.

"How fast can this thing go?" she asks.

"Faster than a Volvo," he says.

Jack punches the gas and races up the ramp to Interstate 95. The Camaro's engine bucks and thunders like an unbridled horse. The final remnants of his anger flow from his foot into the accelerator, pushing the muscle car to its limits.

Mattie grasps her armrest. "Now that's what I'm talking about."

Jack swerves between cars. A semi-truck blocks his way for a while. At first chance, he pulls past it at high speed, but a super slow car pulls ahead of him. He slams the brakes. He needs to calm down. He needs to slow down.

He takes the next exit.

"What are you doing?" Mattie asks.

"It's not safe to stay on the highway."

"But it's the fastest way."

"We'll get there before noon." He points to the clock in the dash. "We have over three hours. There're too many cops on the freeway."

"I don't like it."

"I know, but if we get stopped, we'll never make it in

time."

He heads east until the suburban homes give way to sprawling trees and marshy grasslands. He turns south onto a two-lane highway, pacing the Camaro just over the speed limit.

"Can't you go faster now?" she asks.

"Hey, what's that?" Something is crossing the road in the distance.

"I don't know. I guess it's too bad Calvin is gone. He had incredible eyesight."

"No, you did the right thing. He was starting to be too scared of everything. Loose lips sink ships."

She leans forward. Peers out the windshield. "Oh, I see it. Yeah, he was scared of everything. Especially those."

"Those what?"

"Up ahead. That's an armadillo crossing the road."

"Oh."

"No, wait." She almost presses her nose against the glass.

"What?"

"Make that two armadillos crossing the road. Maybe three."

CHAPTER FORTY-NINE

Mid-afternoon in Matanzas, and the streets are covered in blood. It's a massacre. Ah, but that is a lie. Not all the streets are covered in blood. Only this alley. And not the entire alley. Only this puddle.

Dmitri squats over the puddle.

The rain stopped an hour ago.

A drop of blood falls into the puddle.

He's suffering a nosebleed.

He looks up.

They're coming for him.

He runs to the street. Cars stream down the road, bouncing, jerking, and splashing over the potholes. He searches for the black panel van. The Red Star Society. The men who will one day fill the streets with blood, not just the puddles.

But not these streets. Not at first.

Havana will be first.

Dmitri left Havana and came to Matanzas. Why?

Was it the crickets in his head? Did they tell him to come

here? Why haven't they left?

Because, he thinks, *he hasn't forgotten the launch code.*

He stares up at the sky. The gray rainclouds move as if they're trying to escape. Everyone knows the clouds emptied on Matanzas an hour ago. They won't get away with it. They rained, and now they're running away, and everybody is wet.

Dmitri doesn't know why he's in Matanzas.

His brain feels like a wind-worn wheat field, drying in the sun, turning deep shades of yellow and brown. He has sand in his pocket. Days it took him. It's coming back now. It took him days to hike here.

He steps back into the alley, puts his back against the wall, and squats down. He lets his hands fall between his knees and closes his eyes. He can meditate. He can stop the imaginary wheat field wind, but he can't stop the crickets chirping. There must be some reason he left Havana and came to Matanzas.

A ship in the bay blows its horn. It must be a large ship because the Matanzas Bay is far away. The clouds don't care. They're still trying to get away with rain.

With his eyes closed, Dmitri doesn't even know if the clouds still hang in the sky. He has sand in both pockets. Flashes of the ocean and beachfront fire pits shoot through his conscience. He walked to Matanzas from Havana along the coast. He slept on the beach every night. He had to leave Havana because the Red Star Society had finally found him. *They* weren't supposed to find him, but their new leader is relentless. He had to leave because Carlos told him to. But that's not true. Carlos left years ago.

Dmitri closes his eyes tighter. He strains. Every joint in his body aches.

The new leader of the Red Star Society is real. That man will stop at nothing to have the number. That's why . . . that's why . . . what?

The number. The launch code. It's on the leg of that baby girl.

Joy fills his heart.

He remembered.

Dmitri actually remembered something, and it was something important, and it was something in the past. It's not now. He can picture the tattoo. He remembers being free to die after sending the baby girl to the US. It's wonderful. They can't take his memories away after all.

He lets the wheat field in his brain expand, and his memories blow backward over time. It's like breathing into a balloon, but he has plenty of air. It's as if the crickets are sleeping.

He came to Matanzas to see his daughters because they work here, but they don't work here anymore, do they? No. They worked here ten years ago. It's 2008 now. Or, 2009. Or—it doesn't matter. They're dead, and it's his fault. He should have killed himself a year ago when he put the launch code on the baby girl's leg.

But, he couldn't forget the code. The crickets wouldn't let him.

He put the code on the girl so he could die and trick the Red Star Society into thinking the code and the missile's location had died with him. Then, they would have stopped killing everyone he loved.

Ah, but he couldn't do it. He let himself live, and because of that, his daughters are dead now.

His grandchildren are dead now.

The Red Star Society, with their new leader . . . they're killing everyone.

Something squeaks. Toenails tap on the pavement.

Dmitri has a strong urge to run. He wants to stand up and run. *They're* coming after him. He opens his eyes. A rat stares at him from across the alley. The hideous thing rises onto its haunches and holds its paws to its chest. Its fur is wet. Its eyes are black beads. Its eyes look like fish eggs, and Dmitri is hungry, and *they're* coming for him.

He stands. His body aches too much to run, but he moves as fast as he can. He charges toward the other end of the alley. Toward a brick wall.

They won't find him, but—his memories. They're still there. A much as he's tried, he can't forget. He can't forget the code. The launch code. Because of this, the Red Star Society has killed everyone he ever loved, but—

No they haven't.

Not everyone.

The baby girl's name was Lucía. She'd be two years old now, and she's alive. She's got to still be alive. She was adopted according to his plan. He remembers his plan. She lives with her family in the US. She has the code now, not him. Ten digits. Eight tattooed on the back of one leg, the remaining two tucked away elsewhere. That was Dmitri's mistake. He should have had all the digits put on her hip, but hiding them there had been a second thought.

Yet, she is safe, and he loves her, and the code is her burden now, not his.

So, why is he still running?

Because, even if he could forget the code, they still think he knows it. And he does know it. He can't let them have it. Damn his mind. Damn his memory. Damn the crickets. The plan with the baby girl didn't work because he can't forget. Why can't he forget? Oh no, he's forgotten why he can't forget.

His chest aches. He's walking too fast. He slows down to catch his breath. The end of the alley is up ahead. It's a dead end. The clouds continue to scramble across the sky. Some of them have changed from a pale gray to a bright white. Disguises won't help. Everyone knows they were responsible for the rain. The Red Star Society could be approaching from behind, so Dmitri keeps moving. He keeps walking toward the dead end.

The Red Star Society has killed everyone he ever loved.

No they haven't.

Not everyone.

Carlos, his long-time friend. He must have made it to the US by now. Years ago, Carlos didn't believe the Red Star Society had taken over where the Black Crickets had left off. He'd tried to help Dmitri. He'd told Dmitri to visit his daughters in Matanzas. He was a good friend, but Dmitri didn't listen.

No.

Dmitri did listen.

He listened last week, and that is why he's here.

Oh, no. It's happened again.

It must have been 1990 when Carlos told Dmitri to come to Matanzas. Not last week. Not 2008. Not now.

Dmitri's memories keep overriding his realities.

Where are his daughters now?

His brain swims. The back of his throat swells. He tells himself to think in the past and stay in the present. He repeats this until real memories tumble out of his thoughts. He does his best to see his life in chronological order.

And he tells himself that what he sees is not now.

It was then.

He had a son before he had his daughters. Ana gave birth

to his son before Klara and Kamilla came along. His son played with Carlos's son in the countryside where Ana and Dmitri lived. His son went to the US. Carlos's son also went to the US. Carlos said so. Then, years later, Carlos tried to go to the US. Dmitri doesn't know if he made it.

Not everyone is dead.

Dmitri doesn't think his son or Carlos is dead.

Not yet.

He keeps moving toward the end of the alley. His breathing is easier now. His brain continues to unravel his past. His life isn't exactly flashing before his eyes, but it's not far from it.

Before he married Ana, he was in the Black Cricket's prison. They wanted the code to launch the missile, but he wouldn't give it to them. Carlos rescued him from that prison. What a good friend Carlos was.

No.

Carlos *is*.

Dmitri rubs his fingertips together as he continues down the alley. He remembers how the wire felt when he held it in his hand. The wire he used to connect the missile to the control panel. He remembers typing the number—the number he made up—into the panel and setting it as the launch code. Youthful rebellion. When they sent him to Cuba in 1962 after receiving his degree in engineering, he didn't know he'd be installing nuclear missiles aimed at the US. He thought if he could sabotage one missile, maybe they'd think all the missiles were defective. Maybe he could stop world annihilation.

Youthful ignorance.

His father's pride had lifted the orchids outside the church of the Sign of the Blessed Virgin when Mother Russia selected Dmitri to go to Cuba. The memory of walking with his father outside the church kept Dmitri sane during his prison years. Most of the 1960s. He remembers how the Black Crickets had taken his freedom then, but he hadn't allowed them to take his childhood memories.

They can't take his memories.

Ah, but they have.

Just last week, he thought it was 1990.

No.

They didn't take his memories, but they—

They haven't taken his memories, but they did take his mind. He's losing it, and he knows it. The crickets agree, jumping throughout the wheat field in his mind.

Dmitri stretches his arms out wide. He continues toward the brick wall at the end of the alley, his chin held high.

The new leader of the Red Star Society will find him in Matanzas. If not, the leader will eventually find Dmitri's son in the US and kill him. The leader will find Carlos and Carlos's son, and if he hasn't already, he will kill them. He'll stop at nothing to have the code. It's not likely he will find the baby girl Lucía, but if he does, he'll have the code. But will he get it all? Will he discover the two-digits on her hip? Either way, he will eventually kill her and everyone around her.

Dmitri takes no solace in attempting to save the world by having hidden the code. In doing so, he allowed the Red Star Society to kill his family. And, his dearest friend.

What a good friend Carlos was.

No.

Carlos *is*.

Carlos must still be alive.

But if Dmitri doesn't find the strength to kill himself soon . . . every last person he ever loved *will* be dead.

If the new leader gets the launch code, everyone in the world will die.

Dmitri comes to the end of the alley, his arms still outstretched.

He walks up to the wall and presses his chest against it.

The brick is cool on his cheek.

His head angles upward.

The clouds are gone.

It appears they got away with raining on everyone after all.

CHAPTER FIFTY

YANS

"Why don't you kill me now?" Yans asks.

"You have a lovely family." One of the Red Star Society guards stands next to a closed garage door just behind Yans. "Especially that little boy. Little Tomás."

The wooden, three-legged stool beneath Yans has stability problems. If he leans too far in any direction, the stool threatens to fall over. These men—these babies—bound his hands behind his back, sat him down, and removed his blindfold only moments ago. If they're planning on taking over the Red Star Society, they should just kill him now. He won't let go of his leadership responsibilities easily or at all. It doesn't matter what they've planned. They left his sister bleeding in the driveway of her mansion yesterday, but Yans has kept his temper in check. He is still their leader. He will continue to be their leader.

This coup will fail.

"I don't recognize this facility," Yans says, looking around. "Is this a warehouse? No one told me about this place."

"There's a lot you do not know," says the older man.

"There's more *you* don't know," Yans tells him. "Or realize."

High above, the only windows in the warehouse let the morning light shine inside. The windows run in a single row just below the ceiling, keeping most of the light from reaching Yans and these corrupt Red Star men. They breathe in the shadows. Two young guards stand on either side of the garage door. It's connected to a garage door opener. A luxury not seen in most facilities. The older man wears clean Red Star fatigues and stands within spitting distance of Yans. Of course, Yans would never spit on the man. He'd kill him for his insolence, but he'd never spit on him.

The man holds an AK-47 above his round belly. He has a flabby chin. He's a less than stellar representative of the Red Star Society. Gray and black whiskers bespeckle his face, and his sun-drenched forehead exhibits deep wrinkles. Copper-colored canyons and crevasses forged by time. Yans saw him at least once before, but never talked to him. As the leader of the Red Star Society—soon to be the leader of Cuba—Yans hasn't had time to talk to everyone. It just wasn't possible.

"We know about the nuclear missile," the man says.

"Everyone has known about the missile for quite some time." Yans lifts his chin. Squares his shoulders. "Who are you?"

"You know me. I am Ramon Acosta."

"Of course. Of course. I remember you now, Ramon." He doesn't remember him. Yans shifts his weight toward the front of the stool. "Could you free my hands? It will make the conversation easier."

"No." Ramon speaks with confidence. "We cannot trust you. Not after what you did to Ernesto and his son."

"I believe they are vacationing in the countryside."

"We know. They're near Guanajay. We also know they're on a *permanent* vacation."

They shouldn't know that.

"We also know where the nuclear missile is located."

They absolutely shouldn't know that. "I'm not surprised." Yans shifts his attention to one of the guards. "Did you think I'd be surprised?"

"We also know you have found the launch code on a girl in the US."

They absolutely, definitely, without a doubt, should not know that. They must have gotten to Darien. It's his men in the US who have Lucía. He knows where the missile is located. He's been talking. The *idiota*.

"When the girl arrives in Cuba"—Ramon clasps his hands behind his back, turns, and circles Yans—"we want you to launch the missile. One thing you do not know . . . we have been stockpiling radiation suits for months. After the launch, we will occupy Florida."

"You fools." Yans struggles, but he must keep his temper in check. "You'll never take over the US this way. The world will condemn us."

"We only want Florida."

"Florida?" Yans's anger vanishes. He laughs uncontrollably. "Florida?" He can't help it. He laughs wildly. "Have you been to Florida?"

"No, I haven't."

Yans hasn't laughed like this in years. "You can't be serious. At least attempt to take New York. Or Virginia." He howls. "Florida? *¡Ay, dios mio!*"

Ramon stops circling Yans and stands directly in front of him. He wears a stupid grimace like he doesn't understand.

"Florida is probably the most worthless place to occupy." Yans catches his breath. "*Maine* would be better."

"We're occupying Florida so we will have real negotiating power. The missile is not enough unless we use it. The US has never taken us at our word. This time, we're starting with action."

"We don't need to attack anyone." Yans rocks the stool forward toward Ramon. "The missile and the launch code will be enough. No one needs to die."

"We've waited over sixty years since the revolution. The world will listen to Cuba."

"The world will retaliate. They'll destroy us."

"This is where you're wrong."

"Yeah," a guard says. "You're wrong."

"Be quiet," Ramon says.

Yans can't remove the smile from his face. He's still thinking about Florida. Worthless swamplands and decrepit old people. Alligators and armadillos. He winks at Ramon. "Hard to find good help, isn't it? I suppose you're the new leader."

"I'm not taking over. We want you to launch the missile, and we want you to continue as our leader."

Yans should have expected this. He thought it was a coup, but it is not. They recognize his power. Of course they do. Why would they have ever wanted someone else to lead Cuba? It's his destiny. But if he is the man behind a nuclear strike, the world will condemn him. Not them.

"I will not do it," Yans says.

"We think you will." Ramon waves his hand.

One of the guards crosses the room and disappears down a long aisle.

"Florida . . ." Yans mutters. Tears from his laughter still

stream down his cheeks.

"You may not like Florida, but the US will want it back. We don't want to keep it. We want to bargain with it—use it to join the world economy and prosper. Once and for all." Ramon eyes Yans. "Castro never had the courage."

"Take that back." The heat of his ancestry rises up his neck.

The guard returns.

"*Tío. ¡Tío* Yans!" Tomás calls for his uncle.

The guard pulls Tomás along by his shirt collar. He's dragging the future of Cuba by his shirt collar. Yans's nephew has a bruise on his cheek, and he's stumbling down the aisle at the hands of this—

Yans leans forward hard, stands, and charges Ramon. The stool shoots out behind him, slamming against the garage door. Bent over and hustling, his hands bound behind his back, Yans buries his head in the man's round belly. They tumble to the floor. Yans kicks his way onto Ramon's chest and sinks his teeth into that flabby chin. It tastes like a saltless fried egg.

Ramon yells in pain.

A guard pulls Yans off him.

Ramon stands. He puts his hand over the wound. His body shakes. "You bit me." Blood runs down his neck.

"Let Tomás go, or I'll kill you."

Yans tries to rush Ramon again, but the guards now have him by both arms. He gnashes his teeth. He spits on Ramon. The guards pull him back. Ramon's blood runs over his lips.

"You will launch the missile as the leader of the Red Star Society, or we will kill your nephew." Ramon wipes his bloody hand off on his uniform. Slob.

"No. I won't do it."

"*Tío*," Tomás implores him. "Help me."

"Your sister is already dead," Ramon tells Yans. "She bled out on her driveway."

Tomás turns red. Tears explode from his eyes. He cries out, "*¡Mamá!*"

Yans stops struggling. He stands up straight. He puts his chest out and holds his chin up. He is a Rivero. They cannot do this to a Rivero. "I will not launch the missile."

"Please, reconsider. Your nephew won't be next. He'll be last. We'll murder his sisters next. Then your relatives in Santa Clara. Then—"

"Let him go."

"When we're finished, there won't be a Rivero left alive in Cuba. They'll be extinct."

"Let him go now, or suffer the consequences."

Ramon waves his hand.

The guard pulls Tomás back down the aisle.

"*Tío!*" cries the boy.

"It will be okay, Tomás," Yans calls after him. "I won't let them hurt you anymore."

"What says you?" Ramon asks.

"If I agree to launch the missile, my family will die when the world retaliates. You have nothing to offer me. Let my nephew go and allow me to negotiate with the US as planned. The threat of a nuclear war is all we need. We don't need to start one.

"You're wrong," Ramon says.

"Yeah." One of the guards jerks Yans's arm. "You're wrong."

"Listen to me." Yans clears his throat. He coughs up some of Ramon's chin. "No one ever needs to know you did this. I will tell everyone my sister went on vacation. Let me and my nephew go, and this never happened."

"We not only stockpiled radiation suits for the attack, we have filled multiple fallout shelters with food and supplies. As the new leader of Cuba, you and your family would be protected from the world's retaliation. We will give you one of the shelters."

The guards force Yans back onto the stool. This is not defeat. It's a choice. Family outweighs everything and everyone. Millions may die at the hands of these imbeciles, but the Riveros must live on. Yans does not come from a worthless lineage like that crazy man, Dmitri Belkin. The first bearer of the launch code. That man deserved to have his entire family killed.

The world deserves to have the Riveros live on.

"Still not convinced?" Ramon asks.

"No."

"If you force us to kill your family, we'll kill you last, and we'll launch the missile anyway. You don't have a choice."

"Let Tomás go, now."

"We'll let you go, but we're keeping your nephew until after the missile strike."

Millions will die at the hands of these imbeciles, but not the Riveros. To be specific—millions of Floridians will die. That's not such a bad thing. Worthless Floridians. There is a chance the world will not let the US retaliate. A chance Cuba could come away from this and prosper the way Japan did after World War II.

Yans has never liked chance, but it's all he's got.

"I'll do it." He stands. "Like you said, I have no choice. Now let me go."

CHAPTER FIFTY-ONE

Jack hovers the Camaro around ninety miles per hour. Mattie will yell at him again if he slows down, but maybe the armadillo in the distance has forced her to reconsider the rush.

The armadillo moves onto the road from the right, heading for the center line. Three more follow behind it.

Jack speeds up.

"Slow down," she says. She puts her hand on Jack's shoulder. "Don't hit it."

"I can steer clear." Jack crosses the center line. As far as he can see, the oncoming lane is clear. Just a few more seconds, and he'll pass the armadillos.

"No." She digs her nails into his shoulder. "Look—they're coming from the other side, too."

Ten. Fifteen. Too many to count. A barrage of shimmering, armored bodies rush onto the left side of the road like a river, their plating glinting in the sun like a million tiny mirrors. He's never seen a pack of armadillos move so fast. He's never seen a *pack* of armadillos, period. He makes the half-second decision to hit the six armadillos on the right side of the road, but they've multiplied also.

The road is a scaly sea of beady eyes and pointy ears.

Suddenly, they disappear in darkness.

Random shadows cover the road.

A flock of birds has decided to join the action. They fly overhead, blocking out the sun.

Jack hits the brakes.

Mattie screams. She braces herself by grasping the dashboard with both hands.

The Camaro swerves sideways and slides toward the horde. Jack looks out the driver's side window. He's parallel with the animals. The tires squeal. The birds fly past the chaos, and the armadillos begin flipping into balls. They look like bowling balls.

Something goes *bang* against the undercarriage.

Another *bang*.

And another.

The front end finds traction and noses toward the side of the road.

Jack spins the wheel, choosing to travel off-road and down an embankment over hitting the ever-piling armadillo balls. He almost makes it. His front tire explodes just before the Camaro leaps down the embankment. They spin sideways, sliding on the grass. At the bottom, the Camaro tips up on Jack's side. Mattie's seatbelt keeps her from falling onto him. The earth holds still for a moment, and then the Camaro falls back onto its wheels with a *crash*, bouncing Mattie. She touches her forehead. The windshield is cracked. She's checking for blood, but none exists. Only a bruise.

"Are you okay?" Jack asks.

"I'm fine."

She opens her door.

Jack tries to open his, but it's jammed shut. The hood is completely crumpled. His beautiful Camaro . . . it's destroyed. This gully is the end. The final resting place for his proud machine.

"Are you coming?" Mattie leans over the passenger seat and offers her hand to Jack. "We've got to keep going."

He climbs out her side. His head is still spinning. He gazes up the hill to the road. A lone armadillo unballs itself and walks away.

"Did you see that?" Jack asks.

"How could I miss it?" She trudges up the hill.

"I mean . . . there were so many of them."

"Calvin warned me." She reaches the road and puts her hand on her hip. Uses her other hand to shield her eyes from the sun. "I think I see a restaurant up ahead."

"Calvin also said something to me about them once, but who would have believed him? He said something like this happened to his dad, but he was talking crazy."

The armadillos are gone. The live ones, anyway.

Mattie ignores the carnage. She steps over one of the smashed animals as if it were a pothole. She struts past the line of bodies as if they're not there. She can be so cold when she's in a rush.

"Mattie, wait."

"We can get help up ahead," she says. "It looks like a biker bar. Maybe someone can give us a ride."

Jack runs to her. Grabs her arm. "Are you sure you're okay?"

She whips around and pulls her arm away. "I don't want to talk about it." She has tears in her eyes. "Calvin can never know this happened to us. We can't give him the satisfaction. It's too . . . too . . ."

"Ridiculous?"

"No." Her face crumbles. "Tragic." She points at the dead armadillos. "I should have listened to him. You were right. I should never have let him go. With his bird-like eyesight, he could have seen them in time and warned us. Look at this." She bites her upper lip. "They're dead. They're all dead because of me. I'm an animal killer. Wherever I go, I end up killing animals."

"That's ridiculous." Jack hugs her. Holds her tight. "This whole thing is ridiculous. You couldn't have known. Nothing about this makes *any* sense. Armadillos don't travel in packs."

"But I did know. I just didn't believe him." She pulls away, sniffs, and wipes her face.

"No one would have believed him," Jack says. "No one in their right mind would ever have believed him. You're not an animal killer."

She turns and heads for the biker bar. "We're wasting time." She moves fast. "I want a cigarette."

"You don't smoke."

He glances over his shoulder. Steam rises out of the gully. His car is dead. He catches up to her and walks beside her, not knowing what else to say. He hugged her, but he's unsure whether she hugged him back. It happened so fast. He wasn't paying attention.

He doesn't know how to help.

Like something out of a sixties B movie, a long line of motorcycles guards the entrance of an obvious biker bar. Timber siding on Old West architecture. A wooden platform with poles supporting an awning that spans the roof beneath a sign reading, FULL THROTTLE SALOON. As they draw near, rock music mixed with howls and hysterics blares over a pair of old-timey batwing saloon doors. "Back in Black" by

AC/DC. One of his favorites. It's not even noon yet, but Jack supposes it's five o'clock somewhere.

"So, which one will it be?" she asks.

"What do you mean?"

"Which motorcycle should we take?"

CHAPTER FIFTY-TWO

MATTIE

Several motorcycles in front of the Full Throttle Saloon have only one seat. These won't work. Worse, most of the seats have no cushioning—leather on metal—and most of the bikes have no windshield. The one at the end of the row, though, has large saddle bags and a raised, cushioned seat for a second passenger. It's different. I like it. I wasn't paying attention to the brands when I walked by, but this one appears to be the only Honda.

"We can't steal a motorcycle," Jack says. He stands near the entrance.

"Why not?" I ask. "We're running out of time. We've got to go to Miami and find that port before noon. That's what the creepy old Cuban guy from the strip club said. We only have until noon."

"Do you know how to hot-wire a motorcycle?"

"Jack, please. We've got to go."

He shakes his head. Some private investigator he is. He doesn't even know how to hot-wire a motorcycle.

I'm not letting those Latinos take Lucía to Cuba.

"C'mon," I say.

He takes hold of my elbow and stops me from entering the saloon. "Where are you going?"

Some horrible rock song from the 1980s blares out the entrance between the quaint batwing saloon doors, and the stench of beer and sweat follows it. I've always thought the combination of beer and sweat is what testosterone must smell like.

And then there's the smell of smoke. Cigarette smoke. I want a cigarette. I thought I was over it, but . . . I'm going to get a contact high when I go in here. That will have to be enough. As good as it smells, I'm not starting again. Or am I?

God, I want a cigarette.

I pull my arm free of Jack's grasp. "If you won't steal a motorcycle, you will have to buy one. I'm going inside to find a seller."

"Hold on. I'm not buying a—"

"I know you have enough cash for one, or at least enough for a down payment. Expense it to your client. Make him reimburse you. I don't care." I throw the doors open and barge inside, shouting over my shoulder so Jack can hear me. "We don't have time to argue about this."

My eyes adjust to the light. Neon beer signs run along the ceiling and above the bar, casting a dismal but colorful glow on the walls. Faded posters hang everywhere. Denim-vested men stand in groups, their tattered clothes covered in patches and pins. The floor is sticky and littered with empty beer bottles, bent bottle caps, and nasty cigarette butts. I slow down and stroll toward the two pool tables in the corner. I can't believe these guys are allowed to smoke in here, but they have that rebellious attitude on their faces. They think they can do whatever they want because they know how to drive things with two wheels.

I think they're ridiculous.

"Wait," Jack says. He's hot on my heels, murmuring urgently into my ear. "We shouldn't be in here."

"I'm not leaving without a ride to Miami."

"They're all looking at us."

He's not wrong. It's not like I'm so beautiful that men stare at me when I walk into a room, but they often look. I'm used to it. It happens to women all the time, especially in places like this. But again, Jack's not wrong. An abnormal amount of eyes are upon us. It's not because I'm good-looking. It's because we're not members of their little club.

The song ends, and a biker walks over to the jukebox. He glances at us before turning around and pulling his wallet out of his back pocket. It's chained to his belt loop, and a set of keys dangle from it. He feeds a few bills into the machine and punches the buttons. An empty dance floor separates the jukebox from a makeshift stage. A chalkboard sign reads, TUESDAY NIGHT: MACK AND THE MURDERERS.

I bet their music is delightful.

The biker turns around and leans against the jukebox. He crosses his legs and relaxes his shoulders. Metallica's "Fuel" begins to play. He makes eye contact with me and tips his head back, encouraging me to join him. He's taller than Jack, but his pencil frame says he weighs less than me. He's got patchy, auburn facial hair and a Confederate flag on his cap. Grease stains mark the knees of his jeans. His boots are made of black leather. They're the kind of boots people wear on motorcycles.

My eyes are drawn back to the keyring hanging from his wallet chain. Keys. The chain hangs sloppily, one end clipped to his belt loop.

"That's our guy," I say.

"Hey, baby." The biker rubs the knuckles of his right hand on his vest. "How you doing?" He completely ignores the man at my side. I'm so glad Jack is here.

"What kind of motorcycle do you have?" I ask.

"So personal, already?" He grins. He looks me up and down. "What kind of caboose do you have?" He eases off the jukebox, leans to the right, and eyes my ass. He's repellent, yet I'm still pleased he seems to approve. "My name's Teddy. What's yours?"

I glance around the room. Just as I thought. I'm the only woman here.

"We need a bike," Jack says. "I'm willing to pay you to borrow it. We can return it tomorrow."

Teddy keeps his eyes on me. "You got a cigarette?"

"No. I quit last week."

"How about you start again?"

Jack pulls his wallet out. It's thick. He's paid cash nearly everywhere we've been since he started expensing things to his client. For some reason, I think he doesn't want to be traced, but I wouldn't know why. He could probably buy Teddy's motorcycle, but if he wants to rent it, more power to him.

Jack pulls some bills out of his wallet and holds them out to Teddy. "Is this enough?"

"Wait, Jack." I push the money away from Teddy. "What kind of motorcycle do you have? It's not one of those with a single seat, is it?"

"No." Teddy steps closer to me. "I've got a great big one with room for two, if you know what I mean. How about we dance while Dad here goes and gets us a pack of cigarettes?"

A smoke does sound good.

Jack returns the bills to his wallet and folds it closed.

Oh, no.

He's got that look on his face.

I can barely see the bulge in his waistline, but it's there. He's got his gun with him, and he's getting angry. He doesn't like Teddy.

"A great big one with room for two?" I ask.

"Oh, yeah . . ."

I touch Teddy's shoulder and give Jack a wink. "Tell me more about it. Is it a Honda?"

"God, no." He takes a step back. "Oh hell, no."

"I saw a Honda out there. Is it that one?"

"I told you hell *no.* I ride a '82 Harley FXB Sturgis Shovelhead with a smokin' V-Twin and mag wheels. I'm not a poser."

At the risk of losing what little I have left of my breakfast, I move in close to him. I press my hips against his. I hold my breath, expecting the worst, but he actually doesn't smell bad. "I've never danced to Metallica. Is it even possible?"

"It's more than possible, baby."

I pull him by a belt loop onto the dance floor. "Will you give me fuel?"

"Oh, baby." He jerks his body up and down to the music. And I thought I was a bad dancer. "I'll give you *fire.*"

"Will you give me that which I desire?"

"You know it!" He bumps his crotch into my stomach, tips his head back, and howls. "*Woo hoo!*"

I grab his keys and pull on them as hard as I can. The chain yanks the wallet out of his pocket, and I keep pulling, but the chain won't break. His belt loop won't break. I jerk on it again and throw him off balance. As he staggers, Jack knocks him onto the floor. Teddy tries to catch himself, but his hands splay wide, and his head hits an empty beer bottle, sending it spinning toward the bar.

Teddy rolls onto his back just in time for Jack to jump on him and straddle his chest.

I think I heard a rib crack.

Jack lifts Teddy's head off the floor by his collar and punches him in the face.

The other bikers are gawking and shouting at Jack, but nobody's trying to stop what's happening. They seem to be enjoying the show.

I still have a hold on the keys, and I yank on the chain, and the belt loop gives way. His wallet flies into the air and slaps me in the face.

Jack punches him again.

I run outside.

What the hell does a Sturgis Harley look like?

Three of the motorcycles have a Confederate flag sticking up from their back seats. The key doesn't fit in the first one.

Jack comes running out of the saloon. "That one." He scrambles down the steps and beats me to a midnight black bike with two seats. "Over here."

I throw the wallet-chain-key mess to him, and he catches it in both hands as he throws one leg over the bike.

"I was going to try that one next," I say. It has a flag.

Jack sticks the key in the ignition. It fits. He jumps on and starts the engine.

Teddy and two of his buddies rush out of the bar.

I hop on the back and wrap my arms around Jack. He's so solid.

He hits the gas, and the back tire throws dirt in Teddy's face.

We head out on the highway.

The motorcycle is so fast.

The wind holds my hair back and fills my lungs. It's fresh, cool, and comforting. I'll never want a cigarette again. Not when I can breathe like this.

I hold Jack tight against my chest.

Teddy's wallet dangles on the chain hanging from the ignition. It bounces on the pavement as we rocket toward Miami. It's not nearly as thick as Jack's wallet.

CHAPTER FIFTY-THREE

Kindness comes in many forms. Sometimes, it's a loving touch to a person's cheek. Other times, it's a simple, well-timed "Thank you."

Last night, it came in the form of a hot dog.

After the Cubans went to the Marlins game, their leader returned with a hot dog. It had ketchup on it. Kindness always feels stronger on the heels of pain and suffering, and Lucía's stomach had been on the verge of exploding. He brought her a pretzel, also. One of those big ones with giant chunks of salt. He fed her. He held her hair out of her face while she ate.

He was kind.

But, if he were truly kind, he would have let her go.

On the bright side, if they're willing to feed her, maybe they won't kill her. She'd thought they were going to sell her to someone—to some sex fiend—but when they didn't, paranoia took hold. She imagined being shot in the head execution-style in an abandoned warehouse. She was very tired at the time, right before the leader fed her. The food put her to sleep. Fast asleep. Dead asleep. Hours must have passed by because she feels so much better now. Her torn-up rib cage is healing, her head is no longer throbbing, and her heart is filled with hope.

Her lips are cracked, and her mouth is a desert, but other than that, she's stronger than she's been in days.

Her heart is filled with hope.

The back doors of the van open, and the leader stands there, blocking most of the bright sunlight. "We're here."

Lucía leans forward and tries to see around him.

He motions for her to come to him.

He didn't close the doors.

He's taking her outside.

This could be her chance.

She steps out of the van, her hands zip-tied behind her back. The air reminds her of a trip to the beach when she was eight years old. It had been a Disney World vacation, but they spent one day on the sand. The briny air stung her nose then, and it stings it now. Her sinuses are raw from tears draining into her throat. She's thirsty. Birds cry overhead. Waves crash below. A path runs down a short hill, ending at a dock. A boat big enough for several people bobs up and down with the waves. She knows it can carry several people because it *is* carrying several people.

Oh, no.

Everyone on the boat stops moving when they see her.

Her heart sinks.

They're waiting for her.

The paranoia returns.

They're taking her out to sea so they can—

The leader snips her zip tie, and her hands spring free from behind her back.

She turns to face him. Maybe he'll be kind. Maybe he'll

change his mind and let her go. Maybe he won't put her on that boat, kill her, and dump her body in the ocean. Maybe he won't, but she doesn't want to find out.

The doors to the van behind him hang open. Behind the van, shacks constructed from a patchwork of rusted scrap metal and splintered wooden pallets litter a hill. Some large, some small, but all ugly. Patches of worn and stained carpet are nailed over the openings for doors and windows. The occupants don't seem to be home, or they're hiding.

"That way." The leader points at the boat below.

"Please, don't do this."

His phone rings. He grasps her wrist and squeezes it so tight that she almost yells. He holds onto her while putting the phone to his ear.

"*Hola. . . sí*, Darien. *Buena . . . medianoche* . . . La Boca . . . *Sí. Sí . . . ¿mal tiempo?*"

He gazes up at the sky.

Lucía kicks him in the shin as hard as she can and rips her arm away.

He drops the phone and shouts something in Spanish while she sprints along the van's driver's side. She must run fast, but the hill is steeper than it looked. She must hide somewhere. She must make it to one of those shacks.

Her mind is quick.

Quicker than her feet.

She plans to run inside the nearest shack and immediately out the other side. Then, she'll turn left and run as far as possible before the leader catches up and spots her. With some luck, she can duck into another shack and hide under something. There should be blankets or boxes or something she can hide under.

She nears the front of the van, and the driver's side door

opens.

The Cuban she fears most—The Breather—steps out and wraps his arms around her.

She screams in his face.

When she runs out of air, he screams back in her face and laughs maniacally.

"Stop it," the leader says.

He pulls Lucía away from the monster.

"Let me go!" she screams.

"Don't try that again." His voice is eerily calm. "We're just going for a little boat ride. No one's going to hurt you."

He has kind eyes.

But he's not kind.

If he were truly kind, he'd let her go.

CHAPTER FIFTY-FOUR

YANS

Time drags on.

It always does this when nothing can be done. Yans sits on the wooden, three-legged stool, waiting for someone to come for him. Ramon left the warehouse an hour ago, but the two Red Star Society guards stayed. They stand watch by the garage door.

Yans sat on the stool all night with his hands bound behind his back, and he waited. Ramon forced him to give his word. He will launch a nuclear attack. Then, Ramon left, and now . . . Yans waits.

Somewhere, on the other side of the warehouse, hidden away, they have Tomás. Yans will save his nephew by starting a war with the world. He *will* do it. He gave Ramon his word, and he *will* honor his word. All he needs is the launch code. He needs Darien's men to deliver Lucía.

He needs to leave here. The idleness is killing him.

A faint moaning floats down the aisle. It could be poor Tomás.

Yans lowers his chin to his chest.

It could be the ghost of Dmitri Belkin.

Too much idle time causes evil things to happen. Things like regret. Regret serves no one. Regret is a weed crawling up the tree of *now* in an attempt to strangle the future. Yans believes in this truth, yet he wishes he'd found Dmitri sooner. One month sooner, and none of this would be happening. Darien's men would have found Lucía one month sooner. He would already have negotiated with the US, and New Cuba would have become his.

One month sooner, and he wouldn't have agreed to start World War III.

The moaning comes again, and it is painful. It might not be coming from within the warehouse. It might only be in Yans's head. He regrets relaxing at his sister's mansion yesterday.

He regrets it, and he waits.

He listens to the faint moan of time.

Time drags on.

Finally, the garage door opener comes to life, and the door slides upward, releasing an ear-splitting whine. Someone needs to oil those rails.

A guard pulls out his pistol and points it at Yans.

The other guard snips Yans's zip tie.

He wrings his wrists to ease the pain. Red lines have formed where the tie had dug in.

The garage door stops moving, and one last moan floats down the aisle.

He stands, staring at the guard with the gun.

"Go," the guard says. He waves toward the morning sunlight shining in through the door. "Your man is here with a car."

"May God have mercy on you when this is over," Yans

says.

The guard keeps his gun trained on Yans and follows him outside.

Darien leaps from an SUV and runs to Yans. He pulls his gun out.

"What have they done?" he asks.

"Return to the SUV." Yans glances over his shoulder. The guard is still there.

"Lower your weapon," Darien says. He is aiming his pistol at the guard. "Do you know who this is?"

Yans puts his hand on Darien's wrist and makes him lower his gun. "He knows who I am. We must leave now. Everything is okay now. Get back in the SUV."

Darien cocks his head.

"It's an order, Darien."

Darien stows his weapon and hops in the driver's seat. "Where to?"

"Command."

He glances at Yans's wrists. "What did they do to you?"

"It doesn't matter now."

"If they did anything else . . . I will go back. Let me know who, and I—"

"I know what you did, Darien."

He taps the brakes and steers the SUV around a sharp corner. "Oh."

"Yes. You told them about the missile. You told them about Lucía."

"They already knew."

"They couldn't have known." Yans focuses on keeping his anger at bay. He wants to reprimand the boy, but he needs him. He needs Darien more now than ever. "Think about your conversation with them."

"I swear, they already knew." Darien briefly closes his eyes and shakes his head as if he's reliving the conversation. "They knew."

"Watch the road."

"Sorry."

"They knew the missile existed, and they knew we needed a launch code. Everything else, they assumed. They fooled you. They gave you their assumptions and guesses, and you filled in the blanks."

"I did not mean for that to happen. I am loyal to you, *señor*. You and you only." He spins the steering wheel in the middle of an intersection and makes a U-turn.

"Where are you going?"

"I'm going to make this right." He presses down on the accelerator. "I'm going to make them 'un-know' everything I told them."

"Stop. It's too late. Pull over there."

The exhaustion of sitting on that stool all night hits Yans. His back suddenly aches. The moaning from the warehouse haunts him. His wrists burn. He must launch the missile when he gets the code, and he can't trust Darien. The problem is not Darien's commitment to the Red Star Society. It's his intelligence.

Darien parks the SUV on the side of the street. "What do you want me to do?"

"If this faction of insolent men had not risen up within the Red Star Society and demanded my attention, and you did what you did—you said what you said—to them or anyone, I would have killed you by now." He locks his eyes on Darien's. "You know that, yes?"

"I know," he says, in a boy's voice.

"I need you to be *mi mano derecha*."

"I am your right-hand man."

"They want me to launch the missile without warning. They want to attack Florida."

"Oh." Darien lets out a laugh. "Wait." He wipes the smile off his face. "You're serious. Florida?"

"I know. They're a bunch of buffoons, but that will work in our favor. I attempted to talk them out of the attack, but in the end, I agreed."

Darien puts the SUV in park and shuts the engine off. "You're not going to do it, are you?"

"No."

"That is . . . wait. *No,* you are? Or, *no* you aren't?" His eyes have become bloodshot. He grips the steering wheel as if he's still driving.

"I'm not going to launch the missile."

"I have family in Florida."

"I know. You needn't worry."

Darien ought to worry. His family in Florida must die. Yans gave Ramon his word, and he will honor it. He will not regret this. Yans will preserve the Rivero lineage. Darien's family can go to hell. While Darien's family is suffocating in the mushroom cloud that's become Miami, Yans's family will be eating plantains in a bomb shelter in New Cuba. Everyone in Yans's family except his sister, Suelo, of course. It's okay she died. She fulfilled her womanly duties twelve years ago when she gave birth to Tomás.

"Do you promise?" Darien asks.

"I'm giving you my word. I will not launch the missile. But, I need your help. I need the Red Star Society to believe I will launch it when we receive the code. If you talk to them again, don't listen to what they say. Don't let them trick you."

"I can do that."

"They must believe you."

"They will."

"Where are your men now?"

"Excellent news. They have Lucía on a boat near Miami now." He pulls out his cell phone and taps the screen. "They should be setting off for Cuba anytime, if they haven't left already. They should arrive by midnight."

"Any problems so far?"

"None. Nothing can stop them now."

CHAPTER FIFTY-FIVE

JACK

"We've got to stop them, now." Mattie shouts over the rumble of the motorcycle. She shouts directly into Jack's ear, and it hurts. He eases off the gas. She points over his shoulder. "Look down there. Isn't that her sitting on that boat?"

It is her.

Lucía.

They've finally found her.

She's sitting on the front deck of a boat at the end of a narrow wooden dock.

She's surrounded by the Latinos.

Jack puts the bike in neutral and coasts behind the nearest hovel, getting out of sight as quickly as possible. They've been cruising near the shore, looking for the port, for about half an hour. Several paths lead down this hill, winding between chaotically constructed shanties and ending on a sandy coast. The first path has a dock and a boat at the end. He doesn't know the history of this place, but the top of this hill looks like it houses homeless people. No, that's not quite right. Those haphazard shacks are better than the cardboard and blanket structures he's seen elsewhere. This is not a tent city, but it's not far from it.

He kicks the stand out with his foot and rests the bike on it. *What a thrill ride.* After taking the bike offroad to evade the bikers who chased after him and Mattie, he hit the highway and traveled to Miami at breakneck speed. His heart is still racing. He swings his leg off the bike like James Dean and smooths his hair back. The sensation of riding for the past three hours tingles in the backs of his legs, but it's okay. It's invigorating. He's still pumped. Ready to go. He's ready for a fight, and he's ready for this to be over.

This is his last PI job, and he's going down in a blaze of glory if he must.

Mattie joins him at the end of the shack. Together, they peer around the corner.

"She's just sitting there," Mattie says. "It doesn't look like she's tied up or anything."

Two Latinos stand on the boat's deck next to Lucía. She sits in a chair. They're talking with her. She's waving her hands as she speaks. The man on her left is evil. He's the one who took Jack's gun away in Stanley's trailer.

Jack is going to take more than that away from him.

A black panel van rests on the hill at the end of the path leading to the dock. It looks familiar, but Jack doesn't remember from where. It must belong to the Latinos because there are no other cars around.

"You're right," Jack says. "They don't have her bound and gagged or anything. All I need to do is get her in the water. Are you a good swimmer?"

"That's not a good idea."

She recedes from the corner of the shack and puts her back against the wall. If she leans too hard, Jack's afraid the little building will fall over. He takes her hand and pulls her toward him.

"I'm going down there," he tells her. "I'm going to take them by surprise, but first, I need you to sneak into the water and be ready to catch her."

"What? Are you insane?"

"No. I'll throw her off the bow, and you can swim her to shore."

"Then what?"

"Then, the two of you run like hell."

"What about you?" She splays her hands out wide. "Did you see all those guys? You'll never get to her."

Jack looks around the corner again and counts. Two Latinos sit on the front deck, and five mill about on the sides and back.

"I can do it. I've got my gun."

"Big man with a big gun. They'll stop you, and I'll have to rescue both of you. Or just Lucía, if they kill you."

"Then what do you suggest?"

"I can't believe I'm saying this, but maybe we should call the police now. We've found her."

"No." Jacks shakes his head. "Absolutely not. I'm not going back to jail. Do you want to go to jail?"

"No."

"Trust me. If the police come, they won't do anything about Lucía. They'll arrest us on sight. You stole a car, and you made me steal this motorcycle. They want us, not her."

She gazes at the ground. "I guess you're right."

"You know I'm right. C'mon. Let me do this." He reaches into his waistband and grips his gun. "Please. I *so* want to do this."

"No. There are too many of them. Can you swim? If you

got to her and jumped in the water, could you pull her to shore?"

Jack has never had a lesson in his life. Swimming was a luxury other kids had growing up. Kids whose stepfathers didn't beat their mothers. Kids whose real dads weren't evil like those Latinos down there. Like Stanley Owens. Jack can't wait to rescue Lucía so he can go after Stanley. This is his last PI job, but he has unfinished business. The grip of his gun sends a thrill up his arm. It's go time.

"Jack." Mattie puts her hand on his shoulder. "Are you okay? Do you know how to swim?"

"No."

"Then you'll have to walk her off the boat. That means we need to get rid of them. How about I create a distraction?"

"We don't have time for that. They could take off for Cuba any minute now. They could just ignore you and leave."

"Don't worry." She narrows her eyes and purses her lips. "Do you still have that cigarette lighter?"

CHAPTER FIFTY-SIX

No one has ever described me as a fearful person. Not to my face, anyway. One of the things I like about Jack is that he's never been afraid of me. Not yet anyway.

And, not now.

He hands me his cigarette lighter.

The portrait of Bob Marley on the casing has a scratch.

Live for yourself, and you will live in vain. Live for others, and you will live again.

I live for Lucía. We're saving her today.

"What are you going to do?" Jack asks. "How are you going to distract them?"

I run to the rusted-out oil barrel across the way. It's stuffed with trash. Cardboard, glass shards, broken boards, rusted nails, and—rags. Lots of rags. I grab the blackest one I can find, hoping it's soaked with oil.

"You'll see," I say. "You try to get as close as possible to the boat without being seen and wait for my signal."

"What signal?"

"I don't know. I'll shout *caw-caw* or something."

"Like a bird?"

"Yeah, like a bird. Do you have a problem with that?"

He shakes his head and peers around the corner of the shack toward the ocean. He closes his eyes briefly before breaking into an all-out run. He crosses the path, ducks down, and hides behind a smaller shanty.

I look around the corner at the opposite end. Not much has changed on the boat. Two cowards are talking to Lucía. The others are tying things down and putting chairs away.

They're getting ready to leave.

I've never flown in a helicopter and have no desire to do so, but I have seen how people duck and run to them in the movies. I wonder if it's really necessary to avoid getting sucked up. There's no helicopter here, but I run to the van as if it were one.

I'm in luck.

Not only is the driver's door unlocked, it's cracked open.

I pull the fuel lid lever and slink down the side of the van to the gas hole.

Gas hole?

Is that what these things are called?

Never mind. I don't have time to look it up on Google.

I hold the lighter near the rag.

Bob Marley—don't fail me now.

The rag takes to the flame faster than I thought, and I stuff it down the gas hole.

Gas hole? What the hell is this thing really called?

I run.

Jack had better be near the boat by now.

"Caw, caw," I shout. "Caw, caw!"

I sprint down the hill, waving my arms.

The cowards turn their heads toward me. The ones with

guns raise them and take aim.

"Caw, caw!"

I reach the water's edge and turn around.

The van explodes in a burst of fantastic fire, sending shards of metal and debris across the hillside. The flames spread out, consuming the surrounding grass in an eerie orange glow.

I dive into the water near the boat and swim close to the hull where the gunmen can't see me.

Footsteps hammer down the dock.

I swim to the other side of the boat and find a rope. The climb hurts. My biceps haven't hurt like this since high school gym class, but I'm not stopping. My toes slip on the side as I pull and kick my way onto the deck.

Lucía sits on the chair. She's alone. Why doesn't she run?

Black smoke escapes the van's blown-out windows, rising into the sky. The cowards race around like ants on fire, looking for me.

Jack stands on the shore near the dock. He sees me looking at him, hunches his shoulders, and raises his hands palms up. He's afraid of the water.

"Mattie!" Lucía cries out.

I go to her.

I grasp her arm and pull her up, but the moment she stands, she falls to her knees.

Those cowards tethered her left ankle to a hook with a thick, white rope.

"Jack!" I call out. "Help me."

One of the gunmen hears me and comes sprinting down the hill. He runs past Jack and leaps onto the dock.

Jack runs after him.

I work the knot. The rope won't slip through. Pinching

and pulling, my fingertips lapse into a sharp pain and cease to be effective.

Jack chases the gunman onto the boat, and they disappear behind the enclosed bridge. I can't see them through the windows. I don't know what's happening.

I grip Lucía's ankle and attempt to pull her foot free from the rope.

"Ow!" she shouts.

Jack yells something.

A *crash* comes from behind the bridge.

Punching sounds.

Lucía jerks her leg up and down. She screams, but her foot won't come free.

A gunshot goes off.

I grasp her chin and turn her face toward mine. "It's okay. I'm getting you out of here."

Someone slams me from behind. Rigid arms wrap around my torso. I stumble forward—one step . . . two steps . . . three . . .

My shin hits the railing, and I go over the side of the boat.

Whoever hit me is going to pay for this.

I surface, gasping for air.

The ant cowards stream down the hill and up the dock onto the boat.

Lucía sits down in her chair.

The man Jack chased stands next to her, holding an AK-47 to his chest, watching me.

Bubbles emerge from the water to my side, followed by Jack's head. *Oh my God.* He's the one who knocked me into the water. Now he's splashing around like he's drowning, and I realize he probably *is* drowning. He's sucking in as much water as air.

Bullets fly, hitting the water around us.

I wrap my arm around Jack's neck and pull him underwater.

The gunfire stops, and I struggle to pull Jack toward shore. He keeps trying to surface, but I won't let him. As soon as he can reach the sand with his feet, he breaks free and sticks his head out of the water, gasping desperately for air.

The gunmen on the boat have lost interest in us and are preparing to shove off.

Jack gasps. He looks at me, and I slap him. "Why the hell did you push me into the water? I almost had her free."

"I saved your life."

"No you didn't. You messed it all up. I had to save your life."

"I told you I didn't know how to swim."

The boat's engines start.

We trudge through the shallows to shore.

The boat turns and powers away, leaving a wide wake.

The salty air clings to my lips. The briny water stings my nose. The sight of Lucía growing ever smaller as the boat heads toward the horizon hurts my heart.

"There she goes," Jack says.

A bird flies overhead, and I swear—I'm not kidding—I swear it cries, *Caw-caw.*

"This isn't over," I say. "We're not done."

"I know." He flashes a devious smile at me.

"We can still stop them. We know where they're going, and I'm not afraid of them."

"I know." He grins. "If anything, they should be afraid of you. You know how to make bird sounds."

CHAPTER FIFTY-SEVEN

The sunlight burns Dmitri's eyes when the Red Star Society guard pulls the bag off his head. He tries to shield his face from the sun and wipe the tears away, but they zip-tied his hands behind his back when he let them catch him.

Dmitri glances around. Takes in the scenery.

His heart rattles.

No.

It can't be.

The hill is overgrown. The main building no longer stands by the stairs to the prisoners' cells. Crumbles of concrete peek up from the dense foliage in a line that used to be the main building's back wall.

No.

It can't be.

They've taken him back.

The wind blows dirt in his face, and it feels like crickets crawling. They're going up his nose, trying to find a moist place to hide. The wheat field inside his insane brain has grown thicker. It makes him think he's in places he's not, doing things he can't possibly do. He shakes the crickets off his face, but they were never there. They were nothing more than a feeling. They were never real.

But this place is real.

This place has played host to his nightmares since the Black Crickets imprisoned him here in the 1960s, and it's as real as anything he's ever dreamed. It's as real as anything he's ever seen. He has returned to hell. Yanking himself forward, he screams and leans on his toes and twists his shoulders and shakes violently.

The guard jerks him backward, and he lands on the ground.

The other guard opens the door to hell. The stairs lead downward.

Dmitri kicks his feet and attempts to sit up, but he lacks the abdominal strength to do it with his hands tied behind his back. He rolls onto his side.

"Looks like it'll be easier to carry him down."

"I agree. He can't weigh much."

The guard by the door takes Dmitri's ankles. The other guard picks him up by his armpits. It hurts, but not as bad as the thought of being locked in that cell again.

Dmitri wanted to get caught, but he didn't want this.

Dark patches of moisture stain the concrete walls of the stairwell. The daylight vanishes behind him as the guards carry him below. He kicks and frees his right foot, but the guard quickly regains control. Dmitri's ankle pops. His neck pops. His skin is thin. He has almost no muscle left. Living on the streets, eating out of trash bins, and his age—the crickets sometimes tell him he's still in his twenties, but he must be somewhere north of seventy. If the guards aren't careful, they'll tear him apart, and that would be okay.

It's what he's wanted for a long time.

The ocean refused to take Dmitri's life. Countless times, he attempted to drown himself, but the current kept carrying him to shore. He stood on countless buildings but couldn't bring himself to jump. Twice, the best rope he found broke when he attempted to hang himself. He could never find anyone who would give him drugs or shoot him with a gun, and it wouldn't have worked anyway. His will to live, forged by years spent surviving the mental anguish of the jail cell below, always won.

The guards carry him into the dark.

Knowing he had to die so the world could live hadn't been enough. After tattooing the launch code on the baby girl's leg, Dmitri tried desperately to forget what the numbers were. Sometimes, the crickets would help him forget the code, but then they would tell it to him again as part of some sick game. As long as he knew the code, the world wouldn't be safe. He decided, once again, he must die in order to stop the new leader of the Red Star Society. He decided to make the new leader think the code would be lost forever if Dmitri died, but after so many failed attempts at killing himself, there was only one way. Let the Red Star Society catch him in hopes they'd accidentally kill him before extracting the code from his mind.

It wasn't supposed to be like this.

They weren't supposed to take him here. It's not fair. They were *supposed* to kill him, not imprison him. Not here. Certainly not in the hellhole that dominated his nightmares for the last fifty years.

He screams.

The guards drop him onto the floor of his old home.

Caged lights illuminate the corners of the ceiling. They

weren't here before. Shelves in the back have replaced the iron platform he used as a bed. The shelves are stocked with food, and a man sits on the other side of a table. Gold and silver pins circle the brim of the man's cap. The guards don't have any pins on their caps.

The man must be the leader. The new leader of the Red Star Society.

Dmitri screams again.

The guards prop him up and seat him across from the leader.

The faint scent of mildew and decay lingers in the air. Some of the food on the shelves must have rotted, but it smells good to Dmitri. He's always hungry. As a test, he pushes himself backward with both feet, forcing his chair to slide away from the table. The guards react. One guard shoves Dmitri's seat back under the table, forcing Dmitri's bony chest against the table's edge. The other guard slaps the back of Dmitri's head.

But then, he finds it. Dmitri runs his big toe along a groove in the floor beneath the table.

"I've wanted to speak with you for a long time." The leader sits upright in his seat with his back as straight as a ruler. His gaze is unwavering, and the scar on his cheek demands respect. "Why haven't you wanted to speak to me?"

"I will speak to you now, but not here." Dmitri glances at the floor near the stairwell. The area where he once drew pictures is now covered with dust. His career as a tattoo artist started here. He remembers a sun he drew on the floor. A Russian sun. He glances down at his legs. He's wearing his prison rags. He looks up. The leader has white freckles, like Carlos.

The leader *is* Carlos. Dmitri isn't in his jail cell anymore.

The crickets.

Dmitri *is* in his old jail cell.

The crickets are at it again. It's not 1968. It's . . . it's . . . it's now. Two thousand and something.

"Please," Dmitri says. He's on the brink of tears. "Not here. I'll talk to you anywhere but here."

"You're in no position to negotiate. Tell me what I want to know, and I promise I won't kill you."

"But I want to die."

"I want to know where the missile is located and how to launch it. What is the launch code?"

Dmitri runs his toe along the groove in the floor. He shakes his head.

The leader nods at one of the guards.

The guard puts a pistol to Dmitri's cheek.

"Shoot," Dmitri says. He closes his eyes.

"Tell me where the missile is." The leader's voice rises. "What is the launch code?"

"Shoot me, please."

The leader stands. He waves the guard away. He shoves the table across the room. He steps forward and goes nose-to-nose with Dmitri. His breath smells like *frijoles*. Dmitri is hungry, so he licks the leader's lips.

The leader jerks his head away and seizes Dmitri's neck. He chokes Dmitri.

Death, at last.

"Tell me the launch code," the leader hisses into his face, and releases his hold on Dmitri's throat.

Dmitri gasps for air. "I forgot it. I can't remember it. Take me somewhere else, and I'll tell you."

"You're never leaving here." The leader glances around the room.

Dmitri stares at him.

"Wait a minute," the leader says. "You know this place, don't you?"

Dmitri's heart begins to hammer inside his chest. He trembles.

"Yes," says the leader. "You were here before." He takes a step back. A sickly grin worms its way across his lips. His hideous scar bends like a slug.

Dmitri covers the groove in the floor with his foot. His heart continues to hammer. Maybe he'll get lucky and have a heart attack. This can't go on much longer.

"If you don't tell me what I want to know, I will leave you locked in here forever."

"No!" Dmitri yells.

"Where is the missile?"

"You're standing on it!"

The leader looks down.

Dmitri lifts his foot reluctantly.

Within seconds, the guards have removed the panel and exposed the tunnel leading to the missile. One of the guards disappears down the hole to check it out.

"Now," Dmitri shouts, "take me somewhere else. Please."

The leader takes Dmitri by the throat again. He could snap Dmitri's neck so easily. Why won't he just do it?

"Do it." Dmitri's voice is barely above a hush. "Do it. Do it."

The leader lets go of Dmitri's neck. "What's the code?"

"I told you. I don't know. I can't remember it. You're going to have to kill me."

"Tell me the code, and I'll grant your wish."

Everything slows down.

Dmitri looks deep into the leader's eyes, then at his facial scar. It's white and wormlike. It's a caterpillar. A slug. A big freckle.

A big white freckle.

The crickets begin to jump around inside Dmitri's brain, but he doesn't care. He wants out of here.

He blinks.

More freckles appear on the leader's cheeks. He's got white, snowflake freckles. He's come to help Dmitri. It's Carlos, his old friend. They're working together at the automobile recycling plant. Carlos wants to know the code, but Dmitri has forgotten it.

"What is the launch code, Dmitri?"

"Shh." Dmitri glances at the workers standing over by the shredder. "My name is Feridun. Remember?"

"What are you talking about? Just tell me the code."

"I do not remember it. But I gave it to a girl. I put it on her leg and sent her to the US."

"Her leg?"

"It's a tattoo."

Carlos smiles.

Dmitri has made his friend happy.

"What's her name?"

"Lucía."

CHAPTER FIFTY-EIGHT

JACK

A narrow strand of sand separates the shantytown from a much nicer port. Jack didn't want to leave the motorcycle behind and walk along the beach to get here, but Mattie insisted they'd find a boat faster on foot. With every passing second, Lucía's kidnappers thrust her closer and closer to her fate in Cuba. Jack agrees with Mattie about the nuclear missile. If it exists, it's so old that there's no way it will work. And, when it doesn't, the kidnappers won't need Lucía anymore.

Evil men do evil things.

They will kill her for sure.

Unlike the waters of that shantytown, this place has several docks and dozens of boats. Some are sleek and modern, with shiny paint and smooth curves, while others are weathered and worn, bearing the marks of many journeys. They range from small, single-person vessels to large, luxurious yachts. Jack picks one in the middle and runs towards the dock.

"Wait up," Mattie says.

He boards a boat similar to the Latino's but smaller. It

has an enclosed bridge, and two engines hang off the back. He hopes the smaller size means greater speed so they can catch up with Lucía. Painted in red on white, the words *HOME AWAY FROM HELL* run down the side in italics. The boat has a modern antenna on top of the bridge, and every surface shines. It must be new because the porcelain-white hull doesn't have so much as a scratch on it.

He stares at the controls.

Mattie comes up behind him.

"Do you know how to start one of these things?" he asks.

"You push that lever forward to make it move. I know that."

"Here it is." He presses a button labeled START/STOP, and nothing happens.

"Hey," a man's voice says. "What you doing there?"

Jack's muscles tense. He wants this boat.

A young man stands on the dock, waving and smiling. "That's not your boat, man."

Jack and Mattie exit the command cabin and go to him. He's in his early twenties, Latino, denim pants crudely cut at the knees to make shorts, a tight retro-black Rolling Stones T-shirt, and a face out of a magazine like *GQ* or *Esquire*. His thick eyebrows aren't too thick, and his masculine, pouty lips aren't too masculine or pouty. He's one of those guys who's never had a problem attracting ladies.

Mattie's expression confirms Jack's assessment. The guy is hot.

"This is Mr. Underhill's boat," the man says. "What you doing?"

"We thought it was for sale." Mattie casts her gaze up the dock as if she'd seen a for-sale sign up there. "It's for sale, isn't it?"

"No. No way. This is Mr. Underhill's *Home away from hell*." He glances up the dock. "And I know Mr. Underhill. Believe me, you don't want him to catch you here." He hurriedly motions for us to get off the boat. The moment we do, he extends his hand. "I'm Fernando." This man never stops smiling. "You want a boat. I'll get you a boat. You don't have to steal one."

Mattie scowls. "We weren't stealing it."

Jack shakes Fernando's hand. "I'm Jack, and this is Matilda."

Mattie slaps Jack's shoulder. "Mattie."

"Okay, Matilda." Fernando's smile widens along with Mattie's scowl.

"You have a boat?" Jack asks.

"Let me show you."

Fernando's boat is a far cry from the *Home away from hell*. Deep, black scrapes and scratches give way to rust-colored streaks running down the side. The command cabin has a broken window. Faded teal paint spells out the word CATALINA near the bow. The air lingering around this floating misery smells like burning brakes.

"Does it run?" Jack asks.

"Faster than a cheetah," Fernando says.

"How much?" Mattie asks.

"It's not for sale, but I give tours. I'm very reasonable."

"Give him your money, Jack," Mattie says.

"Look at that hole over there." Jack hurries to the back and points at a gaping cavity in the stern. "It'll never make it."

"The waves never go that high," Fernando assures him. He makes a fist and hits the C in *Catalina*. "She's solid as a rock."

"We don't have time for this." Mattie grabs Jack's wrist.

Her hand is clammy but firm. "Give him your money, now. We've got to get going."

So many cleaner, nicer, newer, meaner vessels bob up and down all around, and *this* is their only option?

It's their only option because of time. Because Mattie is always rushing him for time.

Jack knows that's what he needs.

"They're already gone," he says. "We're not going to catch up with them no matter which boat we take. I'm sure we can find something better."

"Catch up with who?" Fernando asks.

"Right," Mattie says to Jack. "It doesn't matter which boat we take, so we should take this one. Now. And, besides. This one comes with a captain. Do you know how to get to Cuba?"

"What's in Cuba?" Fernando asks.

"Hey, Dandy." A slim young man strutting down the beach calls out, his hands in his pockets and the wind fluttering his jacket. "How's it going?"

"Fast and furious, my friend." Fernando gives him a thumbs-up.

"'Dandy'?" Mattie says.

"That's just a stupid nickname. You can still call me Fernando."

"Okay, Dandy." Jack loves it when Mattie grins. "Do you know how to get to Cuba?"

The male model's ever-present smile vanishes. He pauses. The gears turn in his head. "How much money do you have, *Matilda*?"

"I don't have any, *Dandy*. But Jack's got a ton."

"No, I don't."

"Give him your money, Jack."

"I don't trust him, and I definitely don't trust his boat."

"Hey, Rodo," Fernando calls out.

The man strutting down the beach stops and turns around.

"You can trust me, right? You feel me?"

"Yeah, yeah," the man says. "Everyone trusts Dandy."

Fernando's smile returns and puts Jack at ease. Jack hates that someone named Dandy is putting him at ease. He doesn't want to relax or trust this man-child. He hates feeling like he's being played. He considers taking the boat by force and leaving now, but Mattie is right. They need him. Neither of them has any idea how to get to Cuba.

But if he's not patient—if Mattie can't be patient—they're going to make a mistake.

"Have you gone to Cuba before?" Mattie asks.

"Yes," Fernando says. "Many times."

Jack doesn't believe him.

"We've got to go." Mattie gazes across the bay. "She needs us."

Jack pulls his wallet out, counts out some bills and hands them to Fernando. "I'll give you the other half when we arrive, *Dandy*."

"All aboard!" Fernando pockets the money and helps Mattie step onto his boat. "Get ready for the tour of a lifetime. You're never going to forget this."

CHAPTER FIFTY-NINE

As long as Fernando calls me Matilda, I'm calling him Dandy. I hate the name Matilda. I should think of something worse to call Fernando than *Dandy*, but I can't seem to come up with anything good. My first thought was *Stupid-head*, but that name is . . . it's stupid.

Dandy stands at the helm, steering the *Catalina*. It's so stereotypical for the super good-looking guys to have oversized egos, but here I am . . . judging someone again. I don't know Dandy well enough to judge his ego, but he clearly doesn't lack confidence or looks. In every way, he's physically balanced. Not too tall or short. Not too muscular or thin. Not too energetic or lame. When he reaches up high for something in the cockpit, his shirt lifts, and I see his abs. They might be too defined, but I'd never complain about that.

His boat, on the other hand . . . it's *unbalanced*. The one place to sit—a built-in bench across the back deck—lost its padding years ago. Rusty upholstery nails poke through the stained vinyl cover. I'm not going to sit there anytime soon. The cramped cockpit only has room for two, but at least it's enclosed. The windshield isn't cracked, so that's good. It's yellowed and warped, but not broken. A searchlight sits above a few dials and controls. It's not like a car with headlights, but I suppose it works the same to see at night.

The flat horizon meets the clear sky miles ahead of us. We're nothing more than a tiny black bug buzzing across the water toward an angry island nest. What little I know of Cuba is that they're angry. I could be wrong, but I've always had the impression they hate Americans. I don't care.

I only hate the men who took Lucía.

We're going to save her next time.

The pungent stench of gasoline mixes with the salty air and decaying wooden deck odor. A hatch is latched shut near the back. This can't be the original flooring. It looks like cheap plywood painted with even cheaper house paint.

Jack and I stand just outside the cockpit, holding onto the walls for balance. Dandy has his back to us and hums a song, occasionally spinning the wheel to avoid oncoming currents. We're going full speed.

"How often does this thing break down?" Jack asks.

"Never," Dandy says.

"That can't be true." Jack throws me a look. "What's up with that big hole in the hull? I think I saw bullet holes, too. I can't believe this thing floats at all."

"It hasn't broken down yet today, man." Dandy slows the boat, locks the wheel, and turns toward us. "It might never break down again." His warm smile gives me no reason to doubt anything he says. It never leaves his face. He should be doing something else with his life, like selling insurance or timeshares.

"How long until we arrive?" I ask.

"Before tomorrow."

"Seriously. How long?"

"Before midnight. About ten hours."

"That'll be good," Jack says. "It'll be dark, and they won't see us coming."

"By then they probably won't be on their boat anymore," I say.

"I meant nobody in Cuba, period, will see us, not just the Latinos. We can dock in the dark and run to shore without anyone seeing us."

"No docking," Dandy says. "I'll get you close, but not too close. I'm not losing my boat to them."

After Jack and I absorb this news for a minute, he leans toward me and reminds me in a lowered voice, "Mattie, I can't swim."

"I know," I whisper. "Believe me, I know." I strained my shoulder hauling his sorry butt back to shore only hours ago. He's a big, strong guy with the buoyancy of a rock. There must be some way to get him on shore.

"Does this thing have a dingy?" I ask.

Dandy cocks his head. "A what?"

"A lifeboat or whatever." I glance around. "An inflatable raft, maybe?"

"You have your life jackets. They float."

"That's not good enough." Jack furrows his brow. "We'll be sitting ducks."

"You mean floating ducks." Dandy chuckles. "Right? Because you'll be in the water floating?"

"We get it, *Dandy*. Hilarious."

He smirks. "Thanks, *Matilda*."

He's such a jerk.

"We can't rely on these vests," I say. "It will take us too long to swim to shore with them on, and someone will see us."

"No worries." Dandy strides to the hatch in the rear deck and opens it. "I can provide a deep underwater experience." He pulls out a scuba tank. "For an extra charge, of course."

"No way," Jack says.

"Would you rather get shot trying to swim to shore?" I ask.

"Floating like a duck," Dandy says.

Good *God*, he's not funny. And Jack's defiance irks me. I'm rescuing Lucía no matter what it takes. If it's to be, it's up to me . . . but—I've never been to Cuba. I've never been anywhere. I'm not sure I can do this by myself.

"Wait a minute, man." Dandy has lost his smile. "You serious? You said *get shot*. No one said anything about guns or getting shot."

"We'll do it." I reach through the hatch and pull out a wetsuit. "I know how to scuba dive. All we need to do is teach Jack how."

"No way." Jack raises his hands and takes a step back. "I'm not putting that on."

"Oh, don't be such a gas hole," I say.

"Gas hole?" Jack says.

"Yeah, you like it? Gas hole. I made it up."

"Hm," he mutters. "Gas hole. I do kinda like it, but I don't think it'll catch on."

Dandy gets a funny look on his face and saunters into the cockpit.

"What are you doing?" Jack asks.

"I'm checking how much gas we have."

Jack steps up next to Dandy. "And how's it look?"

"No worries," Dandy says, stepping back out. "I got enough to get you close, just not as close as I thought. You'll be able to scuba underwater the rest of the way. Besides, I'm not going to get shot at. My *Catalina* has enough bullet holes."

The engine backfires with a *bang* and sends a cloud of black smoke into the air.

We startle.

I grab Jack's elbow.

He turns toward me.

"You *will* learn how to scuba dive and help me, won't you, Jack? I can't do this without you."

CHAPTER SIXTY

Jack let me sleep on the bench at the back of the boat. He's sleeping on the floor below me. I only woke up a few minutes ago beneath a star-covered sky. We've been traveling for hours. The ocean out here smells like citrus as much as it does brine, and there's a muggy chill in the air, but it's not so bad. It's refreshing.

Ouch.

Every so often, an upholstery nail sticks in my side. Jack and I are using our scuba suits to lie on, but whenever mine shifts during the night—*ow*. I hurt.

The bench was too narrow for the two of us. Otherwise . . . who knows? We might have spooned. I can hear him breathing on the floor below me.

Across from us, Dandy stands at the helm, steering this wreck. His silhouette splits the headlights shining over the ocean ahead. My stomach churns. It refuses to digest the soggy burritos he shared from his lunch cooler.

The night sky holds so many stars. Many more than I have ever seen from land. Not only stars but clusters of stars. If not for *Catalina*'s chugging motor, the peace right now would relax me. But, I'm not relaxed. We're not there yet, and I don't know what will happen when we arrive.

Jack tried hard earlier when we stopped to teach him how to scuba dive, but his defiant nature fought him every step of the way. He looked good in the wet suit, but refused to stay underwater for long. He panicked getting in, and he complained until he got out. He learned some basics, but—I don't know what will happen when we arrive.

When we arrive in Cuba.

When we find Lucía.

"How'd you sleep?" Jack sits up.

"What time is it?"

He checks his cell phone. "My phone's almost dead."

"Mine too. I'm trying to save battery by not turning it on."

"Thanks." He smirks. "Let's waste my battery."

"What time is it?"

"Almost 10:30." He glances toward Dandy. "We must be getting close."

I swing my legs off the bench and stand.

Suddenly, the *Catalina's* engine peters out.

Dandy takes his hand off the throttle lever.

"We're stopping," Jack says. He rushes to the cockpit.

I follow.

"What's going on?" Jack asks.

Dandy points straight ahead. "See that light?"

"Yes."

A shimmering light no bigger than the tip of my pinky finger glows in the distance.

"That's Cuba. It's a city that way. The one you wanted. La Boca." He points at the darkness slightly to his right. "You'll want to dive and go that way to shore so they won't see you."

Jack's face has gone white.

This is not good.

Dandy turns on the deck lighting and drops to his knees.

"What are you doing?" I ask.

"That's really far away," Jack says, peering off toward shore. "Let's go closer."

"No can do." Dandy turns a wing nut on the deck. I hadn't noticed before, but the deck has two wing nuts. He turns the second one and opens a hidden hatch. "I'm not staying."

"What?"

"Watch out." Dandy motions for us to step out of the cockpit's entryway. He pulls a deflated, yellow rubber raft from below deck and drags it toward us. He lied. I specifically asked if he had a dingy, and he told us we had to scuba dive. This makes me mad, but what's worse is Jack's right. We are way too far from shore to leave now.

"Where do you think you're going?" Jack asks.

"Put your scuba gear on." Dandy returns to the cockpit, pulls an oar out of the hatch, and slings it onto the deck by the raft. "You don't have a lot of time." He pulls out an electric air pump and plugs it in.

"You've got to take us closer." Jack waves his hand in the air. "You've got to be kidding us."

Dandy fastens the pump to the raft and turns it on.

I shout over the pump's buzzing. "What the hell are you doing? You said you didn't have a raft. Are we all taking it to shore?"

"No." He glances up at me. He has no smile. Fear dances in his eyes. "Put your scuba gear on. This boat can only carry two people. I suppose one of you could come with me." He gazes beyond Jack at the command cabin. "I loved this boat. It's a shame, but it's not worth my life."

Jack grabs him by the collar and hauls him up so his face is close to his own. "Tell me what you're doing now, or I'll take your life."

"There." Dandy points over Jack's shoulder away from Cuba. "Look there."

We turn.

A pinlight bounces on the horizon.

Dandy breaks free of Jack's grip, bends down, and pulls on the inflating raft to help air flow into it.

"Who's that?" I ask.

"It could be anyone," Jack says. "The Coast Guard. Cuban authorities."

"What about fishermen?" I say. "Maybe it's tourists."

Dandy disconnects the pump and throws the raft into the water.

The pinlight has turned into a headlight. They're coming in our direction.

"It's not fishermen," Dandy says. He throws the oar into the raft, grabs the lunch cooler, and climbs over the side with it. "If one of you is coming with me, come now."

I look at Jack. I can't imagine he'll make it to shore using the scuba gear. "Go with Dandy."

"No. I'm not leaving you."

Dandy's taken a seat in the raft and slipped his oar into the water. "Goodbye."

"You can't just leave us here," I say. "We need you to cruise the coast with us. We need to find Lucía's boat. Don't you want the rest of your money?"

Jack steps away into the cockpit.

"I'd rather stay alive. They want to take my boat, and they

can have it. The things they do to people who resist . . . it's unimaginable. If they ask, give them the keys." Dandy paddles into the darkness. "I'll take the rest of my money if I ever see you again. I hope you enjoyed the tour."

He's gone before I can yell at him about taking all the food.

Jack switches the helm's searchlight on and aims it at the oncoming boat. I'm not sure he should have done that, but I'm as eager to see who's coming for us as he is.

"Who is it?" I put my hand on his shoulder. It's hard to make anything out.

"Give us your keys." The command bellows over the waters from the mysterious vessel. "Give us your keys." It's coming from a loudspeaker. It's a man's voice with a Spanish accent. "Give us your keys."

I can hear an engine now. It's getting louder quickly.

Jack finds a pair of binoculars.

"What do you see?" I ask.

"I can make out about ten, maybe thirteen men. Only one seems to have a uniform on." He lowers the binoculars and shuts the searchlight off only to realize the deck lights have been on the entire time. "Where's the switch to the deck lights?"

"I don't know."

"We need to disappear."

"Stay where you are." The oncoming boat's loudspeaker unnerves me. "Prepare to give us your keys."

"It's not the Coast Guard." Jack finds the deck lighting switch and flips it. "And it's not the Cuban authorities or the military."

"Who is it, then?"

"I think they're pirates."

Pirates? Like the kind who say, *Arrrrgh?*

"Are you sure?" I hope against hope. "Are you sure it's not a pirate-themed tourist tour? Did you see a parrot?"

He turns to me. "There's no parrot." The pale light illuminates his darkly decisive eyes. "I saw guns. Lots and lots of guns. Big guns. It's a big boat with tons of wooden boxes. And guns. I've heard about these. They take over boats and sell them on the black market to drug dealers and traffickers."

"What are we going to do?"

"We need to disappear."

CHAPTER SIXTY-ONE

YANS

No one in the Red Star Society would suspect Lucía's arrival tonight. Not in La Boca, this insignificant port west of Havana. Only Darien could have told them, and Yans has kept his *mano derecha* close—very close—since Ramon made Yans agree to launch the missile. If Ramon or his men hurt Tomás in the slightest way, they'll meet their god in Guanajay like the others.

Yans can still hear his nephew's cry.

Tío, help me!

Yans changes his mind. Those men are already doomed.

Florida is doomed. All Yans needs is the launch code and directions to his family's bomb shelter.

He gazes at the city lights of La Boca in the distance and pushes the image of his nephew locked away in that dilapidated warehouse out of his mind. Tonight is too important for distracting images such as that. It's almost over. After years of searching for the launch code, fortune arrives tonight. He's made it so.

Yans turns back toward the ocean. He stands next to the

Chinese SUV at the top of the beach. The driver waits behind the wheel. Yans holds his back straight, his hands at his sides, his chin high, and Darien stands at attention on his right. Darien—his righthand man, to his right.

Two of Darien's men tether a raft to the dock below.

They have her.

They have *someone*.

Yans keeps his emotions at bay. He won't forget what happened earlier this week. He'd sworn then that fortune had brought him Lucía, but when the code on that girl's leg didn't work, he had to make Darien take her to her grave in Guanajay. It could happen again tonight.

The dock has few lights, and the lights are dim. Darien instructed his men to land on the periphery of the port, and they did. His men help their captive onto the dock, and they're doing their job well. They've tied the captive's hands together and put a hood over her head.

It's got to be her.

Lucía the Launch Code.

It's just got to be her this time.

A thrilling sensation rises from Yans's boots, up the backs of his legs, and into his chest. The sensation flows over his face.

The scar on his cheek itches.

He scratches it without breaking posture.

When Darien's men look up and see him standing atop the beachhead, they will see the leader of New Cuba. They will see destiny.

Yans breathes in the sweet night air, letting his chest expand.

Darien's men pull their captive down the dock and thrust her onto the sand.

"Go to them," Yans says. "Bring her up here and send your men away."

"Yes, *señor*."

Darien charges down the hill toward his men.

Good soldier.

The SUV's headlights shine down on the moment. This glorious moment.

Darien approaches the beach party and removes the captive's hood. Curly black hair spills out onto her adolescent shoulders. She's the right age, size, color—everything Yans imagined her to be, based on his years of searching for her. She's wearing a pair of white shorts, and her legs . . . Yans can't see her legs well enough from here. He can't see the tattoo.

Darien takes hold of her tied hands, and his men gaze up at Yans.

Yans runs down the hill.

His scar itches wildly, but he doesn't scratch it. He can't allow himself the distraction.

Darien sees him coming and motions for his men to return to the dock. They obey, which is good because Yans doesn't care about them. He wants them gone. They've served their purpose. He nearly dives face-first into the sand just as he reaches the captive. She jumps back, and then, on all fours, he grabs her ankle.

"Where is it?" Yans asks.

"It's there," Darien says.

He twists her leg.

"Ow," she says. "What are you doing?"

The SUV's headlights are weak, but Yans sees a number. Unfortunately, he can't read it with any confidence.

"We should go," Darien says. "There's a boat coming."

Yans raises his head. It's true. A skiff buzzes toward the dock. He gets to his feet.

"When we reach the car"—Yans seizes one of the girl's arms—"put her in back with the driver. I want you to take us to the missile."

"Yes, *señor*." Darien takes her other arm.

"Where are you taking me?"

"What's your name?" Yans demands as they drag her up the dune toward the SUV.

"Her name is Lucía," Darien says. "My men verified it."

"No, Darien. You speak when spoken to. I want to hear it from her." He jerks on the girl's arm.

"Ow. Stop."

"What's your name?"

"It's Lucía."

They crest the hill. Darien waves his hand for the driver to get out of the SUV.

"Here," Yans says to the driver. "Take her. Put her in front of the headlights."

The driver—a brawny man with a thick neck and hands like vice grips—takes Lucía by the back of the neck. He shoves her ahead of the SUV, and she drops to her knees.

Yans crouches down for a better look at her tattoo.

No.

No, no, no.

He shakes his head and covers his face.

"What's wrong?" Darien asks.

Yans stands. He trusted Darien. Despite Darien's prior foolishness when talking to members of the Red Star Society, Yans trusted him. But, now . . .

Bad soldier.

Headlights appear on the horizon. More than two. More

than four.

"We should go," the driver says.

The Red Star Society has found them.

Yans glowers at Darien. He wants to snap the boy's neck.

"What's wrong?" Darien has the fear of God on his face.

No.

It's better than that.

He has the fear of Yans on his face.

Rumbling tires slam against potholes in the distance. Engines rev, and headlights bob up and down. Plumes of red dust obscure La Boca's city lights behind the oncoming convoy of SUVs.

Yans finds this highly distracting.

"Load her into the back," he says.

"Wait," Darien shouts. "What's wrong with her?"

Yans strides to the passenger side. "Darien. Drive. Now."

"Not until you tell me—"

Yans stops, pulls his pistol out, and aims it at Darien.

Darien puts his hands up.

"You said your men verified it was her. Lucía. They verified it, yes?"

It looked like Darien said *Yes*, but Yans couldn't hear him over the increasingly loud engines of the Red Star Society.

"What?" Yans shouts.

"Yes." Darien nods, yelling, "They verified it. That is Lucía."

"Then why does her tattoo only have eight numbers?"

"What?"

"Eight numbers, you orange-picker. There should be *ten*."

CHAPTER SIXTY-TWO

MATTIE

"Give us your keys."

I startle.

Last time, the give-us-your-keys command came from out in the ocean away from Cuba. It came from the pirate ship. Now, the command comes from the other side of Dandy's boat, and it doesn't sound like it's coming through a loudspeaker. It sounds like they're using a megaphone. I turn toward Cuba—toward the distant lights of La Boca Dandy told me about.

"Give us your keys."

I run to the scuba gear hatch. It takes me a moment to find it in the dark. Jack shut all the lights off in hopes we could "disappear."

It didn't work.

I find the hatch and open it.

Jack lowers his head and enters the cockpit. He switches the searchlight on and sweeps it over the waters between the *Catalina* and the pirate ship.

Dandy is long gone in his secret dingy.

If I ever see him again, I will make him pay.

"Jack!" I shout. "Come put your wet suit on."

"There's no time." He turns toward me. "They're already here."

"What?" I throw his suit onto the deck.

"Two of them are coming in a canoe. They must have left a while ago when we first saw the pirate boat's light. We've been tricked."

"Don't move," one of the men in the canoe calls out. "Give us your keys."

I run to Jack.

"Can you swim to shore?" he asks.

The lights of La Boca look a thousand miles away, but I wouldn't swim in that direction anyway. Like Dandy said, I'd have to swim in the other direction to avoid being seen. I'd have to swim into the darkness and hope to hit shore before drowning from exhaustion. If the island curves away from La Boca in the wrong direction, the shore could be very far away.

Very, very far away.

It doesn't matter.

Lucía needs us.

Whether I like it or not, if it's to be, it might be up to me.

But, it can't be.

I can't go it alone. I can't leave Jack.

I won't leave Jack.

"Come with me." I pull him to the side of the boat.

He jerks his arm away.

"I know you're afraid," I say, "but—"

"I'm not afraid."

"Okay. Okay. You're not afraid, but you also can't swim. Just let me pull you to shore."

"It's too far." He takes the gun out of his waistband.

"You'll never be able to do it."

I want to hug him. He looks so angry. He looks like the night he tried to kill Stanley Owens, but I know him better now. He's not angry. He's scared. He's a scared little boy trying to protect his mom from his stepfather. He's trying to protect me from the pirates.

I don't need protection, if it means we must separate.

I need him.

"It's called the dead man's carry," I say. Or the fireman's carry. That's what I should've gone with. "Ignore the name. You're not going to die."

"I'm not going with you."

"You said you wouldn't leave me."

"I'm not. You're leaving me."

And with that, he places his hands on my shoulders.

He shoves me hard.

I stumble backward, turn, and fall, catching myself on the edge. My upper body leans over the water, and I push down to avoid falling in. A light shines over the murky waves below.

It shimmers.

"Give us your keys."

The pirates approach me in their canoe. One is significantly taller than the other, and they both have big guns like Jack saw through the binoculars when we encountered the pirate ship. They're coming right toward us.

Right toward me.

I push back from the edge, but Jack grabs my ankles from behind.

"Stop!" I scream.

He dumps me into the ocean.

Despite the most intense adrenaline dump I've ever had, it's surprisingly cold in the water.

Up is down. Down is up.

I rotate my arms, trying to get my bearings. Trying to float to the surface. I finally determine which way is up, but I'm blocked by the bottom of the pirates' canoe. Muffled voices. They're yelling at each other.

I need air.

I have no choice.

I swim away from Dandy's boat. Away from the pirate canoe, toward Cuba.

My lungs burn, and I keep swimming. I've got to get as far away as I can before I come up. The swelling in my chest threatens to stop my heart. I let a little air out, and it makes me want to let more out.

I didn't want to leave Jack, but he made his choice. He threw me into the water to save Lucía. They'll probably kill him, but . . . he made his choice.

It's up to me, now.

I surface.

Gunshots ring out.

I didn't go far enough. I gasp.

More gunshots. The water next to my head explodes. The bastards are firing at me.

I fill my lungs with air, and I dive. I dive deep, and I keep diving, and diving, and . . .

It can't be.

The pirates must have a searchlight like Dandy's. A brilliant beam slashes back and forth, penetrating the deep, and I see him . . . a gray creature with a round body and flippers drifts by me. Its wrinkled face and whiskers turn in my direction. The animal's soulful eyes meet mine. It's not Hank the Manatee, but it might as well be. All the regret and remorse pile on top of my will to make it out of this alive. If this were a movie, I'd grab a flipper, and the beautiful beast would take me to shore.

But this is not a movie.

If it's to be, it's up to me.

I hold my breath and swim.

When I come up for air this time, I'm well past the pirates. They're on the *Catalina* with Jack, guns raised. It's a standoff. All I can do now is swim to shore and save Hank.

I mean, Lucía.

I'm going to rescue Lucía.

The La Boca city lights glow to my left. I use them to guide my swimming to the right. The creepy strip club Cuban—Carlos, I think—said the missile was east of La Boca, where Dandy had promised to take us. I swim in that direction. My years of lessons and practice pays off. I'm out of shape and exhausted, so I slow down to rest occasionally, but I never fully stop.

I dive under a few times, looking for my manatee friend, but I never see him again.

An hour or more passes. Finally, I make it to shore and collapse on the beach. The packed sand hurts my back, but the citrus scent of the ocean air invigorates my body. I breathe freely. I catch my breath.

Then, it hits me.

I'm alone.

I'm alone in a foreign country. Not just a foreign country, but Cuba. They most likely won't be a fan of my presence here. And I don't have anything with me. My cell phone disappeared somewhere along the way. I have no gun. No knife.

I don't even have a pair of tweezers, and I left the Bob Marley lighter back in those Floridian slums.

I have nothing.

I sit up.

The beach stretches endlessly in both directions. Based on the city lights to my left, shining far away, I'm generally where we wanted to land. Where we thought the Latinos would take Lucía—a missile silo hidden in the nearby hills. But I never planned on looking for her alone. If the Latinos did take her here, they could be here now, lurking in the dark. I head for some bushes up shore. I need to hide. Take some rest.

A man's voice startles me. "Are you okay?"

I freeze.

A light shines down from atop one of the hills.

Someone carrying a torch and moving in my direction. He's seen me. There's no point in trying to hide in the bushes now. I move toward him until the glare of the torch subsides. He's older, probably mid-forties. Touches of gray, slender, and strangely well-dressed for someone lurking around a Cuban beach at midnight.

He's also tall and moves fast.

He's practically running down the hill.

I'm not so sure being alone was a bad thing.

I don't know this person.

"Let me help you," he says.

He speaks English well but has an odd accent. I can't quite place it. Otherwise, he seems perfectly normal. I have no reason not to trust him, other than I don't know why he is here. But it's too late to run, and I don't have the energy. He holds out his hand, and I take it.

"Are you okay?" he asks.

"I'm fine." Something about him still makes me nervous. I brush the water off my shirt. I don't know what to say.

"Are you sure you're fine?" he presses.

"Yes, I'm fine. I just forgot my tweezers, that's all."

"Oh." He raises his torch and gazes over the ocean. "Where's Jack? Will he be coming soon?"

"Jack? You know Jack?"

"Yes. Your partner, Jack Clark. What happened to him?"

CHAPTER SIXTY-THREE

JACK

Jack Clark couldn't understand anything the two pirates said except for, *Give us your keys*. They said it over and over like it was the only English they knew, and it drove him insane. He gave up trying to talk to them a while ago because they couldn't understand a word he said, either. Fortunately, before they boarded the boat, he'd had the presence of mind to dump Mattie into the ocean and run to the cockpit. While the pirates fired their weapons at her, Jack took the keys from the ignition and hid them. If all these men wanted were those keys, then that's the last thing Jack would give them.

He needed to buy Mattie time to reach the shore.

She hadn't wanted to go alone, but it was the only way. After seeing her swim earlier today, he had no worries pushing her into the ocean. The pirates shot at her, but no way did they hit her in the dark. She's too strong a swimmer. He saw this when she tried to teach him how to scuba dive. He's glad she showed him how to dogpaddle, but not because he learned how. Because it reaffirmed his hatred of the water. No way will he ever go in the ocean again. He will never do it.

He looks away from the pirates toward the water.

Never. Never, ever, ever, will he go in the ocean again.

"Give us the keys." The tall pirate sits on the back bench next to Jack's gun. He has his own gun trained on Jack. The other pirate—Jack has taken to calling him "Stumpy" because he's so much shorter than his *compadre*—put his gun away a while ago. He has a troll grin and broken teeth, and he keeps stroking the blade of a hunting knife. Outnumbered, Jack surrendered his pistol shortly after they boarded the boat.

He's not a threat to them anymore. All they want is the keys to the boat, and they won't stop asking for them, and they're not getting them. Not until Mattie has had time to swim to Cuba.

Stumpy stands up next to the tall pirate, and he's still not as tall. They wear matching canvas vests with torn, long-sleeved undershirts and ragged shorts. It doesn't appear as if their pirate ship has a shower.

"Give us your keys."

"You're a broken record, you know that?" Jack sits in the middle of the deck near the scuba gear hatch, his legs folded and his hands on his lap. "You've been saying that for over an hour."

The shorter one points to the side of the boat.

A light beams across the water, and another pirate canoe emerges from the dark.

The pirate ship Jack had seen through Dandy's binoculars earlier carried one man in a uniform. Now, this man stands erect in the canoe. He must be the captain, and he has a *compadre* with him.

Great. The more, the merrier. More *Give us your keys* crap.

Stumpy waddles over to the side and helps the two men out of the canoe.

The captain says something to the tall pirate in Spanish, and lieutenant tree-trunk shakes his head. The captain has jowls that wiggle when he speaks. He's angry. He turns toward Jack.

"Where are the keys?" He speaks English better than the other men.

"I don't have them," Jack says.

"Where did you put them?"

"You speak English?"

"Yes." He taps his *compadre's* shoulder.

The beefy *compadre* pulls out his gun and walks over to Jack. He has a thin mustache and scraggly chin hair that's not worth keeping. He smells like diesel.

"I didn't put the keys anywhere," Jack says.

Stumpy stops stroking his knife and rubs his fingertips together.

"Hey." Jack slips his wallet out of his pocket. "How about some money?"

The captain's *compadre* puts his gun to Jack's head.

"Hey, it's just a wallet."

The *compadre* presses his muzzle harder into Jack's temple. Stumpy grins.

"Here." Jack removes a wad of cash from his wallet. Now, he's glad Dandy left in such a hurry without asking for the rest of his tour fee.

Stumpy extends his hand and steps toward Jack.

The captain turns and slaps the little man.

"Can you call this guy off?" The gun to Jack's head is becoming annoying.

The captain waves his *compadre* away.

"We don't want money," the captain says. "We want your vessel."

"Well, you're not getting it. Any minute now, my friend will come back with the police."

The captain bursts out laughing. His flabby double chin bounces up and down. The other men look at him, and he translates.

Now, they're all laughing.

"What's so funny?"

Stumpy shakes his head and returns to stroking his knife.

The tall pirate stands and looks out over the water toward La Boca. He says something to the captain.

"No one is coming for you," the captain says. "My men shot your friend when she tried to swim away."

"No they didn't. There's no way."

There is no way. Mattie escaped. She swam away, under the water, way away from their bullets. She must have. Suddenly, Jack realizes he'd made a split decision to throw her overboard.

"Now"—the captain holds his hand out—"give us the keys."

Jack stands up.

Everyone tenses.

They jerk their weapons, reaffirming their murderous intentions.

"I don't care if they shot her," Jack says. "She's not the friend I was talking about." It's possible Dandy didn't return directly to Florida. It's possible—not likely—but possible. The Coast Guard or Cuban authorities might have stopped him, and he might have told them about the pirate ship. "Do you think it was just her and I on this wreck? Do I look like I'd own a heap like this?"

Again, the captain bursts into laughter, this time shaking his head. His jowls swing. His belly isn't huge, but it wobbles along with his cheeks. He's fat for a pirate. And, again, he translates, and again, everyone joins him in his merriment.

They squeal with glee like the pigs they are.

The captain strides into the cockpit, motioning for his *compadre* to make Jack follow. Tears of laughter stream down the captain's cheeks. He locates the searchlight above the command panel and switches it on.

"What are you doing?" Jack asks.

The captain's *compadre* shoves Jack in the back.

Jack stumbles forward and peers out over the bridge.

The captain runs the searchlight across the waves until it illuminates the pirate ship in the distance. A rope dangles over the side and ends at an inflatable raft.

It's Dandy's raft.

Jack squints.

"Is that your friend?" the captain asks. "The one bringing those authorities?" He hands the binoculars to Jack.

Jack raises them to his eyes.

In the searchlight's beam he sees Dandy lying motionless in the raft.

The raft moves with the waves, butting up against the pirate ship, but Dandy lies motionless.

Jack focuses the binoculars and sees blood on Dandy's chest.

"We shot the woman, and your friend isn't coming back with the police. He's dead."

Jack lowers the binoculars.

"Now, give us the keys."

Stumpy shouts, "Give us the keys!" He brandishes his hunting knife and forces his way into the cockpit.

Jack glances over Stumpy's head at the scuba gear hatch.

The tall pirate takes notice.

Mattie's had enough time to make it to shore if she's still alive.

And, she *is* still alive. She must be, or all this was for nothing.

Jack wants to act, but he knows he should have patience. He needs to do the right thing. And, to know what that is, he needs time to think—

The tall pirate kneels and opens the hatch.

Jack rushes past Stumpy toward the hatch and hits the tall pirate at full speed, knocking him over the edge. Water splashes onto the boat, wetting Jack's shoes.

The captain yells something, and a gun goes off. The shot came from the captain's *compadre*.

Jack reaches into the hatch and grabs a wet suit.

He grabs a life jacket.

A sharp pain shoots into the back of his shoulder, and Stumpy lets out a terrific cackle.

The keys to the boat rest at the bottom of the hull, just out of reach.

Blood streams down the back of Jack's arm and cools his skin. It gives him goosebumps.

He rolls away from Stumpy.

Still cackling, the little man attempts to stab him again but misses this time.

Jack stands.

The water stretches out before him.

He clutches the life jacket and wet suit to his chest.

He promised himself he'd never go into the ocean again.

Never, ever, ever.

Stumpy cackles once more.

A gun blast deafens Jack.

Everything goes silent.

CHAPTER SIXTY-FOUR

MATTIE

The strange man's torch casts a flickering glow on his stoic features, highlighting the sharp angles of his jaw and the curve of his cheekbones. His piercing blue eyes shine and dance in the light, reflecting the flames like precious stones. He appears to be friendly and fit. Nothing to worry about. Shadows define his broad shoulders, and the torchlight catches on the strands of his graying hair, flickering wildly and giving it a golden tinge. He stands tall, with a confident posture and a peculiarly dark complexion. His latte-colored skin contrasts with his blue eyes.

Something's not right about the way he looks.

The hills behind him form a crescent along the beach, blocking my view of La Boca. It's miles away. Too far to run.

But, do I need to run?

He has a radiant, friendly smile. He has not said or done anything bad to me. I really don't have any reason to run away.

Not yet, anyway.

"What happened to Jack?" he asks. "Why isn't he with you?"

"Who are you?"

"I apologize." He holds out his hand. "I'm Colter Tremblay. Lucía's father."

Everything Jack told me about his client hurtles through my head. This man doesn't look anything like I imagined. He doesn't look like Lucía, then I remember. I think Jack said something about her being adopted.

I take a step back.

"It's okay." He lowers his hand. I wasn't going to shake it. "Let me explain."

"How do you know who I am?"

"Jack told me about you. Certainly, he must have told you about me."

His shiny polo shirt has a logo with two golf clubs overlapping each other in an "X." He looks like someone who could afford all the expenses Jack said he was sending to his client. But he could also be an impostor. Someone pretending to be Lucía's father. He could be working with the Latinos who took her.

"He did tell me about you, but . . . I don't know."

"Here." He pulls his cell phone out, gives it a few swipes, and holds it up so I can see it. "This is you."

The screen displays a picture of Calvin and me standing by A.J.'s Pub & Grill, that awful restaurant where we first talked with Jack. My hair looks better than I thought. I remember catching Jack taking pictures of Dory's license plate after he thought I tried to run him off the road.

"Jack sent me this picture of you the other day," Colter says. "I have his phone number if you want more proof."

"No. I believe you."

"Good. Jack told me all about you." He raises the torch and gazes at the ocean. "Thank you for helping him try to find my daughter. Where is he?"

"What are you doing here? Jack didn't say anything to me about meeting you."

"He doesn't know. I haven't spoken with him since yesterday. He told me the men who took Lucía might be coming to this location." His eyes glisten in the flickering torchlight. "When I didn't hear from him again, I took the next flight and arrived a little while ago." He glances over his shoulder. "I'm glad you're here. I know where they took her."

"Up there?"

"Yes, but—where's Jack?"

"Bad news." I turn toward the ocean. "We were attacked by pirates. He stayed behind so I could get away."

I turn back toward Colter in time to catch a scowl flashing across his face, replaced immediately by that stoic smile.

"That's Jack," he says. "I'm disappointed he's not with you, but this is why I hired him. He's a hero." He nods toward the hills. "Well. Hurry. We haven't much time, and I need your help."

"Hold on, Mr. Man. I'm not going anywhere." I glance back at the beach. The starlight makes the surf glow. White foam rolls up the shore. "We should wait to see if Jack escaped."

"These pirates . . . did they have a large ship?"

"Yes."

"And weapons?"

"Yes."

"We shouldn't wait."

An emptiness thuds inside my chest. He's right, but I don't want to admit it. The last time I saw Jack, he was in a standoff. It was two against one on Dandy's boat with a ship full of pirate bastards in striking distance. Nothing burns me more than giving up.

"Mattie, we can rescue Lucía if we go now."

I don't want to go with him. Something still doesn't feel right. "Go without me. You don't need me."

"Yes, I do. I saw two men take her into a bunker when I arrived earlier. While I was deciding what to do, they left the bunker without her. I think she's alone, but I'm unsure. I need you to come with me and warn me if they return. I'll go inside, and you signal me if someone comes."

I stare at the breaking surf.

"He's not coming, Mattie. You know that."

"Okay," I say. "Let's go."

He trudges up the hill, and I follow.

My lungs ache from the swim, but I'm okay. I can do this. We don't need Jack.

That's bull.

I need Jack.

The smooth sand gives way to rocks, sticks, and dry, chaotic debris scattered along the coastline. It's so dark out here. I wish I had something to defend myself with. We round a slight corner, and Colter stops.

"Keep quiet," he whispers. "The door is over here."

He moves slower now, and I follow, staying a couple of paces behind him.

Sure enough, we come to a door painted the same color as the hillside. Claustrophobic Cinnamon. I once had my nails painted at a goth nail salon, and they had all kinds of interesting names for their colors.

I wish I had a nail file right now. Something. Anything. Tweezers.

"See it?" he asks. "Come closer. We don't have much time. They could come back any minute."

He holds the torch near the door and slowly turns the knob.

The hinges creak, but not too loud.

A set of concrete steps descend into the earth.

Colter steps inside and turns toward me. His bulk fills the stairwell. His broad shoulders nearly touch each side. He can probably hold his own in a fight, but I should have asked if he had a weapon.

Never mind, it's too late now. We're not turning back.

"I'll make a noise if someone comes," I say.

"Like what?"

"I'll shout, 'Caw, caw.'"

"What's that?"

"It's the sound a bird makes when somebody is in trouble."

He cocks his head and grasps my arm. "Did you hear that?"

"No."

"Come." He pulls me into the stairwell. "I hear someone."

"Shouldn't we close the door?"

"There's no time."

He hangs onto me all the way to the bottom. He has a strong grip. My heart races. It's all happening so fast. We burst into a room, and I finally free myself of his grip. I push past him. He swings his torch, and the light casts sinister shadows on the walls.

"Where'd you go?" he asks, waving the torch, searching for me in the dark.

I slink backward until I run into something. It rattles like metal shelving.

"Just a minute," he whispers. "Stay still."

Every nerve in my body is ready to run. We're just waiting for my brain to shoot the starting pistol.

Suddenly, a light turns on.

Colter stands next to the stairwell with his hand on a light switch.

"Why'd you have to pull me down here?" I rub my elbow. "That hurt."

"I heard someone coming. Please, believe me." The whites of his eyes turn red like he's going to cry. He doesn't look like the kind of man who cries.

"I didn't hear anyone," I whisper.

"Watch out." He steps toward me. "They're holding my daughter down there. This is our only chance." He drops to his knees.

"What are you doing?"

I step aside, and he lifts a wooden plank from the floor.

A crude tunnel appears where the plank had been, leading into the earth.

"She's down here." His voice catches. "Please, you must help me save her."

"How'd you know that was there?"

"I don't fit," he whispers. "You need to go in first. I'll get stuck if I try."

"Oh, hell no. I'm not going in there."

He stands.

A strange blankness comes over his eyes.

His stoic features consume his face.

I've been had.

He pulls out a gun.

"Crawl inside, Mattie. I'm not going to ask you again."

CHAPTER SIXTY-FIVE

Lucía should be getting ready for her high school graduation. All of her friends are getting ready.

Instead, she's sitting on a hard wooden chair with her leg chained to a table. The older man, the one they call Yans, said to chain her right leg to the table. He said they might need to cut off the other one, the one with her tattoo, if she becomes unruly.

Lucía is beyond unruly.

She's had enough.

First, her boyfriend, Wyatt, broke up with her. He kidnapped her. Yeah, that's what he did. He did it weeks ago. She just didn't realize it at the time because of the drugs he'd slipped her. Then, he punched her in the face and took her to Salt Springs to sell her to a fancy Asian man. And then, these other guys showed up, and they kidnapped her. They took her to a ballgame, but not quite. While they ate hot dogs and cheered on the Marlins, she sat tied up in a van, starving to death.

That was yesterday.

She spent most of today tied up in a boat. When they took her out of it, they pulled the hood off her head, put her in an SUV, and then blindfolded her. She's so sick of being blindfolded that she could scream, and she did scream. Again and again, she screamed, but it never helped. When they took the blindfold off, she was staring down a hole in the ground. They shoved her into it, and she landed in this room.

That was the last time she screamed.

She's not going to scream anymore.

They closed the hatch to the hole behind her and sat her at this table.

Now—and she doesn't know when "now" is, or where she is exactly, but she thinks she's in Cuba—she sits on a hard wooden chair with her leg chained to a table in a claustrophobic room with a madman staring her down and a missile standing beneath a large steel door. The missile has a nuclear symbol on it.

She's had enough.

She should be at a sleepover with her friends.

She should be putting on makeup and trying on her graduation gown.

"My father's coming for me," she shouts. "He's going to stop you!"

Yans stands over her, his hands on the table. His breath smells sickly sweet like rotten tomato sauce. He has the most hideous scar on his cheek. It looks like larvae. She ought to be scared of him, but she's not. She's all out of fear.

"Your father is nowhere near here," he growls.

"Is that thing on your face going to hatch, or what?"

"Insolent *gringa.* Your father is as good as dead."

"No, he's not, and even if he was, it doesn't matter. He sent someone for me. They'll be here any minute."

She pictures Mattie and Jack rushing into the room, guns blazing.

"They're as good as dead also." He slams his hand on the table. "Now tell me, where's the rest of the code?"

One of the soldier boys in the corner jumps. The cute, younger one. His name is Darien. He drove the SUV here while the ugly one sat next to her in the back. The ugly one is like, you know, super busted. He stands next to a row of wooden crates. The crates have the words STORAGE, FOOD, DRY GOODS, AID, and other things stamped on them. She doesn't know what these guys are planning, but everyone looks scared. Everyone except for Yans and her.

She ought to be scared, but she's not. She's had enough.

"I don't know what you're talking about," she says.

"The other two numbers." Yans points down. "You have eight on your leg, but there should be ten."

"For what?" she asks. "How do you—why do you think that?"

"Darien." Yans stands up straight. "Search her."

"My men patted her down already. She doesn't have anything on her."

"No." Yans strides over to him. "Search her for the rest of the code."

"Search her?" he whispers. "Why? We don't need it. You said you weren't going to launch the missile."

The ugly soldier raises an eyebrow. He glances at the missile. A twisted expression crosses his face.

"Speak when spoken to!" Yans yells. He smacks Darien.

"You did speak to me."

"No, I commanded you." Yans rests his hand on his gun's hilt in his belt. "Search her for the other two numbers."

Darien marches toward Lucía.

The ugly soldier stays by the crates in the corner.

Lucía crosses her legs. She will not let them see her other tattoo. No way. Not down there.

"I'm sorry," Darien says.

"Why?"

He pulls her up until she stands. "Take your clothes off."

"No."

Darien glances at Yans.

Yans nods.

Darien slaps Lucía.

She slaps him back.

He grasps her shirt collar and slaps her again, hard.

A terrific pain shoots into the bruise Wyatt put on her cheek, and she almost passes out.

"Stop." Yans pulls his gun out. Aims it at Lucía. "Where's the rest of the code? What's the rest of the code? Tell us or die."

Darien grasps her collar with his other hand and tears her shirt off.

She wraps her arms around herself.

He spins her, looking all over for another tattoo. All he finds is the one of Mickey Mouse on her back shoulder. He tugs on her bra strap.

"No!" she yells and sits down. "I'll tell you. I'll tell you."

"What is it?" Yans lowers his head to his pistol and closes one eye. He aims directly at her head.

Darien leans down and mutters, "*Lo lamento*."

"It's zero-seven." She's had enough, but she doesn't want any more. Not if it means being stripped naked. Why, oh why, did they put those numbers by her crotch? "It's zero-seven. I swear."

"Prove it," Yans says.

"I can't. You'll have to believe me."

"We have to be sure. We might have only one chance left to input the correct number."

"Why are you doing this?" Darien asks Yans. His lower lip shakes. "My family in Florida—you said—"

"Never mind what I said." Yans lowers his gun and strides over to the missile. "The full number, then, is 2086345107. Is that correct, Darien?"

"I—I don't—"

"Check her leg. Read them off."

Darien does as he's told.

Yans flips a metal panel open.

The panel looks like the circuit breaker box from home. Lucía wants to go home. She wants to wear her graduation gown and pretend none of this ever happened. Where's Jack? Mattie? Her father sent them for her. Why aren't they here? What happened to them?

The ugly soldier says something in Spanish to Darien.

"I'm afraid so, *compañero*." Darien's entire body shakes. "*Yans*. Por favor. My family!"

Darien said his family was in Florida. He said—Lucía realizes now what's going on. Yans said her father was as good as dead. He said everyone was as good as dead. He's got a nuclear missile. A freaking nuclear missile.

"Two." Yans thrusts his index finger into the box.

The box *clicks*.

"Zero." He thrusts his finger into the box again.

Another click.

"Eight."

Another click.

The ugly soldier slips out of sight behind the row of crates.

"Six."

Another click, then a *grunt*, but the grunt didn't come from the box.

It came from behind Lucía.

Yans looks up.

Lucía turns in her seat and strains to see the hatch in the wall.

"Keep going," a man's voice says.

It sounds like her father.

"I told you he was coming for me."

CHAPTER SIXTY-SIX

Dmitri wins the argument. He knew he would. The slums of Havana are no place to raise children.

He and Ana move out of their inner-city hovel and find a hovel in the countryside. A small, one-room shack. Small, but safe from the Red Star Society. Ana reminds him farmers don't want tattoos on a daily basis, but he doesn't let that deter him. He works on his art and shows it to everyone he meets until he finds a taker. A farmer's rebellious son. Then, another farm boy wants ink done. Word spreads about the man named Feridun who works magic with a needle. He's a success.

A small success in a small place, but a success.

People travel from the cities to his hovel in the fields and pay him well, but it's still not enough to live on, so he takes on odd jobs as a farmhand. Every day, he strolls through the pastures on his way home, feeling like a free man and picking flowers for his pregnant wife.

He loves Ana as much as he loves his freedom. He's freer and freer every day as the thought of the Red Star Society finding him in the countryside melts away. His paranoia lifts.

Freedom reigns.

"Push!"

Ana bares down, grits her teeth, and pushes. She sits on the floor with her back against the kitchen wall and pushes again. And again. And, out he comes. Dmitri's baby boy. Blue eyes like his father's. Black hair like his mother's. His skin is a blend of both. Beautiful.

Beautiful and wet.

Dmitri cuts the cord and ties it like the neighbor lady had described. She was supposed to have been here, but Ana's labor came on too fast.

Dmitri wraps the baby in a blanket. Though they'd planned for this moment for months, he doesn't know what to do next. Ana reaches out, crying, and takes the baby away from him. She clutches her child to her chest.

Dmitri stands up. He glances over to the corner where they've set up the bassinet. They have diapers ready to go. Blankets. Baby clothes. He's never taken care of a baby before. The crying, he is sure, is normal, but it's also gut-wrenching.

He drifts over to the bassinet and gazes down.

The crying will stop soon. It must stop soon.

Soon, they'll put the baby in the bassinet, and he'll sleep quietly. Dmitri will watch him sleep. Dmitri will be a good father, and he'll watch his son sleep in peace. Dmitri will watch him sleep the way Dmitri hasn't slept since . . . not since before the Black Crickets held him prisoner in that hellhole.

The baby's crying intensifies.

Dmitri covers his ears.

He blinks, and the bassinet changes. Instead of the pale blue oval filled with a soft white blanket, he sees a rusted iron platform. He sees the bed from the jail cell the Black Crickets made him sleep on.

He closes his eyes.

He shakes his head.

"Come here, Dmitri. Come look at your son."

"No, you whore!"

"What? What's wrong?" Her voice catches. "No. Not again."

Dmitri's chest heaves. He's got to calm down. This is supposed to be the best day of his life. His first child. His future.

But, no. His past won't leave him alone. He's going to be a bad father.

He paces, pressing his hands against the sides of his head.

"Please," Ana cries out over the baby's wailing. "You can stop it!"

She's right. She's seen him suffer like this before, and she's right. He *can* stop it. He pictures the time before the Black Crickets took him. He pictures Russia. His father. The cathedral. The Russian sun.

"Come here," she says.

The baby has stopped crying.

Dmitri opens his eyes.

She has her pinky in the baby's mouth.

He goes to her.

"I'm sorry," he says. "It's the memories." His temples ache. "You know."

"I do know, but it's okay now. You're a father. Look at him." She holds the baby up. "Just look at him. He loves you."

"I love him."

She giggles and gently rocks her son side-to-side, gazing into his eyes. "You love your daddy, don't you? Don't you, Colter?"

CHAPTER SIXTY-SEVEN

After Colter forced me to climb into that tunnel, I fell through a hatch at the bottom and caught myself with the heels of my hands, but my face still hit the concrete floor. The first thing I see when I lift my head is Lucía's long hair with tight coils running down her back, stopping just above her white shorts. It's her. I can't believe it. It's really her. I've pictured her again and again ever since the Latinos took her from me in Salt Springs, seeking her out on every sidewalk, alleyway, and road we passed. And now, I've found her for sure. That's her. Definitely. She's seated at a table with her back to me near a soldier standing next to a stack of wooden crates. The soldier is young and has terror written all over his face.

I lower my head and gaze straight ahead.

They've chained Lucía's leg to the table.

She can't go anywhere, but at least we're finally together.

Then I hear Colter come through the hatch behind me. *What a liar. He fit.*

He drops onto the floor behind me.

Before I can stand, he sticks his foot in my back and

shoves me down. I roll onto my side, and he points his gun at my chest.

"What is this?" a Cuban man asks.

"Sorry I'm late, Yans," Colter says. "I had to address this problem on my way in." He rocks my body with his heel.

I attempt to squirm away, but he grabs my hair, pulls me all the way up to standing, and presses the muzzle of his gun to the back of my head.

The Cuban man who spoke—Yans—stands beside a control panel. He has this attitude about him, but he's just another coward. He wears a fancy uniform and has his shoulders back like he thinks he's all great and powerful, and . . . my God. Maybe he *is* powerful. That creepy Cuban, Carlos, from the strip club—he wasn't lying. A wire runs from the control panel by Yans to a missile. The missile has a nuclear symbol on it and no signs of rust. In fact, it looks brand new, and . . . this guy was trying to launch it. He was trying to start a world war.

"Dad!" Lucía cries out. "Help me."

I have a migraine, and her crying out loud doesn't help.

"You're not late," Yans says to Colter. "You're not supposed to be here."

"I didn't want to be," Colter says, "but you know why I've come."

"Dad?"

"The payments," Yans says.

"Right. You stopped making the payments."

"Yes."

"So, you have the launch code?" Colter asks.

"Yes."

"But not the entire launch code."

"No. I have the entire launch code." He has this thing on

his cheek. A scar. It makes a funny shape when he smiles. "I'm glad you joined us, Mr. Tremblay. It will make things easier." He glances at the soldier by the crates. "Darien?"

The soldier pulls out his pistol and aims it at Colter and me.

"What the hell is going on?" I ask Colter. "Aren't you going to help your daughter?"

Colter shoves me forward.

I resist. The muzzle digs into my head, but I don't think he'll shoot me. Like all the others, he's a coward underneath. I twist my shoulders and try to step away from him, but his grip on my elbow doesn't give. I stop resisting. He does have a real gun, and though he's a coward, it could go off by accident.

He shoves me again and again until I'm standing next to Lucía at the table.

She gazes up at me with tears and hope in her eyes.

Darien glances at the crates. At first, I thought he was trying to tell me something, but now I don't think he saw me looking at him. But, maybe I'm wrong. Maybe he's hiding something. Or someone.

"Here's what's going to happen," Colter says to Yans. "You're going to walk away from the missile and release my daughter. Then, we'll all leave together, and everything will return to normal. I expect to see a deposit covering the last two months by Friday."

"Your arrogance has defeated you," Yans says. "You don't realize the significance of this moment. You do not matter. The New Cuba is at hand." He steps over to the control panel. "What is the next number, Darien?"

"Please. I don't want my family to—"

"Wait, I remember. It was three, wasn't it?" He pokes his

finger inside the control panel. "Three."

"Stop!" Colter shouts.

"What will you do if I don't?" Yans asks. "Shoot your guest?"

"I'm not his guest!" I shout.

He laughs and pokes inside the panel again. "Four."

I look down at Lucía's tattoo. The number reads, 20863451. Number five is next. He's almost finished.

I glare at him, and he glares back.

"We don't need another stripper, do we?" he asks. "Do we, Darien?"

"Who are you calling a stripper?"

"Five."

"And what's that on your face?" I ask. "It looks like a giant bird dropping."

This gets Yans' attention. He looks up at me. "Darien?"

"Yes?"

"Shoot them."

In a fluid motion, Colter removes his pistol from the back of my cranium, steps around me, and fires two shots at Yans.

The blasts assault my hearing.

I throw myself over Lucía and wrap my arms around her shoulders.

Yans falls backward to the concrete and grips his chest.

Darien aims at Colter and fires his weapon.

He misses.

Colter drops to the floor and covers his head.

Darien fires again and again.

Concrete dust clouds spring up with each shot.

He squeezes the trigger until his gun clicks empty.

Colter gets to his feet, fires, and makes a direct hit. Darien puts his hand over his abdomen and slides to the floor. His back rests against the wall by the crates, and blood streams between his fingers. He stares at it in disbelief.

I pull on Lucía's leg chain. When it doesn't give, I crawl under the table and watch Colter's feet approach Yans. Like Darien, blood streams between Yans's fingers, but he was shot in the chest, not the stomach. He winces. Licks his lips.

He's not so great and powerful now.

"Darien," Yans shouts. "*¡Disparale!* Shoot him. Shoot him."

"No," Darien says, weakly. "*Nunca.* Never."

"Who else has the code?" Colter asks.

"You'll never get your money," Yans says. "The Red Star Society will never pay you. They want the missile launched. It must be launched."

Darien moans and makes eye contact with me.

I crawl over to him.

"*Mira,*" he whispers and tilts his head toward the crates. "Do you see?"

I peer between the boxes, and a pair of desperate eyes peer back at me. Someone else is here.

Darien unhooks a keyring from his belt and hands it to me. I count six keys and clutch them in my hand.

"Then I no longer need you," Colter says to Yans and aims his gun at the Cuban General's face. "When you arrive in hell, say *hola* to my father."

"Dmitri was *loco,*" Yans says, "but he didn't go to hell. You shouldn't dishonor your father's memory. He loved you."

"I hated him. I should thank you for killing him."

"You disrespectful fool. Had he not been your father, you'd have nothing. He would never have sent you that girl. The payments you so dearly miss now would never have started. Dmitri was *loco*, but he had some honor. Something you do not have. He could have sent her to anyone, but he sent her to you. Don't thank me for killing him. Thank him for the launch code. Without it, you couldn't have blackmailed me all this time." He laughs. "The code drove your father insane, you know. He carried that burden his entire life, and now it's yours. They'll be coming for you now." He glances at Lucía. "And her."

"Who? Who else knows about the code? About the missile? The Red Star Society? Russia? Do they know this location?"

Yans coughs and blood sprays from his mouth. "No. Only Darien and I know." He chokes. Little blood bubbles burst on his lips. "They'll be coming for you now."

"I doubt that." Colter holds his gun with both hands, aiming it at Yans's wormy cheek scar. His forearms tense.

"History will remember me." Yans closes his eyes.

I turn my head away.

"Daddy, no!" Lucía shouts.

The blast reverberates throughout the chamber.

I cover my ears, but I'm too late to keep the sound from enraging my migraine. I crawl back to Lucía and begin the process of elimination. One of these keys must fit the lock on her leg chain.

Colter strides over to Darien, gun raised.

"No!" Lucía cries. "Don't kill him."

"Quiet." Colter stops. He points his gun at his daughter. "This is all your fault."

"I didn't know what the number was for," Lucía says. "Please."

"You should never have run away. You and I are going to have a long talk when we get home, little lady."

The first three keys didn't fit. I try the fourth.

Darien leans forward and lamely reaches out for Colter's ankle.

Colter aims his pistol at the top of Darien's head. "Who else knows the code?"

The fourth key doesn't fit. I try the fifth. The sixth.

Click.

"*Abandonarlo.*" A Cuban soldier emerges from behind the crates, weapon drawn.

The lock falls away from Lucía's ankle.

"Lucía," I whisper to her. "Come with me." I head for the hatch.

She turns to follow, but Colter catches her by the wrist and draws her to his chest.

My eyes are drawn to Yans, slumped on the floor by the missile. Part of his head is missing.

"*Lo siento,*" Darien moans. "*Mamá. Lo siento.*"

The Cuban soldier from behind the crate puts his hand on Darien's shoulder.

Colter has Lucía's neck in the crook of his arm and his gun to her head. He pulls her past me to the hatch. She chokes and coughs and kicks the floor with her heels, though they barely reach as he drags her through the doorway and into the tunnel. He's such a liar. He has broad shoulders, but he fits inside it just fine.

I want to grab her ankles and stop him from taking her away, but I force myself to pause. To think.

Tugging on her will only make things worse. He might accidentally shoot her.

They disappear into the hatch and up the tunnel.

I turn toward the Cuban soldier, and he aims his gun at me. "*Ve ahora.*"

I raise my hands. "Come with me," I say. "I need your help."

He looks sadly at Darien and shakes his head. He wants to stay with his friend. He lowers his gun, pulls a towel off a shelf, kneels, and places it over Darien's wound.

I don't have time to wait for Nurse Nightingale here.

I need to save Lucía.

I check my body for bullet holes.

I'm clean.

CHAPTER SIXTY-EIGHT

Dmitri has made his friend so happy. Carlos grins ear-to-ear while one of their co-workers mans the shredder. In the distance, the car crusher crushes cars. The warehouse workers dismantle totaled vehicles. The sun is out, and Dmitri has made his friend so happy.

"Her name is Lucía," Dmitri says again. "She has the number on her leg."

The shredder shreds car parts into ... into shredded wheat.

Oh, no.

The crickets are in Dmitri's head again. Their scratchy legs scuttle throughout his mind, jumping at conclusions, making up stories, places, and things that are not real. He's truly gone insane. He reaches for Carlos. He puts his hands on his friend's face and wipes away the snowflake freckles. All but one comes off. It's a large one. It's on Carlos's cheek. Dmitri rubs it harder and—

This is not Carlos.

The freckle is not a freckle. It's a scar.

Dmitri turns his head, and the automobile recycling plant spins. Baby blue walls emerge from the ground, surrounding him in an oval, and his heart rattles. A baby cries, and Ana wants Dmitri to hold their son Colter, but he can't. Dmitri is too small. He's only the size of a baby, himself. He's lying on a soft white blanket in a baby blue bassinet.

He's a baby.

He's trapped.

The crickets laugh at him.

The Black Crickets have locked him in a bassinet.

He wipes his face, and—no. He's not in Colter's bassinet.

The man standing before him is not Carlos. And he's certainly not Ana.

This man has pins on his cap. Military pins. He's the leader of the Red Star Society.

He's Yans Rivero.

"Where is this *Lucía*?" Yans asks.

The crickets scamper away, and the baby blue walls come down. Sanity has returned. Dmitri sits in a chair at a table in his jail cell, but his iron bed is gone. It's not 1968. He's not young. The veins in his arms run like sewer pipes from his hands to his shoulders. He can see through his creped skin.

Yans has brought him back to hell.

He's in his old prison cell.

His heart rattles against his sternum.

But does Yans know about the tunnel?

Dmitri gazes at the floor.

Yans knows.

The wooden plank leans against the wall, and the tunnel to the missile is wide open.

"Let me out!" Dmitri screams. "I can't stay in here."

He tries to stand, but two hands come down on his

shoulders, forcing him to sit back down. His wooden chair screeches on the concrete floor. He wishes the crickets would return. Anything would be better than being here.

"Where in the US is this girl?" Yans asks.

"What girl?"

Somehow, Yans knows about Lucía. The crickets must have told him. But Yans thinks Dmitri sent her to the US. He doesn't know the truth. Valeria took Lucía to Canada. She took her to Colter along with the launch code. Dmitri remembers having the tattoo put on Lucía and telling Valeria something about it, but he doesn't remember the details. He knows he told her the number was of great importance, but he can't remember if he mentioned the missile or not.

"Don't pretend you don't know," Yans says. "You just told me the number is on a girl you sent to the US, you insane buffoon. Now, tell me—where in the US?"

Dmitri bows his head and shakes it.

This is funny.

Yans grasps Dmitri's chin, lifts it up, and uses his other hand to clap Dmitri's ear.

The crickets in Dmitri's mind spring to life and explode, their skeletal bodies eradicating the wheat field in his mind.

"Where is she?" Yans shouts.

"You'll never find her." Free of the crickets, a euphoric feeling washes over Dmitri.

"Tell me, or I'll kill you."

"Please. Kill me."

"Tell me or I'll kill your family."

Dmitri bursts into laughter. "She is my family. She's like my granddaughter." He cackles and coos and laughs at the dry hoarseness of his own voice. "Besides, you already killed my family."

"You're not making any sense. Apparently, I haven't killed all your family." Yans sighs. "I know you had a son, and now you're saying you have a granddaughter."

"No, I'm not saying that. The crickets said that." Tears stream down Dmitri's cheeks. He grins widely. "You'll never find my son. I can't even find my son."

"He went to the US, didn't he?" Suddenly, Yans raises his eyebrows as if realizing something important. "He went where you sent the girl, didn't he? Does he have the girl? Is she your granddaughter?"

"Maybe." Dmitri sniffs. He chuckles to himself.

"Stop laughing."

"I—I can't."

"Why?"

"Because you'll never find her. Or him. You can't kill them if you can't find them."

It's true. It's so true.

And, it's hilarious.

It's more than hilarious now that the crickets are gone.

Yans will never find Colter or Lucía in the US because they didn't go there. Colter went to Canada. He adopted Lucía and hired her mother, Valeria, as his housekeeper. He changed his last name to Tremblay. Lucía Tremblay should be about ten years old now, but Yans doesn't know that. He doesn't know anything. He's the insane buffoon.

The number is safe.

Yans smacks Dmitri's other ear.

The room spins.

He's still in his jail cell. It's now, but it's hell, and it's not funny.

Sitting here, trapped . . . it's not funny.

The walls close in.

His throat constricts.

He's got to get out of here.

"Tell me where your son is," Yans says, "or—"

Dmitri throws himself onto the floor.

The soldier leaps on top of him.

"Stop!" Yans yells. "You'll kill him."

The soldier rams the heel of his hand into the back of Dmitri's cranium, forcing Dmitri's face into the concrete floor, shattering his cheekbones.

"Stop!" Yans bellows.

The pressure of the man leaves Dmitri's back, but he can't stand up.

His neck doesn't work.

He can't inhale anymore.

It's a relief.

"What have you done?" Yans asks.

Dmitri's heart stops rattling.

A wounded cricket crawls across the floor, and Dmitri closes his eyes.

CHAPTER SIXTY-NINE

LUCÍA

"You killed him," Lucía says. "You—you shot him in the head."

"He was going to blow up the world."

She plants her feet in the sand, flexes her thighs, and refuses to move.

Her dad gives her a solid shove from behind, and she stumbles forward. He's got a gun pointed at her back, but he won't use it. Will he?

Daddy?

She turns to face him.

"I did what had to be done," he says, still pointing his gun at her. "Now walk."

"Where?"

"That way." He waves his weapon. "Down the beach." He holds a torch in his other hand and waves it as well. "I have a car around the bend."

The torchlight illuminates his face. His jaw, cheekbones, and brow catch the light, creating sordid shadows. He doesn't look like her father, but it is him.

She turns around and walks in the direction he'd gestured her toward. The sand on the beach is packed and covers a steep incline down to the shore. The surf crashes in the dark. The dock where she landed with the Cubans isn't within sight. They'd taken her hood off just long enough to replace it with a blindfold before they marched her to the bunker. She can't remember how long the walk took to come here.

"Where are we going?" she asks.

"Home. Now, walk."

"What happened?" She staggers along the slanted ground. "Why are you doing this?"

"You can ask your mother when we get there."

"Mom? She's back from Europe?"

"No. Your other mother. Valeria."

A sickness rises within Lucía. It begins just above her groin and envelops her stomach. She slows down and puts her hand on her belly.

"Don't stop," he says.

"What are you talking about?"

He sighs. "You might as well know. Valeria is your real mother. You were going to find out when we go home anyway. I had to tell her what you did so she could help me find you. You know, she thought she saw you at the airport in Miami the other day, but she was wrong. She's so worthless."

Now her stomach twists into a knot because what he's saying . . . it makes sense. Too much sense. Lucía had always felt a connection to Valeria until middle school. When Lucía became a teenager, she began avoiding her housekeeper. Before then, Valeria had always been the one to take care of her. Her—oh, it's so weird to think of her this way—"other" mother was always on trips to Europe, promoting a line of cosmetics. Valeria was the one who had fed, bathed, and played with Lucía. Valeria had taught her how to read and write before she was five.

And, Valleria's mole.

Oh, God—the old housekeeper's mole.

When Lucía was seven, they'd laughed at the coincidence. Valeria had the same-sized mole in the same place as Lucía. That wasn't a coincidence. Lucía regrets trying to cover it with a Mickey Mouse tattoo now.

Or maybe not.

Valeria could have told the truth anytime throughout Lucía's life, but she didn't. Instead, she cooked and cleaned and let Lucía think she was a servant. A stereotypical Hispanic housemaid.

Lucía's stomach moans. It groans.

"I don't understand," she says. "If she's my mom, where did I come from? Why didn't anyone ever tell me? You said I was adopted."

"You were. We adopted you. We shouldn't have, but we did."

"Why not?"

"Because look what you've done. My God. You almost caused World War III."

"Huh? I didn't do anything."

"You did everything." He raises his voice. "You did everything wrong. I hid you from him for years, and this is what I get. You take off and run to the last place on earth you should ever be, and I have to come fix everything. We almost lost it all tonight."

"I didn't run here." She stops, turns—juts her chin out at him. "I was drugged. They kidnapped me. Don't you care?"

"Of course I do. I'm here, aren't I?"

"Then why are you pointing that thing at me? Don't you—"

"I can't trust you to not run again."

"What are you talking about?" she screams. "Why haven't you hugged me? Why are you treating me like this?"

"Shut up and go." The torchlight flickers, casting jumpy shadows on his features. "I'm done pretending. I've done enough, letting you live with us all this time, paying for your private school—the pool, your clothes, your cell phone. I was even planning on paying for your college, but you decided to run away—sorry, I mean 'get kidnapped.' Now, you'll miss graduation, and I have to start over now with a new dictator." He scowls, steadies the gun in his grip. "Now, move."

"No. I don't understand. I'm not going anywhere until you—"

She sees him glance at her leg.

The damned tattoo.

The crazy man in the bunker had wanted the numbers on her leg . . . and near her groin. He'd wanted them so he could launch a nuclear missile. When her dad came to save her, he'd asked for money first. Her dad was a hero, right? Like he'd said, the crazy man had needed to be stopped.

But her dad had also demanded that the man deposit money in his bank account before asking for her to be freed.

He's not her father. He's a monster.

"You don't love me, do you?" she asks. "You came here for money, not me."

"Move!"

"You were blackmailing him somehow, weren't you? You were keeping me away from Cuba, lying to me about my real mother, you . . . my whole *life*"—she slaps her calf—"it's been about *this*. My whole life has been about this, and you never even told me what it was. You knew what the numbers were for, and you never told me."

"You should thank me. I could have written those down a long time ago and gotten rid of you."

"Ah!" She scoops up a handful of sand and throws it at him. He raises his hand to shield his eyes. "Why didn't you?"

"Because of your mother. I couldn't take you away from her. She loves you."

"*Valeria?*"

"No, the other one. My wife. Now, go."

"Explain. I'll go if you explain."

"Okay, fine." He keeps his gun trained on me as I turn around and begin to walk. "Before you were born, we couldn't have kids of our own, then we met Valeria. She brought you to us, and we adopted you. None of us knew what the numbers were for until it was too late. You were ours, and your mother fell in love with you." He wipes his forehead with his forearm. "Then, Yans contacted me. I couldn't very well make you disappear at that point. Like I said, it would have crushed your mother."

The waves crash on the shore.

The life Lucía thought she'd lived crumbles like a sandcastle inside her head.

"Then what?"

"I moved us to Canada, and you're right. I blackmailed him. I told him I had the launch code for his missile. I told him I'd tell the US government Cuba had a nuclear weapon if he didn't pay me." An intense, fevered stare takes over his face. "Then, because of you and your boyfriend, Wyatt, Yans found you in the US and stopped making the payments."

"I hate you!"

"I should have killed you a long time ago. They know

about you now.

The sick feeling in her stomach slips away, and an emptiness like she's never known replaces it.

The waves crash on the shore.

The dock is so far away.

Canada is a distant memory.

"Move," he says, gesturing again with his gun. "That way."

"You're not taking me home, are you?"

CHAPTER SEVENTY

Dog paddling to Cuba took way too long, but Jack made it. No regrets. Those pirates got what they wanted, and if he hadn't jumped in the water, they'd have killed him. They'll eventually find the keys to Dandy's boat in the hull and leave. They can take the boat and sell it to some drug dealers, which is all he thinks they ever wanted. Good riddance.

They didn't want him.

But Mattie does.

She *needs* him.

She must be around here somewhere, but it's tough to see. It must be just after midnight, the only light coming from the moon and stars, reflecting off the water. He drags his feet up the beach. His right shoulder hurts worse than his left, but they both ache from fighting his way to shore, and his knees hurt like hell, too. He's getting older. Getting here has taken a lot out of him. Every time he feels his age, he thinks of *Lethal Weapon*—"I'm too old for this shit."

And he is.

After this, he swears—he double-dog swears—he'll never

do PI work again.

But right now, Mattie needs him.

Or, does she? Maybe she didn't make it.

His entire body aches.

Maybe the Cuban authorities caught her when she made it to shore.

Jack shudders to think she didn't make it, so he doesn't let his mind go there.

La Boca lies around that bend to the east. The city lights reach into the night sky faintly. It's a good hike from here, but he could make it. He could turn himself in and retire from the PI business sooner than later. That is, if they let him go back to the US. He's not exactly supposed to be in Cuba, and he doesn't know the laws. One thing's for sure. If he did return, the US authorities would have a heyday with him because of his past, plus this little adventure.

Nope. It's not worth it.

He'd rather wander in the dark and hope to find Mattie.

She must be around here somewhere.

Muffled voices come from the other side of a bluff. He hunches over and creeps up to the top. The faint scent of salt gives way to an earthy odor. Rotting bark and weeds. He lies down in a cluster of tall, slender weeds—their tips resembling wheat, swaying in the gentle breeze—and listens.

He can't tell what the voices are saying. It sounds like a man and a young woman. He peers over the bluff, and a flame—a torch—bounces along the beach, and—he pushes his shock and surprise to the side. He's certain that's Colter's voice. *What is Colter doing here, unless . . . unless he came to find his daughter.*

Jack stands and makes sure his eyes don't deceive him, squinting in the dark.

He's right. It's true.

The search is over.

The torchlight flashes up just enough to show Lucía's frizzy hair.

Colter and his daughter stroll along the beach.

She's safe.

Jack rushes toward them.

This nightmare is finally over. Colter probably won't pay him now, but it doesn't matter. This thing stopped being about the money a while ago.

Lucía is safe, and that's all that matters.

"Hey," Jack calls out. "Over here."

Colter glances over his shoulder, and then continues to walk behind Lucía. For some reason, she doesn't turn around.

Jack approaches them. He was already out of breath from the swim, and now he is gasping because of the quick jog.

"You're too late, Jack," Colter says.

"I can still help," Jack says. He sucks in a deep breath. He's getting too old for this. "I'm so glad you found her. Are you okay, Lucía?"

"It was with no help from you. You're fired."

"I understand."

"You can turn back and leave us now."

"But—" The waves crash on the shore behind him. Where the hell does he have to go?

Colter and Lucía continue to walk away from Jack along the shoreline, strolling close together, obviously happy to be reunited. At least, Colter looked happy before he turned away. He holds the torch behind Lucía, making it hard to see her face.

"Are you okay?" Jack asks. "Did they do anything to you?"

Lucía doesn't respond.

Jack takes a couple of quick steps to catch up.

"I don't need your help anymore, Jack." Colter doesn't sound as happy as he'd looked only a moment ago. He growls, "Go away."

Something's not right.

Wait.

Maybe he's overreacting. Colter has every right to be angry with him. Jack failed. Jack wasted Colter's time and money, and Colter had to fly to Cuba to do the job himself. Still, Jack's intuition tells him something is wrong here, but he needs to make sure.

"Are you listening to me?" Colter asks.

Jack grasps Lucía's arm.

She turns toward him and moves her lips. In the faint light, she appears to mouth the word *Help*.

Colter pushes her down to the sand, wheels around. and takes aim at Jack.

Shocked by Colter's sudden movement, Jack freezes for a second before hitting the sand and speed-crawling toward the bluff.

A bullet sprays sand into the breeze just ahead of Jack, and he stops crawling for a moment. He changes direction, stands, and instinctively reaches for his gun, but those pirates took it in the standoff. It's on Dandy's boat with Stumpy. Those bastards.

"Stop!" a woman's voice shouts from behind Jack.

Colter looks beyond him, trying to see the woman in the dark.

Jack knows by the woman's voice who she is. It's Mattie. She's alive. She's okay. He wants to turn and see her glorious red hair, but he doesn't dare take his eyes off Colter.

"Jack," she cries out. "Stop him!"

Colter fires his gun at Jack again, and misses again.

"Go back!" Jack waves over his shoulder. "He's got a gun!"

"Thanks for that, Captain Obvious. I hadn't noticed that blast just now."

Colter fires at Jack yet again, and this time, he doesn't miss. Jack's leg explodes in pain, and he goes down.

He wraps his hands around his thigh. With every heartbeat, his leg sprays blood into the ocean air. He can't make it stop. Colter hit something major.

Jack leans back and rests his head on the sand.

Nothing has ever made him so woozy so fast.

CHAPTER SEVENTY-ONE

I've never taken my shirt off so fast in my life. Maybe, once or twice in college, after a night of partying, but that was for an entirely different reason.

"Mattie, go after her." Jack lies on the sand, bleeding. "I'm okay."

"No you're not."

I kneel down beside him. A massive puddle of his blood has formed in the sand under his leg, and his leg is still pumping. He's lost a lot of blood already, and he's still losing it fast. I wad up my shirt and press it to the wound. The blood soaks through it almost instantly.

"Mattie," he says wearily, "go . . ."

"Can you hold this?" I put his hand on the shirt. "Press down."

"Okay." He presses the shirt against his leg with both hands.

"I'm going to get you help."

"Go after her."

"Give me your gun."

"I lost it."

"I'll be right back." My heart hurts for him. "You hold on."

He nods.

If it weren't for Colter's torch bobbing in the dark, they'd be out of sight. He's made it a long way down the shoreline with Lucía, forcing her to walk along the ridge now. La Boca lies around the bend ahead. I glance in the other direction. Running that way would be safer, but I didn't see any lights over when I was on Dandy's boat. The lights of La Boca were the last thing I saw before Jack dumped me into the ocean.

Jack had to do it.

The pirates were going to kill me for those keys.

Jack saved my life.

Now, I've got to save his.

I need a hospital, or an ambulance, or a doctor, or—I need Colter to get out of my way so I can get help.

"Hey!" I shout. "Where do you think you're going?"

He can't hear me.

I sprint up the sandy incline toward the ridge. I need a weapon. Something to stop him. But all I have are occasional pebbles and wimpy sticks beneath my feet. The debris crunches as I run toward Colter and his gun. And, Lucía.

"Hey! Stop!" I shout.

Colter's torchlight stops bobbing in the dark.

I run faster.

They turn toward me, and their faces glow in the torchlight. "Come any closer," Colter calls, "and I'll shoot her."

This slows me down.

"Mattie, help!" Lucía cries.

Her voice sends chills over my arms and shoulders.

I slow down until I'm merely walking. I don't want to rush this.

He moves the torch to the left and right. He's struggling to see me in the dark only aware of where my voice came from. This is good. If I run as fast as I can, maybe I can take him by surprise. Maybe I can slam into him and knock him away from Lucía before he can pull the trigger.

I speed up, but—no.

I need to think this through. I can't possibly run faster than he can pull a trigger.

My foot slams into something hard and I'm pitched forward. I stumble and go down face first onto the hard-packed sand.

A deafening sound caroms off the ridge.

I think he shot at me.

My big toe hurts like it's broken.

I roll over to see what brought me down, and there it is— a weapon.

Well, actually . . . it's a coconut.

"Go away!" he shouts.

The torchlight starts moving up and down like he's walking away again.

Coconut in hand, I hobble, hunched over, down the incline onto the looser sand so it'll be harder for him to hear my footsteps. My toe throbs, but the pain recedes quickly. Again, I consider speeding up and slamming into him. This time, I have a coconut I can hit him with.

But . . . he has a gun.

In a game of "Rock, Paper, Scissors, Coconut, Gun . . ." gun would beat everything.

I'll have to attack from a distance, but I'm horrible at throwing. I should have stayed in softball when I was younger.

I gain on him.

He has his gun pressed against Lucía's spine. He glances back along the ridgeline, and doesn't see me down below. He's unaware that I'm closing in on him.

One wrong move—one sound—and I'm dead.

A firm grip on the coconut with one hand isn't possible. It's too big for that. I could throw it with two hands, but then I'd look ridiculous. I always looked ridiculous doing my between-the-knees-granny-throw in basketball. I should have stayed in basketball when I was younger.

"Don't do this, Daddy." Lucía is weeping ahead of me.

Jack is bleeding behind me.

I raise the coconut—no. I can get closer. I *have to* get closer. I pull it back down.

Colter jerks his head in my direction.

I crouch over, but I don't know why. There's nothing for me to hide behind.

He sees me and startles at finding me so close to them. He drops the torch.

The fire falls to the ground.

I raise the coconut.

He aims his pistol at me with both hands.

Lucía runs down the incline in between us. "Mattie!"

"Get out of the way!" I shout. She's going to get shot.

Colter hesitates. Lowers his gun as he looks at her.

It's my chance. My only chance.

I throw the coconut with all my might.

He turns his head back just in time for the spinning orb to crash into his face.

Direct hit.

He falls flat onto his back.

"Take that, you coward!" I charge forward and pounce

onto his chest.

The coconut has split his forehead wide open, but his eyes aren't closed.

I make a fist and swing at his chin, but he catches my forearm.

His grip is crushing.

He reaches for his gun with his other hand, but Lucía beats him to it and stands over him.

She takes aim. Her hands shake. Her shoulders shake. Tears leap from her eyes. "I'm sorry, Daddy."

I free my arm and punch him as hard as I can driving my fist into his nose.

His cartilage *cracks*.

His eyes close.

"I got him," I say. I turn to her. "You can put the gun down."

She trembles, still aiming at him.

"Lucía. Put the gun down."

"No." Her eyes swim in a sea of tears.

"*¡No te muevas!*" A man dressed head to toe in a blue uniform races toward us along the ridge. "*¡Manos arriba! Policía.*" Several more men, all with weapons, sprint up the beach.

Lucía takes a step back.

I stand with my hands raised.

"*¡Suelta el arma!*" The frontrunner points at Lucía.

She tosses her gun toward the ocean and raises her hands.

Colter lies there with his eyes closed.

I hope the coconut left a permanent mark.

"Help," I say. "I need help. My friend's been shot." I wave down the beach toward Jack.

The policemen halt a safe distance from us, guns raised.

No one responds to me.

"Please," I say. "Does anyone speak English?"

"I do." The policemen part down the middle. "I speak perfect English, Mattie."

"Calvin!"

I run toward him.

"*¡Para!*" shouts one of the officers.

I stop. "How'd you find us?"

"We were out on that ship." Calvin points at the ocean. If a police vessel is lurking in the dark, I can't see it. "We thought you were on a boat. Boats aren't near as good as cars. I saw you on the beach and said, 'There's Mattie. See her hair? It's red.'"

"That's impossible," I say.

"No it's not. There was that torch, and I have 20/10 vision." He blushes. "Where's your shirt?"

CHAPTER SEVENTY-TWO

Colter, that coward—they put him in an ambulance. He's only suffering a concussion, they say. The police should have just jammed him into the back of one of their cars. They should have beat him up for what he did. Instead, they handcuffed him and gave him a bed to lie in. They probably gave him something to drink, too.

I've always been against police brutality, but—he shot Jack.

"Jack's awake now," Calvin says, "but they'll be leaving soon. The main one—a doctor, I think—said it's touch and go."

I peer past Calvin at Jack's ambulance. It's parked at an angle on the parking lot, next to one of the sand dunes. The back doors are open, spilling a harsh white light onto the pavement. The chaos inside the ambulance has subsided. Earlier, the paramedics rushed around with determination and fear on their faces. Jack wasn't conscious when they loaded him up. After they started sticking him with needles and attaching things to his body, I couldn't watch.

They didn't want me to watch, anyway. Not after the surly paramedic with the dirty pants yelled at me and told me to wait over here after I leaped into the ambulance.

I don't know why I did it. Something I'd never felt before took me over, and the next thing I knew, I was inside the ambulance.

I've been waiting at a distance ever since.

"What about the other guy?" I ask Calvin. "I think his name was Darien."

"He's not awake, but he's alive."

The paramedics had used large canvas blankets to carry Darien and Jack across the sand. They'd tried to drive the ambulances onto the beach, but the field of sand dunes blocked them. They arrested the other soldier, the one who'd stayed behind to help Darien, and left what was remaining of Yans in the bunker.

I wish I could thank Darien for giving me the keys to free Lucía, but I'll likely never have the chance. He might not live.

But Jack is going to live.

He *has to* live.

I *need* him to live.

My hands haven't stopped shaking since I punched Colter. I should have hit him even harder. I should have encouraged Lucía to shoot him instead of stopping her. She wanted to shoot him.

She wanted to shoot him really, really bad.

"Thank you for checking on Jack for me," I say. "They don't want me over there."

"They're afraid of you," Calvin says. "You shouldn't have jumped inside."

"I know."

"Was this a Mattie, *if it's to be, it's up to me* kind of thing?"

"No. I wasn't trying to save him." I feel like crying again. "I just wanted to see him."

He nods, considering this. "So, are you two together now? I had a girlfriend once. We kissed. It was no big deal."

"I don't know what we are, but—thank you. Thank you, Calvin."

"For what?"

"If you hadn't brought the police, Jack would have died on the beach."

"I didn't bring the police. They brought me. I tried to take that Uber you bought me, but they pulled us over. I didn't think anyone had believed me about the missile. Honest. I didn't want to tell them anything. I didn't want to break my promise."

"I'm glad you did."

"Okay." He nods again. "And I'm glad you rescued that girl. I'm sorry I left you."

Lucía sits wrapped in a blanket, talking with one of the officers. She'll be talking with someone about this for the rest of her life. I can't imagine a world with enough therapy to help her.

I considered seeing a therapist once to talk about losing my job over Hank. My manatee problems seem like nothing now.

All I want is for Jack to be okay.

Two of the paramedics climb out of the ambulance, leaving only one behind. My eyes well with tears, and I find myself on my feet. Again, I'm propelled forward by an unstoppable need to be with him. It's a force I have no control over.

I glide over the sand, each step moving faster than the one before.

The last paramedic leans out of the ambulance and grasps the half-door on her left.

I break into an all-out sprint. "Wait!"

It's the surly paramedic. She slams the left door closed against me, but the right side is still open.

I jump into the back and scramble to Jack.

"*¡No puedes estar aquí!*" the paramedic yells.

Jack's eyes are open. He's breathing comfortably. He looks so peaceful. It's as if he's never been angry a day in his life.

It must be the drugs.

The paramedic comes toward me.

Jack is strapped to a bed, but he's able to bend his arm at the elbow, grip his oxygen mask, and take it off.

The paramedic reaches for me.

"Get out!" I say, shoving her backward.

She falls down inside the ambulance, but one of her legs slips out the back. She tries to keep her other leg inside and stretches her arms out, reaching for something to hang onto, but fails. She tumbles to the pavement and lands with a *thud*.

"Mattie," Jack says.

"Don't talk."

I press my lips against his, and my life turns into a love story.

ENJOYED THE CRISIS?

If so, I'd love to hear from you. Please send me an email at topaine@topaine.com and let me know your thoughts. If you'd like to hear about upcoming releases from me, follow me on Amazon, BookBub, or sign up for my newsletter at:

https://topaine.com

You can also connect with me on:
    Facebook – https://facebook.com/topaineauthor
    Instagram - https://instagram.com/t.o.paine
    Twitter - https://twitter.com/topaine

A review on Amazon, Goodreads, or BookBub would mean the world to me. Reviews are the single most important factor in an author's success and longevity. If you enjoyed this novel, please consider leaving a review, even if it is only a line or two. I would very much appreciate it.

ALSO BY T.O. PAINE

The Delusion
    "Don't believe everything you read on the internet. It'll drive you crazy. Literally"
The Excursion
    "Escape was never an option."
The Resentment
    "A Wickedly Sharp Suspense Thriller"
The Teaching
    "A thriller based on the author's experience living in a cult."

ACKNOWLEDGMENTS

Thank you!

Dear Fearless Reader, thank you so much for joining Mattie, Jack, and Calvin on their adventure from Florida to Cuba. Readers like you make the world of fiction a wonderful place.

I also want to thank my editor, David Downing, my incredible ITW critique group, my pre-release review team, and most of all, my tenacious first reader, Kim. I'd likely be lost somewhere in Florida without her.

GET AN EXCLUSIVE BONUS STORY

There is always a FREE short story, novella, or full-length novel available on my website. Come on over to:

https://topaine.com/free

ENTER TO WIN A GIVEAWAY

Several times a year, my publisher and I sponsor giveaways as a thank you for reading. Past giveaways included Kindle Paperwhites, Amazon Gift Cards, Headphones, my novels, and novels by other authors. Check out the current giveaway at:

https://topaine.com/giveaway

ALSO BY T.O. PAINE

THE DELUSION

"Don't believe everything you read on the internet. It'll drive you crazy. Literally."

This year's Psychological Research Award winner, Emma, ponders the years she's spent meeting her professor's demands. Then he goes missing and her work is to blame. Now, she must rescue him before the world destroys itself.

THE EXCURSION

"Escape was never an option."

Charly Highsmith is a survivor, but when a blizzard traps her neurodivergent brother with a murderous hunter high in the Colorado Rockies, survival takes on an entirely new meaning. It's not about what God gave you. It's about your ability to adapt.

ALSO BY T.O. PAINE

THE RESENTMENT
"A Wickedly Sharp Suspense Thriller"

They killed her husband. Now, they're going to kill her son. The Resentment is an emotionally charged thriller about anger, addiction, and redemption with more twists than a night on the town. You're only as sick as your secrets . . .

THE TEACHING
"A thriller based on the author's experience living in a cult."

They had her life planned, but when a mysterious girl goes missing, the search just might end her life. The Teaching is a suspense thriller set in a cult where there is no death, and there is no dying. Or is there?

ABOUT THE AUTHOR

T.O. Paine is an award-winning author of fast-paced thriller suspense novels. He is a member of International Thriller Writers and holds a master's degree in computer information systems. When he is not writing, you can find him running and cycling through the mountains of Colorado, USA. T.O. has run fifty marathons in fifty states, ridden his road bike over 10,000 miles up 10,000-foot mountains, and completed an IRONMAN.

* 9 7 9 8 9 8 6 6 9 5 8 5 3 *